THE CROCODILE MAKES NO SOUND

A LORD HANI MYSTERY

N.L. HOLMES

WayBack Press
P.O.Box 16066
Tampa, FL
⇑

Quotes from *The Instructions of Any* and *The Instructions of Amenemope*
from *Ancient Egyptian Literature* by Miriam Lichtheim, with permission.

Cover art and map© by Streetlight Graphics.
Author photo© by Kipp Baker.

This book is dedicated to my husband, with gratitude

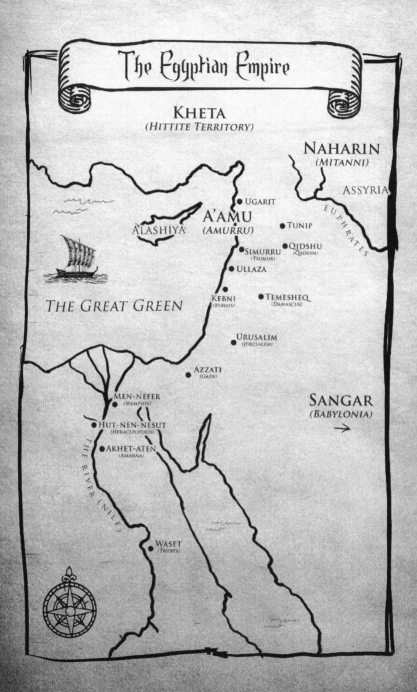

The Egyptian Empire

KHETA
(HITTITE TERRITORY)

NAHARIN
(MITANNI)

ASSYRIA

EUPHRATES

• Ugarit

A'AMU
(AMURRU)

ALASHIYA

• Tunip

• SIMURRU
(TSUMUR)

• QIDSHU
(QADESH)

• ULLAZA

THE GREAT GREEN

KEBNI
(BYBLOS)

• TEMESHEQ
(DAMASCUS)

• URUSALIM
(JERUSALEM)

• AZZATI
(GAZA)

MEN-NEFER
(MEMPHIS)

SANGAR
(BABYLONIA)
→

• HUT-NEN-NESUT
(HERACLEOPOLIS)

• AKHET-ATEN
(AMARNA)

THE RIVER (NILE)

• WASET
(THEBES)

HISTORICAL NOTES

THIS STORY TAKES PLACE DURING the period of Egypt's history known as the New Kingdom, when the country had become an empire, with holdings in Nubia to the south and throughout the Levant to the north. It begins around 1346 BCE, four years into the solo reign of Akh-en-aten, author of widespread religious "reforms", replacing with the Aten the Theban gods Amen-Ra and his family and gradually most of the Egyptian pantheon. Although this new religion is sometimes called monotheistic, it was more precisely monolatrous. That is, Akhenaten didn't deny that Amen and the other gods existed, he simply decreed that the Aten was the only god Egypt would worship henceforth. Scholars are divided over the idea of a coregency in Amenhotep III's later years, but I have accepted that there was one and settled on a duration of five years. Since Akhenaten is known to have reigned seventeen years, this would move his death date earlier than the commonly accepted one.

The reign of Akhenaten marked a nearly unimaginable

overturning of values and customs millennia old, a testimony to the absolute power of the king. But judging by the speed with which his "reforms" were reversed after his death, we must assume that relatively few people really bought into them. We may imagine that those whose livelihood was interrupted by the reforms would have bided their time impatiently and maybe hastened along the fall of Akhenaten's support.

Many authors accept that the mysterious "Greatly Beloved Wife" Kiya was the Mitannian princess Taduhepa, originally sent to Akhenaten's father Amenhotep III. Her name suddenly ceases to be seen at a certain point, and all her monuments had her name chiseled out and that of one of the king's daughters put in its place. Baket-aten is thought by some to have been her child; others make her a late daughter of Tiyi.

The prolonged sojourn of Aziru in Egypt and his prompt defection are recorded in the Amarna letters, a collection of diplomatic correspondences preserved at Akhetaten (today Tell el-Amarna). The real Hani's role in this is, of course, unknown.

As for the *medjay*, scholars today refer to them as policemen—that is, a force to keep the domestic peace and deal with civilian crime—even though we know that a police force in the modern sense was an innovation of the nineteenth century.

CHARACTERS
(Persons marked with an * are purely fictitious)

HANI'S FAMILY

A'a*: the doorkeeper of Hani's family.

Amen-em-hut: Nub-nefer's brother, Third Prophet of Amen.

Amen-em-ope known as Pa-kiki* (The Monkey): Hani and Nub-nefer's second son.

Amen-hotep known as Hani: a diplomat.

Amen-hotep known as Aha*: Hani and Nub-nefer's eldest son. Later takes the name **Hesy-en-aten**.

Amen-hotep known as Anuia: wife of Amen-em-hut, a chantress of Amen.

Amen-mes known as **Maya***: Hani's dwarf secretary and son-in-law, married to Sat-hut-haru.

Baket-iset*: their eldest daughter.

In-hapy*: royal goldsmith and mother of Maya.

Iuty*: a gardener of Hani's family.

Khentet-ka*: Aha's wife.

Meryet-amen*: Mery-ra's lady friend.

Meryet-mut*: Amen-em-hut and Anuia's daughter.

Mery-ra: Hani's father.

Mut-nodjmet*: Pipi's eldest daughter.

Pa-ra-em-heb known as **Pipi***: Hani's brother.

Pen-amen*: son of Amen-em-hut, Hani's nephew.

Neferet*: Hani and Nub-nefer's youngest daughter.

Nub-nefer*: Hani's wife, a chantress of Amen.

Sat-hut-haru*: Hani and Nub-nefer's second daughter.

Other Characters

Abdi-urash: the brother of Aziru, who shared his sojourn in Kemet.

Akh-en-aten (Amen-hotep IV): known by his throne name **Nefer-khepru-ra Wa-en-ra.**

Apeny: wife of Ptah-mose and, in this story, *weret khener* of Amen-Ra.

Aper-el: vizier of Lower Egypt.

Ay: father-in-law and probably uncle of Akhenaten, who held considerable power under his reign and that of his successors, eventually becoming king.

Aziru: leader of the *hapiru*, who became the first king of A'amu.

Djefat-nebty*: woman physician in attendance on the royal harem.

Djehuty-mes (Thutmose): famous sculptor in the reign of Akhenaten.

Ineni*: wife of Djehuty-mes.

Keliya: Mitannian diplomat.

Kha-em-sekhem*: a sculptor in the workshop of Djehuty-mes.

Khuit*: neighborhood healer.

Kiya: Mitannian princess named originally Taduhepa, married first to Amenhotep III then to his son, who made her his Greatly Beloved Wife.

Mahu: chief of police under Akhenaten.

Ptah-mes known as **Mai:** high priest (First Prophet) of Amen-Ra.

Mane: diplomat assigned to Naharin (Mitanni).

Nefert-iti Nefer-nefru-aten: queen and later possible coregent of Akhenaten. She was probably his cousin on the maternal side. Her name means "the beautiful one has come."

Pentju: Chief physician of Akh-en-aten, priest of the Aten.

Ptah-mes: former vizier of Upper Egypt, First Prophet of Amen-Ra, and mayor of Thebes, current high commissioner of northern vassals (this last office fictitiously ascribed to him).

Rekhet-ra*: daughter of Djehuty-mes and former wife of Kha-em-sekhem.

Si-mut: Second Prophet of Amen-Ra.

GLOSSARY OF GODS

Amen-Ra: Amen, or— more properly—Imun, the Hidden One, was a local god of Thebes. When a Theban dynasty came to power in Egypt, Amen became the high god of the entire country and was merged with the all-important sun god **Ra.**

Ammit: "The Devourer", a monster who consumed the souls that didn't prove worthy in the judgment that followed death.

Aten: The Aten was originally just the visible disk of the sun in the sky. Amen-hotep III claimed to be himself the Aten, that is, the *manifestation* of the sun god. His son took it a step further and worshiped his father as a kind of purely spiritual high god, not to be depicted or approached except through Akh-en-aten himself, the sole mediator.

Bes: An ugly, lion-like dwarf god, protector of children.

Djehuty: Thoth, the god of scribes and judge of souls, often associated with ibises or baboons.

Djeser-ka-ra: The divinized king Amen-hotep I, who was worshiped as a patron of healing.

Hapy: The god/goddess of the Nile inundation. Because he/she represented the totality of fertility, Hapy was thought of as hermaphroditic.

Haru: The solar god Horus. The king, while alive, was considered to be his avatar, except under Akh-en-aten.

Hut-haru: Hathor, a multi-purpose feminine deity— goddess of beauty, joy, music, and sex, welcomer of the dead, and personification of the gentler aspects of the sun. Her name means "mansion of Horus."

Im-hotep: Originally an Old Kingdom official responsible for the building of the Great Pyramid, he became the patron god of physicians.

Inpu: Anubis, the god of embalming.

Ishtanu: Hittite sun god, one of several divinities of the sun worshiped in Hatti.

Khonsu: God of the moon, a son of Amen-Ra, seen as the protector of travelers.

Ma'at: Both the goddess and the concept (with a lower-case *m*) of truth, cosmic order, and right.

Meret-seger: "The lover of silence", goddess of the desert where the dead are buried on the west bank of the Nile.

Mut: The consort of the god Amen-Ra, considered a motherly protector.

Ptah: The creator god of Men-nefer.

Sekhmet: The lion-headed goddess of plague and hence of healing. She also represented the murderous power of the sun, a kind of malicious alter-ego of Hat-hut-haru.

Serqet: The scorpion goddess who protected from poisonous stings and from illness generally.

Seshet: The goddess who personified writing.

Shu and Tefnut: The male and female principles, twins and spouses, first of all the gods to split off from the primal All. They represented Air or Light and Moisture.

Ta-weret: "The Great One," the hippopotamus goddess who protected women and children.

GLOSSARY OF TERMS AND PLACES

A'amu: Called **Amurru** by its inhabitants, this was a kingdom on the Mediterranean coast north of Byblos and south of Ugarit.

Akhet-aten: Horizon of the Aten, the new capital city built by Akhenaten.

Akkadian: The language of Babylonia and Assyria, used as a universal diplomatic language. Its cuneiform writing system was also adopted by nearly every neighbor of Egypt and used to write a variety of languages.

bulti: Tilapia.

deben: A unit of weight, equal to 91 grams.

dja: A unit of volume, equal to about 1/3 liter.

Djahy: The southern part of the Levant, more or less Roman Palestina.

djed **pillar**: A pillar erected in a summer festival and also during the *heb-sed*, thought to represent the spine of Osiris. It symbolized stability.

Double House of Silver and Gold: The royal treasury, although much of the wealth of the kingdom was not in the form of precious metals but of commodities.

doum palm: A type of palm tree bearing large edible fruit.

electrum: A naturally occurring alloy of gold and silver much prized by the Egyptians as white gold.

Feast of Drunkenness: An annual festival commemorating Hut-haru's attempt to wipe out mankind, frustrated by getting her drunk. It was celebrated by inebriation, thought to open participants to a mystic perception of the goddess.

Field of Reeds: The pleasant land of the blessed dead.

Gem-pa-aten: One of four Theban temples to the Aten constructed by Akh-en-aten before abandoning that city as his capital.

Great Green: The Mediterranean Sea.

hounds and jackals: A board game played by two people, using carved stick-like pieces that slotted into the fifty-eight holes in the board.

Ipet or **Opet**: "Shrine," a Theban festival held yearly at Luxor which renewed the divine soul of the king and reaffirmed his affiliation to Amen.

Ipet-isut: The great temple of Amen-Ra at Thebes (Karnak).

iteru: A unit of distance, equal to about a mile.

Iunu: Heliopolis, a city in Lower Egypt sacred to Ra.

ka: One of the elements of the human (or divine) soul, which survived death. It seemed to be the vital essence and determined the nature of the person, human or divine. The king was thought to have a divine *ka*, renewed annually in the Ipet Festival.

Kebni: The Egyptian name for Byblos, a large city on the Mediterranean coast. The natives called it **Gubla**.

Kemet: What the Egyptians called their country. It meant the Black Land, because of the rich black alluvial soil of the Nile Valley. They also referred to Egypt as the **Two Lands**.

Kharu: The area represented today by Syria. The name refers to the Hurrian (Mitannian) population, but most people of Kharu were Semitic speaking.

Khent-min: The city of Akhmim in Upper Egypt, home of Queen Tiyi and her family.

Kheta: Hatti Land, the kingdom of the Hittites, an increasingly powerful empire in Asia Minor.

medjay: Originally a Nubian tribe used as policemen, it came to indicate the police in general.

Men-nefer: The city of Memphis, capital of Lower (Northern) Egypt.

moringa: A tree bearing beans that were pressed for oil.

Naharin: An empire in inland Syria and northern Mesopotamia which had been very powerful but was falling apart at the time of our story. Also known as **Mitanni**.

nebet per: mistress of the house, a title used for any married woman, regardless of class.

Nekhen: A town sacred to Horus in Upper Egypt.

Per-ankh: The House of Life, scribal school run by the priests of Amen-Ra at Thebes.

Peret: The four-month winter season, or season of "growth."

Per-hay: The House of Rejoicing, one of Akhenaten's palaces in Akhet-aten, named after his father's palace at Thebes.

The River: The Nile, which had no name nor any personification as a god.

Sangar: Babylonia.

Sau: Saïs, a town in the Nile Delta sacred to Sekhmet.

senet: A board game for two people similar to checkers.

shebyu **necklace**: A special gold necklace granted to favored servants of the king which marked an elevation of their social status.

Simurru: Tsumur, a city in Kharu that became the capital of the new kingdom of Amurru.

Speech of the Gods: Writing; in our story used to distinguish hieroglyphics from script.

sycomore: Not the *sycamore* or plane tree, but a species of very large fig with edible fruit.

sunu (m.), **sunet** (f.): A physician of a scientific sort, as opposed to priestly or magical practitioners of medicine.

Ta-abet: second month of the season of Peret.

Tunip: A city on the Orontes River, vassal first of Egypt, then of Hatti.

Tushratta: King of Naharin.

Wag Festival: An annual feast of Osiris, during which the dead of the family were honored.

Waset: "City of the Scepter," the city of Thebes, the capital of Upper (Southern) Egypt and seat of Amen-Ra's worship.

Weighing of the Heart: The judgment of the soul after death, in which the person's heart was put on a balance against the feather of Ma'at. If it was too light or too heavy, the soul was thrown to **Ammi** to devour.

Wepet-renpet: New Year's Day.

weret khener: Head of the musical establishment of the Ipet-isut, a post held by aristocratic women.

weshket collar: A broad, originally floral, necklace composed of rows of beads.

CHAPTER 1

A LREADY THE THIRD MONTH OF *the summer season is upon us,* Hani thought as he gazed about his garden. The Black Land had begun to pray for a successful Inundation—for high waters and their rich forerunners, the red and green waves, to fecundate the fields.

Once, the people of Kemet had prayed to Amen-Ra and Hapy, god of the flood. Now Hani wasn't sure to whom they were officially expected to offer their prayers and gifts. To the Aten, he supposed, the only god formally recognized by their king, Nefer-khepru-ra. Certainly not to Amen-Ra, the Hidden One, whose name and cult had become anathema. Hani's beloved city of Waset, once the capital of the Upper Kingdom and home of the world's greatest temple, had emptied as the bureaucrats had departed for the new City of the Horizon, and the tens of thousands of priests and lay employees of the god, left without occupation or income, had grown more and more restless. More and more dangerous.

"That I should have lived to see such a thing," Hani said, shaking his head.

Much had changed in the four years Nefer-khepru-ra had ruled alone after the death of his father, Neb-ma'at-ra the Magnificent, and Hani, for one, would have said none of those changes were good. His family tomb had been desecrated. His wife, a chantress of the Hidden One, had been locked out of the Ipet-isut, great temple of Amen-Ra, along with all the other clergy. Hani had been forced by his conscience to drop out of active service in the diplomatic corps, no longer able to enforce a foreign policy he neither understood nor respected. But no one had seized his property, at least, so he still had his garden—his retreat, his hidden place of safety, his little slice of the Field of Reeds on earth. Drawing a deep breath, Hani let his eyes flow fondly over his garden—the trees he and his brother had planted thirty years before, the flowers, the long pool where his beloved ducks played, and the cool whitewashed house set in the middle, where he and Pipi had played as children and now Hani's own children lived happy lives, as they would until they grew up and moved off to their adult homes.

Dawn had just begun to spread its sweet pale light over the walled garden. The birds awakened, twittering and calling. Qenyt, his pet heron, stalked silently around the perimeter of the pool in search of unwary frogs, lifting her burnished legs with angular grace. In the sycomores, the crickets were falling silent, and the cicadas had not yet begun their roar. Hani drew a deep breath until the farthest corners of his lungs filled with the pure, fragrant air of morning. This was his favorite hour. Despite the disturbing news that every new day inevitably brought, dawn restored his sense of balance, of *ma'at*, and his certitude that everything would be all right in the end.

Having mentally sung his little song of joyful greeting to the rising sun, like the baboons of Ra, Hani made his way back through the mat that hung over the door of the house to keep out the flies. No one else was up yet except for some of the servants; he could hear the splash of water in the kitchen and a small thunder of wood for the oven dropped on the earthen floor. No longer did Pa-kiki, his second son, have to get up at dawn to go to school at the House of Life—the Per-ankh was closed, along with the temple that housed it. Hani and his father, both scribes, were putting the finishing touches to the boy's education. Soon Pa-kiki would go to Akhet-aten to live with his brother and work at some low-level job in the Hall of the Royal Correspondence, beginning his rise through the ranks.

Hani planted himself in front of the little shrine in his salon, where a small statue of the Hidden One, and homely images of Ta-weret, the Great One, and the dwarf god Bes—protectors of women and children—were honored with flowers and bowls of grain. These days, every shrine was supposed to feature some stele of the Sun Disk and the royal family, even in private devotions, but he didn't feel that kindly toward his ruler and his ruler's god. If he brought an Aten stele home, Hani could imagine what his wife, Nub-nefer, would say, she whose father and brother had each served as Third Prophet of Amen-Ra. Yet Hani was uneasy about giving some officious visitor an opening to carry dangerous tales about his lack of loyalty. He had enough against him already. *Perhaps I ought to get at least a small one...*

Hani drifted toward the kitchen, following his nose. He hoped the heavenly fragrance of baking meant the cook would soon take some fresh bread out of the oven. Hani was hungry—hungry for bread and hungry for life. It was dawn in the season before the Inundation, after all. Time for good things to begin once more. One could believe, on such a morning, in the cycle of creation—that after the grim, confusing years of the immediate past, good would roll around again.

✦

Later that morning, Hani's secretary and son-in-law, Maya, arrived, ready to begin dictation. The little man, too, was in a twinkling mood. *He and Sat-hut-haru must have had a rousing evening.* Hani chuckled. It still seemed impossible that his seventeen-year-old second daughter was a *nebet per*, a mistress of the house, and she'd traded her maiden's braids for the long locks of a married woman.

"Good morning, Lord Hani. I have these fair copies of the letters for you. Shall I read them aloud for your approval?" Maya seated himself cross-legged on the floor and unhitched his pen case from his shoulder. Thanks to the understanding of his superior, the high commissioner Lord Ptah-mes, Hani had been permitted to work in a domestic capacity rather than resign outright from his post. He hadn't been sent abroad for a year and had seen to his duties from home, showing up at the capital from time to time—just often enough not to be conspicuously absent from the roster of assignments.

"Go ahead, Maya. I'll stop you if I hear anything I want to change."

Maya unrolled the first of the documents and began to read it aloud, but Hani's thoughts drifted in and out as he remembered the troubles of conscience that had bumped his career off the expected road. "Let me look at that, son," he said, reaching out a hand. "I'm distracted and didn't absorb it." He took the papyrus from the secretary and began to read. He had to anchor his attention firmly to avoid slipping away again—to the garden, to the river, to the reeds where the wading birds he loved awaited him.

All at once, Hani was conscious of a rush of bare footsteps and a swirl of skirt bearing down on him. He dragged his eyes away from the letter to see that Neferet, his youngest, had approached with her usual impetuosity and was standing in front of him, hands on hips.

"What can I do for you, my love?" he said, smiling at the sight of her dressed like a young lady, her child's sidelock transmuted into the tiny braids of maidenhood. *I can't believe it. The last of our children, almost grown.*

"I've decided something, Papa," she said earnestly and seated herself on the floor beside him, pulling up her skirt to cross her legs with greater ease. At thirteen, she was still the stocky, broad-shouldered little hoyden he loved, despite the dress. "I've decided I want to be a physician—a *sunet*."

"Is this something new? I don't believe you've ever mentioned it."

"I thought you wanted to be a horse," said Maya with a straight face. Hani tried not to laugh.

Neferet shook her head impatiently, sending her braids flying. "Oh, that was when I was a little girl. I mean, I did

27

want to be a chantress of Amen, but…" She shrugged, with an eloquent lift of the eyebrows.

Although the impossibility of serving the Hidden One these days was a serious matter, Hani smiled nonetheless, because Neferet took after his side of the family and couldn't carry a tune. Neither was she especially lissome, should she be inclined to serve as a temple dancer. Her dance style had about it more enthusiasm than grace, her father thought tenderly—unlike her two sisters.

"Why, that's a noble aspiration, my dear. You'll have to study hard. Perhaps the priests of Sekhmet at Sau have a school that accepts girls."

"I'm smart. I'm smarter than Pa-kiki. Do I have to know how to read and write?"

"I honestly don't know. Most doctors seem to, but I'm not aware of any women in the scribal schools, so maybe women physicians don't."

"We could teach you, couldn't we, my lord?" offered Maya with a glance at his father-in-law. "You wouldn't need to know the formal Speech of the Gods, just script."

She set her elbow on her knee and propped her chin on her fist, staring first at Maya then at her father. "I wonder if there are doctors who take care of animals."

"I can't imagine there aren't," Hani said, recalling his days as an army scribe. "The king's fancy chariot horses certainly had a doctor." He cocked an eyebrow at her. "But in the army, they're all men."

Neferet nodded pensively. "What about cats and pet herons?"

Hani was so overcome with affection for this suddenly serious girl that he reached out and tugged her braids with a smile. "I don't know. You could start a whole new specialization. Be the first heron doctor."

"I could." She got to her feet, seemingly unaware, or untroubled, that her skirt was caught up in the crack of her buttocks. "Let me go talk to Qenyt and see what she thinks about it."

Maya, at his side, was tee-heeing openly. Hani managed not to laugh until his youngest daughter had skipped away. *Don't ever change*, he thought, his heart full.

The two men settled back to work. The sun had swung from one side of the room to its noon position—its long matutinal shafts growing shorter until they no longer pierced the clerestories—when Hani crawled to his feet and stretched. "I guess we're finished for the day, Maya. You can make good copies of those letters I just dictated, and we'll go from there in the morning. At the end of the week, I'll take them up to the Hall of the Royal Correspondence."

"Count on me, Lord Hani." Maya knelt to gather his writing implements and rolls of papyrus. He looked up at Hani with a sudden anxious expression. "Sat-hut-haru and I are having dinner at Mother's tonight."

Concerned by his look of unease, Hani asked, "Is there a problem with that?"

The secretary stood and brushed himself off. He said in a hesitant voice, "I hope Sat-hut-haru won't be disappointed. Mother just lives behind her shop. It's nothing like your house."

Hani had noticed that Maya had never invited his bride to his mother's home, and now he was beginning to get a sense of why. "Sati knows she's a goldsmith. Why would she be disappointed?" But Hani realized that Maya must harbor all sorts of anxieties about his artisan-class birth, having married, as Maya had done, into the scribal class, where no one was ever permitted to forget that their way of life was best. "Do you think we've raised her to care about such things? She loves and admires your mother."

"But she's never actually seen the house. She'll picture me growing up there, and it will make her think of how different our pasts were." His brow was pleated with insecurity.

Hani clapped a fatherly hand on the little man's shoulder. "Give her credit for seeing through that sort of thing, Maya. You're a scribe now, and that puts you in the ruling class. The more credit to you for having done it on your own."

"Thanks to you, my lord." Maya cast doglike eyes of gratitude upon his father-in-law. "Thanks to you for everything, or I'd never have been able to stay in school. I'd be keeping Mother's books in the back of the shop."

Hani had served as Maya's patron, sponsoring the higher education of a promising student who wouldn't otherwise have been able to advance to the ranks of the House of Life. Touched by the young man's gratitude but a little embarrassed, too, Hani mumbled self-deprecating noises. "It's you she's married, my friend, not your mother's house. Don't worry about it. If I'm wrong, I owe you a... a pot of beer. No, some of that wine I sent back from Kebni last year."

Maya threw back his head and gave a great hoot of laughter. "It's a deal, Lord Hani." He let himself out the door with a bit of the old swagger back in his steps.

Hani was shaking his head in affection and pity at the

sensitivity of the young when his wife, Nub-nefer, glided in, barefoot and silent, from the back of the house. She was still trim and beautiful, with great fringed black eyes and a perfectly bowed mouth.

"Ah, my dearest. There you are." He opened his arms to her, his heart expanding, and she pecked him on the cheek.

Her face was puckered with the effort to control her laughter. "Neferet has decided she wants to be a heron doctor. I thought you would be pleased."

"It's a step up from wanting to be a heron," Hani said with a grin. "Our little girl is growing up."

"No point in even taking her ambitions seriously at this age. They change every day."

"Perhaps, although it wouldn't be a bad thing to have a physician in the family. I mean, one who treats humans, not herons."

Nub-nefer looked at her husband, wide-eyed. "Do you mean that? You think she should really study medicine?"

He shrugged cautiously, feeling he had stepped into a trap. "If that's what she wants, why not?"

"But, Hani, who ever heard of a woman doctor?" She made an exasperated noise. "She might as well treat herons, for all the patients she'd get."

"Yet there are such, my dear. I know I've heard of it. I think the priests of Sekhmet at Sau may accept girls for study."

Nub-nefer gave him an accusatory look. "Have you been encouraging her in this scheme, Hani? Because she said exactly the same thing."

"No, I swear, my love. Today is the first time I've even

heard she was interested. And maybe it's just a whim. But if she is interested, why shouldn't she pursue it? She's smart."

Her lips pursing, Nub-nefer hummed dubiously. Hani maintained a prudent silence until his wife finally blurted, as if ashamed to have to say it, "Isn't it a little working-class—a woman going to patients' houses with a basket of herbs? A village healer, for the sake of the Hidden One?"

"Male doctors are scribes, my doe, and often priests. They have very elevated status. Wouldn't it be the same for women doctors?" Hani didn't want to sound argumentative, so he used his best mild, reasonable, diplomatic voice.

"Who's going to teach a girl to read and write, Hani? Don't set her expectations high just to have them dashed in her face, please."

Hani wanted to laugh, but he saw that Nub-nefer was really concerned for her passionate little girl, so he said gently, "Her father, grandfather, both brothers, brother-in-law, and all her uncles know the Speech of the Gods, my dear. She won't lack for teachers."

Nub-nefer turned her eyes away, brows contracted. She murmured, "It doesn't seem feminine to me."

"To me, the mystery has always been why doctors are male, when men generally have so little feeling for the sick or weak. I think a feminine touch would be much superior."

Nub-nefer seemed to debate with herself in silence. Then she said stiffly, "I see I can't argue with you, dear. Your mind is made up."

"Not at all. And it isn't *my* mind at stake here. It's Neferet's. She's only thirteen. She may very well change goals. In a year or two, she may prefer simply to get married and forget all about the scribal life. And that would be fine.

But if she persists, I think we should support her." He turned Nub-nefer's chin back toward him. "Don't you?" He smiled at her beguilingly, and she seemed to soften in spite of herself.

"She'll probably be obsessed with some new scheme before the end of the year." Nub-nefer sighed, no doubt hoping it would be so, and shrugged.

Hani bent to kiss the sweet slope between her shoulder and neck. He thought of Neferet, groping to find herself, of Maya, so concerned that his wife think well of him, and of his own eldest son, Aha, desperate to impress the king. "I pity the young."

"Well, I pity the old," said his father, Mery-ra, from the doorway. "It's a hard walk here from Meryet-amen's in the sun."

"I've told you to take my litter whenever you need it, Father," said Hani in mock severity. "But oh, no. You want to look manly in the sight of your lady friend. You're too proud."

Mery-ra chuckled, his belly bouncing. "Or too forgetful. I'm afraid I'd leave it there."

"I doubt if she'll break it up for firewood the first time that happens," said Nub-nefer dryly. "I leave you gentlemen to your mischief. I need to go cauterize some wounded animals." She headed for the rear of the house but then, at the door, turned back. "Would *you* go to a woman doctor to be treated, Hani?" She disappeared into the kitchen.

"Are you sick?" Mery-ra looked at his son in surprise.

"No, no. It was a rhetorical question. Neferet has been talking about wanting to be a *sunet*, and Nub-nefer wants me to admit that no one would ever go to a female doctor."

33

"Women would, I should think. I'll bet the king's harem has a female doctor."

Hani looked at him, impressed. "An excellent idea, my noble father. I may ask around."

Mery-ra pursed his lips to hide a grin. "The next time you're in the king's harem, eh?"

Hani set off for the bedroom, but his father called after him, "What under the sun did she mean about cauterizing animals?"

With a laugh, Hani said over his shoulder, "She's going to start lunch. It's a little medical humor."

⸎

The next morning, Maya appeared for work in a golden mood, a spring in his step and a snippet of song on his lips. The evening had gone splendidly, and he could see he'd worried for nothing about how Sat-hut-haru would confront his modest childhood home. She was better than some shallow, spoiled rich girl; he should have known. She'd admired his mother's skills and looked around with fascination at the neat compaction of workshop and living quarters, oohing and aahing over everything as if it had been palatial. They had encountered a slightly awkward issue of size that he hadn't even thought to worry about in advance—because Maya and both his parents were dwarfs, their few pieces of furniture were low, and Sati's knees had to turn aside so she could sit at the table. But she managed the maneuver with such adorable grace that no one would have thought it was a compromise.

What a girl. Her bones are silver, and her flesh is gold, like a goddess, Maya thought, pride swelling within him. And of

34

course, Mother's servant was an excellent cook, so the meal had been as much a work of art as the magnificent jewels she turned out for the king and his ladies.

"Good morning, Maya. You look radiant. Things must have gone well last night after all," Lord Hani said with a wide smile that bared the gap between his teeth. His little brown eyes twinkled.

"Oh, yes, my lord. Your daughter was the perfect guest, as I should have expected. Mother gave me these for you." He presented the little meat pies she had wrapped in linen for Sati's parents. "She said to stick them in the oven for a few moments to heat them, although I like them cold."

Hani sniffed the package. Then he unrolled the wrapping and extracted a pie. "Perhaps I'd better make a judgment about that." He bit off half the little triangular pastry and chewed, his eyes closed in ecstasy. "There's cumin in them. And tamarind. Sublime! Be sure Sat-hut-haru learns to make these delights!"

Maya beamed. "I will, my lord. With pleasure."

Hani scoffed down the last of the pie and licked his fingers. "Before we start work, let me ask you something, my friend. Does your mother happen to know of any women physicians?"

Maya twisted his mouth in reflection. "I have no idea, but I can ask. No one is sick, I hope?" Then he remembered Neferet's new ambition and answered his own question. "Ah, to study with."

Hani nodded and prepared to seat himself then seemed to have second thoughts. "Would In-hapy mind if we disturbed her briefly this morning to ask, do you think?"

"Not at all, my lord." Maya hung his writing case,

which he had just removed, back on his shoulder, and the two men headed for the street.

"You know, I thank Khonsu the Traveler every day that I'm not somewhere in Kebni or A'amu right now and that I'm able to perform these little services for the children," Hani said as they walked along with their mismatched strides. He was a broad, thickset man whose heavy, rolling gait made Maya think of a wrestler or a sailor. He was *solid*, in every sense. Maya loved him—adored him—far more than the father he barely remembered. "They'll all be grown and out of the house soon, and how sad I would be not to have any memories of their childhood."

"I guess we should make offerings for Lord Ptah-mes, eh, my lord? It's thanks to him you were given a domestic assignment. And me too," Maya added, heat rising up his cheeks.

Hani glanced down at him from the corners of his little brown eyes. They were crinkled with a knowing smile. "'Take a wife while you're young, that she make a son for you,' eh, Maya? 'She should bear for you while you're youthful.'"

Maya gave the sort of salacious laugh men indulged in when they talked of making sons. He and Hani walked along in companionable silence through the modest neighborhoods of working-class Waset—narrow streets closely packed with small walled properties—almost windowless houses of one or two stories in whitewashed mud brick, more or less well maintained. On the rooftop terraces, women hung laundry, shelled beans, and pounded grain. Men led donkeys loaded with supplies that could barely pass between the walls, while children ran up and down the street on errands or in that rare happy escape from the necessity of work. People called to one another or sang as they labored. The neighborhood was never silent and never without smells of cooking, smelting, and brewing. This was the world Maya had grown up in, a far remove from the quiet garden of Hani's family home and his numerous servants and his country house and his boats.

Maya wasn't sure how he felt about his neighborhood and his home. He both loved it and felt a little shame at its humble dimensions—and the attached workshop, with its inescapable reminder that here people toiled over forges and with dirty substances that hardened their hands and bowed their backs. Still, he'd passed a more-or-less happy childhood behind these walls that he now saw before him.

The gate was locked. It was a goldsmith's shop, after all, and too many valuable things lay within—things that belonged to the king—for just anyone to be able to pass inside. Maya hammered on the door then whistled and yelled, "Mother! It's Maya." The stalwart old Nubian who guarded the gate unbarred it and grinned as he saw his young master. Maya and Hani passed through into the court. "Is Mother here?"

"She is, little master. Inside."

In the square of light from the door, In-hapy, Maya's mother, was bent over the worktable along with a number of men and boys, all of them big people except her. Hair covered with a scarf knotted at the back of her neck, she was perched on the high stool where Maya had seen her every day of his life, her nimble fingers plying a file against something tiny. Sparkles of gold dropped to the table around her as she worked.

"Mother!" Maya called. "Do you have a minute? Lord Hani wants to talk to you."

She looked up and laid down her file, delight widening her eyes, which had been squinting against the flying gold dust. "Son! My lord!" She slid from her stool and came to greet them, bowing before Hani as if they weren't the in-laws of a married couple.

"In-hapy. Blessings on the mistress of the house," Hani said heartily. "I hope I'm not inconveniencing you. I promise not to keep you long."

"Not at all, my lord. Come into the back, where it's quieter. Can I offer you beer?"

"No, thanks. I just wanted to ask you a question, then I'll let you get back to your work."

In-hapy waddled before them through the mat-hung door into the house proper and urged them to seat themselves on the packed-earth floor strewn with cheap rugs and cushions.

I need to buy her some stools, Maya thought, a little irritated. *But she can afford them herself.* The fact was, his mother was quite prosperous. *I suppose she's just never even thought of how low-class it is to receive guests on the floor.*

"Let me preface this by saying I don't know any women other than my wife whom I might approach with a question like this. And I know her answer already." Hani gave his amiable gap-toothed grin that made him resemble a small naughty boy. "Do you happen to know of any female physicians?"

Maya's mother put a pensive finger to her mouth. "Let me think. I hope none of your family is sick, Lord Hani."

"No, no." He laughed. "Neferet, our youngest, suddenly

wants to be a doctor, and I promised her I'd try to find someone for her to apprentice herself to."

"Well, yes, in fact, there's an old woman in the neighborhood who knows a good bit about healing. I don't know if you could really call her a doctor. She's surely no scribe. But everyone goes to her for potions and unguents. She's had plenty of experience."

"That should be a good place to start."

"Her name is Khuit. She's a widow. Her husband used to be a brewer who worked for the temple." She looked up at Hani with a significant spark in her eye. "Good thing he's already dead, says I."

"Good thing indeed." Hani got to his feet and dusted off his kilt. "Where does she live, do you know?"

"Go to the corner in this direction," she said, pointing vaguely toward the entry. "Then down that alley to the fourth or fifth house. I no longer even remember which one. Thanks be to Sekhmet, we've all been healthy. The last time we went there must have been when Ipy got a stone fleck in his eye, and he's all grown up now."

"How's his eye?" Hani asked, a smile trembling on the corners of his mouth.

"Perfect. He's my best journeyman. Sees like an eagle." She turned to her son. "Maya, you may remember which house, but in any case, you can ask."

"Thanks, my dear lady. May the Lord of the Horizon keep you in good health." Hani dipped his head gratefully.

In-hapy bobbed up and down in a respectful bow. "And his blessing on you and yours, my lord."

Maya leaned over and pecked his mother on the cheek.

"Thanks for the dinner the other night. Sat-hut-haru loved it."

The old woman's wrinkled face lit up in delight. She waved at the men as they made their way out the gate under the benevolent gaze of the Nubian.

"I don't suppose she'll ever just call me *Hani*," said Hani when they were out on the street once more.

"I think that would be very hard, my lord." Maya laughed, realizing he had the same problem. He could never address his father-in-law as his social equal. "Habit dies slowly. 'Stand according to your rank,' as you put it so well in your aphorisms."

"That's all right. I can't call Lord Ptah-mes just *Ptah-mes* either, although I think that would please him."

They tromped down the dusty unpaved street to the first alley and turned to their left. Maya started counting houses. There was an empty lot, now planted with lettuce and cucumber, where a residence or maybe two had clearly been torn down, and that confused him. He stood, staring in annoyance at the broken row of houses.

Then a distant memory clicked in. He pointed. "It's there—the one with no whitewash."

They approached the faded door and knocked. No one answered. They waited a decent length of time, then Hani knocked again. "Anyone home?" he called. "We're looking for Khuit." He turned to Maya. "You're sure this is the house?"

"Yes, it's the house, love," a rattly old voice said at their backs. The two men turned. Maya recognized immediately the wispy little bowlegged figure with a basket over her arm who confronted them. Khuit was exactly as he remembered her from his childhood—a shrunken little monkey of a woman who looked as if she had been left for forty days in the embalmers' salts. She was dark and shriveled, with a toothless mouth and bright, twinkling eyes. "What can I do for you, love? Ah, it's my little sweetheart, In-hapy's boy too. Come in, come in."

They followed her into the tiny low-ceilinged salon hung all over with pungent, musty-smelling drying herbs. Baskets of roots gave off a dank earthy odor. There was hardly room to walk through all the jars, baskets, pots, mortars, and cutting boards laid on the tables and on the earthen floor with no apparent order. A striped cat with round golden eyes watched the invaders from the midst of the clutter.

"My name is Hani son of Mery-ra. I understand you're the healer in this neighborhood."

"I am, I am. And have been for forty years. Need an enema?" She cackled, and Maya felt a hot flush creeping up his cheeks. He hoped Hani didn't think this was the sort of person his mother consorted with.

But Hani laughed, seeming at ease in this world so different from his own. He looked extremely large in the tiny, cluttered room. "No, thank you. I'm here because my daughter wants to become a doctor. Mistress of the house In-hapy suggested you might be able to apprentice her to you so she could learn something about medicine."

"Well, then, I have had an apprentice or two over the years. Girls don't seem so inclined to be healers anymore. Everybody wants to marry a rich man. Don't ask me why."

"Neferet is a very independent young lady," Hani

assured her. "Needless to say, we'll pay you. Can I offer you a goat, or would you prefer something like grain?"

"A goat, my lord. A little she-goat. My little she-goat died, and sometimes there's nothing like milk to cure a sick person."

Maya, who caught an avaricious gleam in the old woman's eyes, figured there was probably nothing like a little milk for the doctor either.

"Very well, my good woman. I'll have her brother bring Neferet tomorrow morning, if that suits you."

They made their goodbyes and set out down the road again. Hani said, "I need to go to Akhet-aten tomorrow, but you don't have to come. Just finish those letters and help Neferet with her writing lessons. I should be back in about two weeks. And keep working on that son." He winked sideways at Maya, who felt a surge of resolution.

He might even have puffed out his chest a bit. "With pleasure, my lord."

※

Nineteen days later, Hani disembarked from the ferry that had borne him back from Akhet-aten and made his way home through the deserted streets of Waset, victim of a curious sensation of foreboding that churned in his stomach like an ill-digested meal. He realized the moment he entered the house that something terrible had indeed taken place. From within came the loud, distraught weeping of several females and Mery-ra's voice crying, "When did this happen?"

Hani's heart began to thunder—the wild, flapping wings of a trapped bird. "Nub-nefer?" he called anxiously.

"Is everyone all right?" And of course, first in his fears was that something had happened to Baket-iset, his invalid eldest daughter.

But then he heard her, too, saying, "Oh, poor Auntie!" And he feared lest it might be Nub-nefer's brother, Amen-em-hut. Everyone expected from moment to moment that he would be arrested or beaten or worse.

Hani pushed his way into the salon to find the entire family gathered there with Anuia, his sister-in-law—as he had feared—sobbing hysterically in Nub-nefer's arms. His wife looked up as he entered, tears running down her cheeks but her expression resolutely strong. Neferet swooped down on her father, hugging him close.

Hani squeezed her to him with one arm. "What is it, my dear?" he called across the room to his wife, unable to keep the fear out of his voice.

"Amen-em-hut," she murmured brokenly. "He's disappeared."

Anuia let out another howl. "They've killed him! I know it!"

Hani's stomach clenched with dread. *Oh, great Hidden One, say it isn't so. He's only defending your honor.* His brother-in-law, a priest of Amen-Ra, had refused to accept the closure of the Ipet-isut. He had obdurately complained about the heresy of the king to anyone who would listen— even murmured the dread word *assassination*. He was marked for the enmity of the government in every way.

With Neferet still on his arm, Hani approached his wife and hugged her and her sister-in-law, enfolding them both, as if he could really protect them from harm by this gesture. "Calm yourself, Anuia, my sister. Tell me what has happened."

Nub-nefer guided the hysterical woman to a stool lest she crumble completely. Anuia's homely face was deformed with weeping, her hands fluttering as she passed them aimlessly over her wig, her face, and her breasts as if searching for something—some perch, some rest. "Get Auntie a cup of water, my love," Nub-nefer instructed Neferet, who darted away.

Hani squatted at Anuia's side. "Calmly, now. What happened?"

"He... he was called up by the *medjay* two weeks ago. They interrogated him, warned him they had informers who knew what he was up to and that the king was watching him and that he'd better not try anything. And when he came home, he had a horrible bruise on his cheek and was limping, but he wouldn't tell me what had happened. And the next morning, he was gone." Her ragged words ripped completely into a yowl of fear and grief. "They've killed him! I know it!" She folded over her lap, face in hands, bawling pitifully.

Hani hauled himself to his feet, dread a lump of lead in his stomach. He and Nub-nefer locked eyes. His wife was near the edge of despair, he could see—she was exceedingly close to her only brother, who was just two years her senior—but the mother in her struggled to stay calm for the sake of those who depended on her. The suffering in her tear-reddened eyes struck Hani to the heart. *How gladly I would take your pain upon myself, my love. Yet there's nothing surprising in any of this.* Amen-em-hut had made no effort to restrain his criticism of Nefer-khepru-ra's suppression of the cult of the King of the Gods.

"Maybe he's just hiding," Hani suggested hopefully. "Have you checked your country place?"

Anuia managed to say, "That was the first thing I did, Hani. He's not there. None of the servants have seen him. None of the other priests know where he is, either, and he hasn't been seen anywhere around the Ipet-isut. The gates are locked anyway—he couldn't have gotten in—and the estates of the god have been taken over. There are soldiers everywhere." A wave of sobbing shook her. "He would have told me if he were going to hide someplace. He would have told me. He must be—"

"Let's not jump to that conclusion, my sister," Nub-nefer urged her, massaging her shoulder. She was trying to convince herself first of all, Hani knew. Neferet reappeared with a tall cup of water. She offered it to her aunt, who guzzled down a long draft, splashing it all over her bosom. Anuia passed it along to Nub-nefer, who drank with the same desperation and returned the cup to her daughter.

"Where was the last place you saw him?" Hani forced himself to ask calmly.

"In bed with me, the night before he disappeared."

"Well, the soldiers certainly didn't take him out of the bed while you slept. He must have gotten up safely in the morning. Wouldn't one of the servants have seen him?"

Anuia shook her head, dabbing at her swollen nose with the back of a hand. "He's been having trouble with his stomach. Sometimes he gets up in the night and walks around when he can't sleep."

45

A ripple of unease lifted the hair on Hani's neck. "Outside, you mean? He leaves your property?"

"Sometimes. He walks around the streets. He says it helps him clarify his thoughts."

Foolish man, Hani thought grimly. *With the city as tense as it is now, anything could happen on the streets alone in the wee hours.* He forced himself to smile. "Someone will have seen him, then. I'll ask some of your neighbors' gatekeepers. Maybe the neighborhood watchman."

But Anuia said bitterly, "We hardly have any neighbors, Hani. They've all moved off to *that* place. That hellhole. Where that awful—"

"Enough, my sister." Hani laid a gentle finger over her lips. "Don't get yourself in trouble too. The children need you." He felt an urgent necessity to get away from such misery. Amen-em-hut might just as easily have been the victim of footpads or the desperate unemployed as of the royal police. Hani hoped the priest's body wouldn't float ashore from the River somewhere.

He kissed Nub-nefer and patted Anuia on the back. "I'll go ask around."

"I'll go with you, son," said Mery-ra from behind him. Hani had almost forgotten he was present.

"Thanks, Father. Let's go to Amen-em-hut's house and start with the servants."

"I want to go, too, Papa," said Neferet.

Hani's first reaction was to say no, but there was really no reason why she couldn't accompany them. It would be light a long while yet at this time of year. "Tell your mother where you're going and that I said it was all right."

The girl swooped upon Nub-nefer and whispered

something to her. Hani's wife looked up sharply and caught his eye. She gave him a weary nod as if she was too drained to argue.

Neferet charged back to her father. "I'll take my medical basket."

"Your what?" Hani asked.

"My medical basket. If we find Uncle and he's wounded, I may have to treat him."

Hani and his father exchanged a look that under other circumstances might have been amused. "A generous impulse, my dear," Hani said neutrally, but he had no expectation of finding the missing priest, wounded or otherwise.

They set off through the back streets of Waset, which were noticeably abandoned since the move of the capital. Many of the large walled houses of bureaucrats were empty, the whitewash peeling and the fading gates surrounded by weeds. Most of the inhabitants who remained were probably priests or lay employees of the Ipet-isut and other temples—servants of Amen, Mut, or Khonsu. The fact that they were now unemployed showed in the unkempt facades. Untended mud brick had already started to crumble. Painted gateways needed touching up. The smaller houses, jumbled cubes of unwhitened brick, had already begun the sad, slow march toward ruin. An occasional ill-fed dog roamed the alleys, and the few people Hani saw as they passed seemed furtive and suspicious. No one offered a friendly greeting as they might once have done. Even the intrepid Neferet edged closer to her father as they walked. Hani thought about Amen-em-hut wandering these streets alone in the dark and feared the worst.

"This is what our proud millennial city has come to, eh?" Mery-ra said, speaking for them both. He blew a heavy breath out through his nose, and Hani echoed it.

"I'm afraid Amen-em-hut must have embittered himself the more by his nocturnal rambles," Hani said.

They arrived at the gate of his brother-in-law's villa, a splendid property that testified to the generations of Nub-nefer's ancestors who'd served the Hidden One for liberal recompense. It was defiantly well maintained. Hani knocked on the gate, hoping a doorkeeper would still be on duty. He'd never had the heart to ask Amen-em-hut what kind of toll the closing of the temples had taken on his finances.

Soon an old man opened the peephole. "One moment, my lord."

Hani heard the unbarring of the door from within, and soon it swung wide. Beside the doorkeeper stood Amen-em-hut's twenty-one-year-old firstborn, Pen-amen. His eyes, red-rimmed with sorrow, widened at the sight of his aunt's family. "Uncle Hani! Uncle Mery-ra! Neferet! Mother and Father aren't here."

"We know, son, and that's why we've come. Your mother's at our house and has told us about your father's disappearance." Hani clapped the youth on the shoulder, suddenly forced to swallow hard, unable to find adequate words of comfort. He said in a lower voice, "I told Anuia we'd come and interrogate the servants, ask around the neighborhood. Maybe we can find some clues to where he might be."

The young priest's drawn face lit up with hope. He was devastatingly handsome, taller than his father and just as good-looking, with beautifully modeled lips and great dark eyes set like jewels in a perfectly sculpted copper face. "We're all so distraught—we don't know what to do. Mother just woke up two weeks ago, and he was gone. We kept thinking he'd be back, but..." His lip rippled. "I've come back home to help Mother and the youngsters."

"Good. She needs support."

Hani's nephew walked the men and girl back toward the house through the garden, a splendid place full of shrines and pools. It was a little formal for Hani's simple taste but a delight nonetheless. Everything was neat and clipped to perfection, the paths raked, flowers deadheaded, the shrines whitewashed and decked with bouquets. *The Hidden One and his family must still feel welcome here, at least,* thought Hani affectionately, observing a bowl of grain set out on the step of one of the little buildings. Neferet pointed with a snicker at a pair of sparrows that had claimed it for their own and were gleefully throwing the husks around as they rooted for the best kernels. It made Hani feel especially kindly toward Amen-em-hut that he took his gardening so seriously.

As if he'd heard Hani's thoughts, Pen-amen said, in a voice tight with tears, "Father loves his garden. It's all he's had to keep himself busy since they shut down the temple liturgy."

"He'll be back to enjoy it again, I'm sure," Hani assured him.

"Will he, Uncle?" Pen-amen's eyes were bright with desperation. "It's been two weeks..."

"Have you asked the servants if they saw or heard anything that night?"

"I did. No one observed any unusual sight or sound. Father didn't show up for breakfast—that was the first time they realized anything was amiss."

Hani shook his head gravely. That didn't sound good. "Tell me, my boy. Which of the neighboring houses are occupied? I want to talk to the gatekeepers, see if they heard anything the night he disappeared. When exactly was it, for that matter?"

"It was the eve of what should have been the Festival of Hut-haru. I remember that because we all talked about how few feast days the people have anymore that aren't celebrated solely in the new capital. Father had come back from the office of the *medjay* all bruised and limping, and Mother had made him drink some water lily tea for the pain and suggested they go to bed early. She was nearly hysterical when she saw him, but he wouldn't tell us what had happened, except to say the police were watching him and wanted to convince him to keep his mouth shut."

"I have my medical basket with me," Neferet informed her cousin earnestly. "If he needs more water lily, I can give him some."

"Why, thanks, Neferet," Pen-amen said, looking distracted.

"We have to find him first, little duckling," Mery-ra reminded the girl, laying a grandfatherly hand on her shoulder.

"The nearest inhabited house is the one with the sycamore fig sticking up over the wall. Go north toward the center of town and you'll see it. The owner's name is Nemty-em-saf."

"Thank you, Pen-amen. Let's head out, troops."

"Do you want me to go with you?" Pen-amen offered.

"Aren't you here with the children?"

The young priest nodded reluctantly. "Maybe Neferet would like to play with Meryet-mut; then I could come along."

Hani steered Neferet toward the door. "My dear, why don't you keep your cousins company so Pen-amen can help us find his father?"

"But, Papa," she protested, shooting him an afflicted look. "What if he's hurt and needs medical attention?" Her dragging feet and piteous glance said, *Please don't make me play with Meryet-mut. I'm thirteen.*

But Hani was adamant. "There's my good grown-up girl."

Reluctantly, she stomped into the house, and the three men returned to the gate and into the street.

As they made their way up the dusty lane, empty and silent except for the rhythmic buzz of cicadas, Pen-amen said, pointing, "It's that place right up there. They're the only ones who still live in the neighborhood full-time. All the bureaucrats have moved. Sometimes people come back on holidays, but no one would have had a gatekeeper on duty the night Father disappeared except Nemty-em-saf."

"It's a city of ghosts," Mery-ra said sadly, staring around.

"Men-nefer is even worse," Hani informed him with a grim lift of the eyebrows.

They stopped at the overgrown gate of Nemty-em-saf, and Hani pounded on the faded door. After what seemed a very long time, they heard footsteps approaching, and a stringy middle-aged woman in a scarf swung back the panel. "What is it?" she demanded brusquely. "Oh, Pen-amen! It's you. Come in. Forgive my appearance, dear." She tried to straighten herself up and twitched off her apron.

Hani could hardly believe that the wife of anyone who owned such a large house would have no servants to answer the gate. But without the offerings made to the Hidden One day and night, his priests were left virtually without income. Hani nodded respectfully to the woman, who, despite her apron and working-class scarf, seemed to be the mistress of the house herself. "My lady, I'm Amen-em-hut's brother-in-law. I don't know if you're aware that he's disappeared?"

She gasped in horror, clapping her hands over her mouth. "They've got him, then!" she cried. "Oh, I told my husband he wouldn't last long, being so open about his protests. But may the Great Ones bless him for it. That's what we all say, Pen-amen. We all admired him."

Having noticed her past tense, Pen-amen said in a pained voice, "We hope he's still alive."

"I want to ask you, or whoever may have been guarding the gate the eve of the Hut-haru festival, whether you heard anything. He may have gone walking in the early hours of the morning." Hani watched the woman's face as she gnawed her lip in an effort at recollection.

"It's been weeks," she said apologetically. "There's been a lot of noises at night these last few years. Gangs of ne'er-do-wells breaking into properties and such. I wouldn't have known it was him even if I heard something. But I'll ask my husband."

"Thank you, my lady. Ask any of your friends who live in the area, too, if you would." Hani shepherded the other two ahead of him back into the street. They stared at one another, fighting down discouragement. "Where to now, Pen-amen?"

The young man looked around him in desolation. "All the rest are empty. If we just knew which direction he was walking..."

"I don't think this is going to tell us much, Hani," Mery-ra said. "We'd have to cover the whole city unless we knew where he was going. Assuming he really did leave the house by night. Why don't we try to find the neighborhood watchman?"

Pen-amen led the way to the watchman's modest house. It occurred to Hani that the fellow's job must have gotten a great deal easier since the exodus of most of his neighborhood. Other than patrolling the area to keep the peace, his duties consisted of announcing the news, but he was probably under no necessity to traverse uninhabited streets.

"Perhaps he can notify the neighbors of Amen-em-hut's disappearance so if anyone has noticed anything, they can contact him," Mery-ra suggested.

A little suspicion in his gut made Hani leery of such a move. He shook his head uncertainly. "I almost hate to draw public attention to his absence, Father. Who knows who might hear a watchman's announcement? Do we want strangers to know we're looking for him? Maybe it's better to let them think we think he's dead."

At that word, Pen-amen, at Hani's side, emitted a broken sound. But he caught Hani's eye and said with a resigned nod, "I see what you mean, Uncle. If the *medjay* are looking for him, too, the less they know, the better."

Mery-ra shrugged. "You're the investigator, son."

The watchman's house was a humble whitewashed cube with a second smaller cube on top for an upper floor, leaving the flat roof of the larger part as a terrace. When they knocked on the street door, a man looked down from the roof, hammer in his hand, and called, "What can I do for you?"

"We're relatives of someone in your neighborhood who's gone missing. We wondered if you might have seen him."

The watchman told them to wait, and in a few minutes, they heard his footsteps approaching the door. Soon thereafter, it opened in their faces, and a semi-toothless little man, who didn't seem to be terribly old for all that, bade them enter.

The house was small but self-respecting, boasting a miniature vestibule with a packed-earth floor and a tiny salon beyond. A single column, crudely painted in bright colors, centered it. On the floor beside the column, a woman and a pair of small children who looked like twins stared up, blinded, at the light that streamed in through the open door. Otherwise, the room was dim and stuffy, lit only by a few high, small windows.

"Sure your fellow didn't just move to Akhet-aten?" the watchman asked. "More'n half the neighborhood's gone downriver in the last few years."

"No, no," said Pen-amen. "My father went to bed at Mother's side two weeks ago, and when she awoke, he was gone. He apparently used to walk around the neighborhood in the dark."

"Ah! Lord Amen-em-hut. I shoulda recognized you as his son. Mighty handsome family." The man made an obsequious little bobbing motion. "Always the perfect gentleman, your father, even in the middle of the night."

"You've seen him, then?" cried Hani, cautious hope awakening in him.

"Many times. Don't know which was the one you're talking about, though. He told me once he had trouble sleeping and he liked to walk around a bit. I warned him it weren't safe these days, but he figured he was a priest. If the gods didn't protect *him*, they wouldn't protect nobody."

The man had an open, honest face. It was good to know such a one was walking the streets of the city at night with a big stick. *Although* he's *not very big*, Hani thought with a silent chuckle. *I guess he sounds his clapper for the* medjay *if some large malefactor happens along.*

"This would've been the eve of the Feast of Hut-haru," Hani specified.

"I couldn't say, my lord. It's been a while. The last time I seen him, he was limping, though, 'n had a bruised face. Musta been more or less around the same time."

Hani exchanged a triumphant look with Pen-amen. "That was probably the very night. Did he say anything that might have suggested he wasn't just out strolling as usual?"

The man sucked his sunken cheeks. "Can't think of anything. I passed him not far from his house and greeted him as usual—'cause I've got to know him lately—and he asked somethin' about the wind bein' up. There was a nearly full moon, I remember, and I could see a big bruise on his face. I asked him was he all right, and he said sure. Just had a little accident."

Pen-amen's expression had grown twisted with emotion, but he held his peace.

"Why do you think he asked about the wind?" Hani pursued, an idea forming in his mind.

"The wind on the River, he said. Don't know why."

"Thanks, my man. You've been very helpful." Hani pulled off his faience ring and pressed it into the watchman's hand. The fellow made a pro forma protest but, in the end, received it gratefully. The three kinsmen took their leave.

Once again in the street, Hani said, looking from his father to his nephew, "I think he's somewhere upriver. Did your father sail, Pen-amen?"

"Not a lot, Uncle. But he grew up in Waset, and like all of us, he knew his way around a boat."

"Sounds to me like he wanted to sail upriver and needed to know if there was enough wind. He probably wouldn't have been in shape to row after the *medjay*'s little reception."

"But Mother searched our country place, and all the estates of the god are occupied by the king's soldiers now."

Mery-ra made a dubious moue. "Did he even have a boat?" he asked, and Pen-amen shrugged. "I don't picture Amen-em-hut prowling the marshes the way you do, Hani. Or do you think he stole one from the bank somewhere?"

"I'm sure I can't answer that, Father," Hani said. Still, he felt he had a clue. His brother-in-law probably hadn't been taken by the police from his bed and killed.

After a moment of reflection, Hani said to his father, "We need to pick up Neferet and get home. I don't want the women to be worried about us too."

CHAPTER 2

THIRTY DAYS HAD PASSED SINCE Hani had learned of the devastating disappearance of Amen-em-hut. Hani had tried not to go to the capital any more often than necessary so he wouldn't have to leave Nub-nefer alone with her anxieties. She was a valiant woman—she made an effort not to let her suffering show before the children—but Hani could see from her dark-ringed eyes and hollowed cheeks how afflicted she was. Nub-nefer and her brother were their parents' only two children who had lived. Two years apart in age, they were so much alike even in appearance that Mery-ra irreverently referred to them as Shu and Tefnut, the divine twins. Poor Neferet could hardly get her mother's attention to tell her excitedly what spells and potions she had learned that day, and Hani and Mery-ra found themselves grimly distracted during her and Pa-kiki's lessons. The priest's mysterious fate was an open sore, draining the tranquil energy of the family.

When Hani met with Lord Ptah-mes, he told him about the mysterious disappearance of the priest. "We've looked in the obvious places, but there seems to be no trace of him. It's been a month or more."

Ptah-mes let a heavy sigh escape him. "Listen, Hani. I advise you not to be too openly seen to be searching for him. Amen-em-hut's name is not in good odor at court, and you've made sufficient waves of dissatisfaction. You need to be seen toeing the line." Ptah-mes had witnessed Hani nearly provoking the vizier of the Upper Kingdom to strike him a year or so before. "Dissociate yourself from all the man stands for."

"You're right, of course, my lord," Hani said, but he felt a little rebellious inside. "As you might expect, this is a source of anguish for my wife, though."

"I can't compel you, my friend. But please think about what I'm saying. Things are very tense here, and reprisals will probably be coming. Don't get caught in this." Ptah-mes's thin, handsome face was unsmiling. Something dangerous was clearly underway, and Hani appreciated the warning.

Hani had juggled all this in his mind endlessly on the trip home from Akhet-aten—his wife's grief on one side and the possible safety of the whole family on the other. A terrible Weighing of the Heart through which he couldn't seem to find the perfect course of moral right. *Man does not have a single path; the Lord of Life confounds him,* he reminded himself gloomily.

He was preoccupied as he made his way through the garden to the entrance of his house. The panel was open, the door protected only by the reed mat. Hani put out his hand to draw it aside, only to jump back as his father thrust his head around the edge of the opening.

The rest of Mery-ra was as concealed as his broad physique permitted. "Hani, son. You're home?"

There's something cagey about his manner. What's the old rascal up to now? "As I so frequently am these days," Hani said with a grin. "What are you hiding, Father?"

"Nothing, son, nothing. It's just that there's a little surprise here for you."

"Ah? What's the occasion?" Hani pushed his father gently aside and made his way through the door.

Out of the semidarkness, a familiar yet completely unexpected face appeared in front of him, beaming. "It's me, Hani, old man!"

"Pipi!" Hani cried.

His younger brother, Pa-ra-em-heb, obdurately remained in Men-nefer, former capital of the Lower Land, even though almost the entire government had abandoned it for the new capital. Pipi spread his arms and blocked the doorway. Hani threw himself into his embrace, laughing and protesting his total surprise. They almost never saw one another since Pipi had gone off to the northern capital. Pipi, like all the men of their family, was broad and thick. Never as athletic as his elder brother, he had put on weight since Hani had last seen him, and it spilled generously over his kilt. But his cheerful square-jowled face was unchanged, untouched by the years, as Hani could only hope his own was. With the familial gap between his front teeth, he looked like nothing so much as a mischievous pudgy boy.

"It's good to see you, little brother. What brings you back after so long?" They walked into the salon, arms affectionately over one another's shoulders, with Mery-ra

59

bringing up the rear, cackling his delight—a parade of squat foursquare men who looked remarkably alike.

"Oh, I've been back a few times, haven't I, Father?"

"He has," Mery-ra said.

"But rarely when I've been here," Hani chided affectionately. "I'd concluded you no longer loved me and were trying to avoid me."

"Not so. Purely a matter of coincidence. You're away more often than you're home, from what I understand."

"Or used to be," Hani said. "I'm not missioned overseas so often at the moment."

"Ah ha ha! I told you you'd get tired of traveling!" Pipi tried to goose his brother in the side, and they began to roughhouse, making threatening noises and hooting with laughter like a pair of badly disciplined schoolboys.

"Hani, my love! You're back," called Nub-nefer, who had appeared in the door from the rear of the house. Hani and Pipi fell apart, laughing and breathless. She fixed the two brothers with a wry smile. "I heard all the rumbling and thought we were having an earthquake."

Nub-nefer approached her husband, and they embraced warmly. "Pipi's here," Hani said with a grin, stating the obvious, perhaps to convince himself.

"I know, my sweet. He's been here for two days."

Hani turned to his brother. "Are Nedjem-ib and the children with you, Pipi? Are you here for long?"

"To the first question, only Mut-nodjmet, and to the second, unknown. I'm actually here to ask you a favor, brother." Pipi looked sheepish, like the little gap-toothed rascal he had once been.

Nub-nefer interrupted. "Let's converse over dinner,

shall we, boys? The children are already in the pavilion." She led the way, and the three men followed, still chuckling and jabbing playfully at one another.

"They act like they're six years old, don't they?" Mery-ra said to Nub-nefer, but there was pride in his voice.

"Yes, Father. You've clearly brought them up right." She called out to the children, who were already seated, "Here's your papa back, my dears."

Neferet bounced to her feet and skipped to them, throwing herself on her father. "Papa! Uncle Pipi's here, see?"

"So he is, my love." Hani kissed her and, still dragging her attached to his waist, knelt at Baket-iset's couch. "And how is my favorite oldest daughter?"

"Wonderful, Papa. We've had such fun with Uncle Pipi and Mut-nodjmet."

"Am I your favorite youngest daughter?" Neferet demanded, hanging on him.

"No question about it." He disengaged her and embraced his niece then held her at arm's length. "Mut-nodjmet! I hardly recognize you. You're a grown woman!"

"Sixteen, uncle. And soon to be married."

Hani was prepared to make congratulatory noises over this announcement, but he caught sight of Pipi's face, which looked severely skeptical. Hani raised an inquiring eyebrow at his brother, who rolled his eyes. "We'll talk all about that after dinner, though. Let's see what Mama has prepared for us all."

"Maya and Sati and Pa-kiki should be here by now," said Nub-nefer, her anxiety evident despite her bright tone. Her nerves were raw, Hani knew. After four years, the disaffected of the city of Amen-Ra could still erupt into violence, as the misery only deepened.

Hani declined to feed her fears. Instead, he asked cheerfully, "Pa-kiki's with them?"

"Yes, son," Mery-ra said. "Maya has generously taken over your lessons while you were away. Clearly, an antique like me can't be trusted to substitute. Sat-hut-haru is pregnant, you know."

"Oh, Father," cried Nub-nefer, exasperated. "You're supposed to let *her* tell him."

"Oops." Mery-ra ducked his head guiltily. "Well, I take that back, son. It was a very brief false pregnancy. You know nothing, all right?"

"I know nothing," Hani confirmed. *I can't believe it. My little girl, soon to be a mother. And what if her child is a dwarf, like Maya?* It was in the hands of Ta-weret, the Great One. They would all love the baby just the same, he knew.

They'd barely begun to eat when Hani heard voices in the vestibule—Maya and Sat-hut-haru and the deep voice he had to remind himself was that of Pa-kiki, who had mysteriously turned nineteen at some point, although Hani still thought of him as a boy in a sidelock. The young people burst into the room, and the diners rose. There were enthusiastic and loving greetings all around. Hani observed Maya and Sat-hut-haru clandestinely as they seated themselves at the shared table Nub-nefer had spread for them. *Yes, they have a secretive glow about them.* He braced himself for the announcement.

As if on cue, Maya cleared his throat. "Lord Hani, we have a little good news to impart to you." He and his wife shared an adoring gaze, then both of them stared proudly at Hani. "We're expecting."

"Why, may Bes and Ta-weret bless and protect you, my children!" Hani found it easy to sound surprised. Every time he thought about his daughter being old enough to bear a child, it surprised him. "When is the happy date?"

"Sometime early in the first month of Peret, Papa. We thought you'd never get home so we could tell you."

"I'm sure your mother has already started making the proper sacrifices."

"And *my* mother gave her a beautiful amulet," said Maya proudly. He turned to Pipi. "She made it. She's a royal goldsmith." They passed the new amulet around—a tiny solid-gold Ta-weret, a match for Maya's Bes, which had already saved his life when two would-be assassins had thrown him into the River.

After she'd handled the amulet, Mut-nodjmet said wistfully, "I can't wait until *I'm* pregnant." She was almost the same age as her cousin but was a plump, plain girl with enormous breasts for someone so young. Hani could see her as a wet nurse for twins. In the background, Pipi mouthed a silent cry of anguish, raising his eyes to the sky.

Hani carefully avoided any talk of the pregnancy out of deference to Pipi, for whom the topic was clearly unpleasant, but of course the happy couple couldn't stop working it into the conversation, with a superfluity of medical details. Even Nub-nefer regaled them with stories of her own parturitions. Neferet showed more interest than her father had foreseen. He'd half expected to see her acting out childbirth at table, but instead, she asked all sorts of

63

clinical questions, demonstrating that she had not yet lost interest in a career as a healer.

Pa-kiki shot his father a look of writhing discomfort, and Hani suppressed a laugh. "I suggest that the ladies withdraw to the salon for their midwifery class and leave the men to drink beer in the pavilion," he said, and his son looked immensely relieved.

"That's not fair," Neferet objected. "I want beer too."

"Isn't it past your bedtime?" asked her eldest sister pointedly.

"I'm thirteen," Neferet protested.

Hani fixed her with a grave paternal eye. "I want to talk to Uncle Pipi, my dear. I haven't seen him in years."

She halted whatever riposte had begun to form on her lips and, with surprisingly good grace, danced off, saying, "I'll call the servants to carry Baket."

"That was unexpectedly easy," said Nub-nefer breezily. "She must actually be growing up. Girls, let's adjourn to the salon. Maya, you may want to tell us about your plans for a new room."

Maya followed her order and accompanied the women back into the house, although not without a longing glance back at his half-finished pot of beer. Pa-kiki decided he wanted to go out with his friends, and before long, only Hani and his father and brother were left in the near darkness, sucking their beer with lazy enjoyment. The crickets chirruped in the dark garden, and a whole perfumery of scents that were never perceptible by day drifted over them. Somewhere down the street, in an empty property, a nightingale began its sweet, melancholy song. Hani exhaled a deep sigh of contentment. By his former standards, a two-week absence was nothing, but homecoming was always sweet.

"It's good to be back here," said Pipi after a while. "So many happy memories."

Touched, Hani glanced at his brother, but he couldn't make out his expression in the twilight. "Yes. Thanks, Father, to you and Mother for giving us such a wonderful childhood."

"You owe most of that to your mother, may she bask happily in the Field of Reeds. I was away much of the time," Mery-ra's disembodied voice answered.

"It seems so much harder to do right by our own children these days," Hani mused. "Although I can't complain now that Aha has come back into the fold."

"Was he out of the fold?" asked Pipi.

"He went through a phase of, shall we say, excessive zeal for the king's new religion." Hani honestly didn't know what Pipi's position was on the Aten and his cult. He'd never showed much religiosity in any direction.

"I told you about the tomb," Mery-ra said.

"Ah, yes. Children are always breaking your heart, aren't they?" said Pipi, mournful.

A solemn silence fell. Hani could practically feel Pipi itching to tell his tale. And sure enough, after a moment, he burst out aggrievedly, "Why couldn't Mut-nodjmet have set her heart on some nice young fellow like your secretary?"

"Come on, brother. Out with it. Why are you here?"

Pipi sighed heavily. "Mut-nodjmet is in love with a sculptor who's twice her age."

"A sculptor? That's odd. How did she even meet him?"

"He has family in our neighborhood in Men-nefer, but

65

he actually lives in Akhet-aten. I think he works for some royal studio."

"Well, that could be worse. If she has to marry an artisan, at least he's a royal artisan. He's probably well paid." Hani bent to take a slurp of his beer.

Pipi groaned. Hani was surprised his feckless younger brother even cared if his daughter married an artisan. Pipi had never shown much pride in his birth or, indeed, respected his exalted profession. He and his family lived in cheerful disregard of the fundamental scribal virtue of arrogance.

"It's not that he's an artisan, Hani. It's that I'm not sure he's a good man. I don't want my little girl falling in with someone who won't treat her right. If he takes her off to Akhet-aten, how will we even know?"

"Mmm," Hani grunted somberly.

"She doesn't legally need my permission to marry him, so I try not to seem too opposed to the fellow lest they just run away together. She's fixated on the idea of marrying this bastard."

Although some men would find the amply endowed Mut-nodjmet very much to their taste, Hani wondered if she weren't a bit desperate to find herself a husband. There was something lackluster and unattractive about her, he was forced to admit—dulled, apologetic, as if she assumed no one would find her appealing. Still, she was a good-hearted girl. His pity went out to his brother, who was desperately trying to ward off the shipwreck of his daughter's life.

"What's his name?"

"Kha-em-sekhem," Pipi said glumly. "He specializes in making plaster models of highly placed people—including the king's family—so the master of the workshop can use them for stone statues without them having to sit for months."

"That sounds important."

"Oh, he's apparently pretty rich. And that's what makes it so hard to say no. He's offering a right royal bride price."

"And there you have one thing that makes us all suspicious," Mery-ra chimed in.

"Maybe he's in love with her." Hani said. "An older man like that—maybe he feels he's not much of a catch and he has to sweeten the deal."

"He's thirty," Pipi said dully.

"Oh. I pictured an old toothless man your age," Hani said with a twinkle, hoping to cheer up his forty-one-year-old brother.

But Pipi didn't even rise to the bait. "He's been married before. His wife left him. That worries me."

"Well, maybe she was at fault…"

"Or maybe he was a terrible husband. Mut-nodjmet thinks he's a victim, of course. Like you, she thinks it was all the awful wife's fault."

"Might be worth it to find out the story," Hani said, realizing as the words left his mouth that he had just taken on a job.

"That's exactly why I'm here, Hani. Mut-nodjmet wants to visit her swain in Akhet-aten, and Aha lives there now, right?"

Hani could see a flash of Pipi's little eyes as he turned toward Hani and the house, from which light glowed softly through the clerestories. Nub-nefer and the servants were still up.

"He does," Hani said. "I guess Father has kept you abreast of such things."

"Maybe we could stay with him for a few days while I try to find out something about this fellow, Kha-em-sekhem. What was this divorce all about? I'd like that bride price, but is he really somebody I want my little girl to marry?"

"Who ever pays a bride price, other than some grandee contracting an arranged marriage? I find that strange. Normally, both sides bring whatever they can to the union. This sounds like he's trying to bribe you." The more Hani heard, the more of a bad taste the whole affair left in his mouth. He reached out through the darkness and laid a hand of solidarity on his brother's knee. "If you want me to look into this a bit, I can do that, Pipi."

"I told you he'd say yes," Mery-ra said smugly.

"Thanks, brother. I was counting on that. I don't know the new capital or have any contacts in royal circles." Pipi shifted his heavy body on his stool with a squeak of wood and said in a quieter voice, "I hope… I hope he's upright. I certainly could use that bride price."

Hani was caught by the wistfulness in his brother's words. Pipi wasn't a man who cared about wealth. "Are you in trouble, brother? Do you need gold? Why didn't you say so? Father and I can surely help you out—"

"No, no," Pipi cut in hurriedly. "We're not in need. It's just nice to have a little cushion, you know?"

Hani did indeed know. He'd always been a responsible father of a family, sacrificing and setting aside against an emergency. And thank the gods, he had provided for Baket-iset's care, no matter what happened to him. There was a tidy silo of grain put away for whichever son took her in after Hani and Nub-nefer were gone. It was precisely over the virtue of such economies that he and Pipi had always fallen out. His brother immediately spent every bread loaf of pay that passed through his hands on trivia, and he never troubled to try to advance himself, even when it might bring his family greater comfort and security.

But at no point had Hani ever understood that Pipi was in want. Hani was pierced with sorrow at the thought. It was like a brand of shame burned into his skin—to let his brother suffer without extending a hand. "You've never said anything, Pipi. We'd gladly help. Forget that scoundrel and his bride price. How much do you need?"

"No, no, Hani. We don't need gold. If you could help me investigate this business with the sculptor, you'd have given me all I want of you. And Nedjem-ib too. It's eating her up. You know how mothers are."

"Luckily, you boys never gave *your* mother any heartaches when you were young," Mery-ra said acerbically into the darkness.

"I tell you what," Hani said. "The next time I'm in the capital, I'll look into this fellow's background. Someone there must know him. That will save you making a trip for nothing if he's really so unsavory you want to nip the relationship in the bud."

"Thanks, big brother." Pipi reached over and groped for Hani's hand. When he found it, he squeezed it, and Hani could feel that the gesture was full of emotion. "You're still looking out for me."

＃

As it happened, Hani had a reason to return to Akhet-aten

the next week. It was the grand occasion of introducing his second son to the Hall of the Royal Correspondence. Pa-kiki was scheduled to begin his new job as a clerk in the foreign service. Hani left him at the reception hall, with an embrace and a proud smile, and watched the boy walk straight-backed through the door into the copying chamber. He remembered his own first day as an army scribe, at just about Pa-kiki's age—the pride, the eagerness, the determination to excel—and the bowel-loosening fear. He shook his head fondly. Gone was the unruly lad who had earned the nickname "Monkey." A young man passed through the dark doorway now—into the rest of his life, with all its unknowns. He would live with Aha's family in the capital, his first time away from home.

Hani tore himself away from the lingering afterimage of his son's broad white-clad back, and he approached the scribe on duty at the desk to announce himself to Lord Ptah-mes.

The man said, with his usual sour expression, "He's waiting for you. Enter, my lord."

Hani made a tentative scratch at the door.

"Ah, Hani," said Lord Ptah-mes, opening it. "Come in." The high commissioner in charge of the northern vassals gestured Hani into his office and closed the door quietly behind him.

A cool, elegant scion of the old Theban aristocracy, Ptah-mes seated himself with grace and bade Hani take a seat as well. "How are you enjoying your new assignment?" he asked, a twitch at the corner of his mouth.

"Wonderfully, my lord. I can't thank you enough. I feel

I can look at myself in the mirror again." Hani grinned. "Not that that was ever much of a treat."

A smile warmed Ptah-mes's severe face, then he grew serious. "I'm sorry to say that I have a new assignment for you, Hani. It won't take you away from home, but it will be an inconvenience, I fear. I felt I had to do this, though. The king has begun to notice your absence from the mission roster."

Hani's neck prickled with hairs rising. *Nefer-khepru-ra is watching me that closely? Am I the object of such suspicion?*

"Whatever my lord commands," he said neutrally. "I didn't realize I was under active observation."

Ptah-mes looked down at his ringed hands pressed flat on his knees. "Your brother-in-law's disappearance is being interpreted in a variety of ways. There are those who see it as an attempt by you and the family to hide him from the royal police." He looked up again, and his dark eyes locked with Hani's. "I'll repeat what I have said on other occasions: I think you need to be careful to be seen as actively furthering the king's policies, Hani. Please take this advice seriously."

Hani took a deep breath and swallowed the stubborn refusal that wanted to come out of his mouth. "Absolutely, my lord. I appreciate your insights. What can I do for our sovereign—life, prosperity, and health be his?"

Lord Ptah-mes leaned back in his chair and clasped his hands in his lap. The pleats of his immaculate linen remained as perfect as those of a statue, despite these maneuvers. "I'm sure you haven't forgotten our friend Aziru."

Hani had to chuckle. "No, indeed, my lord." He had spent the last three years of his life in the overseas service, trying to deal with Aziru, the leader of a group of nomads and social outcasts called the *hapiru*. Despite the man's repeated requests to be admitted as a vassal, ruling over the area of A'amu, torn from nearby Kebni, the king had left Aziru dangling so that he was dangerously close to going over to Kemet's enemies. "Has he ever shown up at court?"

"He has. I'm not sure you'll be so happy to hear the rest of this story. He has been admitted as a vassal at last—"

"But that's wonderful! About time!"

"The bearer of the good news should have been you, clearly, since you did all the hard work of preparation and were only held back by the vacillation in... high places." Ptah-mes suppressed the tremor of disgust at the edge of his lips and added blandly, "Instead it was Hotep, the commissioner of Simurru, who had that honor—and who will get the reward for it."

Hani cared nothing for the *shebyu* collars, the mountains of grain, and the gold jewelry that the king might throw to him in a public ceremony. But to see the corrupt and incompetent Hotep rewarded for a diplomatic conclusion he himself had worked hard to achieve—that was infuriating. He could feel the heat stealing up his cheeks and forced himself to laugh, although it came out sarcastic. "The king is loyal to his friends. I guess that's a virtue."

"We both know Hotep should be bastinadoed and stripped of his rank, not lauded. But his father is influential, and he himself has become quite the little personage at court."

Hani shook his head slowly, not trusting himself to speak. He remembered how he had pleaded with the vizier to admit Aziru to vassalhood to prevent him from going over to the Hittites, who were drawing closer and closer to Kemet's northern borders. He'd been told to temporize, to make vague promises to the *hapiru* leader but to grant him nothing. *And now this. I suppose Hotep needs the king's gold now that he's no longer getting bribes from Yapakh-addi.* The latter, a powerful and ambitious grandee, had been broken as a result of Hani's investigation. Part of that investigation had revealed that Hotep was on his payroll. *What a bunch of swine the Living Haru has surrounded himself with.*

Ptah-mes, watching Hani's reaction, said, "But here Aziru is, a vassal at last. Hotep had the honor of accompanying him to the capital, where the newly minted king of A'amu awaits his audience with Nefer-khepru-ra. Only, that audience has been a long while coming—some months now, I'd say. The palace is getting tired of hosting him."

Hani laughed dryly. "It's true he's a lot less mellow than his father. I daresay he's pretty impatient by this time."

"Impatient and suspicious." Ptah-mes examined his fingernails. "The king wants him lodged elsewhere. In some private person's household. Someone who can keep an eye on the *hapir*'s correspondence, sound out his attitudes, perhaps even influence him."

Hani had a terrible suspicion he knew where this was leading. "Ah?"

"I suggested you, Hani." Lord Ptah-mes looked up at him, his dark kohl-edged eyes penetrating. "For the following reasons. One—you already know him. Two—you're just the person to observe him and interpret what you see. And three..." He paused and then added, with emphasis, "Without having to spend time abroad, you will be conspicuously useful to the king by doing this. Life, prosperity, and health to him."

"I see," said Hani, forcing his voice to remain neutral.

Ptah-mes lifted an apologetic eyebrow. "I know this will be an enormous inconvenience. You will receive a subvention for your expenses from the Hall of the Royal Correspondence, of course."

"That's generous." Hani thought of the chaos in his household already—the presence of Pipi and Mut-nodjmet, the constant distraught visits of Anuia, the preparations for Sat-hut-haru's baby, and his efforts to get Pa-kiki and Neferet settled. "I suppose I have no choice, have I?"

"You always have a choice, my friend. Just consider whether refusal is in your best interest."

Hani knew that his superior was doing this as a gesture of protection, and he was grateful. But it seemed to be the final weight on top of a load that had become nearly insupportable to the poor little donkey underneath. The comical image served to restore his sense of proportion. He laughed resignedly. "I accept, of course, my lord. And I thank you for your consideration."

Ptah-mes blew out a heavy breath. "I think it's for the best." His austere face softened with a smile. "Permit me to make you a small offer in return for this sacrifice. When you're in the capital, do me the honor of staying with me. I've built a modest place here, although my wife is reluctant to leave our home in Waset. So for the most part, I'm here alone. Your presence would be no problem at all."

A warm wave of gratitude and affection enveloped Hani. Ptah-mes was by no means the chill, disdainful grandee he appeared to be. "I'm touched, my lord. I've been staying with my son when I'm here, but they have several small children and another on the way, and I know my presence is a hardship. I'll most gratefully accept your offer. I must warn you, though, that I generally have my secretary with me when I come."

"He's welcome, too, of course. The dwarf, is it?"

"Yes. My son-in-law now."

Ptah-mes made a polite noise of interest. "Well, I look forward to seeing you. It's at the southern edge of the city, near the River. Anyone can direct you, and I'll tell the servants you're coming, in case I should be out." He rose to his full height, elegant and once again formal, and Hani, too, got to his feet. "I'll send Aziru to you sometime in the next few days, Hani. This is a real service you're rendering."

"Anything for the cause, my lord," Hani said wryly.

Before Hani reached the door into the inner office, Lord Ptah-mes turned and said, "By the way, the vizier is pleased that your son has joined his staff."

"Pleased, is he?" Hani stared in surprise. They had not seen one another since Hani's near rebellion, and he feared he'd added yet another black mark against his name in the eyes of the government.

"Yes. He interprets it as a sign of your family's loyalty to the administration." Ptah-mes's thin, well-shaped lips drew wide in a cynical smile.

Hani stuffed down the impulse of a complicit smirk and said seriously, "As it is, my lord. As it most certainly is." He bowed deeply and made his way back to the reception room. Maya popped up from a seat in the shadows, and Hani directed himself toward his secretary, struggling to contain the angry laughter he felt rising inside him, his cheeks burning and brows knotted with the effort. "Well, I have my next assignment."

"Overseas, my lord?" Maya asked in trepidation. Whereas once he might have relished an adventure abroad, now the young man was an expectant father. The idea of traipsing around in Kharu, perhaps risking his life, seemed less glamorous, no doubt, than it had even recently.

"No, in Waset. I'll be hosting our friend Aziru for an indefinite length of time." *Probably his entourage as well,* Hani realized.

Maya's eyebrows arched in surprise. "At your house?"

"That's correct."

The two men made their way, with their mismatched strides, across the bleak, sun-scraped court of the Hall of the Royal Correspondence. The smell of baking bread from the royal bakeries drifted past. Hani sniffed, suddenly hungry.

"Let's go back to Aha's and have some lunch. Then we can head off to Waset. Oh, wait," Hani cried. "I was going to look into that fiancé of Mut-nodjmet's. But I don't have time to now. I'll need to tell Nub-nefer about the guests and make whatever provisions are needed. Ptah-mes didn't tell me how many people are involved."

"Is… is this normal, Lord Hani?" Maya asked, pushing back his wig and scratching his forehead. "To put him up at your *house*? With your *family*?"

"I have no idea, my friend. When was the last time anything normal happened in our kingdom?" Hani's tone was still tart, although he'd begun to reconcile himself to the new reality that had settled upon him. Refusal would have brought reprisals, he was sure. And he was better equipped than most people to observe and interpret Aziru's behavior. Ptah-mes had once again done him a huge favor, he had to admit.

            ✦

Nub-nefer's reaction was less angry than stressed and helpless. "A group of strange foreign men in our house? With all that's going on and Pipi and his family here? Oh, Hani..."

"I know, my love. Believe me, if there had been any way to refuse, I would have. But other than going back into the field, this is probably the cheapest way for me to reestablish my loyalty to the king's foreign policy."

She heaved a sigh of capitulation. "We'll need to set some boundaries for them. We have three daughters, after all. And Mut-nodjmet. I don't want the girls to feel uneasy in their own house."

"Of course. And Aziru and his entourage won't be imprisoned here. They can come and go. We'll point out the location of the nearest beer house and brothel."

Hani had hoped to tease his wife back to humor, but she shot him a black look that melted directly into warmth. "Life with you has certainly never been boring, my duck. I need to check the larders and probably have the men bring more grain up from the silos at the farm. How long are these people staying—did Lord Ptah-mes tell you?"

"It could be brief, it could be extended. Aziru's just awaiting word that Nefer-khepru-ra will receive him in audience."

Nub-nefer seemed to have gone off into efficient mistress-of-the-house mode, Hani saw, ticking off on her fingers all the things that needed to be seen to before an unknown number of foreigners descended upon the household for an unforeseeable length of time. He suggested gently, knowing that it would be hurtful, "Perhaps you and Anuia could meet at her house to commiserate, my dear. It might be better not to expose our private sorrows to these visitors."

She stared at him hotly, but her defiance shifted quickly into damp-eyed grief. "Where is he, Hani?" she whispered, clutching at his shirt. "My brother, my poor little brother. It's been six weeks. What have they done to him?"

His heart in tatters, Hani wrapped his arms around his wife and said, in an effort to reassure her, "Lord Ptah-mes said the government believes *we* might be hiding him. That suggests they don't know any more than we, my sweet. I think they probably haven't done anything to Amen-em-hut, much as they might like to."

She looked up at him, her kohl-rimmed eyes swimming. Was she, as Hani was, trying to draw up hope from some well deep inside—from her faith in *ma'at* and the goodness of the world and the care the Hidden One had to have for his faithful priest? Hani held her close, savoring her warmth, breathing her scent of lilies and bergamot.

Nub-nefer sighed against his chest then pushed herself away and said briskly, "I'd better go talk to the cooks and see what we have on hand. We may need to slaughter a calf… certainly stock the pool with carp and *bulti*."

"You'll do beautifully, my love. It will be the highlight of their stay."

When Maya arrived the following morning for Neferet's writing lesson, Mut-nodjmet and Baket-iset were talking together in the garden pavilion. The latter, forever motionless on her couch after a terrible accident ten years before, was a girl as beautiful in face as in spirit. Maya was deeply touched every time he saw her and watched the natural, loving way in which her family included her in their everyday life, despite her infirmity. He felt shame for the occasional times he'd pitied himself for being a dwarf. By all the gods, he was an able-bodied dwarf, at least! A dwarf uncommonly good-looking and literate besides— married to an exquisite girl who was carrying his child. His patron, Bes, had upended the blessings upon him. They were like a sweet-smelling ointment poured over his head or a cone of perfumed wax at a party. Hearing the happy voices from under the grapevines, he resolved to be mindful of his many blessings and to carry them with panache.

He entered the salon of Lord Hani's home cheerfully. The lady of the house, Nub-nefer, greeted him with a smile, but he could see how troubled she was about her brother's disappearance.

"Neferet will be here any minute, Maya dear. How is Sat-hut-haru doing?"

"She's felt a little sick in the mornings, but she said to assure you she'll be over in the afternoon. She wants you to pass judgment on the meat pies she made."

"She's cooking? Who could imagine!" Nub-nefer laid a considering finger to her cheek. "You know, if she needs another servant, a cook, we would be happy to help. She's going to be busy when the baby comes."

"We've talked about that, my lady. I can manage it. But

thank you." Maya wasn't all that sure he *could* manage it, in fact. But he couldn't possibly ask for anything else from Lord Hani. He thought his mother might have something set aside she could lend them. Gods knew what she did with any of what her fabulous royal commissions brought her—she still seemed to live like a pauper. *Not even a couple of stools, by the Lord Bes!*

"Here I am, Maya," called Neferet. She bounded through the door and posed in regal posture, her feet together, her head turned in serious profile, her hands poised with a reed pen and a potsherd. "Who am I?"

"Who are you? Uh..." Maya swallowed hard in momentary panic. The girl was always doing things like this. "Qenyt?"

But she broke her pose and stomped good-naturedly toward him. "No, silly. I'm the goddess Seshet, patroness of scribes!"

Nub-nefer rolled her eyes. "Are you Im-hotep, patron of doctors, when you go to Khuit's?"

Neferet's grin faded, and her look grew troubled. "She's not a real *sunet*."

"Do I detect some disenchantment there?" Maya teased.

Neferet looked up at him defensively. "I still want to be a doctor. But she's not one."

Her mother put an arm around the girl's shoulders. "Is something wrong, my love? You always come home spouting new knowledge when you're there. Are you not enjoying it?"

"I am, Mama. She's very nice, and everybody loves and trusts her. But... some of the things she does—they seem so..."

"Working class?" Maya finished with a brittle smile.

Neferet shrugged, being too young and sheltered to know what that even implied. "Like prayers and spells and things. I don't want to be a priest. Or a witch."

"A witch?" cried Nub-nefer, alarmed. "Is she a witch?"

"I don't know." Neferet looked spooked by her mother's reaction. "How do you know if someone's a witch?"

"I can't imagine my mother ever went to her as a witch," Maya pointed out, a little offended. "She's a successful healer is all."

But Neferet cast her pleading eyes up to Nub-nefer, who continued to stare at her in concern. Maya figured this must be the ultimate worry for the poor woman, as if she didn't have enough on her mind.

"Dearest, you don't have to keep going back to her unless you want to. Don't let Papa pressure you."

"He isn't. But I don't want to go anymore."

Maya felt a crackle of resentment, which he quickly squelched. Just because his mother had recommended Khuit didn't mean he had to defend the woman or that he was somehow diminished by the fact of her insufficiency. He bit back a comment about Neferet being worth more as a horse than a *sunet* anyway and said blandly, conscious of imitating Lord Hani's masterful ambiguity of expression, "Well, let's get to our lesson. Your father will be back soon, and you'll want to impress him with how you've advanced."

"With how much you've taught me," said Neferet.

Damn the girl. Maya shot her a sharp sideways glance, not sure whether she was correcting him or just restating his words. *Does she think I'm doing this just to impress my employer?* "Take dictation," he said, sounding grumpy in spite of himself. And he began to quote Hani's aphorisms:

"Do not sit when another is standing,

One who is older than you,

Or greater than you in rank.

No good character is reproached,

But an evil character is blamed."

"Slow down, Maya!" cried Neferet, scratching away with her pen. She pressed too hard, and droplets of ink flew out and splattered the lap of her dress, stretched across her knees. "Oh no!"

But he plowed on, his breath steaming in his nose:

"Walk the accustomed path each day,

Stand according to your rank.

Rank creates its rules;

A woman is asked about her husband,

A man is asked about his rank."

Nub-nefer snorted in the background, and Neferet, tongue between her teeth, scribbled desperately away. When she had finished, the girl looked up, her face red with effort.

"Now read it aloud," said Maya, implacable.

Footsteps scuffled on the porch, and someone pushed aside the reed mat. "Hello, everyone," said Mery-ra. "It's Pipi and me, back from the beer house." The two big men irrupted into the room, filling it with hairy bellies and the smell of perspiration and beer.

"Grandfather! Uncle Pipi!" Neferet jumped up and ran to them, proudly holding out her potsherd. "Look what I wrote!"

"She managed to escape reading it," Nub-nefer said quietly to Maya.

"Not so," Maya said. "Read it to them, my girl."

She proceeded not only to read it but to act it out—sitting, standing, reproaching, walking—all with great élan.

"Next time, give her a passage with fewer verbs," said Mery-ra, chuckling.

But then Neferet reached the final lines and seemed to realize what she had written. She shot a crafty look at Maya. "A man is asked about his wife. A woman is asked about her rank."

"Outwitted us, she did!" cried Pipi in delight.

"Can I offer you gentleman a drink, or are you full of beer at this hour of the morning?" Nub-nefer said to the newcomers.

"It was a long, thirsty walk, my dear. I wouldn't mind starting over with some water. How about you, son?"

Pipi concurred, although Maya suspected he would just as soon have had more beer.

"Maya? How about you?"

"*Iyah*, a party!" Neferet looked around gleefully then launched into an awkward version of a dance such as professionals might perform at a party, raising her foot high and clapping her hands and swinging her braids as she leaned backward and forward.

"You'll give your patients apoplexy," said Maya dryly, getting to his feet.

Nub-nefer called to her father-in-law on the other side of the room, "Would you say she takes after your half of the family, Father?"

"Let me show you how it's done in our family!" Mery-ra cried, sidling up to his granddaughter and attempting to follow her moves. Pipi joined him immediately, and the three of them danced around in a circle, kicking, swaying their hips, waving their arms, and rocking back and forth with gusto but the most startling lack of grace, warbling some unidentifiable tune.

Maya started to laugh, and then he couldn't stop, laughing so hard his mouth hurt. He could feel snot running down his face and tried to wipe it off, but he was rendered helpless by the extremity of his hilarity. *What must it have been like to grow up with Lord Mery-ra for a father?*

Nub-nefer was laughing too. When the trio had finally concluded their wild dance and dropped, panting and puffing and fanning themselves, onto their stools, she grinned at Maya. "To think I've tainted the children's blood by marrying into this family."

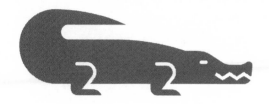

CHAPTER 3

WHEN HANI RETURNED FROM MARKET, where he'd gone to look at some goats to have on hand for milk while the visitors were around, Nub-nefer informed him of two things. First, she said that his father and brother needed a lot of work on their dancing skills. Hani covered his blushing face in pained amusement, being only too able to picture the spectacle Nub-nefer described for him. "Now you see, my dear, that I can't help the way I am. My mother wasn't much of a dancer, either."

"Second," his wife said more seriously, "Neferet doesn't seem to like her apprenticeship with Khuit. Maybe she's getting over her enthusiasm already."

"Oh, she doesn't? Did she say why?"

"She said she thinks the old woman is a witch, and she's not interested in that."

Hani heaved a sigh. It never failed—no sooner did he set foot in the house than some small crisis arose. "I'll talk to her. Unless you particularly want her to become a witch." Nub-nefer pretended to swat him. Then he lowered his voice. "Any word about Amen-em-hut, my doe?"

She dropped her eyes and shook her head. "Still nothing." She looked up, and her lids were suddenly in Inundation, tears spilling over the edges. "Nothing."

"He'll turn up, my love. Have faith." He drew her against him. *Crises, both ridiculous and tragic. Such is life.*

That evening, he spoke to his daughter at dinner. "Your mother tells me you don't want to continue with Khuit, my duckling."

"You haven't given up, have you?" cried Baket-iset. Nub-nefer, who was spooning food into her daughter's mouth, held back while she spoke.

Neferet shook her hands in energetic frustration. "No, it's just Khuit isn't a real doctor. Half of what she does has nothing to do with medicine. She's experienced, and I've learned a lot, but she doesn't know *why* she does anything."

"I'm not sure real *sunu* doctors know why, either. They just read in their casebooks that this has worked, so they do it." Hani could see his careful plans falling apart. Now he'd have to find another lady doctor. "Anyway, I have to go back to the capital in a few days, and while I'm there, I'll ask around. All right, my duck?"

"All right, Papa." Neferet beamed. "You'll be glad when you're old and I can take care of you."

❖

"Hani, my friend!" Mane, the ambassador to Naharin, boomed, opening his arms magnificently and enfolding Hani in a warm hug. "Haven't seen you for a year. Since the jubilee, eh?"

The two men had encountered one another quite by chance in the courtyard of the Hall of Royal Correspondence. "Must be at least that long," Hani agreed, remembering only too well the murderous heat of that day. The astonishing interview with his sunstruck superior, Lord Yanakh-amu, had finally solved his investigation into the death of Abdi-ashirta, the former leader of the *hapiru*. "Anything particular bring you back, or is it just a routine return to the Black Land and the arms of your family?"

"Oh, far from routine." Mane's chubby face grew sly. "Keliya is here too. In fact, he's the main agent of this present visit. He's here on Tushratta of Naharin's behest to pay a visit to his daughter, Lady Taduhepa—Kiya, as she's known here."

"The King's Beloved Wife? Things seem to be looking up for our little princess. She has apparently captured our sovereign's heart."

"Yes, well, Tushratta just wants to be sure." Mane's voice dropped. "Tushratta is by no means happy with our king. I think he's afraid Nefer-khepru-ra is preparing to drop their treaty."

Hani contained the anger that invaded him every time he thought about the king's foreign policy and said neutrally, "I wouldn't be surprised. And Naharin must be uneasy, with the Hittites getting closer and closer to their heartland. So, Keliya plans to do a little snooping while he's here?"

Mane's voice returned to its normal powerful volume. "Oh, that's too strong a word, my friend. You know what a perfect gentleman our good Keliya is."

"I hope to see him while he's here." Hani was genuinely

fond of the young Mitannian, who had become like a brother to him six years before, when the two of them and Mane had made the long journey from Naharin with the little princess Taduhepa.

"That can certainly be arranged." The sly look had returned to Mane's round face, reducing his eyes to slits, and Hani had an uneasy feeling that he was about to become implicated in something. "In fact, the Beloved Wife of the King has requested to see you. You wouldn't object to meeting Keliya in her presence, would you?"

A chill rippled up Hani's back. "She requested to see *me*? Whatever for? I'm trying to avoid the court." And if there were one aspect of court he wanted to evade, it was the inevitable partisan split between the queen and the Beloved Wife, whose ascendant star could not be pleasing to Great Queen Nefert-iti.

"I don't know what for, Hani. Do you think the royal women confide their longings to me? No such luck!" Mane indulged in a hearty bray of laughter. "But I do know that she's powerful at the moment, and if I were you, I wouldn't waste any time in complying."

Hani pursed his lips. He realized he'd just been drafted. "Of course, I shouldn't…" he said suspiciously.

"It will be like old times, my friend," Mane assured him, smiling beatifically. "You and me and Keliya and the little princess."

"Who must be—what? Twenty years old by now?" Hani fell silent, thinking. He couldn't ignore a summons by the King's Beloved Wife, clearly. "You know," he said just above a whisper, "I'm trying to stay beneath the king's notice. My wife's family are priests of Amen-Ra, Mane."

Mane's thick eyebrows rose then pleated sympathetically. "I think I knew that. But... well, what can I say? I'm just the messenger."

Hani nodded, disturbed. When trouble came looking for a person, it came like a crocodile under the water—all at once, there it was, and there was often no way to hide. "All right. When do you want to go?"

"Are you based here in the new capital now? Do you need to go home to Waset to tell your family?"

"I'm staying here with friends for a while, until my business at the Hall of the Royal Correspondence is done. I can go to the palace anytime you want."

"Not to the palace, Hani. To Pa-maru-en-pa-aten, the Sunshade of the Aten."

Hani grunted skeptically. That was too much *Aten* for his taste. "Is this a liturgical meeting, then?" he asked a little sarcastically.

"Not at all, friend. Wait till you see this place. The *maru* is not exactly a temple. It's a place where the Sun Disk shows off what he can do." Mane grinned.

Hani gave a bark of cynical laughter. "I think we saw enough of that at the jubilee. So, give me a time, and I'll be there."

"Right now, Hani. Let's go now, before it gets any hotter." Mane hooked his friend's arm in his and steered him out of the courtyard and into the processional street.

Hani was starting to feel he had been swept downstream by the fierce current of the Inundation. Despite his reservations, he let himself be hustled along the street. He stared around him at this new city, built out of nothing in the desert. It had four years of mellowing on it, the mud brick growing soft under the lashing sand from the desert and even an occasional sprinkle of rain. The colors were already peeling in places. Trees rustled over the tops of some of the courtyard walls, and the scaffolding that had covered much of the architecture had been dismantled. But still, it had a look of rawness. Few real streets intersected the splendid main avenue. When the government moved, people had rushed in so hastily to grab plots and build that the residential sections looked more like a jumble of separate villages than anything planned. Everything was dust and gravel except for the whitewashed splendor of the temples and palaces.

The two men trudged upriver in the mounting warmth of a late-summer morning. Gradually, the higgledy-piggledy density of the city thinned out until their crunching footsteps were the only sound except for an occasional shout from the embarcaderos. A dry breeze mercifully evaporated the sweat that prickled on Hani's temples and basted his sides. He saw the green of fields and beyond that the River, where a cloud of small birds rose and wheeled together across the water. Someone must have brought River mud up onto the desert hardpan to try to grow crops. For the most part, the city lived off farms on the opposite bank. On its way into the capital from some outlying aristocratic mansion, a chariot passed them, leaving them suffocating momentarily in a whirlwind of ocher dust.

We seem to be heading away from all habitation and into the desert. Hani shot an inquiring sideways glance at Mane.

As if he'd read Hani's thoughts, Mane assured him, "We're almost there." He pointed ahead to where a white expanse of wall rose up from the desert, shimmering in the glare like something out of a dream. The men drew nearer, and Hani saw soldiers and priests milling about, departing from and entering its single portal. He shaded his eyes with a hand and gazed up at the walls of the vast, isolated enclosure. No roofs of buildings showed above the whitewashed brick, but trees, mostly palms, waved their inviting foliage. He could suddenly smell water, and it reminded him how thirsty he'd become.

He shot Mane a questioning look. Mane seemed pleased with himself. He drew Hani after him to the gateway, where two of the king's Nubian guardsmen, prinked out in plumes and leopard skin, stood at attention.

"Mane son of Pa-iry and Hani son of Mery-ra, summoned by the King's Beloved Wife," the little man announced.

One of the guardsmen turned away and repeated the announcement to a servant, invisible in the interior, and a moment later, the servant reemerged and greeted the two men with a deep bow. "Our lady will receive you."

Hani and the ambassador to Naharin followed the man through the door into a colonnaded passage, dark and cool, beyond which he could see only the glare of the out-of-doors. Their sandals echoed on the smooth gypsum flooring. Silhouetted at the edge of the colonnade, like a second row of living columns, stood an attentive rank of immobile guardsmen.

And then the three men passed into the Maru-aten itself, and Hani let out a gasp of wonder in spite of himself. It was an enormous walled garden with a big rectangular lake in the middle and trees all around and flowers in dense alternating beds. The place was lushly green, as only cut channels, wells, and the work of innumerable gardeners hauling River silt and manure could make the desert grow. Even the high enclosure walls were embellished with scenes of garden and water, so that Hani was hard-pressed to say where reality left off and illusion began.

At his side, Mane chuckled. "Not what you expected, is it, my friend?" he whispered. Hani could only shake his head, wide-eyed. Birds twittered in the trees and hopped about the gravel paths, delighting in this oasis full of joy.

Ra be praised—it's like the Field of Reeds! Hani thought, overwhelmed. *A place of manifestation of the benevolence of the sun, indeed—call him what you will.* That all of this had been done in only four years, while an entire city rose up around it, seemed beyond comprehension.

The servant stopped them. "One moment, gentlemen, while I notify the Beloved Royal Wife that you have arrived."

As he set off toward one of the columned pavilions that dotted the periphery of the enclosure, Hani stared around, marveling. "I've never seen anything like this. And it's considered a sacred place? I think I understand that."

"No cult is carried out, but it's not too hard to imagine a prayer or two rising from the Maru, is it?" Mane looked mightily pleased at Hani's awed reaction.

The servant reappeared and bade them follow him. They marched across the immaculate walkway and through the plush, well-watered greenery and delicate flowers of late summer, alive with butterflies. A breeze rustled the stiff fronds of date and doum palms overhead. With great strokes of white wings, an egret lowered itself gracefully through the air into the sunken margins of the lake, which were planted as a marsh. Hani drew a deep breath of contentment, even though he knew that whatever had brought him to the royal precinct meant him no good.

They entered an open colonnade that overhung a paved porch. Hani saw the sparkle of water somewhere in the shadows. And before him stood their little princess, her arms outstretched.

"Mane, you got him to come! Hani! How glad I am to see you. It's like old times!" she cried in delight.

But of course, it wasn't exactly like old times. The little girl who would have taken the two men in her innocent arms was now a twenty-year-old woman and the favorite wife of the Great King of the Two Lands. Hani and his colleague folded in a deep court obeisance, one hand to their lips.

When they rose, Hani glimpsed, standing behind the royal wife, his friend Keliya, a big grin on his droopy face. He was unchanged. But Taduhepa—Hani needed to remember she was Kiya now—had changed profoundly in six years. She had grown up. Tall and slender still, with a graceful long neck, she had developed the curves of a woman. Her heart-shaped face and full lips were adorned with artistically applied cosmetics, and her big almond eyes looked twice as enormous edged with kohl. She wore a short Nubian-style wig, angled below the ears to become even shorter in back. It was the latest style, and it had never looked more seductive than upon this glittering young princess. No wonder the twenty-six-year-old king had noticed her among his inherited stable of wives.

"My lady is as radiant as... the Aten of morning," Hani said, stumbling a little over the name he was so reluctant

93

to pronounce. But he couldn't afford to let this visit make him any more suspect than he was. "And this *maru*—it's a setting worthy of your beauty."

"It's extraordinary, isn't it? Nefer-khepru-ra has the most perfect taste, and he's so generous." She was bubbling like any little bride, proud to be loved by her husband. It occurred to Hani that the king's generosity was carved out of the livelihood of tens of thousands of employees of the temples of Amen-Ra. Still, he only smiled.

"But you must be thirsty. How thoughtless of me." Kiya turned and, from a small stand behind her, produced two golden cups and a slender-necked ewer from which she poured out two big drafts. She held them out to the two emissaries. They each accepted with a little bow. The water was ice-cold, Hani realized, chilling his palms.

Hani held his cup up in a toast. "Life, prosperity, and health to our king and to his Beloved Wife."

Mane echoed him in a booming voice, and Keliya, a cup already in his hand, lifted his with them. They all drank, and water had never tasted so delicious. The royal wife gestured to a strew of cushions that lay about, and after waiting for her to seat herself upon her gilded chair, the men took their place on the floor.

The gypsum paving was painted with marsh scenes—calves gamboling among the reeds and wild birds, more natural than life, rising into the sky. The painting was like nothing he'd ever seen; it was so detailed, so delicate that it seemed to flutter in an unseen breeze. Along the midline of the colonnade ran a series of interlocked T-shaped pools—the sacred symbol for *pool*, he noted with amusement, so that they seemed to proclaim their identity with playful aquatic voices.

"Forgive me, my lady. I can't stop staring around," he said apologetically, drawing his eyes back to hers.

"I feel the same way, Hani. This is a place of deep and beautiful magic for me. And it's all mine—only my husband and I can come here without an invitation. The queen has her own *maru*." Kiya's eyes twinkled. "I don't think it's as pretty as mine." She lifted her cup to her lips and locked eyes impishly with Hani over the rim. But when she set it down, her expression had grown more serious, even a little frightened. "I need to talk to you about something, Hani. I hope you can help me. Keliya and Mane thought you could." She shot a worried glance toward her countryman and the ambassador to Naharin.

"We can absent ourselves if you prefer to speak to him alone, my lady," Keliya murmured self-effacingly in Egyptian.

"Do you mind, my friend?" she replied shyly. Keliya and Mane bowed and meandered off to another pavilion some distance away. The royal wife leaned toward Hani. He scented an intoxicating drift of floral perfume. "I may be in trouble." Her adorable face had tensed, her lip caught in her teeth. "You've got to help me, Hani. I need to know what's going on and put an end to it before the king finds out."

Hani's stomach took an ominous dip. "If it's within my power, my lady, you know I'm at your service." He tried to sound reassuring—the royal wife was just a frightened girl, after all, hardly older than Pa-kiki.

If this brings me into conflict with the king... Hani was

95

taut with uneasiness. He could see a shaven-headed priest and several of the royal guardsmen standing at a discreet distance. His visit would surely be reported. He wasn't surprised; he wouldn't have left his own daughter alone with strange men either.

"The other day, two of my countrymen asked for an audience, which I granted. They were mercenaries from Karkemish, former soldiers in my father's army, so I figured I owed them a meeting. Anyone who had been at his side through all that awful civil war—well, I felt grateful. But it was a mistake." She stood up, as if her nerves were twanging too violently to permit her to sit still. Hani rose as well.

"They said they had come on someone else's part but wouldn't reveal whose. They said... they said that my husband was thinking of repudiating his treaty with my father. That Kheta Land was peeling off vassal state after vassal state from Naharin and would soon go for my father's throat. And that Nefer-khepru-ra didn't plan to do anything about it." The royal wife began to pace, her little hennaed hands twisting nervously around her golden cup.

"And they wanted you to intercede for Naharin with the king?" Hani asked.

"Yes. I told them I had no political influence at all. And that's true, Hani. When the king and I are together, he doesn't want to talk about politics even a tiny bit. He rebukes me when I seem to drift in that direction. So I told them that. I suggested they speak to the vizier or to that high commissioner—what's his name? Ptah-mes. Not that Nefer-khepru-ra likes him so much, but at least such things are his business." She was clutching at her cup as if to crush it, until finally, she glanced at her nervous hands and set

96

the vessel with a clang on the water stand. Hani noticed that her slight accent became stronger and stronger as her emotions mounted.

He could see a scenario taking shape that was dangerous in the extreme for the daughter of Tushratta. If the king became convinced that she was lobbying for her homeland against the interests of Kemet—as he perceived them—he would be justifiably angry and perhaps accuse her of trying to drag the kingdom into a war. It could only end in her fall from favor.

"And what did they say then, my lady?" he urged.

Her voice trembling, Kiya said, "They said that if I didn't go along with them, they would... would tell the king something he might like to know about me."

Hani couldn't imagine what a sheltered young girl like Kiya could possibly have to reproach herself about. She'd only been fourteen when she came to the Two Lands, and thereafter, she'd lived in the seclusion first of Neb-ma'at-ra's House of Royal Ornaments and then in that of his successor. "Is it something very serious, my lady?" he asked gently. "Because maybe you could tell the king voluntarily, and then the two mercenaries would have no hold over you."

But the royal wife's crumpling features told it all. She shook her head wildly. "Oh, no. I could never. I was so stupid. Why was I so stupid?" She buried her face in her hands, and Hani heard a sort of broken hiccup that told him she was struggling with tears.

His heart was wrenched with pity for the foolishness of youth. Had she been any other young girl, he would have offered her the same fatherly comfort he might have shown Sat-hut-haru or Neferet. But he dared not touch this one.

He raised and dropped his hands helplessly, not knowing how to respond.

"Please don't tell anyone ever what I'm about to say, Hani." Her voice descended to a whisper of shame. "I… I went to bed with an artisan. This was more than two years ago, right around the time the king noticed me and picked me out for his favor. I didn't know he was going to fall in love with me like he has." She gave a moan of dread. "I'd be in so much trouble if he found out. But I was just bored, Hani. Do you know what it's like to be one of hundreds of royal wives or concubines that never even see their lord?"

Hani had to allow that he did not.

"It's unimaginably boring. And nobody was all that nice to me because I was a foreigner. And the queen—she looks so noble and queenly, but she's just the daughter of a cavalry officer. She can be a real fishwife if she thinks you're at all encroaching on her favor with the king. It was awful. I was going mad with boredom."

Hani made a rueful grimace, unable to think of anything to say that wouldn't sound like a rebuke. It was too late for that. He wondered how she'd even found herself alone with an artisan. Except that the city and the palace, endlessly under construction, had been swarming with them, no doubt. "How did these two mercenaries find out about this, do you think?"

"I have no idea. I don't know on whose behalf they came. Is it some Mitannian? Yet they seem not to mind if they ruin me. And you know what that would mean for the treaty they seemed to care so much about. My father would smash it over his knee." Kiya drew a deep, desperate breath as if her burden had become too heavy to bear. She dabbed valiantly at her eyes with the back of a hand. Finally, she dropped into her chair. In a tiny voice, she said, "Help me, Hani, please."

Hani bit his lip, thinking hard. *Should I agree to help her? One little slip, and I could fall under the king's disfavor— or the queen's—as quickly as Kiya. And what, indeed, can I accomplish?* If she had really been so indiscreet, there was no solution. She could try to buy everyone's silence, but the king could always outbid her. At last, he said quietly, "I'm not sure what you want me to do, my lady."

"Find out who's blackmailing me. Make them understand that I can't help them—that I'm ruined either way. Tell my father even. I don't know. But don't let the king put me away."

Hani shook his head hopelessly. "My lady, I have less than no influence with the king our lord."

"I'm pregnant, Hani." Kiya's voice was raw, even in a whisper. "If this child is a son, he'll be the king of the Two Lands. Don't let them put me away."

Hani's heart sank. No wonder she was so desperate. "Won't that protect you?"

"Not once the queen has found out about everything. She'll twist it until Nefer-khepru-ra thinks it's the artisan's son."

"Are you sure it's not?"

"Absolutely. I haven't even seen him for more than a year. He finished the plaster mask, and I've never seen him since." Her long eyes were tear swollen but desperately sincere.

A spear of suspicion skewered Hani through the

middle. "Plaster mask?" he repeated, hoping that wasn't what it sounded like.

"Yes. You know—he was carving my likeness in plaster so he could use it for stone sculptures later."

"So your artisan was a…"

"A sculptor."

Ammit take him, Hani thought, sinking under a terrible misgiving. "Do you know his name?"

"No, not even. It's not like we had some prolonged affair. Just for the few months he was working on the mask."

"Whose workshop, do you remember?"

Kiya looked frightened by all the questions. "I don't know whose workshop. It's the fellow the king uses for a lot of his statues."

"Bak? Djehuty-mes? Iuty?"

"I don't know, Hani. He has a workshop here someplace." She got to her feet again and took a step toward him. "Are you going to help me?"

"Does the name Kha-em-sekhem mean anything to you, my lady?"

Kiya shook her head, but her eyes widened in fear. Hani said earnestly, "Please be honest with me, my dear lady. I can't do anything for you unless you tell me everything you know, because it's possible this man himself is the one blackmailing you."

She hung her head. "I don't know his name."

We're not off to a good start. So why am I even considering helping her? Hani had to admit that it was, in part, for the sake of his niece.

At last, he said reluctantly, "I'll do what I can if you

promise me to be frank. Anything you know could be of use to me."

Kiya looked up, her eyes alight with hope. "Oh, Hani, thank you! Is there anything I can give you in return?"

Suddenly inspired, Hani asked, "Do you happen to have a female physician, my lady?"

⸙

Hani met Maya at the Hall of the Royal Correspondence, as they had agreed to. He described for his secretary the magical garden that was the Pa-maru-en-pa-aten and told him in broad terms about the interview with the Beloved Royal Wife.

"I think we'll first speak to Lady Djefat-nebty, the royal wives' physician, and then start visiting sculpture studios. It shouldn't take long to ask her if she'd take an apprentice, whereas we may need to spend some time with this Kha-em-sekhem."

"Where does she live, my lord?" asked Maya.

Hani chuckled. "Your guess is as good as mine. We'll have to talk to Kiya's chamberlain."

After a long period of wandering around trying to find the right bureaucrats to talk to, they tracked down the chamberlain, a certain Huy, at the smaller royal residence in the middle of the city. The official told them grudgingly where the doctor lived, and braving the heat of late morning, Hani and Maya set out again for the southern end of Akhet-aten. They found the *sunet*'s villa not long before Hani's stomach told him it was the hour of lunch for those who, like himself, had the luxury of a third daily meal.

"I hope they won't be at table," Hani murmured as they stood at the gate, waiting for the doorkeeper to fetch his mistress.

But the man returned after a moment to beckon them into the house. It was quite an impressive place—a mansion, really—with a newly planted garden surrounding the house. The vestibule was beautifully painted, high of ceiling, and floored with decorated gypsum like the palace itself. Hani and Maya followed the servant into the salon, where, between colorful columns, a man and a woman sat in chairs upon the dais.

Hani made a respectful bow to the lord and lady of the house. "I am Hani son of Mery-ra, attached to the foreign office of the Hall of the Royal Correspondence. I thank you for agreeing to meet with my secretary and me."

The man in his chair was very large—tall and fleshy, with shaven head and ear spools, his full, unexpectedly red lips disagreeably downturned. "I'm Pentju, God's Father of the Aten, chamberlain of the king's house, and physician. This is my wife, Lady Djefat-nebty. She doesn't treat male patients."

The lady at his side looked perfectly capable of answering for herself. She was perhaps five years younger than her husband—about Hani's age—and tall and spare, with an angular, forbidding face imprisoned between the locks of a long wig. She was as unsmiling as Pentju.

Hani assured them quickly, "I'm not here seeking a physician to cure me, my lord, my lady, but rather someone who might be willing to take my daughter on as an apprentice. She's eager to become a *sunet*." He combed their faces with his eyes, but they stared at him expressionlessly.

"She had begun to study with a village healer, but we felt her training was probably not very learned. My daughter is beginning to read and write script—"

"How old is she?" the woman interrupted in a deep, sharp-edged voice.

"She's thirteen, my lady."

Lady Djefat-nebty made a considering frown with her long mouth. "And just now starting to learn to read?"

Hani was tempted to say, "She has wanted to be a horse up to now, and she didn't feel she needed to read," but he refrained, instead nodding polite acquiescence. *Gods, this woman is a tough one.*

"I can't make a decision without seeing the girl. Bring her tomorrow."

"Forgive me, my lady. We live in Waset. It will take me at least a week to bring her back here."

"Well, she can't very well study in Akhet-aten if she lives in Waset, can she?"

Struggling to hold back some sarcastic comment, Hani said mildly, "Fortunately, my son lives here. She can stay with him."

All at once, there came an infernal ruckus from within the house, and a naked little boy of six or so came barreling into the room, dragging a contraption of sticks and rope, clearly of his own construction, behind him. "Mamaaa..." he began in a prolonged whine.

To Hani's amazement, the *sunet*'s sour face relaxed into the lines of purest maternal indulgence. "Sweet one, Mama is busy. I'll be with you soon, all right?" The boy clattered off, dragging his machine. She turned back to Hani, and far from returning to their hostile expression, Lady Djefat-nebty's eyes twinkled with complicit humor. "In a week, then." She rose, and her husband did the same, towering even over his tall wife.

"My thanks, my lady. We'll be here. My lord."

Hani and Maya made their way out the front door even as the lord and lady of the house disappeared into the back. *Doubtless it's the little fellow's lunchtime*, Hani thought with a grin.

No sooner had they reached the street than Maya blew out a heavy breath, as if he had been holding it. "*Iy*. I hope Neferet is ready for that one. The girl'd better learn to keep her mouth shut."

Hani just chuckled. "My guess is our lady doctor isn't quite as ferocious as she seems. What really concerns me is that her husband is a priest of the Aten. Neferet needs to keep her mouth shut for sure."

Hani decided to stop by Aha's house on their way to the sculptors' studios so they could grab a bite to eat. "I feel like that little boy. *I'm huuungry.*" He imitated the childish whine.

But before they reached the road that led to Aha's, they found themselves passing through the city market. The smells of food were too much for Hani. He pointed to a baker's stall. "Let's just get something here and eat as we walk. I'll get bread, if you want to pick out something else."

A short while later, the two men reunited with a handful of olives from the north, wrapped in a big leaf, and a pot-shaped loaf of bread so fresh it was still steaming. "Olives in honor of our old friend Rib-addi," said Maya.

"A generous thought. But how will we eat them without spilling them all? I have it!" Hani tore the bread in two, gobbled out the soft interior of half of it—much to Maya's amusement—and dumped his share of the olives into the cavity. Laughing and savoring the fresh, yeasty bread and salty olives, they made their way toward the southeastern neighborhoods of the city.

By the time they had approached the area where Hani's sources had assured him the sculpture workshop of Djehuty-mes was located, they were licking their fingers and dusting crumbs from the knots of their kilts. "This is the biggest of the studios. If our Kha-em-sekhem doesn't work here, they may at least know where he is."

The workshop was surrounded by a high wall that enclosed the entire corner of the block. Above, Hani could see the second story of the house where the master must live. From within the open gate of the work yard came a cacophony of hammering, metallic screeching, and resounding clangs.

"What do they do in there?" asked Maya, putting his hands over his ears.

"Carve stone, I guess. That can't be quiet."

A little timidly, they moved through the gate and into the court, and Hani had the sudden sense of having happened onto some island of stone people. In addition to statues in various stages of completion, ranging from knee-high to bigger than life-sized, which stood or sat here and there on rollers on the ground or upon sturdy tables, the men at work were so covered in beige dust that they might have been living statues themselves. The noise of chisels and hammers was both deafening and curiously delicate, sometimes stuttering in fast, light filigrees of tap-tap-tapping that made Hani think of a woodpecker at work.

There seemed to be an army of artisans, most of whom were carving away, but others were hauling pieces on sledges, painting finished sculptures, or sawing energetically at nearly raw pieces of stone. Hani found himself fascinated by a whole process he'd never given a moment of thought.

A burly man with a rag tied over his head approached them rapidly. "What can I do for you?" he cried above the din.

"Are you Djehuty-mes?" Hani asked at the top of his voice.

But the man shook his head and pointed at his ear. "Let's go inside."

They followed him into the workshop proper, where more delicate work seemed to be carried out and whole walls of shelving were stacked with statuettes, broken stone body parts, and blocks of plaster. An array of tools lay on a big worktable, where a boy was laboriously sharpening them with fine sand and moringa oil.

"This reminds me of Mother's studio, but on a massive scale," whispered Maya.

The rag-headed man was dust dyed like all the others. His eyes and mouth seemed to be edged eerily with red since the moist lids and inner lips were the only part of him not whitened, including the little square patch of beard on his chin. "I'm Djehuty-mes. What can I do for you?" he said in an unexpectedly high-pitched voice.

Hani introduced himself respectfully then said, "I'm interested in buying a small stele of the Aten for my home shrine. Have you anything already made up?"

The master sculptor led them to a table where such stelai were laid out in plenitude—round-topped plaques of varying sizes. Upon them were depicted the king and queen and their two older daughters, palms raised in worship toward the Sun Disk, who blessed them with his rays, descending with little hands at the ends. The painted figures were executed in sunken relief in the same disturbing style as the statues at the Gem-pa-aten.

Hani refrained from any expression of disgust, picked one, and paid the sculptor. Then he drew closer. "Does a man named Kha-em-sekhem, by any chance, work here, master?"

Djehuty-mes looked uncertain. He wasn't especially tall, but he had a pair of shoulders and arms that wouldn't have been out of place on a bull, if bulls had shoulders and arms.

I could look like that if I hammered stone all day, thought Hani with a hidden grin.

Yet the sculptor's face was mild and soft with large, gentle eyes. He was in his fifties, Hani guessed. Not a young man to be engaged in such heavy work.

"Why are you looking for him?" Djehuty-mes asked in his childlike voice.

"My niece in Men-nefer is hoping to marry him. Her father is a little concerned about a man so much older than she, whose family no one knows, who lives in another city—well, you see what I mean. And apparently, he's been married before. All of which makes our family uneasy. I'd like to ask you what sort of person he is. If he works here, of course."

The sculptor smiled a little shyly. "He does. Before I say anything, let me show you his work. I think that will tell you more about him than I can, not being a man of much eloquence."

He led them into the back of the workshop, which was lit by a row of large clerestories along one side. Behind, through a door hung with a curtain of wooden beads, stretched another sun-washed court. Djehuty-mes approached one of the shelves and pulled out from it a half head in plaster—essentially just the face and throat, unfinished on the back—of a girl with a long slender neck and a heart-shaped face. Her full lower lip and thinner upper one looked as soft as real flesh, and even with no color, the large, heavy-lidded eyes seemed vulnerable and full of longing.

Hani's breath caught in his throat. Flustered by the uncanny likeness, he cried, "It's Kiya!" It was as if the artisan had captured her very soul.

The sculptor smiled. "You've seen her? It's Lady Kiya to the life, isn't it?"

He laid it back on the shelf and pulled out another, while Hani thought, *I'll bet that's the very mask that got our girl into such trouble.*

"Can you recognize this one? Maybe you don't know him."

"By all the gods! It's Ptah-mes!" Hani stared at the sculptor, awed, then back down at the fine, aristocratic features of his superior and friend. The heaviness of the flesh above the eyelid that created a dark shadow. The bony ridge of the nose. The thin, cynical lines around the mouth and at the corners of the nostrils. The man was all there. Hani expected the lips to part in speech. "These are more lifelike than anything I've ever seen, even without being painted. They're... they're unearthly."

"That's the new style we're working on, under the king's guidance. It's something, isn't it?"

"And Kha-em-sekhem made these?"

The sculptor cupped his hand at his ear, and Hani repeated the question.

"He carves stone, too, but he has such a gift for working in plaster that I just keep him on that."

Hani, drawing closer, said in a lower voice, "You just said that seeing these would tell us something about him, Master Djehuty-mes. What did you mean? I see that he's a very talented man, but do you want to say that makes him a good man? A sensitive one, perhaps?"

The sculptor looked ill at ease and made a helpless noise. "I just mean, whatever else is true about him, he has something in here." He struck himself gently on the chest with a meaty fist.

"And what else *is* true about him?"

Djehuty-mes made the noise again and said apologetically, "He's a good-looking young fellow. We can't hold it against him."

"What?" Hani asked.

"Eh?"

"What can't we hold against him?"

"He's fond of the ladies, you could say." Djehuty-mes looked pleading.

Hani stood, digesting this. It was what he had suspected.

A curl of repressed disgust upon his lips, Maya said, "Do you mean he treats them dishonorably?"

Djehuty-mes squirmed. "I don't know much about

his private life, and I don't want to. I just know he always seems to have a girl trailing him. Even when he was married." He glanced at Hani as if reluctant to displease, a childlike sweetness in his broad face. Clearly, he intended no judgment on his employee.

Hani took him by the massive upper arm and asked earnestly, "If my niece were your daughter, would you want her to marry this man?"

But the sculptor held up a hand in refusal. "I can't interfere in his life, my lord. He's a good boy under it all. Maybe somebody who really loves him could find that good."

Hani exchanged a glance with Maya, accompanied by raised eyebrows, sending the message, *This doesn't look promising.* To Djehuty-mes, he said, "Could we speak to Kha-em-sekhem, do you think? I won't keep him long. I'd just like to get a sense of the man."

The master of the workshop nodded agreeably and led them back out into the resounding courtyard. In a corner shaded by the outer wall, a long table was set up with water jars and a basin full of some sloppy white substance that was evidently plaster. A man in a scarf, his slim, muscular back to them, beaded with sweat, was tapping with a padded hammer on a wooden frame that molded a block of plaster. They watched silently as Kha-em-sekhem shook and rapped the mold until, little by little, the plaster block slid out.

"*Yah*, my friend. Do you have a moment?" Djehuty-mes called in a hesitant voice.

The man turned around, his features still so tensely concentrated on his work that he seemed fierce, but instantly, they loosened up, and he grinned. "Master. Gentlemen. How can I serve you?" Congealed droplets of white bedaubed his face and chest, and his sinewy arms were whitened with plaster up to the elbows.

"My name is Hani son of Mery-ra. I'm the uncle of Mut-nodjmet," Hani said without further exchange of courtesies. He wanted to see the man's unguarded first reaction to her name.

Panic flashed across Kha-em-sekhem's face, but then his smile returned, bigger than ever. "Hello. She's spoken of you."

"I'll leave you to your interview." Djehuty-mes seemed eager to escape. He disappeared into the crowd of artisans.

Hani's expression was pleasant, but he minced no words. "Why are you interested in my niece, Kha-em-sekhem?"

The sculptor looked flustered, perhaps offended. He said with a splutter, "Why not? She's a nice girl in a world where there aren't too many of those."

"So nice that you offer her father a bride price? That's unusual, to say the least."

"Well, he seemed reluctant. I thought that might sweeten him up." Kha-em-sekhem smiled, but his eyes were not happy. They darted around the courtyard, squinting into the glare.

Hani found the man good-looking in a rough way that women often seemed to like, with a longish face, strong nose, and high cheekbones. His mouth was long and full and mobile in the extreme. He appeared older than his thirty years—though he might have lied to Pipi about his age. And he seemed to have run through far too many expressions in a short space of time, as if they were masks he put on and took off at will. *There's a fire burning inside him*, Hani thought. *An intensity. Almost a desperation. Does that "good" Djehuty-mes insisted on also exist within?*

"Tell me about yourself, Kha-em-sekhem. Where are you from? Who is your family? Why does such a plain girl attract you—you who must be a connoisseur of faces?" Hani crossed his arms and leaned against the worktable as if he were prepared to stand there for a while.

Kha-em-sekhem compressed his lips, radiating annoyance. He grabbed a towel from his table and wiped his hands. "I'm from Men-nefer. I was visiting my parents when I met your niece. They're sculptors, too, but they make *shabti*s for people's burials. Simple stuff. I apprenticed with my father but pretty quickly got bored. I left against his will—I know, I'm a bad son—and went to Waset, where there were more options. Eventually, I found my way to Djehuty-mes's workshop, and here I still am. When he moved to the new capital, so did I." He shot Hani a challenging stare. "Why your niece, you ask? She looks like a good fertile little mother in the making. Why does any man marry a woman? To have children by her."

He sounds defensive, Hani thought. "So much so you were willing to pay for her. I see." He smiled amiably. "Do you have children by your wife?"

Dusty though the sculptor's cheeks were, the red creeping up them was visible. "By all the demons of the Duat! What is this? Why don't you torture me to get the answers? Yes, I do have children. Two small sons. They went with my wife when we divorced." Kha-em-sekhem's dark eyes snapped with anger.

But Hani saw in him not so much an affronted man as

someone who was reduced to helpless vehemence by the loss of his children. *This is the most honest response I've gotten out of him yet.* "Sorry to be so personal, my friend. But you can understand why our family is a little concerned—a man Mut-nodjmet hardly knows, much older than she, divorced, curiously urgent to have her. Why were you divorced, if I may ask?"

Kha-em-sekhem threw his towel down and stood, unhappy, his chest heaving, as if he were arguing with himself. Then he managed a thin, bitter smile. "You'd better ask my former wife. She initiated the divorce. She left me."

"Infidelity, perhaps?"

The sculptor seemed torn between refusing to answer Hani's questions and losing the girl upon whom he had mysteriously set his heart. He smiled in front of his clenched teeth. Finally, he said, "I have work to do. If you'll excuse me..."

"Are you also looking to have children by the King's Beloved Wife?"

Kha-em-sekhem didn't even manage a semblance of outrage. He stared at Hani, frozen in round-eyed fear.

Hani tipped his head in a genial gesture of goodbye, and with a lighthearted, "Thank you for your time, my friend," he herded Maya toward the gate.

En route, he found Djehuty-mes. While Maya waited by the gate, Hani drew the man aside. "Thank you for your help. I have one last question."

The sculptor stood with his head amiably cocked and his big eyes attentive.

"Do you know the name of Kha-em-sekhem's former wife? Is she in Akhet-aten or Waset?"

"She's here, my lord. Her name is Rekhet-ra. She's my daughter."

Hani gaped at the man, surprise pinning him to the spot. *How can he be so forgiving toward a fellow whom his daughter has fled?* "Would you object if I come ask her some questions one of these days?"

"Not at all. But don't believe everything she says. The divorce was bitter." Djehuty-mes's dust-whitened face creased in his beatific smile. Hani thanked him again and rejoined Maya.

"That Kha-em-sekhem's a slippery bastard," Maya growled under his breath as they passed out into the street once more. "What do you think of him, Lord Hani?"

"I'm not sure. We did get up his nose pretty strongly, so the anger wasn't altogether displaced—"

"Yes, but he has to know the relatives of Mut-nodjmet have the right to some answers. He might have lost her by showing his temper like that."

"He seems desperate somehow—fearful and defensive. Is that an admission of guilt? He's probably a rake, but he loves his children. Not an altogether bad man, probably. Still, I don't think I'd want our Mut-nodjmet married to him." He pondered the confusing fact of Djehuty-mes's continued friendship with the man who had seemingly been unfaithful to his daughter.

Maya's voice dropped, and he said with juicy delectation, "His eyes nearly popped out when you mentioned the King's Beloved Wife!"

"Hmm." Hani smiled noncommittally. "I probably shouldn't have said anything. Now he's on his guard."

"But we can be sure he was the one. We didn't know that before."

Hani realized he'd been striding up the processional road as if he had a destination. "Let's head for the River. We barely have time to get home to Waset and bring Neferet back."

CHAPTER 4

H AVING MADE IT BACK FROM the capital in five days'
time, Hani's intention was to leave Waset again as
soon as possible and head for Akhet-aten with Neferet
in tow, but the will of the king intervened. The morning
after he arrived, there arose a clatter of wheels and the
commotion of raised voices at his gate. Hani went outside
in case A'a, the porter, needed reinforcement, only to find a
secretary of Lord Ptah-mes and a group of retainers edging
a cart full of baggage into the garden. To one side stood
Aziru, flanked by a pair of Amurrites.

Dear gods, they're here. Before anyone could spot him,
Hani dodged back into the house, slipped the new stele
from his clothes press in the bedroom, and set it hastily in
the shrine in front of the statue of Amen-Ra. *Forgive me, my
great lord.* He sighed. *Such are the times we live in.*

He called out to Nub-nefer, "My dear, the guests have
arrived," and brushing down his kilt, he scuttled back out
into the garden and faced the men, who were now gathered
in the gate. "Welcome, my friends."

"Should I take this cart to the barn, my lord?" A'a asked under his breath, and Hani nodded.

The secretary, a pompous little man whom Hani recognized from the Hall of Correspondence, said in the orotund voice of a herald, "Lord Hani, I bring you the king of A'amu and his party."

"Come in, come in." Hani gestured the men before him into the salon, where he knew the secretary would catch a glimpse of the shrine. He turned to Aziru and folded in a low bow. "My lord Aziru. It's good to see you again. I welcome you to my house. Please consider the servants to be your own; if there's anything you need, don't hesitate to ask."

Nub-nefer appeared at Hani's side, beautiful in a long formal wig and beaded *weshket* collar, as if she hadn't only heard of the arrival moments before. Her arms were full of long-stemmed water lilies, which she handed to each man in turn as she said graciously, "My lords, we are honored by your presence. Our home is yours." Behind her stood two of the prettier servant girls with basins and towels, ready to wash the travelers' feet.

"I'll be off, Hani," said the secretary. "Lord Ptah-mes said to see him next time you're in the capital." He turned and disappeared into the darkness of the vestibule, sniffing his flower.

Aziru accepted the water lily with all the polite forms one could wish. He clearly knew Egyptian etiquette and spoke the language with the barest of accents. At Nub-nefer's urging, he and his two men took a seat in the finest chairs, and the servants began to remove their shoes and wash their feet.

The new king of A'amu was a handsome fellow, slim and not very tall but well built—perhaps five years younger than Hani. His dark hair was clubbed up under a gold-embroidered headband, and a neat pointed beard framed his mouth. He looked around him with black eyes that were both warm and cynical.

"My father remembered your hospitality to his dying day, Hani," he said with a dry smile. "I thank you for your welcome... although I hope the sojourn will be brief."

Aziru shot Hani a glance that evoked the long, sometimes painful history between the two men. He might have become a vassal, but he was no man's creature. Aziru—and his father, Abdi-ashirta, before him—had ruled their pack of outcasts and desperadoes with such success that the King of the Two Lands had ultimately had to recognize him as a king.

"Royalty sits well upon you, my lord," said Hani with a grin.

"I don't suppose you could tell me why your king—pardon me, *our* king—summoned me so urgently only to leave me cooling my heels for three months?"

"I could not. Except to say that the divine Nefer-khepru-ra has many exigencies demanding his attention."

Aziru considered this as the servant girl dried his feet and slipped his embroidered leather shoes back on them. "Of which I'm an unimportant part, evidently," he said acidly. He sniffed his water lily. "My lady, I thank you for your gracious welcome. My father was loud in his praises of you and your children, whom he found to be charming and original."

"My lord is free to join us in our familial schedule or

THE CROCODILE MAKES NO SOUND

not, as he chooses," she assured him. "If you prefer to eat in your quarters, that's easily arranged. The upper floor is yours, and the entire property is totally at your disposal."

"Needless to say," Hani added, "you're free to come and go as you wish."

"So not under house arrest, at least. Good." Aziru stood up, kingly in a richly colored tunic woven in bands of pattern. "With your permission, we'll withdraw to get our things unpacked."

"I hope you'll forgive my absence for a few days, Lord Aziru," Hani said, rising as well. "My presence is required in Akhet-aten."

"You have better luck than I, then." Aziru nodded courteously to his host, and Nub-nefer led the men to the stairwell.

⬧

Exactly ten days later, as promised, Hani was back in the capital with his daughter.

Their first stop was Aha's house. Aha had constructed himself a nice villa that would make any young scribe envious. The lad had been briefly under the lucrative patronage of Lord Yapakh-addi, a Fan-Bearer at the King's Right Hand—much to the horror of his parents. But when Yapakh-addi's shady past and even more doubtful present came to light, the king had cut him off and stripped him of his honors and his property.

Aha had come to realize how close to moral ruin his eagerness to advance himself had taken him, and he'd effected a reconciliation with his family. Perhaps he'd found a new patron, or perhaps his friendship with the king's intimates had drawn him into the golden circle of enrichment. Hani thought he probably didn't want to know. Aha had two small children and a third on the way. As his father, Hani couldn't begrudge him a certain amount of ambition.

"So, can I come home on weekends, Papa?" Neferet asked as they stood at her eldest brother's freshly painted red door, a pile of baggage stacked behind them on the porch.

"No, my love. There isn't time to go back and forth. Whenever Pa-kiki comes home, you can come home too."

The doorkeeper returned with Aha at his heels. "Father. Neferet."

Neferet threw her arms around Aha's expansive middle and cried, "I'm going to live with you while I study medicine with Lady Djefat-nebty!"

Aha stared quizzically at his father over Neferet's head as if asking what was going on. They moved inside as a block while the doorkeeper began dragging in the girl's effects.

Hani said, "You didn't get my message?"

"Yes, but I didn't know you meant to start so soon. Neferet, follow Sa-pa-ir, and put your things up," Aha said. When his sister was out of earshot, he turned back to his father, exasperation plain upon his face. "You didn't give me time to send a reply. This is starting to work a hardship on us, Father. Khentet-ka is having some problems with this pregnancy, and she has two other children to take care of. Then you and the dwarf stay with us every few weeks—"

"He's your brother-in-law, son."

"Then Pa-kiki is here all the time, and we have to

feed that bottomless pit. Now Neferet. She's a one-girl sandstorm wherever she goes." Aha held out his hands in a pleading gesture. "I want to help, but by the Dazzling Sun Disk—we don't have any more bedrooms."

Hani swallowed his annoyance and said contritely, "I'm sorry, Aha. It was thoughtless. And I know it was last-minute."

"Why don't you and Mother just build yourselves a little place here? You must spend more time on the River than in your office."

Truer than you know, Hani thought. "You won't have to worry about me and Maya, at least. A friend has offered to put us up when we're in Akhet-aten. Maybe Neferet can use that room."

Aha pressed his lips together with bad grace, forced to a compromise he didn't want. "All right."

Aha is strangely ungenerous in some ways, but he knows he owes the family something. Hani remembered—and Aha had to as well—how Aha had desecrated his father's tomb in his zeal for the king's religious reforms. Hani had stricken him from the family, and the boy had seen the error of his ways and come back—and had been forgiven.

"'What is given small returns augmented,' son. You won't be sorry." Hani smiled warmly and clapped Aha on the upper arms. Under the ample snow-white linen of his son's sleeves, his fingers touched armlets. "I hope Khentet-ka and the children are well. Your mother will make the offerings to the Great One to help her carry the baby."

Aha rolled his eyes with affectionate tolerance. "Those old superstitions?" But he didn't engage his father in a theological discussion. It hadn't ended well last time.

"Thank her for us both, Father. And I'm sorry to sound so niggardly, but I have to think of my own family first." He gave a forced smile.

"Of course, my boy. You're looking well. Eating well, eh?" He patted Aha on his solid belly. "Despite all the hungry adolescents draining your larder. Everything going smoothly at work?"

Aha's smile grew genuine. "Yes, Father. In fact, I've been promoted. I'm second overseer of cattle in the House of the Aten now."

"Congratulations, my son! You always make us proud. Now, if Neferet is set up, I'll take her on to her first session with Djefat-nebty. You know, if the doctor doesn't find her worthy of an apprenticeship, all this may have been for nothing, and you'll have your bedroom back."

As if on command, Neferet's footsteps could be heard galloping down the stairs, and she burst into the room, beaming and eager. "Isn't it time to go see Lady Djefat-nebty yet, Papa?"

He seized her hand. "I suspect it's exactly time. Let's go." They turned toward the door, and Hani shot his son a complicit look over his shoulder. "I'll bring her back soon."

As they walked, Neferet was so full of nervous excitement that she alternately skipped around Hani and danced on her tiptoes at his side. He shook his head affectionately. *I hope she's this excited coming back.*

"How should I act, Papa? You said she's very severe looking. Should I keep a straight face?" She pulled a long, grim expression with fierce eyebrows.

Hani laughed. "No, no, my duckling. Just be yourself. Only"—he remembered that the doctor's husband was a priest of the Aten—"don't talk about the Hidden One or the king or how we feel about things. Can you do that for me?"

"Absolutely, Papa." She slapped herself on the mouth as if to seal it shut. "I will never, ever, even under torture, say anything about the Hidden One or the king or how we feel. May Meret-seger the Lover of Silence put thorns between my toes if I say a word. May my eyelashes fall out and my... my knees turn green. May—"

"I believe you, my dear." He thought in amusement that, at the very least, studying medicine would give her a whole new gamut of curses to call down.

They were in the southeastern outskirts of the city now. Here and there, a walled enclosure, its massive shoulders hunched against the encroaching desert, marked some grandee's villa. Still farther south stood Pa-maru-en-pa-aten, where Lady Kiya awaited some word of her blackmailer. For all that they were entering the third month of the Flood season—the Inundation—the morning was already hot, with humidity hazing the sky over the River to their right.

"There it is," he said finally.

"How will I get here every day when you're not here, Papa?" Her little brown eyes had suddenly started squinting anxiously under their unaccustomed kohl.

"Pa-kiki can bring you before work."

They passed through the gate with its brightly painted frame and the titles of its master carved above—*God's Father of the Sun Disk, seal-bearer of the king, king's scribe, chief of physicians, and chamberlain*. The gatekeeper led them through the formal garden and into the tall doors.

Neferet, usually so fearless, was staring around her with the intensity of a trapped animal.

When the servant reached the inner door, he bade them wait and entered alone. A moment later, he said blandly, "The mistress of the house will receive you."

Neferet fingered the little ankh amulet on her wrist, took a deep breath, and set out at her father's side, striding across the salon as if into battle. Together, they made a respectful bow before the lady Djefat-nebty, who sat— alone this time—upon her tall chair on the dais.

"Lord Hani," she said in her sharp, mannish voice. "This is your daughter?"

"Yes, my lady," he and Neferet said simultaneously.

"My name is Neferet," she finished alone, her voice starting to tremble at the end without her father's to back it up.

There was a stomach-churning moment of silence while the doctor stared at her with her cold eyes. *Oh dear*, thought Hani. *She may be one of those who expect precise and absolute obedience and will hold it against Neferet for answering when she called upon me.*

But Djefat-nebty said firmly, "I like a girl who speaks for herself. How old are you, Neferet?"

"Thirteen, my lady."

"Your father tells me you're learning to read and write. True?"

"Yes, my lady." Neferet seemed to have found her self-confidence. Eyes bright, she launched into a wordy explanation of how she'd just started but could already read quite a few things. And in many hands, too, because her father, her brothers, her grandfather, her uncle, and her brother-in-law were all teaching her.

Hani, his face growing hot, wanted to calm her down, but she wasn't looking at him. Her eyes were fixed on the doctor, and her hands flew with excited description. *Just don't let her start stalking around like a heron*, her father thought. It was all he could do not to burst out laughing. She was indeed being herself.

Finally, Djefat-nebty interrupted. Hani couldn't tell what reaction her severe, expressionless face masked. "I understand you've studied with a village healer. What have you learned?"

"I've learned about a lot of herbs that can be used for things like fever or pain or keeping wounds from going sour. And what to take for a stomach ache and for a sore throat and how to make compresses and extracts and how to splint a broken arm and pull out a tick and—oh, but she also told me things like put a mouse's bones in a bag around a woman's neck if her baby has teething pains and things like that, and I really don't know whether a real doctor would do that. Some things seemed more like a magician would do, and I don't want to be a magician; I want to be a *sunet*. That's why I didn't want to study with her anymore."

Silence.

"Why do you want to practice medicine?"

"Because... because I have a sister who is paralyzed and will be for the rest of her life because she broke her back falling off a boat. There must be lots of people who are sick or injured like that. I want to help them."

Hani stared at his daughter, touched and amazed. He'd never heard her advance any particular reason for her ambition. He had, frankly, assumed it was just a whim that would pass. That this compassion had been fermenting inside his youngest child brought a burn of tears to his nose.

"I see," said the doctor. "Come tomorrow at daybreak." She stood up, a lean, exceptionally tall woman who was nearly as flat chested as a man.

Neferet and Hani looked at each other uncertainly.

"You'll teach me, then?" Neferet cried excitedly, clasping her hands.

"I didn't tell you to come back to beat my rugs." Djefat-nebty's stony face cracked a smile.

Hani said a proud goodbye to his little girl at Aha's door. "Study hard, my duckling, and we'll see you the next time there's a holiday long enough to get home and back. If you want to practice writing, send us a letter." Pa-kiki appeared in the door behind his sister and yanked her braids. She turned, saw him, and fell on him in a rib-cracking hug, the two of them laughing like hyenas.

"You'd better mind your manners," he threatened, "or I'll sell you to slavers bound for Sangar!"

Hani was reassured that with her two brothers around, Neferet wouldn't be too homesick. He just hoped that she would stay busy enough with her studies that she wouldn't get on Aha and Khentet-ka's nerves. The girl loved her little niece and nephew, though. She might even be of some help to their mother.

A bittersweet mixture of loss and joy swirling inside him like clouds of incense, Hani headed toward the River, near which Lord Ptah-mes had said his "modest place" stood. As he strode along, he thought about his family—about the children growing up and finding their way in life. They were each so different yet still so connected to one another. He thought of his Nub-nefer—his pure gold—and their twenty-eight years of marriage and how they had weathered even the shuttering of the Ipet-isut. Nub-nefer still sang every day, determined to keep in practice so that when the Greatest of Shrines reopened, she could take up her sistrum and lift her voice in praise once more. *When. If only.* At least he was here for his loved ones once more.

After asking at the riverbank, Hani directed himself toward the row of fine large houses, more or less next to one another, that backed up onto the greengrocers' fields. From the front, one had the sense of being in a proper city, with a street and close-packed walled gardens. Apparently, the bureaucrats thronging to the new capital had snatched up these choice plots straightaway.

Ptah-mes's house was far from modest. Only a man of old wealth such as Ptah-mes's would think to call it that, although no doubt his ancestral mansion in Waset was much grander. The garden was formal and impeccably groomed, like its master. Hani had no sooner been introduced by the doorman than Ptah-mes himself appeared, dressed in his usual simple elegance with no concession made to being at home—none of the shirtless, shoeless, wigless comfort that ruled at Hani's house. But he was smiling broadly, arms extended.

"Hani, what a pleasure. I was afraid you wouldn't take me up on my offer."

"I can't thank you enough, my lord. I've been staying

127

with my son when I'm in town, but suddenly, he has two of my other children under his roof. He has small ones of his own, and his wife is expecting another. I'm afraid it's straining his filial goodwill." Hani raised a guilty eyebrow.

"Your secretary isn't with you?"

"Not this trip. His wife—my daughter—is expecting. I thought he might like some time at home."

Ptah-mes laughed, a sound Hani had not heard frequently. "Come, my friend. Let's have a drink in the garden. We can talk business or not, as we choose."

Ptah-mes guided Hani through the lofty salon with its cool, understated colors, and into a colonnaded court surrounded on all four sides by grapevine-sheltered porches. A narrow rectangular pool, set into a sunken garden of bushes and flowers, ran along the center of the court. Lettuce was planted between each of the shrubs, a little mound of tender green like a bead on a strand that encircled the pool.

"Your lettuce hasn't bolted. I'm amazed, with this heat. The garden is certainly lovely," Hani said, staring around him appreciatively. "This is quite original."

"I spend most of my time here now. Alas, my wife is not particularly interested in joining me in the City of the Horizon."

I do believe he's lonely, Hani thought in surprise.

"You may not be aware that she is—was—the *weret khener* of the Ipet-isut in Waset." Lord Ptah-mes looked meaningfully at Hani, who widened his eyes in genuine astonishment. Ptah-mes's wife was the leader of the entire musical establishment of the Ipet-isut, ruling over men and women alike. It was a post reserved for women of the highest nobility and was mostly administrative, not actually presupposing any musical talent. So this was how Ptah-mes had been aware of Nub-nefer's position and the dangerous recalcitrance of her brother—Ptah-mes's wife had been her superior! And it made Ptah-mes's conscientious decision to serve the heretical king even more poignant. In fact, Hani remembered, Ptah-mes himself had been some sort of important priest. But all that seemed to have stopped at the same time he ceased to be vizier.

"I had no idea, my lord. Even when I was moaning about my own woes, you never breathed a word. It must have been… difficult." Hani's brows contracted in genuine empathy.

"How long have we worked together? Nearly twenty years? Fifteen, perhaps?" Ptah-mes indicated one of two chairs to Hani, and he swept his long caftan neatly behind his legs and seated himself. "Here, Hani, let me pour you some of this wine. It's nice and cold."

Ptah-mes leaned over to the little table at his side and poured from a tall, slender ewer beaded with condensation into the two bronze cups that sat beside it. He handed one to Hani and lifted his own. "Life, prosperity, and health to our king, Nefer-khepru-ra Wa-en-ra," he said in a loud voice.

Hani nodded, not quite able to bring himself to echo those words, and downed a swallow. "This is wonderful. From your own grapes?"

"No, no. From Djahy. One of the perquisites of office." Ptah-mes smiled dryly. "How is our friend Aziru doing?"

"He's impatient and suspicious, my lord. He and his men play Hounds and Jackals by the hour, and then he stomps into the salon to ask me how long he's going to cool his heels in gilded captivity. I wish I knew. I've promised to take them hunting as soon as I get home. I'm trying to think of other things to do with them to keep him from going completely mad."

"Don't feel obligated to entertain him, Hani. You have your own life to live. Surely, the king won't keep him dangling much longer." Ptah-mes sipped from his cup. "What sort of man is he?"

"Not much like his father, although they share more or less the same goals. Aziru is sharper, harder, less benevolent, I think. Or at least more ruthless in achieving that benevolence."

"Ruthless benevolence, eh." Ptah-mes, cradling his cup in his hand, seemed to savor the idea.

"He's less mellow than Abdi-ashirta, more easily pushed to lose his temper. He can be quite sarcastic. But I'm sure this waiting is legitimately hard on him. After all, he fought for three years to be granted vassal status—"

"And then the king wrote him a bruisingly harsh letter of rebuke for delaying his vassal visit."

"Indeed," Hani said, the old bitterness rising in him. He found himself quite sympathetic to Aziru. "And now this. He's very eager to be away and at work being a king for the first time. He must feel we're testing him."

"As we are."

Hani leaned forward and said regretfully, "I'm just afraid he won't pass the test, Lord Ptah-mes. That he'll go over to Kheta Land after all."

Ptah-mes looked up at him. His dark eyes were humorless. "I've stopped caring, Hani. You should give it a try." He patted the golden penknife at his hip, the gift of the king.

Hani heaved a deep breath. "I am trying. But it doesn't come naturally."

Ptah-mes was silent, then he smiled aridly. "No. You're not made for compromise like some of us."

"Although I pass for a compromiser in my family. We have some very hard heads." Hani grinned, hoping to disarm the seriousness he saw suddenly in his host. "Oh, my lord, I just remembered something unrelated. I happened to be at the workshop of Djehuty-mes, one of the royal sculptors, and I saw a plaster study of you. It was the most amazing likeness I've ever seen. I felt like there was a living person hiding beneath the plaster. Truly uncanny."

Ptah-mes's face brightened. "Yes. That Kha-em-something fellow who does the plaster heads is a real craftsman. I must say, the new style the king is pushing is very attractive—although I'm not sure I want to be remembered for eternity with wrinkles. It certainly holds more charm than the earlier style."

Hani recalled—still with a shiver—the shocking images at the Gem-pa-aten, a temple the king had constructed in Waset when he was coregent. "Are you commissioning statues, then?"

"For my tomb. In Waset. Compromise goes only so far. To be buried on the east bank... I can't. No matter what it costs." Ptah-mes's eyes were opaque with some sorrow his pleasant expression tried in vain to dissemble. Hani observed him with compassion. Finally, Ptah-mes said quietly, "Did I ever tell you why I was removed from the office of vizier?"

131

"No, my lord."

"I opposed the coregent. Not once or twice but habitually. I felt myself secure in the intimacy of the late king, with whom I had grown up and who, I believed, was my friend. I assumed my honest advice was what he wanted, as he had always been an honest man. But it soon became clear that Neb-ma'at-ra was depending more and more on the counsel of his son." Ptah-mes looked Hani in the eye, and even his bronze self-control couldn't completely conceal the bitterness. "I was deposed, Hani. And I was stripped of the high priesthood of the Hidden One. For what cause? No one ever told me. The world was left to imagine the worst. I doubt if I would have remained even in the post of high commissioner of northern vassals had the king not retained enough memory of our long association to protect me from an ultimate disgrace."

Hani made a pained noise, and his distress wasn't solely for the man before him but for Kemet as well, whose faithful and talented servants were treated so poorly.

"This put me on a very delicate footing once the new regime began. I'm sorry I haven't done more for you, my friend. Once, I could have advanced you, but I have to be extremely careful now. I'm suspect at every level. My patronage is the kiss of death."

"Please, Lord Ptah-mes. You've done more for me than you can imagine by relieving me of overseas assignments."

Ptah-mes gazed sadly into his lap, then he took a deep breath and looked up, smiling. "Can I offer you some more of this fine vintage, my friend?"

"Thank you, yes."

"And if I may ask, Hani, why were you at Djehuty-mes's workshop? Are you commissioning a statue as well?"

"*Yahya*! There's a story! My niece wants to marry our Kha-em-sekhem."

Ptah-mes looked astonished. "A sculptor? Are her parents favorable?"

No doubt, the idea of marrying an artisan was completely unimaginable for a grandee like Ptah-mes. Hani shook his head. "They're very uneasy about it. His social class, for one thing. But even more, the man seems to have a shady past where the ladies are concerned. My brother wanted me to investigate him." He grinned. "Pipi is conflicted, because our sculptor has offered him a handsome bride price."

"How strange. It sounds quite louche. I advise caution."

Suddenly, Hani thought about Lady Kiya's connection with the sculptor. He wondered if he should tell Ptah-mes that the Beloved Royal Wife had compromised herself and was vulnerable to blackmail. How he would welcome sharing that terrible secret with someone—especially someone with the connections and experience of the court that Lord Ptah-mes possessed. Ptah-mes certainly wasn't the gossiping type. But perhaps he would consider that his oath to the king required him to make known such a revelation. In the end, Hani said nothing about it. The two men sat in silence, sipping their wine.

"With my lord's permission, I have a few tasks to perform while I'm in the capital," Hani said finally, with a tentative scooting forward in his chair.

Ptah-mes understood immediately and rose, freeing Hani to do so as well. "Of course. I need to get back to the Hall of the Royal Correspondence anyway. I've indulged myself long enough." He shot Hani his bone-dry smile. "Thank you for your company. I find it appalling that two men can work together for nearly twenty years without ever knowing the first thing about one another."

"You're right, my lord. I'm afraid we live in times of suspicion and secrecy." Hani and Ptah-mes clasped forearms in an amicable gesture, and the grandee made his way toward the gate, calling for his litter.

Hani followed and stood in the street, orienting himself. At last, he set off away from the River, heading for the workshop of Djehuty-mes. In the noisy, dust-filled court, he sought out the master sculptor, who left the statue upon which he was chiseling with not so much as a grimace of annoyance and cheerfully accompanied Hani to the door that led into his house.

"Ineni, dear. Lord Hani is here to talk to Rekhet-ra," Djehuty-mes called.

A comfortably plump middle-aged woman emerged from the back of the house and nodded a bow, all smiles. "I'll get her, my love."

What a sweet-natured couple, Hani thought.

A moment later, Ineni returned with an attractive younger woman, soft of face and form, her fuzzy brown hair twisted into rolls that gave it the shape of a layered round wig. "Papa said you wanted to ask me about Kha-em-sekhem," she said, her nose wrinkling. "He said your niece wanted to marry him. Take my advice and warn her away from that dog."

"Now, dear…" said her mother mildly.

"Worse than a dog. We were married for five years, my lord, and he must have betrayed me with as many women.

Every time, he'd swear that he loved only me and that he'd change if I gave him another chance. But he never changed." Her face had grown red, and her mouth hardened and turned down.

Hani could see that she was very bitter. "I'm amazed your parents don't seem any angrier at him." He smiled at the young woman and her mother.

Rekhet-ra cast a reproachful sideways look at Ineni. "Me too. But they always loved him. And I guess Papa needs his skill." Her voice rose aggrievedly. "But imagine, my lord. There he is every day in the courtyard. I can't even go out there. And if he ever got hold of the children, he'd take them away. He was that upset when I kept the boys. It's so hard on me! We're like prisoners!" She took a big sniff in righteous victimhood. "I can't wait to remarry and get away from here."

Her mother laid a sorrowful hand on her arm. "Oh, my lamb, I know it's not easy. But your father thinks of Kha-em-sekhem as a son. We can't just drive him away."

Hani looked at the two women with sympathy. Clearly, Kha-em-sekhem had a weakness, but neither did he seem to be a bad man. These two dear older people wouldn't love him so much if he were truly malicious. He remembered, with an ironic inner smile, that he'd asked Djehuty-mes, "If my niece were your daughter, would you want her to marry him?"

Thinking of the mysterious bride price, Hani asked, "Is Kha-em-sekhem well off financially?"

"That's another thing. Papa pays him well, no question. But he was always throwing wealth around as if he were some great lord. Don't ask me where he got it, but he didn't keep

135

it long. He seemed to feel he had to buy people's respect."
Rekhet-ra was angry, but Hani could see sorrow, too, as if
she pitied her former husband as much as she resented him.
"So we never had enough. He said I was always harping at
him, but I ask you, when you see your children hungry and
their father is throwing bread at perfect strangers...?" She
waved her hands in frustration. "He'd go to a beer house
and buy everyone there a pot of the best. He'd hand a beggar
a *heqat* of grain or a bronze bracelet. He'd come home with
a big piece of jewelry for me when we didn't have enough
to eat. What was going on? He was always trying to buy
me, to prove something, when all I wanted was for him to
be faithful and to stop being so profligate. Now, he's after
your girl, but I'll bet he thinks he has to buy her. He's sick
in the head, my lord. Does a man that talented have to buy
respect?"

Hani listened sadly, starting to feel sorry for the sculptor.
Generosity seemed like more of a virtue than a vice—but to
deprive his family in order to play the bountiful benefactor?
Kha-em-sekhem sounded like a complicated man, and
Hani could imagine that being married to him had been
difficult.

"I thank you, ladies, for your time and your frankness,"
he said sincerely and took his leave, pensive.

That the sculptor was insecure and was always trying to
prove himself was one issue. *Still, where did he get all that
bronze, grain, and jewelry?* Hani thought about Kha-em-
sekhem's foolish indiscretion with Kiya. Perhaps he was the
one blackmailing her. But Kiya's case seemed to be about
political influence, not gold. *And why would a man from
Men-nefer care about the Mitannian treaty?*

Hani heaved a sigh. He thought he knew enough about Kha-em-sekhem's flaws to report back to Pipi, but he wasn't sure what he needed to do to follow up on the Beloved Royal Wife's charge. Perhaps he should speak to the sculptor himself. If Kha-em-sekhem had turned out to be a hardened, misogynistic kind of person, there would have been no point. But he seemed to be a weak man with goodness at the core. Perhaps he could be moved to tell the truth.

Hani retreated to the Hall of Correspondence and busied himself for a while, but shortly before twilight, he headed back to the sculptor's workshop, where he waited outside the gate until the workmen began to trickle out. He wasn't sure he would even recognize Kha-em-sekhem in his natural colors. But sure enough, after a few minutes, a long-faced, wiry man with the lighter skin of the Men-nefer region emerged, and Hani knew him from his shape. He wore a round wig now and was clean and younger looking than Hani remembered, without white dust accentuating the lines in his mobile face. He carried a hempen sack of tools, clanking together, over his shoulder.

"Kha-em-sekhem," Hani called out, hurrying toward him in case the fellow should bolt.

The sculptor froze then made a move to take off, but Hani laid a hand on his neck and guided him out of the stream of departing workmen. "Hello, my friend. I have a few things to ask you. Let's go have a beer."

"I don't have anything else to say to you," Kha-em-sekhem said, his voice tinny with fear.

Hani could feel the tightness in the muscles under his hand, and he hoped that didn't mean the fellow was tensing up to hit him. "I'm not your enemy, Kha-em-sekhem. I just need your help to get to the bottom of something. Where's the nearest beer house?"

"There are few enough in this city of prune-faced mystics," the man grumbled. But he led the way, still secured by Hani's hand on his neck.

It was nearly dark, and the crickets had begun their rhythmic night song by the time Hani and Kha-em-sekhem had made their way into the central city and found the little beer house. The door was open, and lamplight streamed out along with the laughter and conversation and clinking of crockery. *A homey neighborhood place*, Hani thought approvingly. *Not the sort of dive where lowlifes hang out—just workmen on their way home.* He even saw a few women sitting with their husbands, laughing familiarly, as if they were all known to one another.

Everyone looked up when they entered, and someone cried out, "Here's Kha-em-sekhem! Come sit with us, friend." Hani observed with interest the change in the sculptor's manner. He immediately grew loose and expansive; a smile that crinkled his eyes stretched across his face. Even his body relaxed. He waved genially to his friends.

"Don't pay for a round. I want to talk to you unnoticed in some corner," Hani said under his breath. He steered the man toward a dark nook where there were still a few stools unoccupied, and they sat down side by side, looking out over the small room. The low ceiling was made of reeds over the palm-log beams; the floor was of packed earth. Someone had scribbled a game board on the whitewashed wall above the red dado, and Hani saw other graffiti, some of it quite skillful. No doubt, the royal artists patronized the place. Smells of cooking mingled with the yeasty bouquet of the brewer's product, and beside every other person or so sat a big pot of beer on its stand, two or even more straws hanging out.

"Want anything to eat?" Hani asked his companion.

Kha-em-sekhem shrugged. "Sure. But sharing a meal with you doesn't obligate me to anything."

Hani laughed and placed an order with the scrawny boy who sidled up to them. When the lad had left, he turned toward the sculptor and said with a frank smile, "I talked to your wife. She actually described to me a man I would say is good-hearted."

"She did?" Kha-em-sekhem seemed surprised.

"I'm still not sure I want to see my niece married to you, but that's not really what I want to talk about."

Kha-em-sekhem stiffened, his face expressionlessly aimed at the room. His powerful long hands, laid on his knees, grew white knuckled. Hani fell silent as the serving boy laid a plate of endives, a pot-shaped loaf of bread, and a dish of little fried fish before them. A moment later, the lad positioned between them a beer jar, which they were evidently to share, and disappeared.

Hani resumed talking. "No, I want to talk about the King's Beloved Wife." He watched the color drain from the sculptor's face and his throat convulse with the effort to swallow. "That was a superb portrait you did of her. You're a very talented man."

Kha-em-sekhem's eyes twitched toward Hani, and his mouth quirked skeptically. "I think that's not what you want to talk about." He was starting to breathe rather hard.

"Who's paying you?"

"For the portrait? The king." He laughed sarcastically. "Life, prosperity, and health, and all that."

"No, to blackmail her. Because you're in a really dangerous position. You're going to be caught and tortured and killed, while they'll get away free." Hani was venturing out into completely hypothetical waters, hoping to draw the man into some sort of revelation of what was really happening.

"I don't know what you're talking about," the sculptor said tersely. He bit angrily into an endive and wiped the dressing from his lips with the back of a hand.

Hani said nothing, just dropped a fish into his mouth, watching Kha-em-sekhem.

"Who are you, anyway?" the man whispered. Sweat had beaded on his face. Under the angry surface, fear lurked like a crocodile.

Hani shrugged amiably. "One of the officials who brought the Beloved Royal Wife back from Naharin years ago. I feel rather protective toward her. She's suffering. I didn't think you were the kind of man who would use a woman like that."

Kha-em-sekhem hung his head, his mouth slack. "All you gods…"

"In my opinion, you're both being used. Someone knew your weakness for beautiful girls and saw a useful tool. You're the chisel in his fist, my friend. And at some point, he'll throw you away."

The sculptor put his face in his hands and let out a groan.

Hani leaned toward him and said quietly, "I'll do all I can to help you stay out of trouble if you'll help me identify the one who's behind this. If it blows up, it'll drag us into war and pull you and Kiya down with it."

Kha-em-sekhem stared up at the ceiling, agonized, but said nothing. Hani could see by the flickering light of the lamps that his eyes were wet. Finally, the man whispered, "Why should I trust you? Maybe you're the king's man, and the Mut-nodjmet business was just a front."

Hani smiled gently. "No on both counts. I'm really her uncle."

The sculptor stared sightlessly out at the merrymakers in the room, his face wrung by misery, and Hani resumed eating. At last, Kha-em-sekhem said, "I'm not admitting to anything."

"Understood. You're a victim," Hani said through a mouthful of endive.

Another silence stretched out. "You're not going to threaten to break my fingers or something if I don't talk?"

His lips around his straw, Hani grunted and shook his head. The man was finally softening up. "It isn't very private here," Hani said when he had swallowed. "I propose we meet at the house where I'm staying when I'm in the capital. Do you know a man named Ptah-mes? Of course you do—you've carved his likeness."

"He's a vizier or something, isn't he?"

"Used to be. Do you know where he lives?"

Kha-em-sekhem nodded, looking defeated.

"We can either go together right now, or you can join me tomorrow after work. I need to leave for Waset after that."

"Let's do it now."

They headed back through the dark streets lit only by a

quarter moon and the milky light of the stars. Although the sculptor was young and in good shape, his breathing was as heavy as if he were climbing stairs for block after block. Their sandaled footsteps clopping on the packed earth was the only other sound. Suddenly, something large and light colored flashed silently overhead.

Kha-em-sekhem flinched, and Hani smiled. "An owl."

They arrived at Ptah-mes's gate, and the doorkeeper admitted them, since Ptah-mes's servants had orders to let Hani come and go as if it were his own home. Hani saw lights in the house through the treetops. "Let's sit in the garden." The white graveled path still glowed with the last of the day's drowning light, and Hani groped his way to a bench with Kha-em-sekhem at his heels. "Now, my friend. Anything you can tell me will help us to save you."

Kha-em-sekhem sat silently in the darkness for so long that Hani began to wonder if he had sneaked away, but at last he spoke. "It must have been about a year ago now. The person who spoke to me was a servant, although probably a high-level one. He only ever referred to his master as 'the star in my sky.' I had just started working on the plaster bust of the Beloved Royal Wife. He said wouldn't I like to enjoy the beauties of Lady Kiya from closer up, or something like that. That I should figure out how to do so and then anonymously blackmail her to get her to influence the king's foreign policy. I said I couldn't write—how was I going to send a note? He said the star in his sky would take care of that. I only had to slip the note someplace where Kiya'd find it when I was there working on the sculpture."

"How long did it take you to finish the plaster likeness?"

Kha-em-sekhem gave a cough of a laugh. "Less than a

month. But she started thinking of things she wanted me to do—other views, other headdresses, a relief. It went on for about three months. I was getting really nervous. There were priests and guards and handmaids everywhere, and the chamberlain of her household was always prowling around." His voice broke. His hands clenched and unclenched nervously. "Sometimes, we'd keep talking while we were doing it so no one would get suspicious. I'd say, 'Lift your nose a little' or 'Do you want this to be the same color?' I must have been crazy. The danger..."

"This was at the palace harem?"

"Only the first time. *Iy*, that place was guarded like the Double House of Silver and Gold. No, we usually met at Pa-maru-en-pa-aten."

Ah, the place where the Aten shows what he's capable of. "And then, at some point, you left the note demanding action or else. Do you know what it said?" Hani asked.

"No idea. I can't read. My contact just said it had to do with political influence."

"I suppose he paid you, though. After all, you were taking an enormous risk." Hani kept his voice neutral and nonjudgmental.

"He paid me well. In silver, often, or jewelry. I thought Rekhet-ra would be pleased with that, but she wasn't. Nothing I did ever made her think better of me." Kha-em-sekhem heaved a sigh as if he needed air. Suddenly, he groaned. "I've never been so miserable in my life as since this has been hanging over me. I feel like the *medjay* are going to be coming after me at every corner I turn."

In the shadows, Hani made out Kha-em-sekhem lifting his hands to his face. He felt a genuine surge of compassion for the man. No hardened spy but a simple artisan, Kha-em-sekhem was into some nefarious business way over his head. Hani reached out and laid a hand on the sculptor's knee. "Help me to find the person behind this, Kha-em-sekhem, and I'll do everything I can to protect you."

Kha-em-sekhem mumbled a thank-you and then said in a faint voice, "Can I go now?"

"Of course," said Hani kindly. "If you learn anything else, please let me know. It's in your own best interest. By the way, do you know any Mitannians?"

Kha-em-sekhem made a grunt of ignorance and lifted a shoulder, barely visible in the darkness. He unfolded himself from the bench.

Hani accompanied the sculptor to the gate and saw him out then drifted back through the garden, heading for the house. Kha-em-sekhem had given him a version of the affair that was rather different from Kiya's. Hani's ideas were as tangled as a ball of thread Ta-miu had gotten her claws into, his thoughts twisting and flapping and trying to make connections. So he started when a voice spoke his name quietly from out of the dark garden.

Lord Ptah-mes's long white garments appeared against the deep twilight. "I'm sorry, I heard that conversation, Hani. I apologize." He stepped to Hani's side, and they walked back toward the house elbow to elbow. "I was sitting in the dark when you started to talk, and I was afraid it might shut your man up if I rose and left at that moment."

"Ah," Hani said resignedly. "Perhaps I should have told you about this from the start, my lord, but I didn't want to put a strain on your conscience, considering what it deals with."

"My conscience has been under a strain for some years," said Ptah-mes acidly. He and Hani entered the house, which was lit up unto extravagance, as if for a party. "I couldn't make up my mind if I wanted darkness or if I was afraid of it. Have you eaten?"

"A bit."

"Something light, then." Ptah-mes clapped for a servant, who brought them a beaker of wine and cold thighs of waterfowl in a spicy sauce, thickened with ground walnuts. The two men sat in silence while the servant arranged their little tables and poured their silver cups full of bloodred liquid. When he'd left, Ptah-mes said quietly, "Tell me what's going on."

Hani unfolded the events as best he could, starting with his own visit to the *maru*. Ptah-mes listened gravely, giving an occasional nod or lift of the eyebrow. Then he sat for a long space of time cogitating silently, a bird thigh in his fingers, his handsome face expressionless.

At last, he said, "If this unpleasant business can be resolved before it comes to the king's attention, it would spare him a lot of worry. There are other, better ways of encouraging him to take action to support Naharin. I find it hard to believe that Tushratta would have anything to do with this. He would never endanger his own daughter in such a way."

"No. If there are Mitannians involved, other than the messengers or emissaries or whatever those two veterans were, they must be acting on their private behalf." Hani dipped his fowl in its sauce and nibbled off the flesh with his teeth. "What puzzles me is that Kiya is done for no matter what happens. If she tries to influence the king, he'll be angry and put her aside. If she does nothing and the mysterious blackmailer isn't satisfied, he'll probably expose her indiscretion, and she'll be finished in earnest."

"I can think of no scenario that will save her except to strike the blackmailer first." Ptah-mes took a sip from his cup. "How likely do you think it is that you can do that?"

"I can't say, my lord, without knowing *who* he is." Hani smiled but without humor. "She didn't say if they had given her a deadline."

"You know, Hani, this is a very dangerous business for you. Undoubtedly, the king is aware you've visited his Beloved Wife already. You can't be seen to be going there regularly without some good excuse, or they'll start tailing you, and the game will be over."

"I'm aware of that," Hani said grimly as he turned his goblet in his hands.

"As for myself, I mustn't be seen to be involved in this in any way. I give you as much time as you need to work on it, but my name must never come up, even as being aware of what's going on. If I'm questioned, I'll plead ignorance."

"Of course, my lord. And you wouldn't know except through an accident."

"But to have found out as I did and not have reported it…? I am in ignorance, Hani. Is that clear?"

Ptah-mes looked tired and ill at ease. He was several years away from fifty still, but there were times when he looked much older, with his sharp features and narrow lips and the beginnings of bags under his fine black eyes.

Hani said with conviction, "You know absolutely nothing."

CHAPTER 5

H ANI WAS TIRED, TOO, BY the time he made it back
to Waset. The Flood had just begun, and the current
was swollen and fierce. Even with paddles, the ferries were
slow heading south. It occurred to him that he needed to
invest in a nice, small yacht if he was going to be making
the trip back and forth this frequently. He opened his
mouth in a jaw-cracking yawn as he pushed aside the mat
over the front door.

"It's a hippopotamus!" cried Pipi from within. "Look at
that sinister mouth full of tusks as the great beast emerges
from the waters of the River! Be afraid at the sight of its
massive belly that—"

"You no-good rascal!" Hani growled. "Look who's
talking about massive bellies!" He lunged at his brother
and clamped him in a headlock. The two of them struggled
and flailed, thudding heavily and knocking aside the stools,
until both of them had fallen to the ground, weak with
laughter. He looked up to see his father standing in the
inner door with his arms folded.

"I thought that might have been Hani home from the capital, but it seems to be some six-year-old who made his way through the gate." Mery-ra grinned.

"It's another hippopotamus! Catch it!" Hani rushed his father, but instead of flipping him to the ground, he enveloped him in a jolly hug.

"Easy," cried Mery-ra, cringing. "I'm still sore from our dance lesson."

"That was weeks ago, Father," Pipi pointed out, picking his wig up off the floor and fanning himself with it.

"Dance lesson?" Hani asked.

"Yes. When Neferet was here before. She showed us how to be dancing girls."

"Oh, right. Sorry I missed that." Imagining the spectacle, Hani shook his head in merriment.

"But you didn't miss me!" Neferet came pelting in from the porch and hurled herself on her father, who swung her around delightedly.

"Either I'm older or you're bigger, but this isn't as easy as it used to be." Hani blew out a breath. "So, when did you get home, my duckling—and Pa-kiki, too, I assume?"

"Yesterday, Papa. It took foooor-ever."

"I wish I'd known. I would have had you stay another day and come back with me."

"That would have been fun." She tugged at Hani's sleeve. "Come out to the pavilion, everybody. Baket-iset and Pa-kiki and Mut-nodjmet and I are out there."

"Where's your mother?"

"With Aunt Anuia," the girl said as she led the way outside.

Hani shot his father an uneasy glance. "Still no word about Amen-em-hut?"

Mery-ra shook his head, his eyebrows raised significantly.

Pipi, who was trailing his brother, hissed, "Did you find out anything about this sculptor fellow, Hani?"

"Yes. I'll tell you soon."

They found the young people under the shade of the grapevine, laughing and talking. "Papa!" Baket-iset and Pa-kiki simultaneously cried, sending Ta-miu scurrying for cover. Hani kissed them each in turn and Mut-nodjmet, too, and seated himself on the edge of his eldest daughter's couch. "Everything all right on the home front, Baket?"

"Uncle Amen-em-hut's still gone," Baket-iset said in a subdued voice. Then her tone grew more cheerful. "Lord Aziru and his men show up every so often, stomping around unhappily. One of them is very nice. I'm teaching him Egyptian."

"Oh," said Hani, biting back his reservations. No doubt, his lovely daughter enjoyed the attentive company of the man—even if her limbs were immobilized, her heart was as warm and yearning as any girl's—but Hani had no idea who or what the fellow was. He might even be a slave. Hani needed to talk to Aziru.

"And as Grandfather told you in one of his letters, they play a *lot* of Hounds and Jackals."

"Do you feel uneasy with them around all the time, my dear?"

"No, they mostly stay upstairs or go out. It's just the evening when we can hear them walking around." Baket-iset was never bothered by anything.

"So, everyone's home for the holidays, eh?" Mery-ra

149

asked, his hand on Pa-kiki's shoulder. "Wepet-renpet's over. Now the Wag Festival, then our special feast day in honor of Djehuty, and—"

"Why is that our special feast day, Grandfather?" asked Mut-nodjmet, who was sitting cross-legged on the floor like Neferet.

"Patron god of lunatics," said Pipi.

"Of scribes," Mery-ra corrected, clapping a hand over his younger son's mouth. "And then the Feast of Drunkenness."

"*That's* our patronal feast," Pipi declared between his father's fingers.

"Get ready to be woken up in the middle of the night by drums again," warned Pa-kiki with a big smile that suggested he couldn't wait.

Hani looked around. "I haven't been home much in recent years. Do we... do we still celebrate all these feasts of Osiris and Hut-haru?"

"Well, *people* do," said his father. "I don't think the mayor or the king or anyone official does—although you'll notice they gave the chancery the period off. You're not going to stop people from putting little boats at their loved ones' tombs or sending them down the River."

"We're already making the boats." Neferet held up one she'd folded from a piece of papyrus.

"I hope that's no important document you girls have cut up," Hani said, raising a warning finger. "Not the deed to the house. Not Father's *Book of Going Forth by Day* for our tomb."

Pipi pretended to gasp. "It's the will of our rich uncle!"

Through the laughter resounded the boom of the gate clanging shut.

"Mama's back," Neferet cried, surging up and galloping to greet Nub-nefer before she had reached the door.

Hani heard the beloved footsteps crunching on the gravel as she approached, and he intercepted her with open arms. "My beautiful dove! It's so good to be back."

She clung to him so tightly that he feared he'd see her in tears when she drew back, but her face was calm. "I'm sorry I wasn't here, my love, but Anuia was in a bad way."

"Any news?"

"They've found Amen-em-hut's little boat washed up downriver somewhere. The Flood carried it off from wherever it had been."

"Why, that's probably good, isn't it? If he set off in a boat, he's probably hiding."

She smiled, and Hani could see how drawn her face was under the mask of good cheer. "Let's hope it was tied up and not just overturned in some reeds somewhere for a month until the floodwaters dislodged it." She looked around at the gathered family. "Well, I'll go see what we have for dinner. It's like feeding the army these days."

One at a time, the children drifted off to their activities, and Hani was left with Baket-iset and his brother and father. Ta-miu came sauntering back in and jumped on Hani's lap.

"All right, Pipi," Hani said, stroking the cat's fur. "Here's what I found out. This Kha-em-sekhem is not an altogether bad man, but he has a little womanizing problem."

Pipi groaned.

"And he runs through his silver as if it were water."

Mery-ra groaned.

"And he's involved in something that may really come down on his head in a terrible way."

"Ammi take the bastard," Pipi moaned. "It's just as we thought. He's totally unsuitable."

"What's the bride price all about?" Mery-ra asked. "That always seemed particularly odd to me."

"He apparently feels he has to buy people's friendship. It seems to be a pattern. He throws silver and grain and what have you at everyone as if he fears no one will accept him otherwise. He's actually a nice-looking man and enormously gifted, but... well, he doesn't have confidence in himself, I guess. He's not the sort of person to whom you'd want to entrust a young girl who doesn't have any self-confidence either."

Pipi hung his head, cursing under his breath.

"Poor Mut-nodjmet. She'll be so disappointed. She's done nothing but talk about her handsome fiancé," murmured Baket-iset.

"I'm afraid she'll run off with him without waiting for my permission," Pipi said, glancing behind him as if she might be tiptoeing down the path as he spoke.

Hani shook his head. "You've got to convince her, Pipi. Make her understand for herself how unsuitable he is. I don't advise taking her to see him; it might just inflame her. Although I think he might not be so keen to have her at this point. He's in deep trouble."

Mery-ra looked avid. "What's he done, son?"

"I can't tell, but it's certainly a capital offense."

Mery-ra and Pipi stared at one another, eyes wide. Pipi heaved a big sigh. "I guess I have to go give her the paternal talk." He hauled himself up and dragged himself off into the house.

"I forgot to ask Neferet how her first days as an apprentice *sunet* went. And Pa-kiki—his first job," said Hani after his brother had lumbered away.

"Oh, you'll hear all about it at dinner, I'm sure, Papa," said Baket-iset, her voice full of merriment. "They've already started to regale us in great detail. It's lucky Lord Aziru and his men weren't at table last night."

Hani rose, dumping an indignant Ta-miu from his lap. "Do you want to stay out here, my swan, or shall I have the servants take you into the salon?"

"If she wants to remain outside, I'll stay and talk to her," offered Mery-ra. "It's such a nice evening after such a hot day."

"Thank you, Grandfather. I'll stay until dinner, then."

"Oh, son," Mery-ra called after Hani as he started down the path. "They brought a diplomatic pouch last night. I think it must be letters for Aziru."

"Thanks, Father." That decided Hani's next action for him. He needed to read the Amurrite's correspondence and report on anything that might be of interest to the vizier. He didn't think he had the energy to undertake it that evening, though. Several nights sleeping on a boat tied up somewhere along the riverbank weren't very restful. That made him think of Amen-em-hut. *Dear gods, what's happened to the man? Is he even alive anymore? If so, where can he be?*

Although they were so different, Hani was fond of his brother-in-law. Amen-em-hut always made Hani think of a fussy little bird, handsome and diminutive as well as anxious and intense. But he was a good man and fastidiously upright. If anything had happened to him, he was a martyr to his conscience, faithful to the Hidden One he served.

Great lord of heaven. Has there ever been such intolerance in our fair and inclusive land? Has anyone ever gone around shutting down temples and denying gods their meat and drink? We've always welcomed everyone and their gods with them and made them part of our own, because you can never tell whose help you may need.

In the shadows of the salon, he saw his own little shrine. Someone—Nub-nefer, no doubt—had put the Aten stele at the back, behind the statue of Amen-Ra. He had to admit that what bothered him was not the Aten, who had been an object of worship at least since Neb-ma'at-ra's first jubilee. Nor was it that strange way of showing him without a body—just a disk, like the sun in the sky, and little rayed hands coming down. It was the idea that only the royal family really approached the Aten. Hani looked down at the stele, at the image of the king and queen in that disturbing, exaggerated style with locked knees and bulging thighs. *What about* our *prayers? All those priests? Do we—do they—count for nothing? And what happens when the king dies?*

Hani let out a heavy breath. Too many deep thoughts for one night. He looked forward to the next few days of holiday. *Time to get out in the marshes in my boat and see the birds.* Then he remembered that the River was in Flood, and an inundation of disappointment rose in him as it used to do when he was a little boy and his mother said he couldn't have the treat he had been promised after all because he'd been naughty. He laughed at himself. Dinner would restore his good humor.

✦

Aziru and his men were seated at their little tables with the family that night. The *hapiru* leader made an effort to be his more charming self rather than the bitter, bored self who was apparently his habitual guise lately.

"How are things in the capital, Hani?" he asked without letting the implied meaning beneath his words baste them too liberally with sarcasm.

"Hot, my lord. You'll cool your heels much more successfully here."

Aziru flashed a pinched smile, his eyes bright. For all that Egyptian wasn't his native language, he was quick to catch word play. "Your wife has been a charming hostess. I apologize for the disruption this must have caused."

"Not at all, Lord Aziru. I just regret that you're kept away from your own family so long. Perhaps you and your men would like to go hunting in the next few days. Everything will be closed because of the festivals."

The Amurrite looked genuinely pleased. "I'd like that." He leaned over to the good-looking young man at his side and said in his own language, "He says we can go hunting in the next few days. Sounds like fun, eh?"

"A welcome diversion, my brother," the youth replied, his bored face brightening.

"He's really another of your brothers?" Hani asked.

"He is. His name is Abdi-urash. He said your daughter is teaching him Egyptian." Aziru bared his white teeth in a smile. "The other fellow is my secretary, Binana."

"The day after tomorrow is the Wag Festival, and we'll all go over to our family tomb to put, er... paper boats on it." Hani knew that must sound quaint to a foreigner. "You're more than welcome to come, if you like. But after that, there's a day before the Festival of Drunkenness. That might be a good time to go."

"Whenever you like. It's something to look forward to." Aziru occupied himself with his balls of herb-and-garlic-flavored pork for a moment. "I don't suppose any mail has come for us?"

"I haven't had time to look, my lord," Hani said, massaging the truth. He didn't want to make it too obvious that he was reading their correspondence, although Aziru no doubt suspected as much.

The king of A'amu nodded and lifted his cup to his lips. Hani turned to Nub-nefer, who shared his table. "My dear, I forgot to tell you. I know the husband of your *weret khener*."

"Lady Apeny? She's such a grand lady, always so perfectly turned out. You can't imagine how tight a rein she kept on that unruly bunch of chantresses, everyone thinking she's better than everyone else. And the men! I can't tell you! But Apeny cracked her whip, and they all jumped." Nub-nefer smiled with affectionate recollection.

"You liked her, then?"

Her eyes sparkled. "I loved her. She was like a goddess to us all."

"She's the wife of my friend Ptah-mes."

"Friend? Oh, Hani, they're old nobility of the highest rank. He was mayor of Waset when he was only in his twenties, and First Prophet of the Hidden One—although not for long." Nub-nefer gave him a disbelieving look, as if Hani were delusional for thinking such a person could be his friend.

"I know. Ptah-mes grew up at the king's table with the Osir Neb-ma'at-ra."

She stroked her husband's face with proud eyes, melting toward him, then suddenly, her gaze sharpened into a fierce point. She said in a low voice, "Maybe they could help us find Amen-em-hut."

A ripple of unease ran up Hani's spine. "I don't know, my love. Ptah-mes is already compromised. He has to be very careful about what he's seen doing…"

Nub-nefer drew back, nodding desolately. "I suppose so." She turned to her meal, her face downcast and her brows strained.

Oh, my dearest, thought Hani in pain. *We've got to find that man for your sake.*

A burst of wild laughter from where the young people all sat, heads together, made Hani look up.

Baket-iset called, "Neferet's telling us about her medical lessons, Papa."

"Medical lessons?" Aziru leaned toward Hani and raised an eyebrow.

"She wants to be a *sunet*," Hani explained. "She's just apprenticed with the doctor of the Royal Ornaments."

"You have women doctors?" Aziru turned to his brother and translated.

Abdi-urash leered. "I suddenly feel sick," he said in his own language.

"I believe they only treat women. More's the pity," Hani replied in the same tongue.

He glanced back at the children and noticed Mut-nodjmet sitting rigidly, a fixed smile on her plump face. She looked thoroughly miserable, her eyes red and swollen. *Pipi has spoken to her.* Hani sighed.

Pipi was watching his daughter too. Hani leaned around Nub-nefer's back and tapped his brother on the arm. "How did she take the paternal talk?"

Pipi's usually merry little eyes were sad and strained. "It hurt her deeply, Hani. In her own mind, they were all but married. I'm not sure she won't sneak off and try to find him."

"Not convinced, eh?"

Pipi shook his head. He looked up at his big brother, desperation written on his face. "What am *I* going to do?"

An alarm started trumpeting in Hani's mind. He rose from his stool and tossed a sideways nod to indicate that Pipi should follow him. They withdrew to the empty vestibule, and Hani closed the inner door behind him. The hilarity in the salon faded away.

"What is it, Pipi? You're afraid to lose the bride price?"

Pipi hung his head and said vaguely, "It certainly would have come in handy…"

"Not good enough, man." Hani's voice grew rough and imperious like that of the officers he'd known in the army. "Why do you need silver?"

"I… borrowed a lot and need to pay it back."

"Come on. Why did you borrow it?" They were big brother and little brother again, Hani unashamedly wielding the authority of the elder.

Pipi heaved a resigned sigh and peeked up at Hani from

under his eyebrows like a guilty, pudgy little boy. "I bought a horse."

Hani was caught speechless, winded, as if someone had sneaked up behind him and flipped him to the ground. A horse was an almost unimaginable luxury. Only the wealthiest nobility maintained a stable. The stud farms were a royal monopoly. He gaped at his brother.

"I know," Pipi cried as if to forestall him. "It's crazy. I only wanted to drive it once, and then I was going to sell it. I got it at a good price and figured I could make a profit on it."

Hani finally managed to close his mouth. He wanted to turn Pipi over his knee and paddle him, but he forced himself to speak calmly. "If you got a cheap horse, it's because there's something wrong with it. Will the seller take it back if you say you don't need it anymore?"

Pipi shifted back and forth, evading his eyes.

"Don't tell me it was some kind of itinerant horse trader…"

Pipi gave him a guilty look, his lip trembling.

Ammit take the fellow, Hani thought, pitying him but angry at such stupidity. Pipi had never had the sense of a goose about finances. Hani forced himself to draw a calming breath. "Who did you borrow from? How much do you owe?"

"Hani, I've always wanted to drive a horse," Pipi cried defensively. "I know I can't afford to keep it."

"Who did you borrow it from? How much do you owe?" Hani pressed relentlessly.

"A merchant who changes silver and such." He mumbled an exorbitant number of silver *deben*s.

"Lord of light! So much? Is that what you call a good price?" Hani thought that what Mut-nodjmet should really be looking sad about was the fact that her father was on the verge of bankrupting the family. "You'd better hope the king throws you the *shebyu*, the gold of honor, my friend. This is going to be difficult. I'll talk to Father."

But Pipi lurched toward him in misery. "Don't tell Father."

"No, I'm telling him. It'll take both of us to raise that kind of wealth." *I'm not touching Baket-iset's wheat*, Hani swore to himself. He wanted to be angrier at his brother, but Pipi was as irresponsible as a child. Instead, he felt hopeless. The same two parents had raised them with identical values, but people made their own choices. He looked at Pipi's face, sagging with shame and fear, and his anger melted. Hani stretched out his arms and enfolded his brother. They hugged, scarcely drawing a breath. He could feel Pipi's chest quivering with suppressed tears and squeezed him tight.

Suddenly, the inner door opened. The laughter and talk swelled, and Mery-ra appeared in the doorway, a squat silhouette. "What's going on, you two? Another dance lesson?"

"Come here a moment, Father."

Mery-ra closed the door behind him, and the voices were cut off once more. "What is it, son? Something wrong?"

And Hani explained to him what they had to do.

The next morning, the eve of the Wag Festival, Hani

retreated to his kitchen, opened the diplomatic pouch, and pulled out several letters for Aziru. He carefully broke the clay envelopes and slipped out the enclosed tablets. They were written in the Amurrite language in a lacy spatter of tiny wedge-shaped characters that made him think of bird tracks in the wet sand, which were also used for the international diplomatic tongue, Akkadian. Hani knew them both well.

The first letter was from Aziru's queen. There were a few words about the weather and the projected harvest. Then she gave him news about the children. Hani had to laugh; some things were universal. At the end of the missive, she asked her husband to bring her some gold vessels and a parure of jewelry. Unless it was all code, there was nothing political in her communication that might interest the vizier.

He turned to the next one, which was sealed by Aziru's brother, Pu-ba'alu, and his son, Bet-ilu. The two of them were administering the kingdom of Amurru in the new king's absence. Hani skimmed down to a line that grabbed his attention. The men of Kheta were tearing gobbets out of western Naharin. They had ninety thousand troops massed in Nuhasshe, which was a Hittite vassal state as of a year or so ago. The Egyptian holdings on the coast were almost completely encircled. They wanted to know what they should do and asked if the Great King of Mizri expected them to defend their fellow vassals. They'd fortified their border against neighboring Tunip, but without minute-by-minute orders from their king, Aziru, it was going to be touch and go.

Hani looked up and expelled a whistle, the hair rising

on his arms. *Ninety thousand troops? That's an enormous army. If this is at all accurate—and Pu-ba'alu may just be repeating word-of-mouth reports—the men of Kheta are up to something big.*

Ptah-mes and the vizier Aper-el would certainly be interested in this. Hani made a few notes to himself on a broken piece of pottery. Of course, it was also possible that the Amurrites were exaggerating in order to pressure Nefer-khepru-ra into letting Aziru go home, but that was up to Hani's superiors to judge.

Hani swept the broken envelopes into a jar to dissolve and reuse the slurry then stacked the letters in a basket to deliver to Aziru. He had just straightened up from the cook's worktable when a knock on the frame of the door made him start. His first instinct was to be sure there was no evidence of his tampering visible should Aziru enter.

"Sorry, my lord. I didn't mean to scare you." Maya stood in the doorway, his pen case over his shoulder. "Sat-hut-haru came to spend time with her mother, and Lady Nub-nefer said you were in here. I didn't know if you wanted me this morning or not."

"Oh, yes, Maya. Glad you're here. We have a few things to do, so all the work will be out of the way for the feast days coming up. I promised to take Aziru and his men hunting day after tomorrow. I'll need to borrow a chariot, I suppose." Hani thought glumly of the horse standing in Pipi's cowshed, eating up his income. It had come out the previous night that Hani's brother had taken a demotion in order to remain in Men-nefer as part of the local government rather than follow Aper-el's staff to Akhet-aten. Just thinking about his brother's bad judgment was enough to give Hani a headache, although he supposed his own work situation was unorthodox enough.

"Let's see. Would you mind taking these up to our guest, my friend? I want to say hello to Sat-hut-haru." Sending Maya on the errand would prevent Hani from having to answer any probing questions on the Amurrite's part.

Maya slid the basket over his arm and obligingly headed for the stairwell. Hani entered the salon, where the women of the family had gathered. "How is my little mother doing?" he said, opening his arms to his middle daughter. She was already six months pregnant, and against her slim young body, the mound of the developing baby was more than conspicuous.

I hope she's old enough for this, he thought anxiously. Women could die in childbirth; indeed, they often did. *Stop there. Her mother bore five children and had no problems, even though she's so tiny.* He let himself smile confidently.

Sat-hut-haru was beaming. She looked very much the young *nebet per* in her long voluminous wig. "Very well, Papa. I'm not sick in the mornings anymore. We had Khuit work a forecast for us. It's going to be a boy!"

"Khuit forecasts, does she?"

"I told you she was a witch, Papa," Neferet said with a touch of smugness, as if she'd been vindicated.

"But, my dear"—her mother smiled—"that's not witchcraft. In fact, anybody can predict the sex of a baby. Priests do things like that too."

"I don't want to be a priest, Mama." The girl looked sheepish. "Although I have to say, in Khuit's defense, that doctors do put mouse bones around a woman's neck if her baby has teething pains."

Hani laughed in spite of himself, and Neferet added stoutly, "But they know *why* they do it."

"No one begrudges you your apprenticeship with Djefat-nebty, my dear. In fact, she's not asking us for anything, whereas we had to pay Khuit." *And that's suddenly become an issue, alas.* He had bade a fond mental farewell to his dreams of a yacht since last night's decision to bail Pipi out of debt.

"Have you thought of what to name the baby?" Baket-iset asked.

Sat-hut-haru lit up. She gazed at her father like a sunbeam in summer. "We want to call him Amen-hotep."

Hani was so overcome by pride and tenderness that his nose sparked with tears. His oldest son had certainly never wanted to perpetuate Hani's name among his children. But Hani had to say, "I'm touched, my love, but do you think that's wise?"

Neferet cried out, her hands on her hips, "Oh, Papa—not Pa-aten-hotep! Please!"

Hani cringed. "Neferet, my love, please be a little more discreet," he said softly. "We have foreign visitors in the house."

From across the room, Nub-nefer stared at him, a whole complex of terrors within her widened eyes.

Hani glanced at Mut-nodjmet, who gazed silently at her cousin's swelling belly with admiration and longing. Her small eyes were lined with kohl, but nothing could conceal their lack of sparkle. He felt great pity for her. She longed for marriage and children almost at any price.

From the garden came voices, and suddenly, Mery-ra

appeared in the doorway. "Sorry to break up the party, fair ladies—but, Hani, there's a man at the gate to see you."

Hani excused himself and followed his father through the garden to where a scrawny adolescent stood, twisting his hands together and trying not to look too out of place. "How can I help you, son?" Hani asked.

"My lord, I'm from the workshop of Djehuty-mes."

"Yes?" Hani wasn't sure what this presaged.

"He said to tell you that Kha-em-sekhem is dead. He thought you'd want to know, since your niece was in love with 'im."

"May the Lady of the West guide him and Osir accept him!" Hani cried, distraught. He stared at his father, whose broad face looked as dumbfounded as Hani felt. "When did this happen? What did he die of?" *A strong young man like that...*

"We was working on Wepet-renpet, New Year's Day, because we 'ave a lot to do for the king—life, prosperity, and health to 'im—and Kha-em-sekhem didn't show up. The master was afraid 'e forgot it was a workday, so 'e went to 'is house to find 'im. And Kha-em-sekhem was dead." The boy made a little apotropaic gesture with his fingers.

"Any sign of what he died of?" Hani asked again.

"Oh, yes, my lord. Somebody... somebody stabbed 'im. With a chisel. Must've been one of 'is." The boy looked spooked at the thought of being killed with one's own tool.

Hani could imagine how overcome Djehuty-mes must be to lose this man who was not only an important member of his workshop but like a son to him as well. "Thank you, my lad. Tell your master he has our deepest condolences. I'll come see him at some point soon. Do you know where the body is? Have they taken him to the Place of Purification yet?"

"Not when I left, my lord. He's at the master's house."

"I'll be there soon."

The boy took his leave, and Hani turned to his father somberly.

Mery-ra said, "That's Mut-nodjmet's beau, isn't it? She's going to be grief-stricken. Who would want to kill a sculptor?"

"There's more to it than that, Father. You know I told Pipi the fellow was involved in something very dangerous?"

Mery-ra nodded, his little eyes wide.

Steps came crunching down the path, and Maya appeared. "Ah, here everyone is."

"Not everyone. Where's Pipi? This concerns him more than anybody." Hani could see his own anxiety mirrored on Maya's face as the secretary became aware of the seriousness of the two men.

"In the salon with the ladies. Shall I get him?"

"Why don't you?" Mery-ra said. "We need to break it to him before Mut-nodjmet hears."

Maya looked confused, and Hani said in a low voice, "Her sweetheart has been found dead."

"The sculptor?" Maya cried, wide-eyed. "Does this have anything to do with…?"

"Very likely." *Am I responsible for the poor man's death?* Hani asked himself, his gut churning. *Did someone follow me, observe that he talked, and want to get him out of the way?*

Will I be next?

Hani sent Maya back after Pipi, and a moment later,

Pipi burst into the vestibule, his eyes round with concern. "What is it, brother? What's happened?"

"Kha-em-sekhem has been killed. A boy just came from the workshop to let us know."

Pipi appeared stunned, staring from Hani to his father. "Killed? An accident?"

"Probably not an accident." Hani sighed. "Let's decide right now what we want to tell the rest of the family. I say he fell into the River drunk and was savaged by a hippopotamus. Does that meet with everyone's satisfaction?"

"Satisfaction doesn't seem like the right reaction to such a tragedy," said Mery-ra piously.

Hani laid a hand on his brother's shoulder. "Pipi, why don't you tell Mut-nodjmet? In a sense, this may make it easier to let go of him. I wish I could see the body before the servants of Lord Inpu get at it, but there's no way we could get there in time. I don't know how many long-haul ferries will even be running during the holidays."

The men trooped back into the salon, where the others looked up in uneasy curiosity.

"Mut-nodjmet, my dove, come with me for a moment," Pipi said somberly to his daughter, and the two of them exited.

"What's wrong, Hani?" Nub-nefer asked. These days, fear was always close under the surface of her eyes.

"Her sweetheart was found dead. It was a tragic accident."

A collective gasp of horror and compassion met this news. From the kitchen, a shriek of anguish indicated that Pipi had told his daughter.

"Oh, poor Mut-nodjmet," Baket-iset murmured, her voice higher than normal.

It occurred to Hani that she had more than a passing acquaintance with tragic accidents. Feeling guilty, he wished he'd thought of another scenario.

"What happened, Papa?" asked Pa-kiki.

"He, uh, fell into the River while drunk and was apparently killed by a hippopotamus."

Loud sobs poured out of the kitchen.

"Perhaps I should go to her," said Nub-nefer, popping up from her stool and staring anxiously at her husband.

Hani suspected, by the way her face had gone gray, that she was thinking of Amen-em-hut and his empty boat. He nodded, and she lurched away. *Hani, you clumsy fool*, he told himself. *Couldn't you have thought of some other way for him to die?*

It was the first time Maya had been home in Kemet for the Wag Festival in two years. He had forgotten the solemn joy of the prayers to Osir and the trip across the River, malachite waters twinkling with the little white boats let loose by the thousands upon its current. This time was marked by his first trip to Lord Hani's family tomb to lay around the door the little papyrus boats Neferet and Mut-nodjmet had made—facing west, in hope of the family dead's resurrection into the beautiful Duat. The door of the house of eternity was now closed and barred, the repairs to the damage wrought by Aha in a misguided fit of ambition had been completed, and the artists had withdrawn their scaffolding.

All around them, Lord Hani's neighbors and colleagues were making the same journey with their families. Like Hani and his clan, everyone was decked not only with joyous wreaths of flowers but also with the white headband of mourning. Hani exchanged waves with a former priest who lived down the block from him. Maya saw a secretary he recognized from the Hall of Correspondence tottering over the rock-strewn trail to the cliffside tombs of the affluent, his arms full of little boats probably made by his grandchildren. But the numbers were nowhere near as great as Maya remembered from his youth. No doubt some people had come back from Akhet-aten to visit their ancestral burial spot, but not everyone would have been able to—or dared to. Maybe they were no longer sure what place Osir and the kingdom of the dead played in the religion of the Aten. How did darkness figure into the cult of the light? Maya was sure he didn't know.

Now that he had fulfilled his obligation to Sat-hut-haru's family, he would take a detour to his father's tomb.

As the party made their way back toward the crossroads of the western paths, Maya saw Lord Hani's eldest son, accompanied by his two little children, trudging toward them from the River, heads down. Maya's joy tarnished. That arrogant twit Aha—he was already fat, as if he were some rich old scribe who made more grain than he could eat. According to Lord Hani, Aha had a lay post at the Great Temple of the Aten.

"It's Aha!" Neferet cried joyfully and rushed ahead to greet him. She jumped on her brother and clung to him then bent to hug her little nephew and niece, who seemed ecstatic to see her after a few days' absence.

169

"Aha, son! I'm so glad we crossed paths," Lord Hani said, sounding genuinely happy. He and Lady Nub-nefer took turns embracing their firstborn, then Hani picked up the younger boy and his wife took the little girl by the hand. Everyone exchanged embraces with the only family member who had chosen to move to the Horizon of the Aten. Everyone except Maya. The bastard Aha completely ignored him, as if Maya were a servant who had come along to carry the boats. Maya forced himself to smile like everybody else, but a slow fire of offense was smoldering within.

"Uncle Pipi. Mut-nodjmet. I didn't know you were here. Where's the rest of the family?" He always acted like he was bestowing some enormous blessing on a person by acknowledging him.

Here's one of the family right in front of you, you turd, Maya thought grimly.

Lord Pipi tried to act like his usual joking self, but he was clearly still saddened for his daughter. "Oh, I had some business down here, and I, er, brought Mut-nodjmet with me. Nedjem-ib stayed home with the younger ones."

"And look at my little sister! Somebody's having a baby!"

"Somebody's having a baby!" Ooh. Who could that be? Not Pa-kiki.

"Isn't it exciting! The little cousins will be almost the same age," Sat-hut-haru effused in her sweet way, sticking out her belly proudly, oblivious to her husband's resentment. "How is Khentet-ka? Neferet said she was having some problems."

The bastard wouldn't think to congratulate the father.

"Oh, better," Aha said airily. "But she didn't feel like climbing all over the rocks." He looked down at the papyrus boats in his hands as if he couldn't imagine how they had gotten there. "You know how it is, though. The children wouldn't miss it."

Maya noticed Lord Hani glancing at him and then at Aha, his wide mouth stretched into an expression that might have been disgust. Maya hoped he wouldn't make an issue of Aha's snub. That would smack a little too much of forcing two quarreling children to kiss and make up. As far as Maya was concerned, Aha had made it clear he, Maya, was only a nominal member of his family. Once an artisan, always an artisan.

Finally, the ordeal was over. Maya and Sat-hut-haru peeled off toward the middle-class shrines of the dead that sprinkled the sloping land between the River and the cliffs, and the rest of the family headed for the grand tomb of Lady Nub-nefer's family.

"I hope Uncle Amen-em-hut is all right," Sat-hut-haru murmured as Maya helped her navigate the cherty rock-strewn west bank. The sun was high by now and cast their stubby shadows before them at their feet. Maya chose not to dwell on how much shorter his was. "I know Mama is afraid he's one of the dead she's here to pray for."

"I'd be surprised if he weren't in hiding someplace, my sweet. Perhaps he's even fled the country."

"He would have told Aunt Anuia, Maya. He wouldn't have abandoned his family without a word like that."

They came to the small pyramid-roofed shrine that topped Maya's father's grave. It was neatly whitewashed and had several pole bouquets of fresh flowers leaning against it. Mother was always careful about that. She'd had someone paint on it a nice scene of Osir and his father's coffin, face-to-face. Maya couldn't remember if his father, a dwarf, had had such a tall coffin or if that were the artist's invention—Maya had only been a toddler when he died. He saw the little boats Mother and his aunts and nieces had left, and he knelt and added his own.

"Give me yours, dearest. I'll lay it for you so you don't have to kneel." How sweet it was to have a wife at his side for this familial duty! *Gods, she's adorable, with those flowers all around her head. I did pretty well, didn't I, Father? Meet your grandson.* "Do you still want to catch up to the others at your mother's family tomb, or would you rather go on back?"

"No, let's join them. Auntie needs all the support she can get."

They picked their way northwest toward the cliffs. In the distance, Maya saw the cluster of white-clad figures surrounding the opening of Lord Amen-em-hut's splendid house of eternity, already in the purple shadow of the Mountains of the West.

When they arrived at the tomb entry, Lady Anuia and her children, including the ridiculously handsome Pen-amen and his wife, were there. Everyone was weepy eyed and sad. Despite the wreaths, the gathering had more the air of a funeral than one of joyous hope. Lord Hani looked up and smiled at Maya, but his little brown eyes were dark circled, full of sorrow. They approached him, and he put a fatherly arm around Sat-hut-haru.

"Have we had any news?" Maya whispered.

Hani shook his head.

Maya heard Lady Anuia say to her sister-in-law in a wavering voice, "It's been more than a month, Nub-nefer. If he were alive, he'd have gotten word to me somehow."

That's all anyone can talk about. The poor sod's probably long gone.

They hugged all around, and this great priestly family wasn't too good to embrace a working-class boy. Then Lord Hani's party split off and headed back toward the River, while Amen-em-hut's remained to stew in their grief for a while.

Maya guided Sat-hut-haru with a hand on her hip as they navigated the uneven terrain. Lord Hani walked beside her with an arm around his wife, Lord Mery-ra toddled along on the other side with Lord Pipi at his elbow, and Pa-kiki, Mut-nodjmet, and Neferet strode on ahead. The would-be doctor was chattering away and waving her hands, but Maya couldn't hear the topic of her monologue.

All of a sudden, a fluttering hiss sped over his head, like a bird flying low. Ahead of them, just at the heels of the three adolescents, an arrow sprang from the ground with a *thunk*, swaying back and forth, a deadly flower. Maya froze, his heart in his mouth. He could hardly register what had just happened.

Hani whipped around, staring wild-eyed at the cliffs behind them, and cried, "Run, everyone! Toward the River!"

They fled in a disorderly rout, poor Sat-hut-haru stumbling awkwardly, Maya at her side, trying to steady her, although he was no fleet-footed gazelle himself. He could see other people staring at them as they lurched past.

"What happened?" his wife cried, her breathless voice shrill with fear.

"An arrow," Maya panted. "Someone shot right into us from above, up on the cliffs."

They trailed to a stop well out of range from the cliff tops. Gasping for air, everyone stared one at the other, uncomprehending and terrified.

"What was that?" Nub-nefer clung to her husband's arm.

Lord Hani tried to make light of it. "Someone must have been at target practice in the desert. How stupid, on a day when crowds would be at the tombs of their ancestors." His eyes were still a little wild despite his calm words, Maya observed.

Lord Mery-ra, who had bent over, his hands on his knees, trying to recover his breath, rose and shot his son a penetrating stare. Pipi looked confused and frightened. No one said anything for a long space of time. Maya heard no sound in this realm of the Lover of Silence except a dry rustle of wind and the gradually relenting hammering of his heart.

"Let's get back," Hani said finally.

"The servants will have lunch ready," Lady Nub-nefer murmured, almost sounding normal. "Are you all right, Sat-hut-haru, my love?"

"Maybe this means the baby will be a fast runner," Neferet offered. Everyone made the effort to laugh.

But Maya remembered that Kha-em-sekhem had just been murdered and wondered if Lord Hani didn't have a target on his broad back as well.

◈

Hani had tried to shake off the sense of terrible danger

that dogged him. He'd laughed and chattered during lunch in an effort to lay to rest the anxieties of his family, but his own were more tenacious. He saw with pain that Nubnefer's hand trembled as she served around the platter of stuffed dates. Mery-ra and Maya kept staring at him with eyes that suspected too much, but of course, his father was better than anyone at lightening the atmosphere.

"Oh, son, I've found chariots for your hunting party," the old man said after the festal prayers had been concluded. "Meryet-amen still has one that belonged to her late husband, who was a chariot officer. And her nephew has one too. He said he'd be happy to drive."

"Well done, Father. I know Aziru can drive as well. But there's still one too many of us for the two vehicles."

"Her nephew said he'd be happy to take the guests out for you—I told him you weren't a particularly keen huntsman. Seems his family has a property with really good game. They've actually stocked some ostriches out there. He says it's a guaranteed bag." Mery-ra grinned, but his look was meaningful. "I'm sure you have other things to do than run around in the desert. And he, young court buck, loves nothing better than killing animals. He was all excited at the thought."

"Your lady friend has earned my deepest gratitude, noble father," Hani said. The idea of finding himself all but alone in the open desert with a pair of foreigners who didn't know the terrain seemed especially frightening. Hunting accidents were easy to arrange. Whoever the blackmailer was, he wanted to rid himself of the only two others who knew something was going on. Hani had to get to the bottom of that strange business, not only for Lady Kiya's

175

sake but also for his own. "I'll send one of the servants over to coordinate with him."

After lunch, Pipi and Pa-kiki settled down to a game of *senet*, while the younger girls gathered around Baket-iset's couch for a round of gossip. His daughters had been very good about trying to distract Mut-nodjmet from her sorrow, Hani thought gratefully. Since they'd given the serving girls the day off, Nub-nefer and Sat-hut-haru busied themselves with clearing the tables. Seizing the moment, Hani, Maya, and Mery-ra withdrew to the garden pavilion, where they sat staring at one another like three conspirators, no doubt all thinking the same thing.

"I don't like this, son," said Hani's father. "Whoever's nose you've gotten up is ruthless. What exactly was that Kha-em-sekhem involved in? Is this some underworld gang you're mixed up with?"

"Worse than that," Hani said. "It seems to have something to do with international politics." He wanted to spare his father the knowledge of this case that might be dangerous even for him, but perhaps the old man needed to know what was hanging over their heads, the better to defend himself. "You remember I said our sculptor was involved in something with a capital punishment attached to it?"

Mery-ra nodded avidly. He loved to know the dark secrets of the court, but Hani was confident he would never speak of them to anyone. His father had been a military scribe for forty years, and Hani had reason to think he'd been in on more than one state secret. He wondered if Mery-ra might not even have served occasionally as a spy. If Maya knew, there was no reason Mery-ra shouldn't.

Hani leaned toward his father and said in a quiet voice, "Kha-em-sekhem had an affair with the Beloved Wife."

Mery-ra's little eyes grew round as plums.

"But let me start at the beginning." Hani told his father how someone had suggested to the sculptor—through an intermediary—that he compromise the royal wife and then leave a blackmail note, which that person would provide. He recounted the history of the two Mitannian veterans and their mysterious master and their demand for an intervention with the king on behalf of Naharin. He pointed out the discrepancies between Kha-em-sekhem's and Kiya's versions of events. "I suspect she's afraid she's pregnant by this man and wants to recast the whole story to make that an impossibility."

Mery-ra whistled. "She's trapped, isn't she? Either she's put away for fostering the interests of a foreign power, or she's punished for cuckolding the king. How did you get sucked into this mess, my boy?"

"Mane brought me a message saying she wanted to see me. I guess she still thinks of me as a sort of father figure." Despite the heat of the afternoon, Hani felt a cold chill pass up his back like a draft. "I don't think there's anything I can do for her. Now that Kha-em-sekhem's dead, I have nowhere to look for clues. And the only way to free her from her dilemma is to obliterate the blackmailer before he can tell anyone."

"You need to find an assassin," Maya said, pounding a fist into his palm like some ruthless little street thug.

"But I don't know who my target is." Hani shrugged helplessly. "Although he apparently knows *I'm* involved. I'm afraid he's giving me credit for being closer to identifying him than the reality justifies."

"You need to find a bodyguard before you find an assassin," Mery-ra said, his tufty eyebrows quirked in concern. "Think of motives, son. Who would want to push the Greatly Beloved Wife for a Mitannian intervention?"

"Someone who is nonetheless willing to sacrifice a Mitannian princess and bring the treaty down around her ears. It doesn't make sense at all."

Maya said eagerly, "Maybe that's their point—to bring Kiya down. Who would be her enemy?"

Hani emitted a caustic noise. "I'm sure anyone with the king's favor has a million enemies. The court's a snake pit."

He stared desolately out across the garden pool, where a small troop of ducks splashed and dabbled. Suddenly, two of them began to peck at one another, and before long, they were in a full-blown battle, beating their wings and trying to push each other under the water, squawking and bludgeoning the adversary with their comic blunt bills while the others paddled hastily out of reach.

The men began to laugh wildly because of the tension that they were holding in. "By the Lord Montu, even the duck pond is a snake pit!" hooted Mery-ra. "I think it's time for Lady Hut-haru to slay us all and start over."

"You always say that two days before the Feast of Drunkenness, Father," Hani said with a grin. The feast actually celebrated the salvation of mankind from the goddess's wrath by getting her drunk.

He picked up a pebble from the ground and threw it into the midst of the squabbling birds. The splash was as effective as slapping a hysterical person. The two ducks broke apart as suddenly as they had begun—perhaps having forgotten the reason for their brawl—and cruised away, ruffling their feathers and emitting outraged quacks that trailed off into a simmering stream of self-justifications.

"I've heard of cockfights, but I didn't know drakes were so scrappy," Maya admitted. He had seen the magnificent spurred cocks Tushratta had sent with his daughter to the late king.

"Oh, these warriors weren't even drakes. They were two females. Maybe they were fighting for the attention of a male." Hani flashed Maya a sly look. "You're newly married, my boy, but this is a message: beware the wrath of the ladies."

The three men laughed knowingly, then sobriety began to descend upon Hani once more. "I need to talk to Lady Kiya again, but I'm sure her visitors are observed, and I don't want to be seen coming and going too frequently."

"If she's so closely watched—and any wife of the king would be—how is it this horny sculptor was able to have his way with her?" Mery-ra asked cynically. "Sounds strange to me that they'd leave her alone with a man long enough to get into something."

"I don't know," Hani mused. "They were at Pa-maru-en-pa-aten. I remember from my own visit that guards and priests were posted all around, but nonetheless, there were spots outside of anyone's sight line. Still, your point is well taken." He turned to his father. "Where are you going with this?"

Mery-ra shrugged, looking innocent. "Oh, I don't know. It's too far-fetched to think our mystery man might have a henchman in the Beloved Wife's household who was willing to look the other way, I suppose."

"Not at all. This whole business has the mark of a court intrigue upon it."

All at once, the image of the two ducks battering one another returned to Hani's mind. *Beware the wrath of the ladies.* A slow wave of shivers lifted the hairs on his neck. "I think I know who the blackmailer may be," he said, his heart sinking.

"Who is he, my lord?" Maya whispered, leaning forward.

"If I'm right, it's not a *he*."

Mery-ra stared at him. "Oh, you're in trouble, son."

CHAPTER 6

MAYA, INNOCENT OF COURT LIFE, wasn't so quick to see the answer. "Who, my lord? One of the Beloved Wife's ladies-in-waiting?"

"Well, it's quite possible one of them is in league with her. But who stands to lose the most if the king's favor toward Kiya continues?" Hani pressed.

Maya's eager face froze in horror. "The queen?"

"Especially now that our girl is pregnant. So far, the queen has only presented her husband with daughters. The minute the King's Beloved Wife gives birth to a son, Nefert-iti's days of influence are over." He shot a sideways glance at his father. "If I were she, I'd try to make my rival trip herself up too."

"You'd better watch your step, son. The power is all stacked on her side."

"She must have thought I was close to unmasking her after I talked to Kha-em-sekhem."

As if just then realizing the risk they'd run, Maya

cried in horror, "Someone must have been following us everywhere we went."

Hani thought of Lord Ptah-mes trying so hard to stay out of the affair. The high commissioner might already have been compromised. *But is my very friendship so dangerous? How could anyone know we discussed the case in his salon?* He longed for Ptah-mes's experienced advice and calm cynicism.

Hani blew a hopeless breath through his mouth. "If this theory is true, then our princess is doomed. The only thing that could save her, as one of us just said, would be to eliminate her blackmailer." He snorted grimly. "That's certainly not on the table. So what do we do?"

No one spoke. Maya's face was anguished, Mery-ra's grave and considering. The jovial grandfather had disappeared into another man whom Hani didn't know very well himself.

Finally, Mery-ra said, "You need to unleash the big dogs, Hani. Find some intercessor at court who is intimate with the queen. Have them beg her—or better still, persuade her—not to go through with her plan to ruin our girl. Even get Kiya's father to make a state visit."

Hani laughed sarcastically. "I think you overestimate my influence, Father. I don't travel in such circles. Even grandees piss themselves at the thought of falling under the displeasure of the Great Queen Nefert-iti. I've only ever seen her silently at her husband's side at my initial audience, and frankly, I marvel that she even knows of my existence."

"Think, Hani. You must know someone." His father pinned him with an urgent stare. "Do you know anyone in the queen's family? What about your friend from Naharin? Could he press Tushratta to make a stink on his daughter's behalf?"

Hani shook his head, thinking hard. "It might be a mistake to reveal that I suspect her—because after all, this is only a theory. But in any case, if we found someone to approach her, they would have to offer her some scenario better than this one to tempt her to pull back." He cast his eyes around him at the grapevine, the garden, and the ducks, hoping for another inspiration. "You know, 'Don't force her to disgrace herself; instead, leave her in favor, let her have her child, and then... something good will come to you as a result.' Present the son as your own, or raise him and make him love you more than her... I don't know."

Mery-ra turned to Maya and said, humor returning, "You're good at embroidering stories, my lad. Think of something."

"If I were the queen," Maya said fiercely, "I'd see to it that my rival didn't come out of childbirth alive. *Then* I'd raise her son as my own and all the rest."

"Well, that's a solution, all right, but I wouldn't want to be the one to propose it to the queen," Hani said, raising his eyebrows. He found it hard to draw a satisfying breath, as if the weight of this awful burden lay upon his chest physically.

"You need an intercessor Nefert-iti trusts," Mery-ra insisted.

"Father, all my friends are under suspicion because they're associated with the priests of Amun-Ra."

"Who's her family?"

"She's a niece of the dowager Tiyi. Their family

183

members are provincial aristocrats—priests and military men—from somewhere farther south. Khent-min, I think. Her father, Tiyi's brother, is a cavalry officer who's now something bloated at court. They call him the God's Father, but he's not a priest—the god in question is apparently Nefer-khepru-ra. That's all I know. I've never met any of them personally except Lady Tiyi." *All you dear Great Ones,* he thought miserably, scrubbing his face with his hands, *my one prayer was to have nothing to do with the royal family.*

"Goodness, son," Mery-ra said with a droll quirk of the mouth. "Your education has been wasted on you. You haven't made any friends at court."

"No, but I seem to have made enemies."

"So, we have three objectives. First," Maya said, ticking it off on his stubby fingers, "is to prove that it is, in fact, the queen blackmailing Lady Kiya. Second, to invent some scenario even more advantageous to her than ruining Lady Kiya. And third, to find an intermediary she would trust to be looking out for her interests."

"Who's willing to risk losing her favor by telling her this," Mery-ra added.

Hani smiled bleakly. "Is *that* all?"

Aziru and his brother and secretary were off to the hunt with Lady Meryet-amen's predaceous nephew. Hani was immensely grateful that he didn't have to accompany the Amurrites after all. Poor Aziru was becoming more and more impatient and caustic as the days passed with no summons, and Hani just didn't have it in him to try to defend the king's foreign policy. He had a sneaking suspicion that

Nefer-khepru-ra had simply forgotten about the vassal king once he was off the palace grounds. Hani had hoped never to have to think again about the disaster that their behavior abroad had become, but it seemed destined to haunt him.

The urgent need to resolve Lady Kiya's dilemma was another thing that haunted him. He'd awakened with a headache that morning after a restless night—not the best preparation for the Feast of Drunkenness, which inevitably resulted in a grand, if sacred, hangover.

Pipi was the only other member of the family up yet. He came lumbering sleepily into the garden pavilion and threw a mock punch at Hani, who fended him off, grabbed his arm, and wrestled him to the ground with a growl. The two of them laughed affectionately as they climbed to their feet and sat side by side.

Hani was glad his little brother was returning to his playful self. Between the humiliation of exposing his financial disaster to his family and the sorrow of his daughter's imagined loss, Pipi had been reduced to a tentative shadow of his normal good cheer, as if he were afraid any attempt at joking might be taken as not appreciating the debt he owed.

"You're up early, old man," Hani said.

Pipi gave a deep sigh of contentment. "I guess there's no more excuse for me to stick around, Hani. Mut-nodjmet's lover is out of the picture, so I might as well take her back. It's been nice passing some time with you after all these years—seeing Father and the house, being here for the festivals and everything. It's like old times."

Hani clapped him on the shoulder, a warm tide of

affection rising in his heart. "You're welcome any time, brother. I don't know why you've waited so long."

"I don't know either." Pipi fell silent. Then he said, "Maybe I felt I... I embarrassed you."

Hani shot him a surprised look. "Why? Because you have a space between your front teeth?"

Pipi stared at him, nonplussed, then burst out laughing. That space was a trait they both shared. After a moment of fond grins, he said more seriously, "I always felt maybe the family was a bit disappointed in me. I never did as well as you—not in school, not in life..."

"I wasn't aware it was a competition, Pipi. You're a good man, and you seem to be a happy one. What finer ambition could one harbor? I envy you. You'll have the Judges of the Underworld in stitches at the weighing of your heart." Hani smiled mischievously.

Pipi's little eyes grew misty, and he fell on Hani's neck, cuffed his head with rough affection, and put an arm around him. "I love you, Hani. My big brother's still looking out for me." His voice had grown dangerously high-pitched, and he took a wobbly sniff.

"Just promise me you'll sell the horse, Pipi. Father will be coming up with a whole barge load of grain and cattle to pay off that debt. But never again, please."

"I swear to you, brother."

They sat in affable silence for a while, wigless, shirtless, and barefoot in the warmth of morning. Pipi's head was closely shaved, the rolls of flesh at the back of his neck stubbled. He'd apparently made a similar perusal of his brother's scalp, because after a moment he said, "I'd forgotten how curly your hair is, Hani. You take after Mother, don't you?"

"Not enough." Hani laughed.

"What do you mean by that?"

"I can't dance any more than you or Father can." Hani stood up and awkwardly pranced a bit, one hand in the air, one at his hip. Seeing Pipi begin to laugh, he tried a few gyrations, clapped his hands, and already breathing hard, launched into a spirited series of kicks.

Pipi immediately jumped up and joined in. Each of them tried to follow the other in their thoroughly graceless and thunder-footed dance, clapping and yelling "*Hai!*" from time to time. They bumped bellies, turned, and bumped butts, laughing like schoolboys and shouting "*Hai!*" louder every time until laughter threatened to render them helplessly weak. They fell apart, panting and full of hilarity.

"Don't let me stop you, children." Nub-nefer had appeared on the garden path, a cup of milk in her hands. She grinned at her husband. "I see you haven't waited until evening to lose your inhibitions."

"We're filled with the goddess, my dear," Hani said happily. He planted a kiss on his wife's cheek. His headache had quite gone away.

She caressed his sweaty face with a hand. "May there always be laughter in our house." She took a sip of her milk. "Have you eaten?"

"No," the brothers answered simultaneously and laughed again, their arms companionably over one another's shoulders.

"I left bread out, not altogether fresh, and there's milk. Help yourselves. The servants have the day off." Nub-nefer seated herself gracefully in the one chair, and the men drifted into the house.

As they passed through the salon, Pipi said, "I think we'll leave today, Hani."

Hani looked at him, surprised. "Before the festival's over? You may not find any ferries willing to go downriver. At least, not with sober pilots."

But Pipi seemed to have made up his mind. "I want to leave on a sweet note. Mut-nodjmet finds Waset a place of bad memories now, and there's no reason to stay. Besides, Nub-nefer has a house full of guests without us."

"Whatever you want to do, brother. It's been a joy to have you. Don't make me wait so long next time."

They found the flat loaves of bread and tore one in half to share. Hani poured two cups of milk. He pushed one over to Pipi and, leaning against the table, drank from the other.

At the door, their father watched, rubbing his eyes. "You lads are up early."

"Pipi's going to take off today, Father. I think I'll go boating in the marshes. I need a break from the city."

"You're leaving us, my boy?" Mery-ra laid a hand on his younger son's shoulder. "I guess it won't be so long until *I* see you again, but don't forget your brother. Waset will always be your home."

Pipi embraced his father, his mouth trembling with emotion. "Thank you for everything—both of you."

"That's what family's for," Mery-ra said tenderly. "Now, if we could just find little Shu..."

"Who?" Pipi looked confused.

"Nub-nefer's brother. The one who's missing," Hani said.

Mery-ra moved off to find himself some breakfast, and his sons finished their bread and milk.

"I'm going to the room to pack and see if Mut-nodjmet is up." Pipi lumbered off into the salon and disappeared from sight.

"Let's go outside, Father. I'll sit with you while you eat." Hani picked up the two cups, and Mery-ra supplied himself with bread.

"Do you think going out on the marshes is a good idea right now, son?" the old man asked uneasily.

"I think the current is steady. It won't be too strong out of the main part of the River."

"No, I mean..."

"It's going to be hard for anyone to follow me through the crowds of merrymakers today. Once I'm in the country, I'll be able to see whoever's around as easily as they can see me."

Mery-ra made a dubious noise.

Hani had to admit that his father had a point. As soon as he was among the reeds alone, he would be vulnerable to the attack of a stalker. "No, wait. I've changed my mind. I'm going to start back to the new capital today. By the time I get there, the people I need to see will be back at work."

"Are you taking Neferet with you, then? She'll be disappointed."

"She can go back with Pa-kiki tomorrow. This will leave me a little more time with Pipi, too, if we can find a boat."

By midmorning, the entire family was awake, laying plans for the evening's festivities. Neferet had trotted out the phallus clappers and was pulling the string to make hers pop up with a loud clack. Before long, she was clapping it in the face of anyone she passed.

"What is this, my dear? Homework for your anatomy lesson?" her father asked in veiled annoyance, having repeatedly fended it away from under his nose.

"No, Papa," she scolded him cheerfully. "It's for the festival tonight."

"It's probably not the only thing of that shape that's going to be popping up once the merrymakers get a few jars of beer in their bellies and the girls start peeling off their clothes," Mery-ra predicted. "Sure you don't want to stay, son?"

"I think the quiet deck of a boat is just where I want to be. I have some thinking to do. Plans..." He lifted an eyebrow at his father. "This is going to require some serious inspiration."

"Maybe you should stay and let the goddess fill you."

"She can fill me on the boat to Akhet-aten."

Hearing him, Neferet cried out, "You're going back today, Papa?"

"Yes, my dear. I have people to see."

"Am I going back with you?"

Hani couldn't tell if her words were a plaint or a plea. "You can wait until tomorrow and come with Pa-kiki, if you want."

But to his surprise, she said, "I want to go back with you. Lady Djefat-nebty just said, 'See you after the holidays,' and I don't know if she means *right* after the holidays or a boat trip later. She thinks I live there with Aha."

Her responsible attitude pleased Hani. He'd been so

distraught by all the drama of the last few days that he hadn't even had the forethought to ask her. "Better to be safe. Pack your bag, then, my dear."

Just after lunch, Pipi made his goodbyes and thank-yous to the family, and he and Mut-nodjmet waited in the garden while Hani and Neferet said their own goodbyes. Hani had expected Aziru and his hunting party to have returned, but they still hadn't shown up. However, the Amurrite was used to his host coming and going and wouldn't be surprised to find Hani gone.

"I hope they bring us some game," Hani said to Nub-nefer with a wink.

Together, the four of them started off to the riverside. Already, the crowds were starting to gather on major streets and in open spaces. It was strange to see a throng outside the gate of the Ipet-isut, even though it was shuttered and its flagpoles empty. The spirit of the festival seemed less joyous and innocent than usual. To be sure, a few instances of mischief were always committed as inhibitions loosened, but this time, he saw a truly nasty expression on some of the faces around him. No small number of those people were out looking for trouble. Having been away in Kharu so much over the last few years, he hadn't celebrated the feast in Waset for at least two years and maybe longer. The difference was noticeable. There were fewer decent, ordinary people of the working class and above. Judging by their clothing, the dissatisfied poor made up a high proportion of the leering faces. Perhaps dissatisfaction and poverty were swallowing up the working class, since Waset had been robbed of its temple economy and the vast number of prosperous bureaucrats who hired, commissioned, and paid people to work for them. He found the change disturbing. *Please let Pa-kiki and his friends be careful. And let Sat-hut-haru and Maya stay home.*

It reassured him to see a *medjay* officer and his leashed baboon threading through the crowd. No one would trifle with the foul-tempered animal. But he was only one officer among many people.

Hani noticed that he and Pipi had, as if by unspoken agreement, moved the girls between them so the pair of adolescents was flanked by two large men. He heard a whistle or two and a few crude remarks at the expense of Mut-nodjmet's conspicuous bosom. The girl blushed self-consciously, her head up and her neck stiff.

Pipi looked downright nervous. "Is it always like this? It's still the middle of the day."

"Never seen anything like it. In the last few years, there've been riots even on ordinary days, though. People are deeply disturbed by the emptying out of the city and its wealth."

Suddenly, the friendly custom of loosened inhibitions didn't seem like a good idea. Hani saw the quays ahead full of boats large and small, many of them loaded with partygoers, shouting and laughing drunkenly and clacking their clappers. He let out a nervous breath. "I just hope there are ferries."

They turned down the first boat that offered itself; the crewman soliciting their business could hardly stand up, he was so inebriated. Farther down the bobbing line of hulls was a large, sleek boat, beautifully painted in black and green, with a high, curved, papyrus-shaped stern. But it ended up being someone's private yacht. They stared at it in longing and admiration. They'd just turned away when Hani heard a voice call his name. He spun and looked back at the deck of the boat. Lord Ptah-mes and a tall, slim woman were standing at the gunwales, waving.

Hani returned eagerly to the water's edge. "My lord!" he called. "Nice to see you."

"Are you going back to the capital?" Ptah-mes was wearing a linen wig cover that drew the locks of his wig behind his ears, and he looked rather unlike himself. He seemed genuinely happy to see Hani.

"We are. My brother and his daughter are with us. We're looking for a ferry with a sober crew."

"Our crew is sober. Come on and join us. We're leaving as soon as they finish loading supplies."

"If you're sure we won't disturb you..."

Lord Ptah-mes assured him they had plenty of room, and the four of them gratefully mounted the gangplank. Hani had some experience of noble yachts, although this one was uncommonly beautiful. He saw that Ptah-mes had exceptional if somewhat austere taste—he'd overseen the construction of Neb-ma'at-ra's magnificent funeral temple, so that came as no surprise. The wide sail was still furled, but between the tall steering oars at the stern was a covered pavilion draped at the back and over the top with a richly patterned fabric from some island in the Great Green. Folding chairs with colorful cushions sat ready for use, with beer stands in position beside them. Otherwise, the vessel was painted in near monochrome with only discreet touches of other colors. A crew as large and businesslike as that of a merchant vessel hustled about, preparing to cast off.

Hani smiled at his friend as he stepped down to the deck. At his side, Pipi gaped about, and the girls seemed awestruck. To Hani's surprise, Ptah-mes embraced him, a smile twitching at the corners of his mouth in an almost conspiratorial way. "Hani, permit me to introduce my wife, Lady Apeny."

"Your servant, my lady." Hani folded in a reverence, a delighted grin upon his face. "My wife Nub-nefer is loud in your praises."

The woman smiled back. She resembled her husband to a striking degree—tall, slender, and aristocratic to the marrow. She had clearly been a beautiful woman in her youth and still was, in a faded way. Hani judged her to be a little older than Ptah-mes, but the fine thoroughbred bones of her face had held up well. "She is too kind. I adore your wife, Hani. Welcome to you and your family."

"My lord, my lady, permit me to introduce my brother Pa-ra-em-heb and his daughter Mut-nodjmet. They've been visiting from Men-nefer. And this is my own daughter Neferet, the one who's studying medicine."

"Oh, how interesting," Lady Apeny cried in the most perfect expression of genuine fascination. "And such a coincidence. I myself am continuing the journey to Men-nefer after my husband stops in the new capital. I would be delighted to offer you a ride for the rest of the way."

Pipi looked overwhelmed. He stammered, "Oh, with all my heart I accept, my lady. You're too kind."

She laughed—a cool, musical laugh that somehow managed to sound both practiced and genuine. Hani remembered Nub-nefer's description of Apeny cracking her whip over men and women alike as the *weret khener* of the Greatest Shrine.

"Girls, I have something delightful to show you, but I ask you to play with it in the cabin down there and not on the deck, all right?" She led the two cousins toward the little cabin amidships while her husband, Pipi, and Hani climbed the tilting deck and took seats under the canopy.

"What a completely unforeseen gift of the gods," said Ptah-mes.

A lurch and sudden bobbing of the stern told them the boat was free from the docks. Hani replied, "Indeed. We were a little uneasy with all the merrymakers around. I wasn't sure we were going to find a boat suitable for the girls. We didn't want to get on the first vessel we saw."

"No," Ptah-mes agreed grimly. "There's a very unpleasant atmosphere abroad today. I wonder if something isn't going to happen."

The man at the steering oars leaned with all his weight to his left, and the boat began to slide out into the current.

"I doubt if we'll need the sail," Ptah-mes said with the air of a host who doesn't let too long a silence fall over his party.

His wife made her way gracefully up the deck and took a seat in the vacant chair at Ptah-mes's side. Hani was struck by the absence of response. There was no exchange of glances, no smile between them, no little gesture. They were a perfect-looking couple dressed in the most exquisite fashion—handsome, well-bred, genial hosts who showed no hostility toward one another. But they were completely alone, both of them. It made him sad. He wondered if the move to Akhet-aten had come between them to this extent, symbolic as it was of Ptah-mes's compromise with the Aten.

"I have a puppy in the cabin," Lady Apeny said with a smile. "The girls were enchanted."

"It's for our daughter's children in Men-nefer," Ptah-mes explained.

"Ah," said Hani. "Have you other children, my lady?"

"Yes," she replied. "Seven altogether—one of them in Men-nefer, one in Nekhen. Now that I have more leisure, I visit them frequently."

She means, now that the Ipet-isut is shut and the cult of the Hidden One forbidden. Lady Apeny had managed to say it without bitterness, but Hani wondered what was in her heart and how much of it she blamed on her husband and men like him.

They chatted emptily of one thing and another as the magnificent boat slid down the fast-moving current—past the green palm-tufted banks and open farmlands, the whitewashed villages and tasseled marshes. Hani could feel his tensions washing away with the growing *iteru*s of distance between him and the City of the Scepter.

At last, Lady Apeny rose and said apologetically, "Forgive me, gentlemen. I'm going to see about something for our dinner." She made her way, swaying with the movement of the vessel, to the cabin amidships.

A moment later, Mut-nodjmet appeared on the deck and called, "Papa, you've got to see this irresistible creature!" Her face was alight with happiness, and Pipi seemed beside himself with surprise. He popped up, saying, "My pardon, my lord," and bumbled his way across the swaying deck to the cabin door.

Once they were left alone, Ptah-mes said quietly to Hani, "How is it going, my friend?" They both continued to gaze, squinting, out over the River, which was sparkling with the long rays of evening sun.

"Aziru's brother wrote to tell him that ninety thousand Hittite soldiers are massed just outside our borders."

"They're preparing to invade Naharin," said Ptah-mes with a sigh. "I doubt if that number is accurate, but certainly, they plan to take Naharin."

"Pu-ba'alu claims that without Aziru's brilliant strategy dictating their every move, they can't resist. He begs to know if they're expected to try to guard our other vassals."

Ptah-mes snorted. "No one's going to attack our vassals. They're going to go over to Kheta willingly, as soon as they see we're not making a move to defend our borders. Tunip is already gone."

Hani made a noise of disgust. He reminded himself not to care. After a moment, he said, "The sculptor Kha-em-sekhem was murdered."

Ptah-mes shot a penetrating sideways glance at Hani. "When?"

"On New Year's Day, my lord. And then someone fired an arrow at me from the Western Mountains as my family and I laid boats on my mother's tomb."

Ptah-mes made a grim noise through his nose. "Be careful."

Hani said levelly, "I have a theory about who the blackmailer is."

"Oh? Do I want to know, even in my complete ignorance of the matter?"

"I doubt it." Hani hesitated and whispered, "I think it's

the queen." He looked straight at his superior then, hoping to see a reaction of skepticism.

But Ptah-mes's expression was black. "Of course. It would be. You might as well stop your investigation while you're still alive, Hani."

"I don't know the Lady Nefert-iti. Would she do something like that?"

"Naturally. Any royal woman would if she felt her position were threatened. It doesn't mark her as particularly ruthless or ambitious. Although," he added, "she is both. She's her father's daughter."

They settled once again into their contemplation of the banks sliding past as the great yacht leaped downriver. A few small fishing boats clustered in the shallows. Its sail spread, a sleek, sinister military vessel plowed upstream, casting a shadow across the twinkling water. Hani felt the icy fingers of fear squeezing his heart. He wanted desperately not to be involved in this affair.

Finally, he said, "I had thought that if I could come up with some solution that would give her an even better outcome than disgracing the King's Beloved Wife, and if I had someone the queen trusted present that idea to her, she might relent—out of self-interest."

"And what is that solution, Hani?"

"I don't know, my lord, any more than I know someone trusted by the queen who would consent to cross her desire in this way."

Ptah-mes drew a deep, weary breath. He seemed relieved when his wife appeared.

"Gentlemen, I trust you're hungry. The servants have prepared us a little cold supper." She smiled graciously at

Hani without a glance at her husband. "Your brother and the girls know. They'll be up in a moment."

Apeny swept her long, gauzy skirts aside and seated herself with queenly grace.

"Were you aware, my dear," said Ptah-mes blandly, "that the older girl's fiancé was just killed?"

"What? Oh no! The poor child!" Apeny looked genuinely sorrowful. "At least she'll have these few days of amusement with the puppy to help distract her." She leaned toward Hani. "What happened to the unfortunate man?"

"He met with an accident on the River, my lady."

"It was that fellow who did our studies for the funerary statues," said her husband.

"Oh, really?" She looked nonplussed but recovered quickly. "What a loss. He was so talented."

Hani thought, *She's too well bred to show what she thinks of marrying an artisan.*

Pipi and the girls were making their way up the deck, chattering. Hani saw, with a mixture of embarrassment and tenderness, that Neferet was imitating the puppy, her folded hands up as if begging, her tongue hanging. She cocked her head and widened her eyes in pleading at Pipi then turned that pose to her father as they approached.

"Forgive my daughter," Hani said to his hosts with a dry grin, but his eyes were pointedly on Neferet's. "She feels the need to act out everything she sees."

"No, Papa," she said with a magisterial air, crossing her legs and seating herself on the luxurious carpet beneath their feet. "Only adorable things like that puppy. He's going to be a big hunting dog, but right now, he's the sweetest little ball of fur!"

"He's only nine weeks old," Mut-nodjmet added. "He licked my face with his little tongue." It was the first time Hani had seen anything resembling happiness on that drab face since she'd arrived in Waset.

His heart warmed with tenderness. *All any of us want is to be loved.* The incorrigibly unfaithful Kha-em-sekhem— wasn't he always seeking someone who would love and approve him? Hani thought of Lord Ptah-mes and his wife, as cool as polite strangers to one another. But then he considered Ptah-mes's courteously tempered longing for Hani's—or probably anyone's—company. He thought of Pipi's reluctance to let his father and brother know about his debt, as if he might forfeit their love by having been so imprudent. Indeed, Hani thought of the queen and the Beloved Royal Wife conniving for the favor of their husband. What did either of them want except to be loved? It was fatal not to be.

After supper, the girls returned to the puppy, and Lady Apeny went off to prepare sleeping places for the guests while the men sat on the stern deck in the cool of evening. The sun was sinking fast, as it did over the desert, inlaying the western sky with amethyst and coral and carnelian. An occasional constellation of lights was visible on the banks, where some village celebrated the Festival of Drunkenness. Faint music and laughter drifted over the current. Once, Hani heard the belching roar of hippopotamuses. The sailors had lit torches and thrust them into cressets on the long prow of the vessel, like shooting stars piercing the twilight that were mirrored in the waters of the River. Hani found himself lulled by the movement of the boat and the gentle hiss and clap of water against the hull, the illusion of sailing the bark of Ra among the imperishable stars.

He was almost certainly drifting toward sleep when Lady Apeny returned and said quietly, "Hani, I'm going to have the servants make your and your brother's beds here on the deck, if you don't mind. The girls will have more privacy in the cabin with the puppy. Lord Ptah-mes and I will be in a different room. Don't worry."

Hani roused himself to see that Ptah-mes had already departed. Pipi was asleep in his chair, head lolling on his chest.

"Thank you, my lady," he whispered. He rose and roused Pipi, and the two of them stepped aside while the servants spread a thick stack of blankets and cushions for each of them.

"We'll travel all night, then?" Hani inquired, surprised.

"Yes. It cuts the trip in half, obviously. Sleep well, gentlemen."

What luxury—a double crew and a torchlit passage devouring the iterus. He had to admit it didn't seem altogether safe, but it was a transcendent experience nonetheless. Hani stared up at the sky and saw the boat's glittering passage reflected overhead, a heavenly River of stars that draped the black body of Nut, the sky. They were alive. They sang—the souls of those who had joined Ra on his barque, sailing through the night, until dawn restored him to his sovereignty in the sky. What did the Atenists have to say about this majestic living darkness? How did they explain the absence of light? At last, he curled up under his blankets, and lullabied by Pipi's snores, he slept.

As predicted, they reached the Horizon of the Aten in half the time a normal fast boat required for the trip. Hani bade Pipi and Mut-nodjmet a misty-eyed goodbye as they continued to Men-nefer with Lady Apeny. Lord Ptah-mes headed directly home in his litter, while, despite Ptah-mes's offer of hospitality, Hani and Neferet went to find some breakfast on their own. The city seemed remarkably alert on the morning after the Feast of Drunkenness, but from what Hani could see, that festival had scarcely been celebrated here, where the fun-loving Lady Hut-haru was under the ban. Hani remembered Kha-em-sekhem calling it a city of prune-faced mystics and smiled to himself.

They bought bread and dates in the market and ate sitting on the ground in the shadow of one of the lion-bodied images of the king that now lined the processional road in the central part of town. *We probably look like country hicks,* Hani thought in amusement.

Afterward, he walked his daughter south to the mansion of Lady Djefat-nebty and entered it with her. He didn't want to leave her before he knew if the *sunet* expected her. But at the gatekeeper's announcement, the lady herself appeared in a scarf and old dress, ready to work.

"Neferet," she said as if stating the obvious. "We're mixing potions today. Go find an apron."

"I leave her with you, my lady." Hani bowed and was ready to withdraw, but Djefat-nebty stopped him with a word.

"Lord Hani. Before you go, let me say something." Her face was its usual stern mask, and he half feared she would say Neferet wasn't suited for the role of a doctor and should leave. She approached him, as tall as he was, and said in her harsh-voiced bark, "Your daughter is a delight. At last, a girl who isn't a conventional meek little mouse. She has character. We clash sometimes, but that's good. She won't always be a student, and she has to have opinions of her own."

Hani was amazed. His own recollections of his schooldays were that the master wanted unthinking obedience and a sealed mouth—a mouth used only to shout out the passages that had been assigned for memorization. But he was extremely pleased—proud of Neferet and happy that she had fallen into the hands of a teacher who was an unconventional thinker. "I'm honored by your praise for my daughter, my lady. I hope she continues to give you satisfaction."

Djefat-nebty drew down her long mouth as if to suppress a smile that threatened to expose her hidden niceness. She nodded brusquely and turned away, disappearing into the interior of the house.

Still warmed with the pleasant glow of the doctor's praise, Hani made his way back toward town and the working-class neighborhood where the shop of Djehuty-mes stood. He wasn't sure what information the sculptor might have that could be of use, but he wanted at least to express his condolences for the loss of Djehuty-mes's sometime son-in-law. A guilty little voice within whispered yet again that Hani himself might have been the remote cause of Kha-em-sekhem's murder.

He entered the courtyard, which was noisy and dust-whitened as ever, only to learn that the master was busy at the palace. But Djehuty-mes's daughter met Hani at the door of their house. Her soft face was tear streaked, her eyes swollen and red, and she wore a mourning scarf around her locked hair. The two little boys hung on her skirts.

"Oh, hello," she said, her voice nasal from weeping. "You've heard, I guess."

"Yes, and I wanted to express my sorrow. May the Lord Osir receive him in the happy lands of the West."

She nodded, unable to speak.

"Would it be too painful to tell me what happened?" Hani asked. "How he was found?"

Rekhet-ra stepped back from the door and gestured to Hani to enter. He followed her into the surprisingly spacious, well-appointed salon—a testament perhaps to Djehuty-mes's good taste and certainly to the financial success of his art. From the corner of his eye, Hani noted the shrine with its proper stele of the Aten and the royal family. The thought that the Great Queen might be after his own humble head was almost too absurd to comprehend.

"Sit down." Rekhet-ra gestured to a stool and took a seat opposite him. The little boys ran pattering away into the back of the house. She crossed her arms over herself as if for protection. "Why are you asking? Your girl has lost him now."

Hani said in a quiet, confidential voice, "Rekhet-ra, I'm a royal investigator." It wasn't untrue. He had investigated many cases in Kharu and elsewhere. And if he could save the Mitannian alliance by protecting Lady Kiya, this one might even come legitimately under his mandate.

"Will you find out who killed him, my lord?" she cried,

hope lighting up her desolate eyes. "I didn't think I still loved him, but it isn't right that he should end like this."

"Like what?"

"Stabbed in the back by his own chisel."

"In the back?" Hani hadn't expected this.

"He was sleeping on his stomach, as he often did. And someone... nailed him to the bed, almost, with a bronze chisel. He probably never woke up." Tears began to flow again from her slitted eyelids.

"Were there any other details you can remember?"

"I didn't see it. It was my father who found him. He and some of the workmen brought him back here."

Hani found it hard to swallow. "He's at the Place of Purification now, I suppose?"

"Oh, yes. It's been over a week. He wasn't such a bad man, my lord. He just couldn't keep his eyes off the girls."

"I agree, my dear," Hani said kindly. "He wasn't a bad man. He didn't deserve to die like this." He rose to his feet. "Please tell your father how sorry I am about his loss. If there was anything unusual about the room or the body, perhaps he could tell me."

She escorted Hani out, and he thought to himself, *Why am I even troubling them about such things? It was almost surely a hired killer who did the deed. What I need is a clue as to the one behind the murder. I only have a theory, and I certainly can't approach the queen without some kind of proof of her involvement. She could just brush it off and say, "What have I to do with it?"*

He had no reason to go to the Hall of the King's Correspondence since he had already reported to Lord Ptah-mes about Aziru's letters, and he had no desire to drift about this accursed city sightseeing. Especially since someone seemed to have an interest in silencing him as they had Kha-em-sekhem. He betook himself to the back lanes and made his way south toward Ptah-mes's mansion on the River's edge.

CHAPTER 7

P TAH-MES WASN'T HOME, SO HANI sat in the vine-
shaded courtyard and watched ten or so jays coming
over the wall and taking the ripening grapes one by one.
They seemed to be in hot competition among themselves,
screeching belligerently, as if there weren't ample fruit
for everyone. *Even among the birds, there's no peace*, Hani
thought, glum.

He needed desperately to understand what was
happening around the Beloved Royal Wife. Was it, in fact,
the Great Queen behind this attempt to discredit her? And
if so, how could she be dissuaded? Perhaps it would suffice
to warn the king anonymously of the warfare between his
wives; it was certainly being carried out behind his back. *But
then Kiya's infidelity will come out, and that will be the end
of her and the Mitannian treaty.* He found it discouraging
to think that the queen had so little care for the welfare of
Kemet's borders. Of course, the king himself seemed to be
no more concerned. Hani wondered if Ptah-mes had yet
passed along the word about the ninety thousand Hittites

massing on their frontiers—perhaps Aper-el, the vizier, wasn't even back in his office after the holidays. He doubted that that news would so much as make a difference to those who ruled the kingdom, hopeless as the thought made him.

And then Hani had to deal with the fact that someone seemed to be out to kill him. Or had that arrow been a mere warning? Certainly, he'd left any would-be assassin plenty of opportunities, if his voyage into the West were the goal. He heaved a sigh and watched the jays yelling threats at one another.

⹊

When Lord Ptah-mes returned that evening from the Hall of Royal Correspondence, Hani was still sitting in the shade of the arbor, pondering his course of action.

"Oh, there you are, my friend." Ptah-mes eased himself into one of the chairs, and although he was too well bred to groan, he couldn't conceal the painful weariness in his movements.

"I guess the work was stacked up after the long holiday," Hani said sympathetically.

But his superior shot him a somber look. "Aper-el wants to see you tomorrow, Hani."

Hani's stomach tightened at Ptah-mes's expression. "Is it about the news in Aziru's letter, my lord?"

"I don't think so. But I'll let him tell you." Ptah-mes seemed about to leave it at that, but after a moment, he added in a low voice, "He's going to pass along a summons from higher up."

Hani could feel a bitter taste rising in his throat. "Male or female?" he murmured.

"Female."

And here's the confirmation of my suspicions. Hani reminded his host, "You know absolutely nothing about any of this affair, my lord."

"True." No doubt picking up on Hani's fear, Ptah-mes's brittle gaze softened. "It may be something else entirely."

"Of course, my lord." But neither of them was sufficiently innocent to believe that was so.

⚜

The next morning, Hani dawdled over his breakfast so he wouldn't be seen arriving at the same time Lord Ptah-mes did. But it was effort mostly wasted; the court of the Hall of Royal Correspondence was in large part abandoned to the cicadas. No doubt, many of the officials had yet to return from their ancestral homes where they had passed the long holiday.

Hani had stopped to gather his courage for the interview with his superior, the vizier, when the cheerful voice of Mane called out from the street side, "Hani, old man! You *are* back after all!"

Hani turned with a fixed smile on his face. Much as he enjoyed Mane's company, he needed to prepare himself for what was coming. "Mane. I've... er, got an—"

"How was the little vacation? How are the family?" Mane strode up to him with purposeful directness, and although his round cheeks were split in a hearty smile, his eyes were a bit too bright. The two men embraced.

"Look, Mane, I've—"

But the emissary drew closer than normal to Hani and

209

said under his breath, "Our girl is getting anxious. She wants to know what's happening."

Hani whispered, "They're watching me. The queen has sent for me. I can't come back."

"Send a message through me, then. Or Keliya. He's still here." Mane drew back, slapping Hani on the arms in a genial gesture, and said in his usual booming baritone, "Glad I saw you. Let's plan to dine together some evening before you leave."

"Right, Mane. May... may the lord of the horizon bless you." Hani, too, had raised his voice.

"And the Dazzling Sun Disk shed his face upon you. I'll see you soon before we both get away." Mane receded across the court and into the shadow of the buildings, a rotund little figure of perfect good cheer.

Distracted, Hani took a deep, steadying breath and marched into the reception room of the vizier. The hall was still almost empty, its lofty ceiling misted palely by the sunlight that filtered through the clerestories. Hani's steps echoed on the plastered floor as he presented himself to the clerk on duty. The man disappeared and, a short while later, emerged and ushered Hani toward the vizier's door.

Hani entered and bowed deeply, hand to mouth. Lord Aper-el, vizier of the Lower Kingdom and Hani's remote superior, sat upon his chair, his hands resting on its arms. He was dressed in full ceremonial garb—the long kilt high under his armpits, knotted over the chest, and his *shebyu* collars, with their lens-shaped beads, around his neck. Hani was reluctant to look him in the eye; they had not met since nearly a year before, and at that meeting, Hani had provoked Aper-el's displeasure. But the vizier displayed his usual cool, slightly sour expression, nothing worse.

Aper-el was in his midfifties, a former military man of Djahyite extraction with a pale, hawkish face. His piercing eyes stared Hani up and down. "Lord Hani." He had an unpleasantly nasal voice. "I haven't seen you recently. Ptah-mes tells me the *hapiru* are chafing in their gilded captivity at your house, eh?"

"So it seems, my lord." Hani forced a bland smile to his lips, but he was sweating heavily, the beads starting to dribble down his temples.

"Sorry I can't tell you how long they'll be there. Submit a list of expenses, and I'll see to it you're reimbursed."

"I thank you, my lord." *He's purposely torturing me,* Hani thought, amused.

"The queen wants to see you, Hani."

There it is—the coup de grace. "I'm honored by her attention," he said, bowing a little.

"Present yourself today at the House of Rejoicing in the center of the city. That's all, unless you have something to report." Aper-el rose, not hostile but far from friendly.

"I think Lord Ptah-mes must have reported to you about the massing of Hittite troops inland of our northernmost vassals, my lord."

Aper-el nodded once and turned away, already departing through his private door as Hani backed his way from the chamber, bent in a bow, his cheeks burning with apprehension.

He left the scribal quarter immediately, trailed by the scent of bread from the nearby bakery, and made his way with a determined stride toward the processional street and the central palace. *No point in putting off the inevitable.*

To his left across the street stood the bridge that served as a gateway to the royal precinct, its approach now lined by rows of crouching lions with the head of the king. Upon that bridge was the Window of Appearances, where the king and queen stood to throw gold and grain and cuts of meat to functionaries who were being honored for some service. Hani had seen the ceremony when he felt he couldn't avoid it—the joyful recipient borne on his friends' shoulders, surrounded by his family, his colleagues, his tenant farmers, all scrambling for the gold and gifts that showered down from the hands of the living... Aten. Hani no longer knew how the king saw himself or what he wanted to be called, thousands of years of custom having been swept away almost overnight with the abolition of the Hidden One, maker of kings.

He turned right and followed the long, blinding wall of the palace to its north side, where the public entrance lay through a high pylon gate. The red banners were not to be seen upon their flagpoles—the king himself was not in residence. One of many oppressive weights seemed to lift from Hani's shoulders at that thought. *Although the female of the species is often the deadlier.*

The outer gate was heavily guarded, but Hani gave his name and cited his summons by the queen and was permitted to pass. He found himself in a vast, barren courtyard ringed by buildings. Enormous seated statues of the king were in the process of erection all around the edges. In fact, a crew of workers mounted on scaffolds were chiseling away as he passed, and other sculptures were being painted. Hani was too nervous to take a particular interest at the moment, but he reminded himself to see afterward if Djehuty-mes were there with the workmen.

At the end of the entrance court, a second, even more monumental gate awaited, with a ramped doorway, no doubt for chariot processions. Hani took a smaller pedestrian gate well to the side, guarded by exotically dressed soldiers from various parts of the empire. And before him stretched yet another court—a long, tiring exposed approach probably intended to soften up petitioners and foreign delegations before their audience. Hani's knees were becoming a little watery from anticipation. The expanse was all but empty. Here and there, a palace official or a visitor walked, rendered the size of an insect by the enormity of the space. On either side of the main entry of the palace stood two great obelisks with gilded pyramidal caps, flashing in the sun like all-seeing golden eyes.

Hani passed under a colonnaded porch, where brightly painted palm columns and mural decorations of scenes of nature at last relieved the whiteness of the courtyard. More soldiers. He again identified himself. Finally, feeling small and nervous—as he was intended to—Hani was admitted to the reception hall and turned over to a haughty majordomo with a staff in his hand.

"Follow me," the man commanded, and together, they set off through the dazzlingly rich public rooms of the palace, their steps punctuated by the clicking of the bronze-shod staff on the floor. The colors, the gilding, and the luxurious textiles stupefied Hani's eyes. Servants better dressed than the average grandee passed in silence on bare feet, while Hani's sandals clopped as gracelessly as a donkey's hooves through the incense-laden hush. At last, the men paused before a pair of tall gilded doors guarded by Nubians in leopard skins. The majordomo rapped with his staff, disappeared inside, and a moment later returned to usher Hani into the chamber.

Hani entered an intimate throne room. The queen sat within on a tall chair of electrum set with scenes inlaid in colored stones. At one side, two high windows with carved screens admitted a greenish light filtered through palm fronds. Hani was conscious of a swirl of perfume and color all around him, but his attention was fixed on the Great Queen Nefert-iti Nefer-nefru-aten.

It was the first time he had seen her not from afar in ceremonial regalia but wrapped only in the glories of a beautiful woman. She had on a short, angled wig of the same style Hani had seen on Kiya, which set off her long, graceful neck. Her heavy-lidded eyes were painted to perfection, her full lips rouged. But only Khnum the Maker had designed those exquisite cheekbones and the square jaw, strong yet made more feminine by a slight overbite. She lived up to her name; she was the Beautiful One.

Hani tore his eyes away and flattened himself to the floor in a full court prostration.

"Hani," she said in a breathy low-pitched voice. "We meet at last. Rise."

Hani crawled to his feet, conscious of his awkwardness.

The queen smiled, but it seemed calculating, without warmth. "We see too little of you, Hani."

"My lady has only to command," he answered. His initial anxiety over the queen's summons had firmed into his usual diplomatic smoothness.

The queen observed him silently, letting her beauty work its devastating sorcery. She wielded it like a sword. "Someone has told me that you frequent the King's Beloved Wife, Lady Kiya. Is it so?"

"I've seen her once since I brought her from Naharin, my lady. Hardly frequentation, I think."

"And was there a particular reason for that visit?"

Hani's heart began to beat faster despite the fact that he was prepared for this question. "She wanted to reunite with her old companions of voyage. The Mitannian ambassador was in town, and so she summoned me and our envoy to Naharin, who was also in the capital."

The queen nodded thoughtfully. "Is she happy? Is her life going well?"

"I'm sure she's very happy. The favor of the king is the breath of life in the nostrils of all of us who serve him."

"Indeed." Nefert-iti's lips twitched in an unreadable smile. Then, in a frontal attack, she asked, "Is she pregnant?"

Hani spread his hands helplessly. "How could I know, my lady? She didn't look pregnant."

Her voice hardened with an avid edge. "Because there are rumors. And rumors that someone other than the Living Face of the Aten might have something to do with that."

"I would be the last to know, great lady. I'm hardly an intimate of the royal women."

"That is as it should be, Hani. Your duties toward the Mitannian princess ended when you delivered her to Neb-ma'at-ra."

That's a warning. She's the blackmailer, all right.

"I'm completely in agreement on that. I have another assignment now that is quite demanding."

"Good." Nefert-iti rose from her chair. Below the slim shoulders and small bust, Hani saw that she had fleshy hips and a protruding, slightly pendulous stomach. She was, after all, the mother of numerous children—all, alas for her, daughters. But her movements, even in this formal setting, were sinuous and catlike, only enhanced by the fullness of her lower body that was so eloquent of fertility. She was well aware of the effect she had on men. "We understand each other, then. I hope to be able to count on your expertise. One has need quite often of a discreet service."

"I am yours to command, great lady," Hani said gallantly, thinking he was well and truly caught.

"You are dismissed."

He bowed low and backed from her presence. The door opened behind him as if by magic—*Did the majordomo listen to the entire conversation from behind the panels?*—and Hani caught only a glimpse of the queen, still standing before her chair in the magnificent femininity of a mother goddess, before he rose and the door closed with an echoing clang.

❖

Hani had sufficient presence of mind left to remember that he intended to speak to Djehuty-mes before he departed the palace complex. In the enormous courtyard, he sought out the work crew swarming over one of the royal statues. A figure who looked like the sculptor—rag over his head and all—was drinking from a wooden ladle in the shade of the unfinished image.

Hani approached him, and the man looked up. His

dust-whitened face opened in a red smile. "Lord Hani," he called in his high-pitched voice.

Hani clasped his hand, feeling the powerful grip that was belied by the soft face and clear, gentle eyes. "My condolences, master. I visited your workshop as soon as I got back to the capital, but you weren't there. I wanted to tell you how sorry I am about Kha-em-sekhem. Your daughter seems genuinely sad about his passing to the West."

"She still loved him—just couldn't live with him. We've lost a great sculptor, my lord." Djehuty-mes's eyebrows drooped in sorrow.

"I'm sure of that." Hani paused, wondering if it were too callous to probe the artisan for information about his deceased son-in-law. Finally, he said, "When was it he did the study of Lady Kiya? Do you remember?"

Djehuty-mes cocked his head and cupped a hand at his ear, and Hani repeated his question.

The sculptor scratched his head through the scarf that covered it. "I think about a year ago, after we'd done the king and queen and their older children. Why?"

"Just curious. Did he do the queen as well?"

To Hani's surprise, Djehuty-mes grinned and said, "No, I did."

"To protect him from himself?" Hani asked, sharing the grin in the knowing way of one who understood the charms of the queen.

"No, Hani. Because if anyone ever remembers me, it will be because of that face. Her statue will be my masterwork."

Hani clapped the sculptor on his massive shoulder, wished him well in his labors, and set off across the

N. L. HOLMES

courtyard to the pylons that marked the boundary of the palace. He left the royal precinct by the gates through the bridge—the first time, and he hoped the last, that he ever traveled that trajectory. Hani set off down the processional street between the leonine likenesses of the king, uneasy and unable to wash from his mind the image of the queen's body swelling beneath the gauzy folds of her gown. She'd aimed it at him like an arrow. Despite his diplomatic evasions, she knew Kiya had told him about the sculptor, and she was warning him to back away from any investigation. She'd even, he thought, offered him a chance to spy for her.

He didn't know what all this meant for him or whether he should abandon the Beloved Royal Wife's cause. He wanted nothing to do with these battles for the king's favor. He wanted—if the gods cared to know—to live quietly, tend his garden, feed his birds, and enjoy his family. He wanted the king and his wives to forget about his very existence.

Hani trudged down the processional street toward the south, lost in thought. At first, he didn't quite interpret a familiar voice crying, "Lord Hani! Lord Hani!"

Hani looked up, snapping back into the present moment. Maya was waving at him from a distance, then the secretary started to run toward him with his clumsy stubby-legged gait. Suddenly Hani was alarmed, his heart in his throat. *What's the boy doing here? Is something wrong at home?*

He broke into a run himself, and the two of them met, panting. "What is it, Maya? Is there—"

"My lord," the secretary gasped, "Lady Nub-nefer wanted me to come after you. I left the same afternoon you did, on the Feast of Drunkenness. It took me this long to get here." He stopped to drink in a big lungful of air. "There's been a riot in Waset."

Hani's heart seemed to stop. "Is the family all right?"

"Yes, but the gate was damaged. Part of the garden caught fire. The crowds attacked many of the big houses, believing, I guess, that they belonged to henchmen of the king."

"In Waset? Priests, more likely."

"Believe me, they weren't thinking that clearly. They were mean drunk and spoiling for a fight. I don't know who put them up to it, but there are plenty of people reduced to poverty there by the closing of the temples and the moving of the government, and they only needed a spark to set them off. They just wanted to take revenge on someone. It was pretty violent, my lord. A lot of houses burned down, a lot of girls raped, a lot of heads broken. Royal troops were sent in, in addition to the *medjay*."

Hani remembered the military boat they'd seen passing soon after they'd sailed. "How did you get out?" he cried. "You left the women there alone?" His breathing was still labored and not just from the exertion. "You left them?"

"Easy, my lord." Maya looked scared. "Lord Mery-ra told me to go. He and the servants and Pa-kiki and the three Amurrites were mounting a defense, like the last time this happened. My mother was even there. She came early on because she didn't feel safe at home—all the workmen were among the crowd."

Hani forced himself to calm down. A little damage to the garden was nothing if the family was safe. "No one hurt, then? You and Sat-hut-haru were at our house?"

He already knew the answer, but he wanted to hear the reassuring words.

Maya nodded. "My lord, your wife begs you to come home as soon as you can. She was badly upset by the events. She was afraid you and Neferet and your brother and niece hadn't found a boat and were trapped at the docks. There'll have to be repairs made to the gate, and... well, she needs you at her side."

"I've finished what I had to do here, Maya. Come with me to Lord Ptah-mes's so I can pick up my things, and we'll head straight back."

"I went there first. He told me where you were." The two men had begun to walk purposefully.

Hani said under his breath, "I had an interview with the Great Queen."

Maya's eyes grew wide. "Did she admit to anything?"

Hani expelled a breath that he felt as if he'd been holding ever since he emerged from the audience hall. "She's the blackmailer, all right. She subtly told me to let Kiya alone and even—I think—urged me to work for her."

"And if you don't accept that urging?"

Hani raised a cynical eyebrow. "She's too canny to resort to open threats. But the only limit to her power is the desire that the king not find out about this rivalry. She asked me if Kiya were pregnant."

"What did you tell her, my lord?"

"That I'd be unlikely to know." Hani snorted at his own dishonesty. "Oh, and I saw Mane this morning. He's pressuring me to get in touch with our girl again. Says she's anxious to hear what I've found out. I feel like a frog being pulled in two by a pair of herons who both want to eat me."

They strode on, Maya struggling to keep up without breaking into a trot. The day was beating down now, the sun on their backs like a blanket of sheepskin in that broad street with no shade. When his stomach growled, Hani realized it must be midday. They swung through the market and picked up some flatbreads, which they rolled around chickpeas and pickled vegetables and ate as they walked. By the time they reached Ptah-mes's villa by the River, they had brushed the last of the crumbs from their chests.

Hani led the way rapidly through the vestibule and was preparing to cross the salon when he saw Lord Ptah-mes sitting by himself, eating lunch at a small elegantly set table. The commissioner looked up. "Ah, Hani," he said pleasantly. "I see your secretary found you."

"He did, my lord. Thank you for directing him my way. I'm afraid my presence is required in Waset. It seems there were riots. A lot of damage was done, including some to my property."

Ptah-mes rose, looking grave. "I suspected that was coming. I haven't heard whether my place suffered any assault."

"I'd be happy to check and send you word."

"That's kind of you, my friend, but if there's been damage, one of the servants will let me know. Can I offer you gentlemen some lunch?"

"I thank you, my lord, but I'm looking to catch one of the next ferries out. Your hospitality is appreciated, as always."

"Think nothing of it, Hani."

Ptah-mes had to be itching to hear about the meeting with the queen, but he gave no indication whatsoever, just nodded courteously to the two men, who swept off to Hani's room. When they passed through the salon again a few moments later, Ptah-mes had left.

When Hani and Maya finally reached Hani's home, they found the doors of the gate dismounted and the painted stone lintel blackened with smoke. From within the wall came the sounds of sawing and hammering. Hani stuck his head through the opening, and A'a popped up before him.

"Ah, my lord. Look at what happened to us," the old gatekeeper cried, indicating the doorway in disarray.

"Maya told me. It sounds like it was a bad night." Hani stared around him at the trees with blackened branches, the heat-shriveled bushes, and the sooty ash staining the graveled walk. Fortunately, the damage seemed to have been contained within a small area. He and Maya picked their way past the carpenters at work building a new pair of doors for the gate and set off down the ash-strewn path. Before they'd reached the house, Nub-nefer came running to meet him, Sat-hut-haru at her heels.

"Oh, Hani, thanks be to the Protector of Travelers you're all right! We were so worried to think you and Neferet were out in that crowd, maybe looking in vain for a ferry." She threw herself at Hani, and he enfolded her in his arms. "She is safe, isn't she?"

"Safe and sound, my dearest. We ran into Lord Ptah-mes and his wife, who were preparing to set sail in their yacht, and they kindly invited all of us aboard. Lady Apeny even took Pipi and Mut-nodjmet on to Men-nefer."

"Thanks be to the Hidden One. She's such a wonderful lady."

"Yes." Hani thought of the painful chill between Apeny and her husband—yet they were both uncommonly good people. "Djefat-nebty complimented Neferet on her independent thinking."

Nub-nefer looked skeptical. "She did? Well, that's nice." She dropped her eyes, and a smile twitched at her lips.

She's proud in spite of herself.

Nub-nefer turned and indicated the garden around them, raising a suddenly distressed face to her husband. "Maya told you about the riots, Hani? It was terrible. The mayor of Waset refused to provide beer for the revelers— there's no official support for the festival at all anymore, of course—and that touched them off. They'd certainly gotten drunk on something. What must those guests of yours think of the Two Lands? Aziru and his party got back from their trip loaded with game just before the trouble started. Fortunately, Maya and Sat-hut-haru and his mother had come over. They didn't feel safe at home. So at least we had a houseful of warriors to hold back those people."

"My dear, 'those people' are people like us, who long for the restoration of the Ipet-isut," he said quietly at her ear.

"Maybe. But I think there were troublemakers among them. Someone could be exploiting the dissatisfaction for his own ends."

Hani had to admit she could be right. But that smacked of royal politics, and he had no desire even to think about it.

Nub-nefer said in a determined voice, "I want to take

223

Baket-iset down to the country place, my love. I don't feel safe in the city anymore. And besides, I don't like the attention that Amurrite is paying to her."

"He's a prince, my dove. We should be flattered," Hani replied with a smile. "But I take your point. Let me go down and see to setting things up for you. I need to inventory the cattle and grain supplies so I'll know what we can liquidate for Pipi anyway." He gave her a squeeze around the shoulders. "Maybe we should have done this from the start—just turned the house over to the visitors." Somehow, he'd have to stay abreast of their correspondence. He'd have one of the servants bring it down as soon as the diplomatic pouch arrived.

"And you won't believe what's hanging in the cellar. Your friends had just walked in the door with this... this enormous..." Nub-nefer burst out laughing and put her hands to her face, giddy with nerves. "It's a bird as big as I am, Hani. And then the riot, and we didn't have time even to pluck it. What are we going to do with it? I just want to get away!"

"They bagged an ostrich?" Hani laughed with her, but a childlike eagerness to see the thing arose in him. "Maybe the servants can dry it or salt it."

"That's what they're going to do, as they're able. But it will be so tough." Tears of helpless laughter were coming out of her eyes. "Oh, Hani, my love. What a day! Oh, how glad I am you're back." She put her arms around him, and her sounds of hilarity turned suspiciously sob-like against his chest.

"The plumes will be worth a lot. We can exchange them against something more useful."

"And those men were so proud of themselves. I just wanted to scream." He could feel her shaking with wild weeping. "And then we sent Maya off, and no one was sure he got safely away, and poor Sat-hut-haru was crying and saying we'd killed him. It was so terrible, my love. I was so afraid for the girls." She drew back, mopping her eyes with a fist. "In-hapy was a pillar of strength, though. I'm glad she was here."

"Me, too, my dearest. That was a lot for you to carry alone." He caressed her tear-streaked face with his hand. "It will be better in every way at the farm."

"Hani, my boy! Thank the Traveler you're back in one piece," said Mery-ra from the doorway. "Nub-nefer's told you about our adventure, eh? I just came back from Meryet-amen's. Wanted to be sure everything was well at her place." He toddled into the salon, arms spread.

Hani and his father embraced. "I wish we'd stayed here one more night. Not that my personal presence would have made you any safer, but at least we wouldn't have had to worry about each other." Hani had come to the topic he wanted to discuss but wasn't sure how to ease into it. "I, uh, had an interview with the Great Queen."

Nub-nefer's eyes grew wide with anxiety. "Really? Is that good or bad?"

Mery-ra shot his son a narrow look. "Tell. Tell."

"You men go talk. I have things to do. Giant birds to pluck." Nub-nefer squeezed Hani's hand and moved off toward the kitchen. Hani took his father's arm and led him outside to the pavilion, where they seated themselves in the shade. A faint smell of burnt wood still lingered in the air.

"So, is she as beautiful close-up as she is from a distance?" Mery-ra asked.

"She's extremely beautiful, although not in her first youth. I was surprised."

"What—all of twenty-six, like the king?"

"Older, I should think, but maybe I'm wrong. She's clearly a woman who has borne many children. Although somehow that added to her beauty, which is uncanny, I have to admit." He could see her standing before him again, her spreading curves only too visible through the gauzy gown. "She knows how to use it too. I felt like a poor helpless bird in the presence of a snake."

Mery-ra chuckled. "Maybe she doesn't have anything to worry about from your little Mitannian."

"You know, there's something similar about them, although they don't look alike. The long neck, the heavy-lidded eyes."

"Well, of course," Hani's father said as if it were evident. "The king has a long neck and heavy-lidded eyes."

"What? Are you saying men marry women who look like them?" Hani hooted. "Although I always thought you and Mother resembled each other. And Meryet-amen looks like you, too, actually."

"You see? Pipi and Nedjem-ib." Mery-ra sounded smug.

"Me and Nub-nefer? I'm flattered!"

"You're the exceptions that prove the rule."

"Lord Ptah-mes and Lady Apeny, I grant you. They could be brother and sister. But Amen-em-hut and Anuia? Sat-hut-haru and Maya?"

"Well, *some* men marry women who look like them,"

Mery-ra allowed. "The better sort of men." He grew a little red in the face as his argument crumbled under his feet.

Hani realized they'd drifted away from the thoroughly serious content of his interview. "The queen immediately asked about Kiya. She knew I'd visited her. She asked me if Kiya was pregnant."

"How would you know?"

"That's what I said." Hani smiled dryly. "Although, in fact, Kiya told me she was. In so many words, Nefert-iti warned me not to frequent the Beloved Royal Wife. If I understood her, she invited me to spy for her instead."

Mery-ra's mirth had fallen away. "Stay away from those women, son. No good can come from getting involved in any capacity with the king's women."

Hani emitted a humorless laugh. "The very same day, Mane sidled up to me and said Kiya wanted to know how things were going. She wants to see me again."

"No, my boy, no. Avoid those women. Next time, the arrow may not go over your head."

Hani heaved a sigh. "What worries me is that I already seem to be involved with them."

He stood up and wandered to the edge of the pavilion, suddenly filled with tension that needed to be discharged. From the bushes, a silent gray-blue shadow approached. "Qenyt," Hani said fondly. "There you are, my girl." He dropped to his heels and stretched out his hand to the heron, who eyed him, considering, poised in midstep. Hani squatted there for a long space of time while the bird's golden eye looked him up and down. Then Qenyt drifted away at a deliberate pace.

"She's a model for you, son. 'Have nothing to do with these humans.'"

Hani rose to his feet. "I'm going down to the farm tomorrow. I need to inventory the cattle and grain, see what we can offer Pipi. Do you want to come with me?"

"Sounds good. Nub-nefer wants to decamp down there with the girls. She said she didn't fancy Sat-hut-haru giving birth in the midst of a riot."

"I know," Hani said. "That's another thing I need to do—set things up for them. Get the servants to clean up the house, air the linen."

"How appropriate." Mery-ra stood up and joined his son at the edge of the porch. "On the Festival of Cloth."

"Is it already that time of year?" Hani sighed. "The Ipet Festival should be coming up, but I guess we can be sure *that* won't take place. The king doesn't seem to want to receive a divine *ka* from the Lord Amen-Ra."

Mery-ra grunted morosely. Then he brightened. "Have you seen that enormous thing hanging in your cellar?"

"No, but Nub-nefer told me about it. Your lady friend's nephew carried out his duties as master of the hunt very well, it seems."

"Yes. Your friend Aziru has been more cheerful than usual these last few days. A hunt, a battle—it's enough to get a young man's blood pumping. Now we just need to find him a girl."

"Let's go look at the ostrich," Hani said, unable to control the eagerness in his voice. "I want to see the wishbone."

⚱

The next morning, Hani and Mery-ra were awake early, and by midday, they were ready to head upriver the half an afternoon's journey to Hani's country place. But as Hani rose from his lunch, he heard a clatter and voices at the gate. A moment later, Neferet came running into the salon and threw herself into his arms. It took him a few heartbeats to realize she was in tears.

"What is it, my duckling?" he cried in concern. His first fear was that someone had attempted some violence against his family in Akhet-aten.

But Neferet was speechless with loud sobs, clinging to his waist. Hani guided her back to one of the stools he and Mery-ra had vacated and seated himself. She plopped into his lap and buried her face in his chest.

"Here, my love. Tell me what's happened."

Pa-kiki appeared in the doorway, his hands outstretched helplessly. "I don't know what's gotten into her, Papa. She just exploded into my room the other evening and said she wanted to go home. I managed a few days off for the festival and brought her back, but I can't stay."

Hani's stomach clenched with dread. *What could have happened to make a strong, cheerful girl like Neferet dissolve into tears for days?* "Calmly, duckling. Tell your papa what's wrong. Did someone do something to you?"

She shook her head so hard her braids flicked him in the face. Hani saw she was making an effort to regain control of herself. Finally, she looked up, her eyes brimming, her lip caught in her teeth. "I don't want to go back, Papa."

"You know you don't have to, Neferet. But why? You were enjoying it so."

The girl dropped her eyes, and murmured, "It's not like what I thought it would be."

"How so, my love?"

She took a deep breath, as one might before jumping into the water, and said in a rush, "Lady Djefat-nebty has started taking me with her to treat the Royal Ornaments, the ladies of the harem..."

Hani's blood ran cold, but not for Neferet.

"I thought that would be fun. But there was this one older woman whose breast was all eaten out, and she was in terrible pain, and there were worms in it and everything. Oh, Sekhmet have mercy, Papa! You can't imagine how horrible it was. And she was moaning and screaming. Oh!" Neferet clamped her hands to her ears as if she could still hear the poor woman, and her face was twisted with the agonizing memory.

Hani cringed. That seemed like a lot for a thirteen-year-old to have to confront. He said gently, "But at least you were able to help her, my love."

"All we could do was give her poppy juice to knock her out, Papa. And then Djefat-nebty put her hand in that wound and started cleaning out the worms. I thought I'd vomit." Tears started bubbling out of Neferet's eyes. "It's just as bad as Khuit's. I thought with rich people it would be better. There wouldn't be all those flies laying eggs in people's eyes and bloated, starving little children and people whose whole face was swollen up, oozing pus from an infected tooth. But it's the same. It's just the same." She pressed her face to her father's chest again, and he rubbed her back sadly.

"Ah, my little duckling. I'm afraid everybody's the

same, all right, whether they're rich or not, whether they have the king's favor or not." *What a hard way to learn that lesson.* "So that's why you wanted to leave Khuit? There was too much misery?"

"It's the worms I can't take, Papa. And people rotting away alive. I thought it was just poor people, and that if I studied with a real *sunet*, I wouldn't see things like that."

He said quietly, "I think, my love, that if you can't take the sight of misery, you'd better find something else to do than practice medicine. And there's no shame in that. I'm not sure I could do it."

"But…" Her tear-stained visage had regained a little of its stubbornness. "But I want to take care of Baket-iset."

"That isn't always clean either, duckling. Mama and the servants have to do everything for her."

Neferet sat up on Hani's knee and stared at him, her square little face settling into an expression closer to her usual resolution. "Lady Djefat-nebty said to take a week and think about it and then come back or not, depending on what I decided."

"So she knows you're having trouble?"

Neferet nodded energetically then looked up, guilty, from under her bangs. "She said the same thing had happened to her, but I didn't believe her."

"Give it some deep thought, then, my love. Talk to your mama about it. Better still, talk to Baket-iset. Father and I are going to the country place to set it up for Mama and Baket and Sat-hut-haru. They want to get out of the city."

"Can I go too?" She jumped up and began to bounce on her toes, hands fisted eagerly. "It's quiet there, and I can think hard."

"Well…" It wasn't every day Neferet sought quiet.

"Please, Papa? I'll bring my medical basket. You never know when you or Grandfather might turn an ankle or be stung by a bee."

"Ask your mother."

She bounced off to find Nub-nefer, and Hani took his basket of clean clothes and toiletries to the door. He heard Mery-ra clumping in from his room, humming tunelessly.

"You ready, Father?" Hani asked.

"Ready, my boy. Was that Neferet or a herd of wild asses I just heard galloping through the house? Why is *she* back?

Hani told him about the girl's crisis of nerve. "Djefat-nebty is a hard master to expose a little girl to things like that."

"I think she's wise, son. Better that a doctor finds out in advance if sickness is more than she wants to confront."

Pa-kiki passed through the vestibule, heading for the gate. "I'm off to the capital again, Papa. Somebody tell me if Neferet needs to come back up."

"Thank you, son. This is very generous of you. And I've heard never a word of complaint." Hani remembered Aha grumbling over a much less onerous task. He clapped the boy on the shoulder. "Travel safely. May the lord of the horizon watch over you."

Pa-kiki waved cheerfully and disappeared amid the greenery. A few moments later, Neferet showed up with her basket, saying, "Mama said I could go," and Hani, his father, and the girl set off down the dusty lane toward the Great River.

❦

It wasn't so far upriver to the country house. The small ferry got them there in the hottest part of the day and, since the River was still high with its flood waters, left them right at the edge of one of the fields. The black soil, with standing puddles full of rich, greenish water simmering under the sun, smelled of life and plenty. Newly planted lettuces and onions in rows and cucumbers, melons, and lablab beans staked to low fences ran inland from the water's edge. Beyond, Hani saw fields destined for wheat and barley, black and muddy, almost dry enough to sow. He needed to keep that in mind. If the spring harvest was good, they would have more to send to Pipi. But he especially wanted to check the supply in the granary.

At his side, Mery-ra huffed, "Whew. Hot."

"The plants love it." Hani watched a pelican rise and circle over the land and then float above the River as if it were sailing its own invisible stream in the air. He drew a deep breath of satisfaction. "Let's put our things up, and then I vote for an afternoon in the marshes before we get to work."

"It'll be cooler on the water, all right," Mery-ra agreed.

They trudged between the fields, skirted the orchards, and made their way through the courtyard. The farm was strangely silent. "Where is everybody?" Neferet asked.

"Feast day," Mery-ra reminded her. "They're probably all in the village."

They passed the cup-shaped well and big grain silos—whitewashed domes, like a clutch of enormous eggs. Hani remembered the ostrich in the cellar and laughed.

"Why are you laughing, Papa?" Neferet asked.

"I'm thinking of a very big bird Aziru and his men brought back from their hunting trip. You haven't seen it yet."

Hani let them into the house, where they were enveloped by the cool darkness. "Throw your things down anywhere. We can assign rooms later." He dodged into the kitchen—with its own little court, half-roofed with reeds—and looked around to see if any water had been drawn. In the corner, a big jar sweated invitingly, and Hani ladled water into a gourd he always kept hanging on a peg by the door.

"I hope they've left us food," Mery-ra said, peering around. He looked under an overturned basket. "Cheese." A melon and a pomegranate sat in a smaller basket. "No bread?"

"We can get wheat out of the granary and make our own," Neferet suggested.

"I don't think it's as easy as that, my dear," her grandfather said fondly. "Maybe your young knees are up to grinding flour, but mine certainly aren't."

Fortunately, Hani found some dryish flatbreads in the food safe suspended from one of the beams. "We'll be all right tonight. We can have the servants make more tomorrow." He held up the gourd. "To the marshes, loyal troops!"

They gamely trudged back down through the farmland toward the River. Hani was only partially sure he'd left the boats tied up in their usual place of embarkation, at the bottom of a sloping footpath screened by enormous fig trees. Ripe fruit was hanging on the trees, and the whole air was perfumed by the unmistakable honeyed scent of fig. As they approached, a cloud of bossy jays rose, squawking. Wasps circled. Neferet ducked and swatted as she passed.

They emerged onto the bank to find it naked. "Oh, I put the boats away. Stay here. I'll go up to the boathouse." Hani left his father and daughter sitting on the slope in the shade of the fig trees and headed back up toward the fields. "I won't be a minute," he called over his shoulder.

Hani strode up the steep path from the riverbank, enjoying the strong movement of his legs and the action of drawing deep breaths of fresh country air into his lungs, relishing even this brief moment of solitude. Not that he didn't enjoy the company of his father and daughter, but he saw them both a lot—Mery-ra every day—and his household had grown a little too public in the last few months. It was rather like living in the marketplace, with relatives and foreign visitors everywhere one turned. For all that he enjoyed people—as Mery-ra never ceased to remind him when pooh-poohing his desire for an assignment in the archives—he needed to get away.

Hani looked forward with a powerful longing to this afternoon on the River, among the reeds and the ducks. Even with companions, it wouldn't be so constraining as his little garden, where one could never really escape the cries of the children—or more recently, of the Amurrites and snide, sullen Aziru, poor man, smarting under the king's deliberate unavailability. Anuia, in and out, wailing and hopeless. Maya and Sat-hut-haru, who seemed to spend all their time at Hani's these days, chattering excitedly about the baby.

He walked on between the fields rich and wet with the

receding water of Flood season. There was the row of palms he and Pipi had planted as boys, now tall and laden with dates, swaying slowly in the breeze like a line of dancers with weighted pigtails. The sky was as blue as a piece of glass; one could almost reach up and touch it, that exquisite ceiling of the world.

His little shed was just ahead—a square, low, windowless box of mud brick with a triangular vent over the door. He began to whistle a tuneless version of an old song and even broke into the words, since no one could hear him. "My heart devised to see her beauty, while sitting down in her house. Hey-ho, ho-ho… I can't remember the rest of it." He was chuckling to himself as he prepared to lift the bar from the door, thinking already of his little reed boat and the water beneath it and the satisfying effort of paddling against the fulsome swell of the marsh water. But he had left it unbarred.

Hani swung back the door and propped it in place with a bucket, remembering too late that he'd have to carry the boat by himself. He wasn't sure he could get it through the opening very easily. He straightened up—and stared into the feverish eyes of a man clutching a pruning knife in his fist.

CHAPTER 8

H ANI JUMPED BACKWARD LIKE A frightened cat, his
heart thundering, before he could wrap his mind
around what he saw. "Amen-em-hut!"

"Hani," said the priest faintly. He dropped the knife
with a clatter. In the near darkness, he was a wraithlike
bearded figure, wild-eyed and ready to bolt, like a cornered
animal. The room stank of sweat and dung.

"By the Hidden One, man. What are you doing here?"
Hani extended his hands to his brother-in-law, who took
them, trembling. He seemed to have trouble standing up.
Hani supported him to a seat on a sack of manure, where
he slumped wearily.

Amen-em-hut squinted against the light, holding up a
hand to block it. "I'm hiding. What do you think?"

"In my boat shed? Why didn't you go into the house?
The servants would've let you in."

"I don't want anybody to know I'm here, Hani. I've
already endangered you and Nub-nefer by hiding on your
property. I need to go somewhere else. Forgive me."

"Not at all. Your only offense was not asking me for help." Hani put an arm under the smaller man's armpits and helped him stand. "Come inside with me, by all that's decent. Nub-nefer would never forgive me for leaving you here like this."

Amen-em-hut made a broken sound that might have been a chuckle or a sob. "I dared not tell her or Anuia where I was going. I know they're worried, but if the *medjay* interrogate them, it's better they know nothing."

"Of course. But you can't live like this for long. What have you been eating? You're skin and bones."

They moved up the path toward the house through the orchard, shuffling at the priest's pace. He looked terribly weak and sick, holding a hand up to protect his eyes from the unaccustomed light.

"Not much. Your servants very conscientiously lock everything up at night. Fruit, when I could find some. Grain. What I could steal from your pigs."

The poor man, Hani thought, his heart wrenched with pity. *What an indignity.* "Where did you sleep in there?"

"In your boat." Amen-em-hut laughed giddily. "I could certainly use a bath."

"Of course. The house is yours. Use whatever you need. Eat, for the sake of all that's holy. Sleep in a bed. No one would ever look for you here."

But Amen-em-hut seemed unconvinced of that. He shot a worried look at Hani. "I don't want to bring danger down on you and Nub-nefer, Hani."

"Don't worry, my friend. I can send the servants to the city and leave you here alone if you want, but I really don't have any doubts about their loyalty. Why would they even know the police are after you?"

They hobbled past the grain silos and the animal pens and into the garden. Unoccupied, the yard was utterly silent. The servants had fed the geese and the pigs and turned the cows out before they headed to the village for the festivities.

Hani pulled up the door bolt one handed and ushered his brother-in-law into the cool interior. "*Are* the police after you? What happened to make you take off like that, Amen-em-hut? Anuia said they had interrogated you, roughed you up, but that you didn't give her any details beyond that."

He led the priest to a stool. Then he headed toward the sweating jar that stood just inside the door of the kitchen and ladled water into a ewer. He snagged a cup from the wooden shelves hanging on the wall then found the cheese sitting under its overturned basket and brought that too. In a moment, he'd returned to Amen-em-hut and poured him a big cup of water, which the priest guzzled down eagerly.

"They said to keep my mouth shut or they'd shut it for me, and I had no intention of shutting my mouth."

Hani suppressed a sneer of disgust. In his eyes, a bully was always a weak figure. No king of any dignity would descend to threatening his subjects into agreeing with him. Still, he supposed no king would be likely to ignore calls to assassinate him, either. Hani's heart was heavy. This was a complex matter. "You've got to stop talking about assassination, Amen-em-hut," he said soberly. "The king might tolerate objecting to the closing of the Ipet-isut, but he won't allow sedition." He passed his brother-in-law the

N. L. HOLMES

cheese, and Amen-em-hut tore into it with hungry teeth. Hani pulled up another stool and sat knee to knee with him. "He might send the police after your family if he can't find you and the threats continue."

Amen-em-hut looked up, his eyes haggard and uneasy. "Do you think he would descend so low?"

"Absolutely. You all need to get far away from Thebes and stay out of sight. It's going to be the silent who survive."

"Survive? I want to bring the whole regime down, Hani, not just survive. If I have to die to do it, that's a reasonable price to pay. *He* has alienated the goodwill of the King of the Gods. How can anything but disaster lie in wait for the kingdom?" Amen-em-hut's voice, weak with hunger, cracked, but a fierce flame of hatred set his handsome face alight. Hani had seen such a look on his wife's face. Her family was intense.

"If they kill you, that'll be the end of your resistance, my friend. Survival is the best tactic. 'Your silence will overthrow your enemies. The crocodile makes no sound, yet fear of it is ancient.'"

Amen-em-hut snorted. "You and your aphorisms." But he smiled at Hani as if embarrassed by his own fervor. "Listen, brother, let's not argue. I'm grateful to you. You know that, don't you?"

Hani reached across and clapped him on the shoulder. "I do. Let's get you something else to eat."

"Maybe later. My stomach's been hurting a lot. I don't want to overdo it by eating too much at once."

The two men rose. Hani had just opened his mouth to say he would take Amen-em-hut to the bedroom, where he could stretch out, when he heard the outside door swing open. They both froze and stared back toward the vestibule, rigid with fear. Hani grabbed his brother-in-law's arm, ready to hustle him out of sight, but there was no time.

"Papa? Are you in here? Where did you go? We're waiting for you," came Neferet's voice from the darkness of the vestibule.

Dear gods, I forgot all about Father and Neferet, Hani thought desperately.

She burst into the salon. "Papa—oh, Uncle Amen-em-hut! You're here? Everyone's been—" Her astonished face dropped suddenly into worry. "Oh, Uncle. What's wrong? You look horrible. And you smell."

The fear that had stopped Hani's breath dissipated, although his voluble daughter was perhaps the last person he would have wanted to see the fugitive. He said dryly, "I think you need to work on your bedside manner, my girl."

But Amen-em-hut managed a smile. "Hello, Neferet, dear. Give me time to take a bath, and then I'll hug you."

Neferet stared back and forth from her father to her uncle, a grin spreading across her face. "Is this where he was all along, Papa?" She danced around on her toes with relief. "Oh, Mama and Auntie will be so happy you're safe. But you don't look good at all, I have to say."

"Let him get cleaned up, my dear. Uncle's going to be staying here for a while." Hani threw a gesture of the head at his brother-in-law, who tottered into the bathroom, steadying himself against the wall. "I'll find you some clean clothes, my friend," Hani called after him. He stood, both relieved and anxious, facing his daughter while Amen-em-hut rattled around in search of a jar of water in the distant bathroom. "I'm sorry; I forgot you and Grandfather were still waiting by the River, my duckling. I found Uncle here, and we got involved."

"Did someone kidnap him?" Neferet asked in a hushed voice.

"No, no. He just felt he should get out of sight for a while until the police forgot about him." Hani drew her to him and put an arm around her shoulders, looking straight into her eyes, which were still wide with stupefaction. "You must tell absolutely no one that you've seen him; do you understand, Neferet? It could endanger his life. Not even Mama or Aunt Anuia. I'm entrusting you with this like an adult."

She nodded with great gravity. "Physicians never reveal anything about their patients, Papa. That's the first thing Khuit taught me. No one will ever, ever rip any word of this out of me, not even if they torture me with red-hot pincers and put leeches up my nose. May Meret-seger the Silent One bite my feet if I ever, ever—"

"I believe you, my girl," Hani said, hoping this was a sincere oath and not a bit of dramatic extravagance. "Go look in the bedroom and see if there are any clean clothes in the chest that Uncle can use." *He'd fit a dish towel better than one of my kilts*, Hani thought with a sigh. *Six weeks of fighting the pigs for food has left him pretty rubbed out.*

"Hani? Neferet? Where is everyone?" Mery-ra called from the door.

Hani rolled his eyes in resignation. Amen-em-hut's secret was unraveling fast. "In here, Father."

"First *you* disappeared, then Neferet. I was getting a little concerned. What's going on? Why are you up here? The boats are in your shed." Mery-ra toddled in, his face red from the climb from the riverbank. He looked from his son to his granddaughter. "Where is everybody?"

Hani said, "The servants are all down in the village. It's a festival day, remember?"

"Oh, right." Mery-ra's little eyes narrowed. "Why the look of studied carelessness, son? Something going on? A surprise for your old father, perhaps?"

"*I'll* say," said Neferet, looking slyly at Hani from the corner of her eye. But she said nothing further. The three of them stood there, staring at one another, until Hani finally recovered his presence of mind sufficiently to say, "We might as well go on back to the boathouse, Father. It's still not too late to go out."

Mery-ra shrugged. "If you want to. But I can tell you, it's getting hot, whatever the hour."

"Yes, let's go. Come on, Neferet." He hustled the girl before him toward the door.

"But you said to look in the clothes chest—" she objected.

"Let's go."

As they departed from the salon, Hani heard water splattering in the bathroom and the ringing *thunk* of a heavy jug being set on the floor. He caught his breath and stiffened.

Mery-ra looked back. "Who's that? Is one of the servants still here?"

"Probably. Come on, everyone. To the boathouse. You can help me carry the boat, Father."

They retraced the worn path through the farmyard, Neferet skipping ahead. Mery-ra took advantage of her distance to ask under his breath, "What's going on, son?"

Hani could see that the secret was going to come out one way or the other. It made him realize that Amen-em-hut undoubtedly would have to move after all, probably well before the rest of the family came down. He weighed his father's reliability and decided to tell him. He said under his breath, "It's Amen-em-hut. He's been hiding in the boathouse for more than a month. I took him to the house and told him to stay there instead. But Neferet saw him. I don't know how long she can keep from telling her mother and the girls. We need to find another place for him."

Mery-ra grunted. "Little Shu's going to bring trouble down on all of us."

Hani said reasonably, "We can't just abandon him, Father. He's Nub-nefer's only brother. And he's a good man, besides. He's doing a principled thing."

Mery-ra grunted again.

They'd reached the boathouse, where Neferet waited, her medical basket in her hand. "I left it here when I went to look for you. I found a piece of chalk in it for—for anyone who needs it."

"Oh, good," Mery-ra said with a twinkle in his eye. "Sometimes, when I'm out on the water, I get a craving for a nice piece of chalk."

"No, it's for—" She clapped a hand over her mouth.

Hani heaved a sigh. This was why secrets were so hard to keep. "Grandfather knows," he said heavily. "Look, both of you, we need to get our fugitive out of here as soon as we can, but in the meantime, please understand how important it is that no one else find out. Neferet, do you hear me?"

"Yes, Papa." She looked as chastened as she was ever likely to look. "This chalk will help his stomach, though."

"My dear, please don't feed him anything that will make him sick. He's been through a hard few weeks. He needs to eat and rest."

"Djefat-nebty said it would help. In goat's milk. Or was that to make people throw up?"

Hani suddenly felt very tired. It seemed he had no control over any aspect of his life, as if the gods were lobbing him back and forth among them like a child's leather ball. He just wanted all these complications to go away for a bit. He shot his father a look that pleaded for mercy. "You know, it's too hot to go out in the marshes after all. Let's go back to the house and have a pot of beer." Then he remembered the servants were gone. "If I can find it."

Mery-ra suggested, "Why don't we go into the village and see what's happening at the festival? I'd be amazed if there weren't some good food."

"You and Neferet go. I want to talk to... our guest."

"Why won't you say his name, Papa? Nobody's around," Neferet asked. But she took her basket and followed her grandfather.

"Let's get into the habit of not saying it, all right?" He waved to the pair as they cut across the lettuces and headed for the road.

At last, he stood there alone, gazing out over the reeds and trees and, not too far in the distance, the blinding ribbon of the Great River. A mob of frenzied wing-flapping ducks surged up into the sky from its waters. Something had disturbed them. Some of them might not have made it into the sky alive. *The crocodile makes no sound, but fear of it is ancient.*

He turned back to the house lit up rosily by the long afternoon sun, a friendly jumble of cubes where they'd added on rooms here and there over the years as the number of children grew. It was providential that the servants were not around, although they'd no doubt be back before the night was over. He needed to think of what to do about his brother-in-law.

When he entered the salon, he saw Amen-em-hut, looking gaunt but much more himself, shaved and clean, his thick, wavy hair getting so long it almost hung over his forehead. Hani saw that he was graying at the temples. *Damn, the man is handsome even after all that.*

The priest looked up at Hani gratefully. His eyes, so like Nub-nefer's, were circled with dark rings. He was shorter than Hani, but still, sleeping in the little reed boat with its upcurved ends couldn't have been comfortable. "Thanks, my brother. I don't know where to go next, but I can't stay here and endanger you."

"You could stay as long as you wanted, except that the women are coming down the minute I tell them things are ready. I'm not sure Anuia could hide her sudden joy if she knew you were safe here." Hani brought him a piece of the stale bread. "You can toast this if you want. There's more cheese and some salted fish." It occurred to him that priests weren't permitted to eat fish.

"This is fine," Amen-em-hut assured him, dunking a piece of the dry flatbread in his water. "I don't know where to go, Hani. My own place is too obvious."

"Listen, are you sure they're actively looking for you?

My feeling is that the king has forgotten all about you. As long as you don't make any noise, they'll assume you're dead."

Amen-em-hut said nothing, but his face was somber as he chewed the bread with difficulty. He swallowed. "If I make no noise, I might as well be dead." He looked up as Hani started to speak and added, "I appreciate your own tactic, brother, but it isn't mine."

Hani sighed, a little put out. "None of the other prophets are being so obdurate, Amen-em-hut."

The priest snorted scornfully. "Political appointees. That's what you get. My forefathers have held this office for generations, Hani. I would shame my ancestors if I didn't cry out."

"I admire you, my friend. But I see this bringing pain down upon your family. Once you said to me that bad times were coming and that I should protect Nub-nefer. Well, I say the same thing to you. Why make it so hard on them?"

Amen-em-hut hung his head, his mouth a thin line.

He loved his wife and children—not to mention his sister—deeply, Hani knew.

"Just until everyone's forgotten about you, Amen-em-hut. Then pop up in Men-nefer or Iunu or Sau or someplace and yell all you want."

Amen-em-hut bared his teeth bitterly.

"But stop calling for assassination. That's what really has the king's back up. And I can't say it isn't understandable. They'd just ignore the other things." Hani could see his brother-in-law was unmoved, but the consequences of his obduracy were so dangerous that Hani was willing to beg. "I mean, regicide, Amen-em-hut? Can't you compromise?"

The priest stared up at Hani with his black, starved eyes, and he almost looked like a madman. "*He* hasn't enacted the Ipet Festival since he came to the throne alone, Hani. He's not the living Haru. His *ka* is not divine. He's not a legitimate king. I'm not preaching regicide."

"Then who, by all the demons of the Duat, do you think *is* legitimate? No doubt, the queen's father would happily crown himself, but is civil war what you want?" Hani's voice had risen. He felt half-mad, himself, with frustration. He seemed to be beating his head against an unyielding wall. Civil war—that was what was out there waiting for the Black Land. And at their borders, the Hittites slavered. "The king's one legitimate brother is dead, his half brother is weak in the head, and Nefer-khepru-ra has only daughters. Who, Amen-em-hut? Some general?"

"I don't know." Amen-em-hut let out his breath as if he were deflating. "Whoever has the favor of the gods."

Hani sputtered, "But who is that? Be reasonable, man. This isn't just a theological problem. There are real consequences. If you just kill the king, with no one out there to replace him, what in the name of all that's holy do you think is going to happen?"

"That's not my business, Hani. That's for the military and the chancery to decide. I'm a priest. And the gods reject the heretic on the throne of the Two Lands."

Hani's face was burning like a coal. *The man won't listen to reason at all.* He turned away and breathed deeply, seeking to calm himself. He didn't want to be yelling at this poor half-starved worn-down brother-in-law of his, but Amen-em-hut had become a complete fanatic. *Can he really be so unworldly that he doesn't foresee the consequences of what he's preaching?*

Hani forced himself to say levelly, "Do what you think you must, then. But we need to find another hiding place for you. And your family. Because if you insist on speaking out against the king, I can promise you, he'll strike at them."

Amen-em-hut stared at Hani, his eyebrows buckled in pain. "Hide them, Hani," he begged, and his voice was suddenly wobbly, all his blazing confidence drained out.

Hani strode up and down the little salon, trying to jog his imagination. "Where, though? What if we sent your brood down here with Nub-nefer and our children? Would it be too obvious? If they didn't leave the property, no one would know where they were. Would Pen-amen be willing to hole up here, do you think?"

"If he thought he had to in order to keep his mother safe."

"And where do we stash you?" Hani laughed in spite of himself. He was thinking of his little brother-in-law as some kind of holiday surprise for the children. *Where shall we stash it?* He reached out and laid a fraternal hand on Amen-em-hut's thin shoulder. "No hard feelings, right?"

"I'm grateful, Hani—for all you've done for me. Just stash me where I won't be any danger to you." The priest grinned up conspiratorially. Hani didn't think of Amen-em-hut as a man with much sense of humor, but he wasn't opaque. *Poor fellow. I'm glad I'm not him.*

The door banged open in the vestibule, and Mery-ra and Neferet came clattering in, their voices raised in painfully off-key song. They finished the verse at an explosive volume. Hani heard a burst of laughter and the thud of something being dropped to the floor.

"Hani?" called Mery-ra. "We brought provisions for until the servants get back."

"We saw some of them in the village." Neferet stood in the doorway. "We told them to take their time. Oh, Uncle! You're all clean. Can I hug you now?" She threw herself on Amen-em-hut, and he embraced her in return, his eyes dampening.

How he must miss his children, Hani thought, his heart softening. "We're trying to think of a place for Amen-em-hut to hide and quickly, before the others all get here. Maybe his family can stay here at the farm with Nub-nefer and the girls. We're afraid the police might try to get at him through them."

Mery-ra shook his head dismally. But he greeted the priest with unreserved warmth. "How has your vacation in the boat shed been, my boy?"

While his father chatted with Amen-em-hut, Hani helped Neferet carry their purchases into the kitchen. He saw fresh bread and smoked fish and a gourd full of curds. "Thanks for this, my duckling. It should hold us till the servants have time to prepare food. Is this my drinking gourd?"

"We didn't have a pot with us, Papa." She lowered her voice. "How is Uncle?"

"He hasn't eaten or slept well for more than a month. But he's all right. We just need to get him to a new hiding place."

She nodded, furrowing her brow. "What about the other priests? Couldn't they hide him?"

Hani looked at her appreciatively. "Not a bad idea, little duckling. Maybe someone could even let him into the temple precincts."

Neferet looked pleased. "I told you I was smart." She grinned her wide gap-toothed grin.

The four of them ate a frugal supper featuring bread and curds. Neferet picked some lettuce for a salad, but none of them could find oil or green grape juice, so they crunched it down unsauced.

"It's a feast, believe me," Amen-em-hut assured them. "Compared to what I've been eating. Except for the figs. They've been marvelous for the last week or so."

Mery-ra said, "I can't wait till the servants get back and find the beer. Or make it, if there isn't any. I don't know what our young *sunet*'s professional opinion is, but I find water an unhealthy substitute."

"But our well is good, isn't it, Papa?"

"Yes, my love," Hani said, his mouth full of bread. "Amen-em-hut, our girl had a good idea. Would any of your confreres consent to hide you?"

The priest looked up, his eyebrows raised. "That *is* a good idea. I thought of it, in fact, but I'd need to sound someone out, and I had nothing to write with nor any means of delivering a note."

"That's one problem we can solve," Mery-ra said. "Scribes are thick on the ground around here. Not a single person in this room is illiterate, right, Neferet?"

"Right, Grandfather. And I just happen to have in my medical basket a stack of potsherds, a pen, and some ink blocks."

"Take one potsherd before bedtime with a cup of inky water," Mery-ra finished, lifting an authoritative finger.

"Nooo," she said, cheerfully exasperated. "It's to write prescriptions."

Hani said, "I'll deliver it for you, brother. Just say whatever you have to say discreetly, please, in case the *medjay* pick me up and rifle through my writing case."

Neferet mixed up some ink and passed the scribal tools to her uncle. He stared reflectively at the potsherd, chewed the end of the pen, and shaped it into a point with his fingertips. "I'm just going to ask at this point if they know where I could hide. I'm hoping they'll spontaneously offer to cache me, but it would be a lot to lay on someone simply to present myself."

Indeed, Hani thought with a twist of the mouth.

Amen-em-hut began to write, straight-backed and proper as if he were seated in the House of Life. After a moment, he handed Hani the potsherd blackened with his fine cursive. "This person can be trusted."

Hani closed his hand over it without looking. "What excuse do I have to show up at the door of a former priest of Amen-Ra, though? I'm just afraid someone may be tailing me... for another reason."

"Have Nub-nefer deliver it. No one would think anything of it. They're friends."

A wave of reluctance rose in Hani like a case of incipient nausea. "Do we have to get her involved? *I* don't even want to know whose name is on this sherd. How much less my wife?"

"They're following you, Hani, not Nub-nefer," said Mery-ra, to Hani's surprise. "As Amen-em-hut says, if they're friends, no one would think twice if she paid him a visit."

Hani pursed his lips, reluctant. Finally, he said, "All right. Neferet, you can read the name for your mother. I don't want to see it."

"Chances are, they'll just say, 'I'll find you a place to stay,' so you won't know where I am anyway. Any of you." Amen-em-hut climbed to his feet. "My eternal thanks, Hani."

Hani embraced the little man, thinking, *Just don't get us all killed.*

The salon had grown dark as they talked. Hani could see through the clerestory that twilight was upon them, the sweet greenish half-light just before the sky sank into velvety night. A few stars spangled the east. "Why don't you go to bed, brother? The servants will be back any minute, and while I doubt if they even know who you are, I see no point in flaunting your presence."

Amen-em-hut nodded, and Hani led him toward the stairwell. "The room to the left at the top. That's where the children stay when we're here."

The priest turned and took his brother-in-law by the arm. In the darkness, his gaunt face was tense and vulnerable. "May the Hidden One bless you, my friend."

Hani chuckled, suddenly tired and a little giddy. "Which hidden one? You or the god?"

Hani took Nub-nefer aside as soon as he and the others arrived in Waset and told her quietly about finding her brother. At first, he thought she hadn't even understood him, her reaction seemed so calm, but then, suddenly, her face collapsed into a kind of uncontrollable expression of anguish, and tears of relief spouted from her eyes. "Oh, Hani, thank the gods! Thank the King of the Gods. Mut, mother of us all, thank you, thank you!" She smiled through the curtain of tears, her elegant nose running unheeded. "I thought he was dead for sure, Hani. Oh, thank you for finding him, my love." She grabbed her husband's face and kissed it all over.

Hani hated to dampen her happiness, but he had to warn her. "We mustn't tell anyone—not the girls, not Anuia. Especially her. She wouldn't be able to control her joy, and that would be noticeable immediately to anyone who might be watching her."

"But Neferet knows? Then everyone will know. Don't delude yourself."

"Keep her away from Anuia."

Nub-nefer looked up at him with starry-lashed eyes. "That seems so cruel."

"I know, my love, but it's for the good." *The real cruelty is Amen-em-hut's. He's as bad as the king in his way. Everyone else is being sacrificed to his vision.* Aloud, he said, "Neferet will read you the name on this note, then you must pay a visit to your old colleague and deliver it. I mustn't know where you're taking it. Do you understand, my dove?"

"And then he'll stay with them? Can't I even see him before you spirit him away?"

Hani considered this request. What would it cost for the women to move down to the farm before Amen-em-hut moved out? "Perhaps. Let's see how fast things start happening. How close is everyone to being packed?"

"The girls are all ready. We're just taking one handmaid for us all. The other servants can manage, don't you think?"

Hani agreed wholeheartedly, although he never would have dared suggest it. "Neferet, my duckling. Come here," he called.

Neferet bounded into the room, quacking and flapping her arms. "How can I serve you, noble Papa?"

He put a steadying hand on her shoulder. *What kind of father am I to involve her in this dangerous business?* "Read this silently, my dear, and whisper the name of the addressee to your mother. Don't tell me."

She perused it carefully then pressed her cupped hands to Nub-nefer's ear, and Hani heard a hissing of incomprehensible syllables.

Nub-nefer looked up, her face determined. "I'll go right away, Hani, before we leave for the farm. I'll take some of the figs and put the message in the basket, so no one will think anything is out of the ordinary."

"Thank you, my dearest. Then, I hope, we'll have no more responsibility in this matter."

So conscious was he of the danger of their activity that Hani nearly jumped when his father called from the vestibule, "Hani, your friend is here."

"Which friend? Or are you implying I only have one?"

"Oh, I thought you were expecting him. It's that Mane." Mery-ra toddled into the salon as Nub-nefer, knotting a shawl around her shoulders, passed hurriedly into the vestibule.

"Didn't you invite him in?" Hani did his best to conceal the sinking feeling in his middle. His life was like a rickety

N. L. HOLMES

scaffold that was coming apart and tumbling down on his head all at once—with results that might well be fatal.

"He said he'd wait in the garden." Mery-ra followed his daughter-in-law curiously with his eyes. "The homestead is a busy place this morning. Where's the mistress of the house going in such a cyclone?"

Hani pushed past his father grimly. "Where is Mane?" He stumped out onto the porch and saw the emissary standing in the graveled path, a smug grin on his face.

"Hani, old friend. I thought you'd never come see me as you promised."

"Did I promise—" Hani began, but Mane cut him off with a discreet finger to the lips. He said in his usual booming voice, "Lunch is waiting. Did you forget? I hope you didn't eat." He took Hani by the elbow and steered him to the gate.

Hani saw that he was trapped. Everything was happening at once. "Please, Mane, not now. I have so—"

"Keliya is leaving soon. We need to send him off." Mane lowered his voice as they passed through the gate. "Stop resisting me, friend. We're probably being watched."

Hani was too tired to fight. Some ineluctable net was closing around him, and he felt like an unsuspecting duck on the breast of the River. He let Mane pull him along down the lane, but he shot the emissary a dark look. "What's going on?" he hissed.

"Keliya and his men are preparing to take their report back to the king of Naharin. He wanted to say goodbye to his friends. It may be a year before we see him again." Mane continued to burble cheerfully as they directed their steps to the quay. A small fishing boat was waiting for them there. They climbed in, and the steersman pushed off into the current, heading upstream.

"Where in the name of the seven-headed demons are we going, Mane?" Hani demanded as soon as they were well out into the water.

Mane was staring back at the bank behind them with eyes narrowed against the late-morning sun. "A destination I think is safe, but I didn't want to take chances."

Neither of them said anything until they'd put to shore somewhere near the southern edge of the city. "Good. Good," muttered Mane. There they waited for several minutes while Hani fought his rising sense of unwillingness. *For half a* dja *of grain, I'd jump on the next boat and go home*, he thought mutinously. At last, a long, slim private yacht with a grinning Bes head on the prow cruised up to the bank and threw out the gangplank. Mane, still looking around him, led the way up to the deck. The two men seated themselves in the rear pavilion, and Mane drew the curtains along the sides.

"I don't suppose you'd tell me what's going on." Hani thought he knew, but he wanted an explanation. "Is this your boat?"

"No. It belongs to a friend." Mane shook Hani's knee in a jovial gesture. "You know what's going on. If someone is tailing you, this should help lose them."

"You're taking me to Akhet-aten? I'd have liked to have warned my family." Hani shot his friend a look of annoyance. "Did you know the queen called me for an interview? She knows I met with Kiya, and she warned me to stay away. This is direct disobedience."

"Maybe I'm taking you there, and maybe I'm not. And

yes, I did know that." The emissary to Naharin grinned broadly, but Hani wasn't appeased.

"This is no game, Mane. You're in danger, too, you know—if *my* peril doesn't move you."

But Mane just continued to grin. Hani shook his head, as if Mane were some incorrigible child, and blew out an angry breath through his nose.

They slid swiftly, downstream this time, the paddles rhythmically dipping and splashing. Hani could see nothing of the banks, since the curtains were drawn. *He's kidnapped me*, he thought, warming to the idea. *If anyone asks, he kidnapped me.*

The better part of the afternoon had passed before the boat turned toward the shore. Mane rose and drew Hani after him to the side of the boat. They were out in the middle of nowhere—a scatter of little farms and irrigated fields along the River was all that met Hani's eye. Palms and tamarisks waved lazily in the hot wind. A second elaborate private boat stood anchored just off the shore. In the near distance, hazy with sun shimmer, a whitewashed villa stood by itself—some expensive country place—surrounded by trees.

"Who lives here?" Hani asked, trying not to sound sullen.

"Another friend. A Mitannian merchant and his Egyptian wife. This is where Keliya stays sometimes."

They disembarked and mounted the covered litters that stood by under the shadow of a willow. Before long, the heat of the fall sun fell away, and cool shade flickered over the curtains as the litters moved beneath trees. Finally, the bearers set the vehicles down, and Mane emerged, Hani at his heels. They were at the door of the villa he'd seen from the River.

"Enter, my friend," said Mane with a smile, but his face was tense and his eyes cast around him uneasily.

The property was furnished, but it seemed to be vacant—no porter at the gate, no attentive servants hurrying to welcome them in and wash their feet. Then, ahead, in the dimly lit salon, Hani saw Keliya peering toward the door. His lugubrious face lit up when he saw the two men. "Hani!" he cried. "He got you to come!"

"He practically abducted me," Hani said tartly with a sideways glance at Mane. "Where is she? I need to be home by nightfall."

Keliya turned back and said softly in Hurrian to someone in the shadows, "You can come out, my lady. It's our friend."

Hani and Mane entered the room at the same time Lady Kiya stepped out from the other door. She was wrapped in a gauzy shawl that by no means concealed her pregnant condition, a bland, long wig such as any housewife might wear, upon her head. No jewelry glittered at her throat or wrists, and her sandals were plain. Adorned only in her youth and natural beauty, she seemed very vulnerable.

"Oh, Hani, tell me what you've found out," the King's Beloved Wife cried in Hurrian.

The four of them sat knee to knee, more like coconspirators than a royal lady and her court. Hani launched right in without any gallant small talk. "I've found out you lied to me, my lady. And that makes it very hard to help you."

She lowered her eyes then cast them guiltily at the other two men. "I was afraid," she said defensively.

"You told me your... adventure with this sculptor took place two years ago, and *he* told me it was less than a year, a fact I had his master confirm. You said nothing of any blackmail messages before the coming of the two men of Naharin."

Kiya bit her lip, her big eyes frightened.

"Let me ask you again: are you sure the child you're carrying is the king's?"

She put a hand to her mouth, and her eyebrows crumpled. She said in a small voice, "How can I know until I see him?"

Hani pressed relentlessly on. "The queen is the one blackmailing you. And now Kha-em-sekhem has been murdered. Nefert-iti isn't playing around. She knows I talked to you. She knows you're pregnant, and she suspects the child may not be the king's. No doubt somebody in your service is being paid to spy on you. She has you in a very dangerous place, my lady. And I'm in danger too. Her people are watching me now. That's why I haven't come back to you before. Short of assassinating the queen, which is absolutely not feasible, I don't see how you're going to avoid ruin."

"Easy, Hani," Mane protested. "You can think of something."

"I can only think of two things, neither of which is very likely to happen." Hani's voice was as tense as his body. He stared at his two friends accusingly as he addressed the royal wife. "Either we think of some course of action more profitable to the queen than ruining you and then find a person she trusts to convince her of that, or we somehow implore your father to make an intervention that would hold back the king's hand."

Keliya said gravely, "As for the second, King Tushratta has his hands more than full with the Hittites on his doorstep, I'm afraid."

Kiya gave a hiccup of fear.

"But," the Mitannian continued, "there was an issue of some of the agreed-upon goods from Neb-ma'at-ra never being delivered—gold statues, I think. Tushratta has tried several times, without success, to get Nefer-khepru-ra to cough them up. Could that be interpreted as nullifying the marriage?"

"More likely, nullifying the treaty. Our king would like nothing better at this point," said Mane skeptically. "Would he surrender our lady to return to her homeland?"

"I'm afraid her infidelity just gives him grounds for not paying out whatever is still owed," Hani said. "I don't suppose Tushratta'd come for a state visit?"

Keliya shook his head. "Hani, he's in the field against the Hittites as we speak. My homeland is fighting for its life."

"Well, then. Do either of you know anyone who has the queen's trust and would be willing to offer her an alternative to pulling Lady Kiya down?"

Mane laughed bitterly. "First, we have to come up with that alternative."

"My point precisely." Hani sat back, grim to the point of depression.

"Think of something, someone," Kiya cried in desperation, her little hands clenched together.

After a long cogitative silence, Hani surged to his feet. "Every moment we sit here together, we all run an enormous risk. You know where my investigation stands, Lady Kiya. I suggest we disperse and each be thinking hard about a solution. There's no reason to limit ourselves to my poor imagination."

The others stood up in turn. The house had grown quite dark. Outside, crickets had begun to pulse. Keliya retreated with the Beloved Wife while Mane and Hani made their way in near darkness down to the riverbank. One of the sailors was squatting on the bank beside a small fire, and when he saw them approaching, he signaled the boat with a wave of a brand. The crew extended the gangplank, and while the sailor held it, the two diplomats clattered their way on board. Once seated, Hani felt he could breathe again.

"Please don't involve me in this any further, my friend," he said to Mane with a weary sigh. "I'm the target of the royal displeasure in so many ways at the moment it boggles the mind."

"But our girl is in worse trouble still, Hani."

"'Beware of a woman who is a stranger,'" Hani quoted. "Did I write that after we met Taduhepa? Or after she became Kiya?"

Mane chuckled in the gathering darkness. Somewhere behind the Mountains of the West, the Lord Ra sank into a glorious pallor of rose and green.

"I'm serious," Hani said. "I want out. Don't call me again."

"As you like, my friend." After a moment, Mane added

quietly, "The king will probably have her put to death if Nefert-iti tells him what happened."

"Stop it, Mane. You have no idea how complicated my life is right now. You know, the police are looking for my brother-in-law. My whole family is in danger. I don't need to get on the wrong side of the Great Queen." As Hani spoke, he heard how false his rationale sounded. Mane and Keliya were certainly risking their necks as surely as Hani. He heaved an enormous sigh, and as if he'd blown it out, the sun dropped suddenly below the horizon.

"Hani, where were you? I thought we were going to go down to the country place this afternoon, but it's too late now." Nub-nefer met him at the door with a moringa-oil lamp in her hand, partly worried and partly annoyed, her great dark eyes running him up and down.

Hani put his arm around her shoulders and walked through the vestibule with her. "I'm sorry, my love. Urgent business came up. We'll all go down together tomorrow. Does Anuia know? Is she willing to sequester herself there for a while?"

"Yes. They'll follow in a day or two." Nub-nefer's lips twitched in a secretive little smile. "That will give me time to see my brother before everyone else gets there."

"Did you get a reply from the person to whom he wrote?"

"Yes. They'll keep him there for the time being."

"Thanks be to all the gods. I'm afraid any property of ours is too obvious a hiding place. I'm just grateful no one's found him before now."

"In the boat shed?" Nub-nefer's expression grew pained. "Poor Amen-em-hut." Her eyes fell and grew misty. "Sometimes when we were tots, the big boys would try to pick on me—you know how they can be with little children—and he would always stand up to them. It didn't matter that they were bigger than he. He would fight for me." Her voice shook a little, and she took a big sniff.

Hani kissed the top of her head, which was clad only in her own long hair, radiating the scent of bergamot. "I don't doubt it, my love. He doesn't lack for courage." *No, it's prudence he's lacking*, Hani thought. But then he chided himself. *Not everyone has to be a silent crocodile.* "We may have to disguise him to get him safely to his new place of refuge. Dress him up like a woman." He smiled impishly.

But Nub-nefer snorted. "Hani, my dear, women don't dress in layers of wool and veils here the way they do in your northern countries. It isn't easy to counterfeit a woman here."

Hani chuckled and allowed that she was undoubtedly right. To his shame, the image that sprang to his mind was that of the queen. "What has Neferet decided to do? Is she going down to the farm with you, or is she returning to Akhet-aten?"

"I don't think she knows yet. She'll come down with us for now."

Arm in arm, they headed through the silent house to bed, the tiny orange light of the lamp flickering before them.

CHAPTER 9

THE FAMILY ARRIVED AT THE farm like a tribe of nomads, loaded with baggage and even with some of the more comfortable furnishings from the house in Waset. Hani held his breath until the servants, grunting and sweating, had carried Baket-iset down the gangplank of the ferry. They all trooped up the bank by the fig trees, through the gardens, past the cow pasture and the silos, and into the house, which the resident steward and his underlings had prepared. Hani, Maya, and Mery-ra were along to help, but the men would all return to the city as soon as their womenfolk were settled. Hani let his wife quietly into the bedchamber to see Amen-em-hut before the others became aware of his presence. He was due to leave for his new hiding place in Waset that evening.

"My brother!" cried Nub-nefer in a tremulous high-pitched voice as she threw herself in his arms. She clung to him as if she could safeguard him from all the dangers that hung over his head, just as he had once defended her. His eyes were wet, and he caught his lip in his teeth, hanging onto his sister.

"You're so thin," she said at last, holding him at arm's length.

"Hani's accommodations aren't the best." He laughed, with an apologetic glance at his brother-in-law. "But I'm grateful nonetheless." His eyes grew pleading. "How are Anuia and the children?"

"Distressed but well. They're coming in a day or two, just to get out of sight. How I wish she could know you're safe."

Amen-em-hut's face darkened with anguished regret. "Don't tell her, Nubet. It's better she knows nothing if the *medjay* should question her."

Hani sank to a seat on the edge of the bed. "I just wish I understood what has happened to the Two Lands in the last few years. It's not a place I recognize anymore."

"It's easy, Hani," Amen-em-hut said in a hard voice. His handsome features were suffused once more with that brittle anger that had marked him in the last four years. "This all started under the late king. At his first jubilee, he made known that he was himself the revelation of the sun god—the dazzling Aten, the Visible One, the disk of the sun."

"All right." Hani nodded. "But he revered the Hidden One. He even suggested that he *was* Amen-Ra, right?"

"Right—the revelation of the Hidden One, in fact. Among others. The implication was that all the gods were essentially one." Amen-em-hut sat beside Hani. "All fairly orthodox. Just pushing the traditional theology of kingship a little. You'll notice that the first temples to the Aten were here in Waset, next to the Ipet-isut."

Hani recalled the disorienting images at the Gem-pa-aten, with their androgynous portraits of the then-coregent and the statues of the queen with the regalia of kingship. "Explain to me those carvings, brother. I still have nightmares about them."

"Remember how Neb-ma'at-ra already played up all the fertility images around him and his family? Queen Tiyi was everywhere with him, at a comparable scale. She *was* him, the female half of the king."

Hani thought he was beginning to see a path of continuity, but it was a little vertiginous. "So, if taken together, the coregent and his wife were he- and she-king?"

Nub-nefer made a disgusted noise. "And those other statues—something in between?"

"He- and she-king in one body," Amen-em-hut said sourly. "Still not altogether outside of orthodoxy. We have hermaphroditic gods. And they're fertility gods. The fullness of fertility."

Hani groaned. "So where does it all go astray?"

The priest snarled, "When the young king decided that *only* the revelation of the sun god was to be worshiped." He struck an outraged fist upon his knee. "The Visibility. The Hidden Essence was to be abandoned, dishonored. That the whole revelation from henceforth was to be the king and his wife. *They* are the Aten, Hani. It's them we are expected to worship, and them alone."

Hani heard the door click open behind him, and he wheeled, his heart in his mouth, but it was only Mery-ra, who was already in on the secret of the priest's presence.

"Oops," the old man said. "Just wanted to ask where I was sleeping tonight."

"Here, Father. Let's leave them. You and I will talk elsewhere." Hani shut the door carefully behind him, and the two men descended the stairs. At the bottom, having checked that none of the children were nearby, Hani said under his breath, "I'm taking him back to Waset this evening, right after we eat. I'd like to disguise him somehow, but we shaved off his beard, so he can't be an Amurrite. Nub-nefer assures me he can't be a woman."

"Let him be a workman. Dress him in one of the servants' clothes, and put a sack over his shoulder."

Hani nodded in agreement. "Excellent plan. He's a little pale after being in the boat shed for nearly two months—"

"Say he's a northerner. No one will think twice about it," Mery-ra assured him. "Can I go back up with you?"

"Of course. I'll ask Maya if he wants to as well. Although he's become maniacally solicitous of Sat-hut-haru."

"Good for him," Mery-ra said firmly. "I want all my granddaughters to be married to solicitous men."

As if summoned by their reference, Maya appeared from the salon. "Can I go back to Waset with you, my lord?"

"We were just wondering if you'd want to. We'll leave the ladies to their retreat, then. I arranged for the ferry to return at sundown. Father, would you go collect some old clothes and a cheap wig from one of the smaller servants? I can find a sack in the famous boat shed, no doubt."

Maya gave Hani a questioning look.

"For our guest," Hani informed him. "A manner of disguising his identity a bit."

"He's small. You could dress him like a woman," Maya suggested.

But Hani held up a hand. "Can't be done, I'm told. A workman is better. Hidden in plain sight."

He pushed past and made for the door, calling over his shoulder, "I'm heading for the boat shed."

Neferet galloped after him as he passed through the salon. "Can I go, too, Papa?"

"Of course, my duckling." They strode along together through the farmyard and down the path between the gardens toward the River. The colors of the season of Inundation were as bright as wall paintings—gold and intense green and silvery green and deep enamel blue, cut through by the white loincloths of the workmen bent over in the black fields beyond. Hani drew a deep, satisfied breath. He'd been trying for months to get into the marshes, but it hadn't happened yet. Still, just breathing the air of the countryside was restorative.

At his side, Neferet gazed around as she stalked along, squinting against the sun. "I guess I'll go back to Akhet-aten, Papa."

"You think you're willing to encounter suffering, my love?"

"I'm afraid it'll be there no matter where I go," she said philosophically. "Might as well meet it head-on, eh?"

Hani suppressed a laugh and wrapped an affectionate arm around the girl. *She sounds like a grown-up*, he thought fondly. *My little girl is almost an adult.*

"Do you want to come back to the city with me and Grandfather this evening? I can take you to the capital tomorrow."

"I'd like that, yes." She peeled off and skipped back up the slope toward the house, throwing her head and pawing the air like a horse full of spirit—a child again.

They ate an early supper all together, except for Amen-em-hut, who—as one who wasn't officially present—ate in the bedroom. Then the three men and Neferet bade the others goodbye and headed for the riverbank while the priest, disguised as a workman, slipped out and went around through the fields, approaching as if from the village. In his worn kilt and cheap straw-soled sandals, with a goat-hair wig and a sack over his shoulder, even the fastidious Amen-em-hut could pass for a laborer of the less muscular sort, thought Maya. *He's thin enough at the moment to look genuinely underfed.*

"Can I carry your bags, my lord?" the priest said meekly to Hani when they met at the waterside.

Lord Hani laughed. "Well done, man. We should rub a little dirt on your face, and you'd fool anyone."

"Walk more bent over, though, my boy. Try to look weary. Don't look people in the eye." Mery-ra twitched the priest's wig so it covered more of his forehead. "There you go. Be sure to bow when you speak to us."

Neferet could hardly contain her laughter. She stooped her own back and put an exaggeratedly humble look on her face. "I'll pretend to be his poor downtrodden daughter." She turned her long, pitiful face to each of the men in turn and extended a hand. "Alms! Alms for a poor downtrodden girl?"

"Easy, Neferet," Maya said sternly. "This is serious

business. You don't want to expose his disguise." *The girl has to draw attention to herself somehow*, he thought in annoyance. *It's a game for her, but it's life or death for Lord Amen-em-hut.*

Hani just smiled benevolently. In the distance, Maya could see the ferry, with its broad sail taut, turn out of the current and approach the bank, a burnished silhouette against the setting sun. Lord Hani had engaged a big boat because he had needed to load and unload Baket-iset's litter as safely as possible that afternoon.

The sailors lassoed the lines to the pilings along the shore and drew the vessel in close. They threw down the gangplank, and Hani settled the landward end. The four of them marched up, Neferet between her father and grandfather. Amen-em-hut trailed behind, charged with their bags. It gave Maya a certain bitter pleasure to see the pampered priest dragging the baskets and sacks. Maya had always found him a little sharp and dismissive, secure in his family wealth and prestigious position. And he was so absurdly good-looking.

The party took a place on the deck toward the stern, sitting cross-legged in a circle, their "servant" behind them, his eyes modestly averted.

"Neferet has decided to go back to Lady Djefat-nebty," Lord Hani announced.

Neferet nodded and held up a hand as if accepting applause.

"How's Aha's wife's cooking?" Maya asked a little maliciously.

"Oh, Khentet-ka doesn't cook," the girl informed them in a snooty voice. "She has servants. Everything's very *fawncy*. I never know what I can pick up with my fingers and what I have to use a knife for."

"Good training for court banquets," said Mery-ra acidly. "Maybe we know now who's spoiling the boy."

"What boy? Aha?" asked Neferet.

"Has Aha shown you his *shebyu* collar yet?" Maya couldn't resist asking, even knowing that Lord Hani would reprove him.

"Does he have one?" Neferet cried excitedly.

"No, my dear. Maya is teasing." Lord Hani was distracted, gazing out over the darkening river where occasional lights twinkled along the bank, doubled in the water. "It's going to be completely dark when we get home. Did anyone think to bring a lamp?"

No one had. Maya cursed himself. This was one way he could have made himself useful to his father-in-law.

Hani turned to the false servant. "Amen—er, -mes, please get yourself to your destination as soon as you can. I don't want any of us to be on the streets much after dark. Maya, why don't you stay at our house?"

Did he have to give the priest my *name?* Maya thought, a little put out. Amen-mes was his formal name, although he was always known as Maya. Aloud, he said only, "With pleasure, my lord."

The journey wasn't long. The last of the twilight was just fading as they tied up at the quay in Waset. Two sailors jumped out first with torches to guide the passengers down the plank, and once on dry land, they parted company with Amen-em-hut, who melted into the dark streets at a quick pace.

"Goodbye!" Neferet called, but her father hushed her.

He seemed quite nervous now that they were back in the City of the Scepter.

Through the unpaved lanes, they passed in a knot, their footsteps getting faster and faster. The pale whitewashed walls still held a twilit glow, but it was more the memory of light than light itself. Their white clothing seemed to be unoccupied now and moved, ghostly, through the darkening back streets.

Maya started at a bang somewhere not too distant. He could see that Lord Hani and Mery-ra were equally tense—no one had forgotten the frightening riots of the Feast of Drunkenness. Maya noticed that her father and grandfather had bracketed Neferet protectively. Maya was deeply relieved that Sat-hut-haru was safe in the country with her mother to tend her. He hoped his own mother was equally secure, but the apprentice workmen lived around the courtyard, and they and the Nubian doorman would protect the workshop with their lives.

At last, the gate of Lord Hani's property appeared before them. At a knock, A'a opened it, a lamp in his hand, and welcomed them in. Golden light streamed from the clerestory of the house through the trees. *Safe at last.*

Lord Hani set down, with a bang, the baskets he'd taken from Amen-em-hut when they parted. He turned to his daughter. "Tomorrow we set off for the capital, my girl." Then he grinned at Maya. "You and me too. No womenfolk to occupy us at home."

"You're going to leave me here by myself?" Mery-ra objected.

Loosening his shoulders with a painful shrug, Hani

said, "You're welcome to come if you want. But don't you have some sort of duties at the barracks here?"

"Only from time to time. But maybe your friend won't have room for a third person."

"I don't think he'd mind," Hani said.

Maya thought of Lord Ptah-mes's magnificent "modest place" overlooking the River in Akhet-aten. The grandee would never notice another guest.

Hani asked slyly, "But won't Meryet-amen miss you?"

"She's at her country house." Mery-ra put his hands on his hips, looking pleased with the turn of events. "I'll go. I'll say hello to Aha. And I want to meet this Djefat-nebty my granddaughter is studying with."

Hani let his father accompany Neferet to her teacher's mansion in his place. By the time Mery-ra joined them at Ptah-mes's house, Hani and Maya were sitting in the vine-shaded courtyard, although the ripening grapes that had begun to drop threatened to drive them elsewhere.

"What did you think, Father?" Hani asked once the old man had taken a seat beside them.

"I was favorably impressed. She obviously thinks well of the girl, and Neferet has the greatest respect for her. They're going to the House of the Royal Ornaments today, from what I understood."

Hani's good humor chilled. He said uneasily, "I should have known this would happen. I just hope no one asks who the little apprentice's family is. I don't want to remind anyone close to the king that I exist."

"And Djefat-nebty's husband is God's Father of the Aten, you know," Maya said.

Hani nodded, displeased. Then he brightened. "Well, I need to report to our host at his office. I finally caught up on Aziru's mail the last night before we left."

"What's new in the north?" Mery-ra asked, leaning back against the wall and crossing his arms.

"Kheta is swallowing up Naharin. We're going to lose all our northernmost vassals," Hani said somberly then lowered his voice. "And Kiya is losing whatever clout her father's position earned for her. She's becoming politically dispensable. If our king doesn't intend to grant Tushratta our help when Naharin is literally under attack by our worst enemy, it's clear the treaty has no more meaning."

The three men sat in gloomy silence for a moment. Then Mery-ra leaned forward eagerly. "I know who could talk to the queen for you, Hani."

Hani and Maya turned to him simultaneously. Hani's heart stepped up a beat. "Who, Father?"

"Why, Djefat-nebty, of course. She obviously has Nefert-iti's confidence."

"But would she do it? She may care nothing at all for Kiya. Or there may be professional objections to getting involved in court politics." *Or both*, he thought, caught between optimism and fear of getting his hopes up.

Mery-ra shrugged.

Maya said glumly, "We still don't have a plan for her to present anyway."

Ammit take this, Hani thought. *Why am I even occupying my head with such ponderings? I told Mane I wanted out. It's none of my business anymore. The foolish girl has gotten herself into trouble that can't be healed.* "I'm off," he said, rising to his feet.

✦

At the Hall of the Royal Correspondence, Hani was admitted to Lord Ptah-mes's office without delay while Maya waited in the reception room. Hani made his report on the latest correspondence of the Amurrites, vaguely aware of a coolness or tension in his superior's manner.

When he'd concluded, Ptah-mes said thinly, "Do you know where your brother-in-law is, Hani?"

Hani beamed in satisfaction. "No, my lord. I can honestly say I don't. He quitted my premises several days ago and is hidden somewhere else now."

Ptah-mes let out a breath through his nose and stood up to his full height. He stared at Hani expressionlessly, leaving the latter strangely uneasy. Then the high commissioner walked to his window and stared out at the sky. At last, he turned back, fixed Hani with his dark eyes, and said in a quiet voice, "He's at my house, Hani."

Hani, who had risen as well out of respect, felt his stomach catch in his throat as if he'd been thrown from a height. "Your... your house?" He didn't know how to react. *Is Ptah-mes angry about it? Does he hold me responsible?* "How did this happen?"

"He asked my wife if she would hide him, and she said yes."

"All you gods! She was the reliable colleague?" Hani slapped himself on the forehead in disbelief.

"So it seems." Ptah-mes sat heavily and rubbed his face with a long, ringed hand. "As if it weren't sufficiently scandalous for one's wife to hide a man under one's roof, it's a man with a price on his head. A man calling for the assassination of the king." He laughed a little wildly.

Hani was completely abashed. "Oh, my lord, I swear I didn't know this was what he had in mind. I'll take him back immediately. This can only endanger you."

"You'll have to fight Apeny for him, Hani. She's determined to do this at any cost to us. To me."

Ptah-mes looked so grim and worn that Hani felt downright sorry for him. He didn't seem to be furious, as he might well have been. Hani knew only too well the kind of anxiety that followed in the firebrand priest's wake. But at least he was Hani's family; it was Hani's duty to take the risk. Ptah-mes had no connection to him at all. This was no doubt one more stress on his tottering marriage.

"I'm so sorry," Hani said in heartfelt apology. "I told him I didn't want to know where he was going. He had my wife carry a message, and I didn't even ask her about her destination."

Ptah-mes said dully, "I believe you, my friend. The only question is what to do now. I can tell you, the *medjay* are out looking for him. Would they think to look in the home of a former First Prophet of Amen-Ra and the *weret khener*, a woman who has been none too discreet about her positions?" A pained smile twitched at his lips. "And if they looked, would they find our fugitive? And what then?" He lifted an eyebrow. "Would they believe that a woman would undertake such an action with neither the knowledge nor the permission of her husband—a husband, I might add, who has been publicly humiliated by the present king and stripped of his rank and who might be expected to harbor a grudge? We can't demand that Lord Mahu and his henchmen understand the unconventional arrangements of my marriage."

Hani groaned, his hands over his face. "I'm so sorry, so sorry. How did you find out?"

"I showed up unexpectedly in Waset. Apeny wasn't home, but your brother-in-law was asleep in my bed. He explained what had happened. She confirmed it upon her return."

Hani was nonplussed. "He's not... they're not...?"

"How do I know, Hani? That would be the least dangerous part of it if it were true."

"May the Hidden One guide us..." Hani murmured.

"Indeed." Ptah-mes stood again and said levelly, mastering himself with an effort, "I suppose I'll see you this evening at the house here."

"Yes, my lord. My father came with us. I hope that's not one more burden that my family is imposing upon you."

"Not at all," said Ptah-mes with perfect graciousness. "I like your father."

Maya was waiting in the shadowy reaches of the reception hall, reading over a letter he'd been writing. He sprang to his feet as soon as he heard his father-in-law's heavy footsteps emerging from the high commissioner's office.

"Maya, my friend," said Hani in a flattened voice. "Our troubles are contagious."

Once they had passed out into the courtyard, Hani recounted the unforeseen turn of events.

Maya rolled his eyes, outraged. "With all respect, my lord, that priest is endangering everyone he touches."

Hani blew a puff of air from his mouth. "I have no answer for that. We just have to survive."

Mery-ra intercepted them in the garden. "I bought us food for lunch so we don't inconvenience your friend even further, Hani."

"Good, Father. I think we've just about filled the cup of his inconvenience to the brim." Hani clapped his father on the shoulder and pushed past him toward the courtyard.

"What's that supposed to mean, son?" Mery-ra trailed after him. He cast an inquiring look back at Maya, who answered only with an eloquent raising of the eyebrows. "What's happened now?"

"Let's set out your lunch first, and I'll tell you as we eat."

They spread out the stack of flatbreads, pickled vegetables, imported olives, and chickpeas on an unoccupied stool. To one side, Mery-ra set several bunches of grapes and a handful of little pies of some sort. Maya's saliva was starting to run at the smell.

They'd just begun to dig in when Ptah-mes appeared from around the bushes, a tall ewer and a stack of cups in his hands. "Here you are," he said with a smile. "May I join you?"

"By all means, my lord. We were hoping not to inconvenience you any further," said Lord Hani, who vacated the single chair and moved to a stool.

"No inconvenience." Lord Ptah-mes looked pleasant enough for someone whose life had just been put in jeopardy. "I wanted to assure you, Hani, that there are no hard feelings. I know you had nothing to do with this." He poured out a rich red wine for them all from his ewer and handed around the cups.

"What have you done now, Hani?" asked Mery-ra.

"Forgive me, my lord. I don't think I've ever introduced my father, Mery-ra, to you. Or my son-in-law, Maya."

"My pleasure, gentleman," said Ptah-mes, nodding graciously. "I believe we have met, in fact. I hope you've found the accommodations to your liking."

"It's most kind of you to extend your hospitality to us in this way, my lord," said Mery-ra, who was trying to catch Hani's eye.

Hani said in a voice scarcely above a whisper, "My brother-in-law seems to have turned up at Lord Ptah-mes's house in Waset, Father."

"Ah, he knows?" Ptah-mes said. Whatever distress he'd experienced at first seemed to be mastered. He said calmly, "My wife is hiding your son-in-law, Lord Mery-ra."

"Mut the mother of us all," the old man cried, the color draining from his face. "Someone needs to spank little Shu hard."

At Ptah-mes's interrogatory look, Hani explained, "My wife and her brother resemble one another strongly in appearance. This is my father's irreverent nickname for him."

Ptah-mes nodded. "If they catch him, they'll do worse than that to him. And to us, too, I fear." He lifted his cup and said in a louder voice, bright and cheerful, "Life, prosperity, and health to our king."

The others echoed his words in a somewhat vaguer fashion and upended their cups. It was the most exquisite vintage Maya had ever tasted. *These grandees know how to live*, he thought, smacking his lips appreciatively.

"I'm afraid we have a rather simple lunch, my lord, but I beg you to share it with us," Hani said with his big inviting smile.

"With pleasure, my friend," said Ptah-mes, reaching out his ringed hand for a piece of bread.

They ate, not saying much. Ptah-mes displayed unimpeachable amiability despite the bad turn Hani's family had done him. *He's a real aristocrat*, Maya thought. *Look at him. Gold of honor around his neck. A wig that probably cost as much as my house. Who could believe I'd ever break bread with such a man?*

"Tell me, Hani," Lord Ptah-mes said as he poured Hani the last drops from the ewer. "Whatever happened with your niece's fiancé?"

Hani looked suddenly uncomfortable. "Alas, he was murdered." He exchanged a significant look with their host.

"I remember now. My condolences," murmured Ptah-mes.

"As regards my granddaughter, at least, it was for the best," said Mery-ra. "He was completely unsuitable."

"It seemed so. I trust... all that business is behind you, then." The high commissioner didn't even raise his eyes from his cup, but his meaning was clear, and it was aimed at Hani.

"I hope so, my lord, although one of my colleagues in the foreign service recently solicited my continued aid for his client." The two men locked eyes over the rims of their cups. "I'm not sure what I can do for him."

"Probably nothing."

Maya felt he was listening to them converse in code.

"However..." Hani's brows were knotted as if some troubling idea were forcing its way into his head. "My lord, these two men have my complete confidence. May I speak frankly to you about... that matter?"

"But of course. If they understand that I know absolutely nothing about any of it."

"My lord, I've worked in the secret service under three kings, and I can swear to you, you know absolutely nothing about it," said Mery-ra with a complicit smirk.

"Nothing," Maya confirmed.

Hani recommenced. "My brother-in-law was explaining the king's new theology to me the last time I saw him, and all of a sudden it occurred to me that this might be what we were looking for." He stared around at the men, a spark of excitement in his eye. "You recall we hoped to find some alternative plan that the queen might find more appealing than ruining her rival, the Beloved Royal Wife. How does this sound to you? She or her father should convince the king to make her not queen but co-king with him. She would be far above any competition from any other woman, even one loved by the king."

They all stared at Hani with varying degrees of incomprehension and skepticism on their faces.

His cheeks growing scarlet, he hastened to explain. "You'd have had to hear what our friend said about the theology, I guess. How there's a he-king and a she-king, fertility figures making up a whole that is the king—"

"Slow down, son. He-king and she-king?"

"Come on, Father. You remember the images at the Gem-pa-aten?"

"And how. Ah, perhaps I see what you mean. The queen with the crook and flail."

"Yes. The idea is the king's, but we suggest that he make it real, not just symbolic."

"And he'll listen to you?" Lord Ptah-mes asked neutrally.

"No, but he'll listen to the queen. And she'll listen to Lady Djefat-nebty, her trusted physician."

They stared at one another. Maya was unsure what to think, and he didn't want to be the first to express an opinion. He licked his lips, his eyes flicking from face to face.

Finally, Lord Ptah-mes said, "I can express no position on matters theological regarding the Aten, Hani, but it might appeal to Lady Nefert-iti. The question is, will it appeal to the king?"

Hani spread his hands in a gesture of helplessness. "We can't know until we try."

Mery-ra made a pondering hum. "And if you find out that it doesn't? Will you live to say, 'Oops, let's try something else'?"

"I can't read the future, Father," Hani said. "I'm in trouble even if I do nothing."

Another silence descended.

Lord Ptah-mes rose to his feet. "Gentlemen, I leave you, as ignorant as when I came. I'll see you at dinner, I suppose. This time, let me be the host." He smiled one of his warmer smiles and disappeared gracefully into the greenery.

Lord Hani watched him depart and said finally, with a sigh, "I guess I need to pay Lady Djefat-nebty a visit."

◈

Hani waited until evening, when he knew Neferet was released from her duties, and presented himself at the physician's door. Neferet was pale and kept swallowing hard. The *sunet* herself accompanied the girl, her face a stern mask. "Lord Hani. I'm happy your daughter has decided to persevere. The Dazzling Disk help the patient whose doctor doesn't care enough about her to be appalled at her suffering."

"Well said, my lady. I hope her behavior was... appropriate today."

"She'll be fine." The woman crossed her arms like a man. "I'll see you tomorrow, then, my girl."

"Yes, my lady," said Neferet in a weak voice.

Hani was concerned. He'd rarely ever seen his irrepressible daughter so cast down. He looked back at the *sunet*, standing tall and unapproachable in the semidarkness of the vestibule. He said humbly, "My lady, may I speak to you privately sometime about another matter altogether—a matter that has ramifications for the welfare of the kingdom?"

She raised a curious eyebrow and gestured for him to follow her.

"Wait here, my duckling," Hani called to Neferet.

Lady Djefat-nebty walked briskly through the salon, with its dais and throne-like chairs, and into a smaller room painted with the luminous scenes of nature that Hani had seen at the Beloved Wife's *maru*. She closed the door behind them. "What's this about?"

Hani took a deep breath and began. "My lady, I am attached to the foreign office of our lord king's Hall of Correspondence. My sole concern is for the safety and well-being of our kingdom, particularly as regards its allies and enemies. I beg you to keep that in mind—my aims are not partisan in any way. And I would ask that you keep our conversation confidential."

The physician thrust out her lip, considering. She looked curious in spite of her forbidding features.

Hani plunged on. "It has come to my attention that there is a rivalry—understandably—between the Great Queen and the Beloved Royal Wife. Unfortunately, if the queen manages to humiliate the Beloved Wife, the result will be the rupture of the treaty with Naharin and quite possibly the loss of our northern vassals to Kheta." He hoped Djefat-nebty wasn't well versed in what was already happening to the north at the moment, because then she would know how Kheta had emasculated Naharin and that Kemet's vassals were already peeling off. Her expression revealed nothing, but she listened with punctilious attention.

"It's the sincere hope of me and my colleagues and all right-thinking men of Kemet that this can be avoided. The queen has asked me to serve her as I am able"—Hani believed this wasn't stretching the truth too egregiously—"and this is what occurs to me. Since your husband is a priest of the Aten, you can probably evaluate its theological merits better than I. What if the king made of his Great Queen something even more exalted, something no mere king's wife, no matter how beloved, could hope to rival?"

"What is greater than a queen?" the doctor asked pointedly in her mannish voice.

"A king, my lady." He saw her eyes widen then squint thoughtfully. "What if the royal couple presented itself as a

285

male and a female king, perfect in kingship, perfect in the fertility of the Aten?"

"Kings are male, Hani."

"So are doctors, my lady." He watched her expression change from shock to amusement and even, he hoped, approval. "Yet we have had female kings before, just as we have had female doctors. It's not common, but it's not impossible."

"Novel." She stood, digesting the idea in silence, then said, "Where do I come into this?"

"I think both the Lady Kiya and the Great Queen trust you, my lady. Your impartiality is impeccable, and your family's devotion to the cause of the Aten is above reproach. Someone might suspect me of some sort of self-interest, but if the idea came from you, I think those who need to consider it would give it a fair hearing."

She continued to stare at him as if she could read his heart. *And* do *you have some sort of self-interest in this?* she seemed to be thinking.

"If we don't forestall the breakup of our Mitannian alliance, the Hittites will have won the day, my lady. The royal women can save the kingdom."

At last, Djefat-nebty said, "I'll consider it. I assume that when you say to keep it confidential, that doesn't mean I can't weigh its theological merits with my husband, who is trained in these matters."

"That seems more than reasonable. I wouldn't want to suggest anything that wasn't theologically orthodox." It was all he could do to repress a naughty smile at that lie. But his desire to see this plan work was completely sincere.

She nodded and opened the door. "I'll ponder this and get back to you."

Hani emerged into the raw garden of the mansion and saw Neferet squatting in the path, watching something. She rose at her father's approach and cried, "Guess what I am, Papa." She began to nudge something invisible with her head, then her shoulder, then both hands, her feet planted behind her as if she were trying to flip a fellow wrestler.

Hani scratched his chin. "Is this some medical procedure?"

She hooted with laughter. "No, silly. Watch closely." She shaped a globe with her hands then repeated her pushing gestures.

"I give up," Hani said. "What are you?"

"A dung beetle, of course!"

"But of course!" He laughed, partly from the relief of his own tension and partly for joy that Neferet seemed to be restored to her good humor.

She waddled and waded down the path, her hands crawling the air in front of her. "That's how beetles walk."

"How do they talk?"

"They're too small. I can't hear them."

Hani put a fond arm around his daughter's shoulder and squeezed her toward him. "Are you all right, little dung beetle?"

"It's hard sometimes, Papa, but I'm all right." They walked side by side to the gate and out into the street. Neferet said, "You know what Lady Djefat-nebty said? She said that real *sunu*s use magic and prayers, too, because you have to figure out what spirits are troubling the patient before you can treat them. And that people feel better and heal quicker when they know the gods are helping them."

Hani wondered what a woman who had apparently accepted the worship of the Aten thought of praying to Sekhmet or Serqet or Im-hotep or the divine Djeser-ka-ra who had once been the king. No doubt, if it made people feel better, it was good. He liked Djefat-nebty for that. She was a pragmatist. He hoped that augured well for his request.

Finally, they came to Aha's gate. "Grandfather and Maya and I are going back to Waset tomorrow morning, my duck. I'll say goodbye to you here." He folded her in his arms and kissed her head. "I love you, little duckling. I'm proud of your courage."

She squeezed him hard. "I love you, too, Papa. Kiss Grandfather and Maya for me, all right?" She giggled. "Or maybe not kiss them, exactly!"

She scampered gaily into the garden, and Hani watched her until the gatekeeper pulled the red panels shut in his face.

❖

It had been Hani's intention to leave for Waset first thing the next morning. Under the circumstances, he was eager to relieve Ptah-mes of the burden of three of his family members. But Ptah-mes had a message from one of the vassal kings of the north he wanted analyzed, and no one had as much experience in that part of the world as Hani. Having spent the morning at the Hall of Royal Correspondence, Hani decided to stay another day, and he saw Mery-ra and Maya off after lunch.

He told Pa-kiki he would collect Neferet after her lessons again, and that evening, he appeared at the lady doctor's door.

"Papa! You're still here!" cried Neferet in delight.

Djefat-nebty raised an eyebrow at him. "Lord Hani. Come inside for a moment, won't you?"

Hani's stomach clenched in a mix of dread and hope. He followed her inside the vestibule, where she said to him under her breath, "I spoke to our lady the Great Queen."

Hani's heart began to gallop.

"She wants to see you tomorrow."

"You explained the proposal to her, my lady?" he whispered.

"Yes. And I said it was from you. And she wanted to see you." The doctor's long mouth quirked in a wry smile.

"I can't thank you enough, Lady Djefat-nebty." *Although*, he thought, *I would have preferred you to present it as your own idea. I can only hope my name will never come up with the king.*

She gave a bark of laughter. "Whether you have cause to thank me depends on what she says, doesn't it? Good evening, Hani."

He rejoined Neferet, who capered at his side, regaling him with all the things she'd learned that day. There'd been no gravely ill patients, it seemed. He left her at Aha's house and made his way back to Ptah-mes's, eager to tell him that they'd passed the first test—that of securing the Great Queen's interest. But Ptah-mes had sailed for Waset, he was told, so Hani dined alone in the garden and tried to prepare himself for his interview on the next day.

For the second time in his life, Hani walked between the lion-bodied images of the king that lined the northern part of the processional street. At his left, the long white wall of the palace compound was lit like a rosy cliff by the rising sun. Only his ungainly shadow bobbed along it. He thought of Neferet's dung beetle and almost laughed. He was holding up his hands to his temples like beetle horns to see their effect on his silhouette when a palace official passed him, drawing away in horror at his eccentric behavior. Hani chuckled. He felt all fizzy with excitement, like a pot of beer that was close to blowing off its cap in the sun. Yet the queen could easily be angry. He might never walk out of the palace alive.

He presented himself at the first gate and traversed the long court to the second monumental pylon, where he noticed the red banners that signaled the king's presence were mounted. He crossed the interminable court with the obelisks and, entering the dark shade of the colonnaded portico, gave his credentials at the door of the palace reception halls. There he found himself waiting for a long while in the richly colored splendor of the foyer. He noticed once more the utter silence of the place, where even the busy servants moved barefoot and soundless. At one point, a troupe of dancing girls in skimpy costumes of gauze and beads walked rapidly in a jingling line toward the interior of the palace, called, apparently, to some command performance.

Perhaps half the morning had elapsed before the

majordomo approached to say, "The Great Queen will receive you, my lord."

As before, the servant led Hani to the small audience chamber, and two Libyans in tattoos and plume-crested costumes pushed back the lofty gilded doors with a bow. Hani entered, folding in a court prostration. When he rose, he saw that the Great Queen, seated in majesty upon her throne of electrum, was not alone. A man Hani's age or a little older sat in a less exalted chair below her dais. From his high cheekbones, square jaw, and wide, full lips with a slight overbite, Hani suspected that this was the queen's father, Ay.

"Hani, we meet again," said Nefert-iti the Beautiful One in her breathy voice.

"My lady does me too much honor."

"My physician brought me a message from you, Hani. Have you decided at last to make yourself useful to your queen?"

"My lady, my sole hope is to be useful to the Two Kingdoms. To that extent, I am indeed in my lady's service."

The man at the queen's side laughed. "Well said, like the diplomat you are." He rose and took a step forward with a friendly expression on his face—a striking face that exuded charm. "I'm the God's Father, Ay. My daughter and queen has asked me to be present to discuss the novel idea that you are apparently prepared to present."

"I welcome my lord's analysis. I'm certainly not a theologian, but it's my understanding that one of the priests of the Aten has evaluated the plan."

"That's what Djefat-nebty said." The queen unconsciously rubbed her protruding belly with a jeweled hand, and it was suddenly obvious to Hani that she, like Kiya, was in an advanced state of pregnancy.

Hani then described the idea he'd had of elevating the queen formally to a rank equal to that of the king, thus protecting her against any rivalry. She and Ay exchanged a look.

"What do you get out of this, Hani?" asked Ay in his pleasant way.

"Peace, my lord. Secure borders. Allies to help us repulse the Hittites, who are getting more and more aggressive. To break our alliances now by humiliating foreign princesses would be disastrous."

"So, you're still in *her* service?" the queen said with a slight cooling of tone.

"Not at all, my lady. I am in the service of Kemet alone. I see in the king's own theology a way to end personal rivalries to your advantage and to work for the good of the kingdom."

"Of course, the first motive for such an action would be the more perfect revelation of the Aten," said Ay. There was a crafty edge to his smile. He looked like a fox inviting other foxes to collaborate. They might not all walk out of the den alive.

"Of course."

Silence descended over the richly colored room—a busy, thought-pulsing silence as thick as the incense floating upward from the little braziers on either side of the queen's throne. Nefert-iti shot a look sideways at her father from under her malachite-edged lids. He tipped his head ever so slightly.

"Leave us now, Hani," said the queen, rising. "You've

delivered your idea. It's up to others to decide what to do with it."

Hani bowed in silence and, still in a bow, backed from the room, forcing himself not to look up at that intoxicating body before him.

✦

Hani arrived home in Waset to find a letter from Nub-nefer, which Pen-amen had written out for her. All was well. Anuia and her four children had joined Nub-nefer and the two girls, and the days were filled with activity and conversation. Of course, it wasn't all happy. Anuia didn't know that her husband was safely hidden in the City of the Scepter; she was increasingly sure he'd been killed. But she was determined to be brave. Baket-iset was enjoying the country air, and Ta-miu kept her company for the most part rather than wandering off into the fields as she usually did. Sat-hut-haru's pregnancy was proceeding well. She was due to deliver in another month or so. But she was in good hands with all the female relatives around.

Hani already missed his family, but he knew they were safer in the country. He'd settled himself cross-legged on the floor in the salon to write a reply when he heard the opening of the door and voices in the vestibule.

"You home, son?" Mery-ra called. "How did it go?" He toddled in, his face eager. "You're still alive. That's a good sign."

"The best." Hani grinned. "I think it went well. They're considering it."

"They?"

"Lord Ay was with his daughter."

"Oh, that one. They say he's wormed his way into the king's confidence and is using it to get his family's toe in the door."

"So much the better. Our plan is to Nefert-iti's advantage." Hani ranged his writing implements and crawled to his feet. "Though I'd say Ay's family already had its toe in the door, wouldn't you? Isn't he the dowager queen Tiyi's brother? And the king's father-in-law? Wasn't his aunt the mother of Neb-ma'at-ra?"

"You can never have too much toe in the door."

"Of course," Hani said, suddenly sobered, "even as she-king, she might still want to ruin Kiya. I hope I painted the consequences of that move as sufficiently laden with ill effects. Let's hope no one tells her that Naharin is collapsing fast."

"Are you going to let Mane know what's happened?"

"Not until I'm sure the plan is going to be adopted. No point getting Kiya's hopes up falsely."

Hani and Mery-ra walked side by side through the salon. Mery-ra said, "I'm going on to the farm to start gathering the grain and animals for Pipi. I'd like to get up there and back as soon as possible. He hedged about furnishing me details, but I think his moneylender gave him a deadline."

"Excellent plan, Father. I hope he's trying to sell that accursed horse."

"Ah," said Mery-ra, brightening. "I may have a buyer. One of the officers I work with."

"It's not Ay, by any chance?" Hani suggested with a twinkle.

"No, no. No one you're likely to know. A young fellow named Pa-aten-em-heb."

"I hope this famous animal isn't some spavined nag that no one will want."

"Or that it doesn't drown on the way back. I've engaged a barge for a round trip."

Hani shook his head. "That Pipi. This is the last time I'm bailing him out. If some emergency arose all of a sudden, I wouldn't be able to deal with it without selling the farm. I just hope the spring wheat harvest is good. It's not right for a grown man to endanger his old father like this."

Mery-ra made a deprecating noise. "He's not endangering his old father. Most of the payback is yours, son. But he does need to grow up; no question."

Hani stopped at the kitchen door, realizing he had walked there automatically without any real reason. Perhaps the talk of grain and cattle had led him there. He had turned back to the salon when he heard a knock at the front door. A'a's footsteps clopped into the vestibule, then a faint exchange of voices came to Hani's ear. He stopped, curious.

"My lord," said A'a from the inner door. "There's a gentleman here to see you. He declined to give a name."

A little flame of anxiety began to flicker in Hani's breast. "I'll come talk to him there for now, A'a. Thank you."

Mery-ra raised an interested eyebrow from the kitchen door.

Hani proceeded, barefoot, into the vestibule, to find standing there a well-dressed heavyset man of middle age who looked vaguely familiar. "I'm the master of the house. May I help you?"

The man turned toward him a jowly face, cold of expression and devoid of charm. "My name is Mahu, chief of the king's police at Akhet-aten. Is there some place we can talk in privacy?"

Fear tunneled up Hani's back like an icy wave of the Inundation. "You're a little far from your territory, aren't you, Lord Mahu?" he said amiably. "Let's go out into the garden." He slipped into his sandals by the door and led the way down the gravel path, the policeman's heavy tread crunching along behind him. The desire to bolt was almost overpowering. Hani entered the garden pavilion and turned to Mahu, still smiling. "Have a seat, won't you?"

Mahu dropped into the chair with a thud, his meaty paws on the arm rests far from relaxed. His eyes were narrow and overhung by flesh and the tufty excrescence of eyebrow. He never took his gaze from Hani's face.

"Now, what can I do for you?" Hani asked in his smoothest diplomatic voice.

"Where is your brother-in-law, Hani?"

"I wish I knew, my lord. The family thought *you* had him." Hani's heart was beating hard, but he'd settled into the calm, alert state of the negotiator.

Mahu snorted skeptically. "That might have been true months ago. Where is he now?"

"In all frankness, I haven't seen him for a while."

"But you have seen him? When?"

Hani decided a certain amount of honesty was in his best interest. "He'd hidden himself in my boat shed at the farm. I came upon him by accident. He then decided to move. I haven't seen him since."

Mahu cocked his head as if doubting the story. He said sarcastically, "You found him hiding, and you didn't think to report it to the police, eh?"

"Tell me, Lord Mahu," said Hani a little sharply. "What crime is he guilty of that I should turn him in to the police? Of believing in the god he has served all his life? Since when is piety a crime?"

Mahu's eyes narrowed still further, and Hani could see the policeman was angered by his interlocutor's logic. "I suspect, Hani, that you are well aware of the fact that the king wants this man for crimes against his majesty. Why was he hiding if he wasn't guilty of something?"

"What crimes against his majesty, Mahu? Tell me what he's done."

"He has called for the assassination of the Lord of the Two Lands. The crime of regicide."

Hani smiled caustically. "He's guilty of words? Even my children have figured out that the more Papa talks big, the less he's likely actually to do to them."

As if he'd suddenly had enough, Mahu surged forward in his chair, his face disfigured by a snarl. "Don't push your luck, my lord. This disrespect will not go unmarked. Words are often the first step toward actions, and we all know it. Preach regicide long enough, and someone is likely to put those words into practice. And then who's guilty? The man who drew the sword? Or the man who told him to do it as well?"

"So regicide consists of wishing the king were dead. I suppose it constitutes theft to wish I had that gold bracelet of my neighbor's." Hani could feel a cold fury building in him. *What kind of tyranny has my fair Black Land become, that one can no longer think or speak one's mind?* But he dared not lose his temper, because, justly or otherwise, Mahu had power and Hani had none. He forced himself to smile.

"I have ways of making you talk," said the *medjay* chief in a low voice that resembled an animal's growl.

"But I am talking," said Hani. "I'm telling you everything I know. Which happens to be nothing."

Mahu rose abruptly to his feet. "We'll see. You're under arrest. Follow me, please."

Hani's heart seemed to stop. So much for his little joust of words. Remembering the condition of Amen-em-hut when he'd returned from the *medjays'* hospitality, Hani swallowed hard. "As you will. What is my crime?"

"You're a person of interest, Lord Hani. We want to hear what you really have to say."

Hani felt the blood draining from his face. He tipped his head in acquiescence. Mahu gestured him ahead of him, and Hani went docilely. Mahu pushed him in the back.

Say nothing. Say nothing, Hani cautioned himself. *You'll just make him angrier. There's nothing legal in this. He's just angry.*

He proceeded to the gate with as much nonchalance as he could manage.

His father was standing on the garden path, staring incredulously. "What's going on here?" Mery-ra demanded.

"I'm under arrest," Hani said levelly. "For knowing nothing."

Mahu gave him a brutal shove through the open panels of the gate. Outside stood four armed policemen with a baboon on a leash. Two of them grabbed Hani immediately by the upper arms and forced him toward a donkey cart, which stood parked in the road.

"Get in," ordered Mahu, his thin lips set in the downward crescent of a man who suspected he'd been mocked.

Hani obliged, setting his foot on the spoke of the wheel and preparing to haul himself up. The policemen shoved him in unceremoniously, skinning his shins and banging his knees on the floor. One of them bound his wrists behind him. His breath was coming in jerky bursts, anger and fear at war within him. *You're in for it now, my boy.*

Mahu said roughly, "To the River."

The last thing Hani saw before they pushed him facedown in the vehicle was Mery-ra standing in the gate, his mouth wide open in horror.

CHAPTER 10

Maya arrived at Lord Hani's house around the middle of the morning, prepared for dictation. To his surprise, A'a told him Hani wasn't home. The secretary was just debating whether to leave or stay for a while and wait when Lord Mery-ra barreled through the front door in a cloud of dust and sweat.

"Ah, Maya, my boy. Something terrible has happened." The old man's face was grim and anguished, and a wave of fear rolled over Maya, lifting the hairs on his neck.

"What is it, my lord?" he cried.

"Hani has been arrested."

Maya's mouth flew open in shock. "What? Why?"

"I don't know. A man came to the door this morning, without giving his name, and the two of them went out into the garden to talk. The next thing I knew, the fellow was strong-arming my son through the gate, and Hani cried out that he was being arrested." Mery-ra's mouth had grown hard as he spoke, his eyebrows knit in a bar of fierce determination.

"Bes protect us," murmured Maya, his heart in shreds. "Is this about Kiya or about Amen-em-hut?"

"Only the gods know. I just went down to the chief of the Theban police's garrison, but Hani wasn't there. I had heard the bastard say as they left, 'To the River.'" Mery-ra clenched his fists. "I'll bet this was one of the king's police from Akhet-aten."

Maya's legs felt suddenly weak, and he sank to a seat on the floor with a plop. He could hardly close his mouth, the shock sat upon him so strongly. "I can't believe this."

Mery-ra stalked up and down like a caged wild animal. "I don't want to alarm Nub-nefer till we know what's going on. Maybe we should grab a fast boat to the capital."

"Should we... should we warn Lord Ptah-mes in case that's what it's about?" Maya looked up at him.

"Probably. You do that, son. You're faster than I am. Even if he's not there, tell his wife. She's apparently the one who needs to know anyway. I'll go put a boat on standby."

Maya sprang to his feet and jogged out the door and away, his heart in his mouth. He felt as if he'd been smacked in the face—stunned, pained, and offended. *Of all people, Lord Hani, the most conscientious man in the Black Land.* Maya was gasping and panting by the time he reached the great urban estate of Lord Ptah-mes. Hani had pointed it out to him once, although Maya had never entered the majestic gateway. Ptah-mes and his ilk were as high above the lower-level aristocrats, like Hani, as Hani's station was above Maya's own. *Waterfront property in Waset!* Ptah-mes's family must have been here before Amen-Ra became the god of the entire kingdom, back when grandees of Waset had made themselves kings.

But all class consciousness fell away as Maya churned up the road to the grandiose gate. He had a mission that transcended his artisan roots. Panting, he hammered on the panel. A porter in livery appeared, looking askance at the sweat-dripping dwarf on his doorsill.

"Quick, man. Your master or mistress. It's urgent," Maya cried in his most authoritative voice. "Quick! Quick!"

The man disappeared through the garden, and Maya eyed his surroundings. Enormous sycomore trees shaded the path, trimmed neatly—everything relating to Ptah-mes was neat. But the patina lacking in his newly planted garden in the capital buttered the grounds here with the golden softness of ages of wealth.

A moment later, quick footsteps, almost running, came crunching down the path, and Lord Ptah-mes appeared, his eyes wide, his chest heaving. "Maya, I thought it must be you. Come in. What's wrong?"

"My lord, the *medjay* have arrested Lord Hani"—Ptah-mes's face went pale—"and we don't know why or where they've taken him. But just in case, you'd better get you-know-who someplace else."

Ptah-mes stared at the gate as if he expected to see policemen marching in. Then he turned and hustled off, crying, "Come with me."

Maya scarcely noticed the endless manicured gardens and pools that flashed past him as he ran. He was reaching the end of his energy, but Lord Ptah-mes's long legs strode relentlessly on. Maya followed Lord Ptah-mes into a painted portico, where astounded servants drew back at their master's passage.

"Stay here," Ptah-mes directed, and Maya gratefully

stopped in the dim, cool vestibule while the lord of the house stalked into the interior, his form reflected in the polished floor as if in water.

Maya could hear urgent voices in the salon, a man's and a woman's, increasingly raised in argument. Then Ptah-mes's shouted, "And if they torture Hani and he talks, my dear? Get the son of a bitch out of here immediately."

He appeared once more in the doorway, his face red and grim, his nostrils taut with anger. "Let's go. My boat will be faster."

"Lord Mery-ra is expecting me, my lord."

Ptah-mes called his litter bearers and said to Maya, "Take the litter back to Hani's house and pick up his father, then come to the quay. I'll be waiting." Over his shoulder, he yelled, "Out. Immediately."

Maya crawled into the litter, trying to blot from his mind the argument he'd just heard, while Ptah-mes ran down through the garden to his private landing. The men picked Maya up, and off he swayed through the streets in effortless comfort.

He found Lord Mery-ra waiting impatiently in the gate. "Did you find him?"

"Yes. He said to join him on his boat, and we'll all go down to the capital together. It's faster. Here's his litter." Mery-ra climbed in, and to the bearers, Maya said grandly, "To the quays, men."

Lord Mery-ra had seen the yacht before, of course. He hailed it, and the two scribes galloped up the gangplank, followed by the litter bearers. Maya stared around him. *Gods, the luxury! What stories I'll have for Sat-hut-haru!*

303

But of course, her father was in the clutches of the *medjay*. Maya blew out a distraught breath.

Lord Ptah-mes welcomed them. "We'll travel all night, whatever the risk. We may actually get to the capital before the police boat." He was both anxious and angry, his lean face whetted sharp, his mouth a grim line. "This was inevitable," he muttered.

"My lord, I feel sure Hani would never say anything about your role in this," Mery-ra said.

"If they torture him, Mery-ra? Will he be able to stop himself?" But then Ptah-mes seemed to realize the selfishness of his concerns, and he added, "For his sake above all, let's hope they don't torture him. My wife has taken this upon her of her own free will."

They stood tensely at the gunwales until the crew cast off and veered into the stream. Maya heard the rhythmic splash of the paddles that propelled them past other boats just riding the current. At last, their host led them up the sloping deck to the stern, where they seated themselves in the curtained kiosk between the steering oars. Ptah-mes sat preoccupied, staring ahead of him. Finally, he said, "Do you know anything more, Mery-ra? Did they say what this was about?"

"Nothing, my lord. The doorkeeper announced an unidentified guest this morning, and Hani went out to the pavilion to speak to him. The next thing I knew, the man was marching my son to the gate, and Hani cried, 'They're arresting me for knowing nothing.'"

Ptah-mes nodded. They subsided into silence, and the morning passed in that silence, the sun rising in the sky. No one spoke. Occasionally, somebody would sigh. Ptah-mes's face never changed expression, as if it were permanently imprinted with care and anger. Maya watched the grandee surreptitiously, observing his unconsciously graceful gestures and how his clothes never seemed to wrinkle. Perhaps it was because he was slim; there was no straining of shirt over belly or kilt top crumpled from the overflow. *Still, he has to bend his legs when he sits.*

Mery-ra, on the other hand, had something rumpled about him; his wig was always a little askew. He was closer to the ideal of the scribe—sedentary, well fed, cheerful. But even at his age, there was a sense of power in those broad shoulders and big hands. He was surely the image of Lord Hani in twenty years' time.

If Lord Hani lives. Maya felt fear well up inside him, an icy seepage. Hani was so solid, so calm, always in command of things. He was such a bulwark. Maya couldn't imagine a life in which his father-in-law was no longer there, looking out for him and Sat-hut-haru. And their son. *Oh, Great One, please let him live to see his grandson.* Maya could feel his nose begin to burn. *Let him be all right.*

Lord Mahu and the four *medjay* cast off from the quay with their prisoner in tow. Although there was little chance of Hani making an escape from the deck of a boat, they left his hands tied and made him sit on the deck with the baboon staring at him from a cubit away. Hani entertained himself for a while, making faces at the animal, which watched him with world-weary close-set amber eyes and finally turned away in apparent disgust. It scratched behind its knee in an absent way and then examined its nails like a bored human.

Once, it yawned, revealing enormous yellow fangs. *They probably trained it to do that to intimidate prisoners.* Hani tried to picture the baboon raising its hands and ecstatically praising the rising sun, but this was clearly a jaded, soul-hardened police baboon incapable of such sensibility.

After some time had passed, Mahu stumped over to where Hani and the baboon sat face-to-face on the deck and squatted at Hani's side. "Here's what's going to happen," he said in a tone of barely contained hostility.

I shouldn't have antagonized him so, Hani thought, uneasy but resigned to his fate.

"You're going to tell me honestly and completely what you know about Amen-em-hut's whereabouts since we released him last summer. Get up." He barely gave Hani time to put a foot beneath himself before he hauled him up by the neck of his shirt. "Now, talk."

Standing in the midday sun, where Mahu had positioned him so that he had to squint into the glare, Hani said, "He came home from the police barracks in Waset, bruised and limping. He refused to tell his wife what had happened to him, saying only that he'd been told to keep his mouth shut. He went to bed at her side, and when she awoke in the morning, he was gone."

"All right. That's day one. Go on."

"Nobody knew where he was. The family was distraught. We thought *you* had him or that he was dead. After the Inundation, his boat turned up downstream, and everyone figured he'd been drowned. More than a month later, I went into the boat shed at my country house, and there he was. He apologized for endangering my family, and the next day, I think it was, or a few days later, he disappeared again."

"And he didn't tell you where he was going?"

"I specifically told him I didn't want to know."

"Does his wife know?"

"No. He didn't want anyone close to him to know. For this reason." Hani nodded at his bound hands. "I told him to leave the country if he knew what was good for him."

"Do you think he did that?"

"I have no idea."

Mahu looked sly. "You're in the foreign service, Hani. If you were sending a family member abroad, where would you send them?"

Hani pondered that. Of course, he'd done no such thing, but it was interesting to speculate. "Given the situation in the north, I would tell them to go to Kebni or Arwada. Far enough away to be out of sight but not so close to the border to be endangered. Enough Egyptians around not to be completely isolated but not so many as to be running into people who knew them."

Mahu sauntered away then drifted back and glared at Hani. "Do you think that's what he did, Lord Hani?"

"I have no idea," Hani said. "I think it would be hard for him to leave Kemet, but maybe he was desperate enough to do it."

"And if he didn't leave the country, where might he have gone?"

Hani wrinkled his brow as if in thought. "He might have found a way to get into one of the estates of the god. I think he'd feel he had some right to be there." He looked up with a smile. "But that's just a guess."

"Any other family members who might have helped him hide?"

"All his children still live at home with their mother except his son. None of them knows where he is. They all think he's probably dead. And maybe he is."

"And what about his sister?"

No, no, not her, Hani thought, panic flaring. He tried to smile. "She lives with me, my lord. If I don't know, neither does she." His heart had started to hammer.

"What about your children? At least two of them are married."

You dirty bastard. You've studied up on my children? "I know my middle daughter doesn't know. I see her nearly daily. My oldest son lives in Akhet-aten. He's no friend of the old gods, my lord. It would surprise me mightily if he knew and didn't turn his uncle in." Breathing had become difficult. Anger flickered like a cold fire in Hani's middle. *Stay away from Nub-nefer and the children.* He clenched his fists quietly.

Mahu sensed Hani's rage and seemed to enjoy it. "Perhaps we should call your wife in."

Hani fought down the urge to throw himself at Mahu and knock him over the edge of the boat. "She knows less than I. I only encountered him by accident," he said, forcing his voice to remain level. He hoped the *medjay* couldn't hear how his breath shook in his nose.

They fed him at mealtime and permitted him to sleep uncomfortably on the deck. But every day, Mahu asked him the same questions, no doubt expecting to find some telltale differences where the truth didn't underpin his words. For the rest of the time, Hani and the baboon confronted one another in boredom at first, then with a kind of fascination. Hani observed that a big, tooth-exposing grin was taken as a threat rather than an expression of good humor and learned to smile according to the baboon's taste. At one point, the animal reached out a long hand and picked at something on Hani's kilted thigh, examined it, then popped it in its mouth.

The young policeman who was the animal's handler observed the interchange with amusement. "He likes you," he said on the third day.

"Does he have a name?"

"Djehuty's Cub." The man laughed. "Only we can't say that anymore. He's just Cub."

At last, after five interminable days, Hani saw, sliding toward them on the bank, the white walls of the riverside palace and the beige cubes of private dwellings and warehouses that told him they'd reached the capital. The thought of new possibilities made swallowing difficult. The *medjay* might imprison him and continue to interrogate him. Presumably, that was why they'd taken him to Akhetaten. *Surely, Mahu sees that I know nothing.* But they were in Mahu's home terrain now. He had full authority to do whatever he wanted to a *person of interest.*

One of the policemen prodded Hani to his feet. Mahu stood before him, hands behind his back. The boat had started to swing out of the current and draw toward the shore. "Here we are, Hani. I'm going to turn you loose for the moment, but be aware that we're watching you." He gave a disagreeable smile that spread his lips without touching his eyes. "I'm not convinced you don't know more than you let on. Perhaps it will just take a little more motivation to make you share that knowledge, eh?"

His back to the shore, Mahu staggered as the boat slid

up into the shallows with a lurch, and he had to put out his hands to steady himself. Hani forced himself not to sneer— that small discomfiture gave him so much satisfaction. He suspected Mahu wasn't a man who easily endured looking ridiculous.

"I can't tell you what I don't know, my lord," he said mildly.

Mahu flicked a gesture to his men. While the sailors threw down the gangplank and lifted the segment of gunwales that blocked the opening, two of the *medjay* untied Hani's hands and pushed him toward the exit.

Suddenly, Hani stopped, a thought forming that set alight a spark of suspicion within him. "Excuse me, Lord Mahu," he said, turning back. "May I ask how these threats against the king or calls to regicide or whatever they are have been disseminated? Because Amen-em-hut saw absolutely no one, at least during that month or more he was in my shed. He certainly didn't *say* anything to anyone."

Mahu sauntered closer, a dark light flickering in his eye. "They were written, Hani. They were posted in places where the lettered could read them. They were aimed at priests and scribes, I'd say, wouldn't you?"

"Then it wasn't Amen-em-hut!" cried Hani triumphantly. "He had no writing implements. He didn't even go into my house—he just stole from the garden to live. Where would he have gotten papyrus and ink in a boat shed?"

"Perhaps you could tell me."

"I could not. Because he didn't have any. Much as he might have liked to write such calls to arms, it wasn't him.

It couldn't have been." Hani was unable control his grin. *Why didn't I think of this sooner?*

Mahu's eyes narrowed in reflection. Then his thin lips parted in a smirk. "And yet he signed them. Strange, isn't it?"

Hani made a dismissive sound. "Not at all. Anybody could have written the threats and signed his name to them. Do you have them? I could recognize his handwriting."

"And what reason do I have to trust you if you tell me it isn't his?"

A slow burn of anger had begun again under Hani's breastbone. Mahu didn't want to know if Amen-em-hut was innocent. He didn't want to consider any evidence that might exculpate him.

"I'm sure there are other people who know his hand," Hani said coldly. "You don't have to trust me. Confirm it with someone else."

"Who? A priest of the Banished One?" Mahu said sarcastically.

Hani threw up his hands. "I've tried to help you, Mahu. But it seems you don't care about the truth of this matter."

To one of the policemen at his side, Mahu made a gesture so quick Hani could hardly react. The man hurled himself at Hani and struck him, hard knuckled, in the face. Hani reeled back, his stomach in his mouth as he felt himself fall backward through the opening in the gunwales onto the narrow gangplank. All he could think of was Baket-iset toppling from the deck years before. Someone grabbed his feet, and he just avoided sprawling all the way down the cross-staved boards or into the water. But his back and ribs ignited with pain almost as intense as the

311

blow to his cheekbone as they dragged him heavily back over the edge. He groaned as two of the *medjay* hauled him to his feet without tenderness.

"You need to learn some respect for authority, *Lord Hani*," said Mahu, breathing as hard as if he himself had thrown himself on the scribe. "I think I've had enough of your company for the moment. But we know where to find you when we need you." He turned his back, and the soldiers loosed their prisoner's arms. Gasping and staggering, Hani lurched down the plank and onto the land, half his body on fire with pain.

He stared up at the boat while his face began to swell and obstruct his vision. He pressed the back of his hand to his cheek, and it came away bloody. *I shouldn't have acted so cocky,* he thought ruefully. *But I've found out something. There's somebody else out there acting in Amen-em-hut's name.*

Hani tried to plan his next move. He had nothing on him with which to pay the ferry back to Waset. He thought of heading to Lord Ptah-mes's house, but Mahu wasn't aware of his—or his wife's—involvement in the affair, and if Hani were followed, he would implicate Ptah-mes unnecessarily. He figured the least suspicious place for him to go was to Aha's.

Walking was painful and slow. Hani had lost his sandals and his wig, on top of everything else. He limped along, his teeth gritted, his face pulsing, his clothes filthy from his slide down the gangplank—amused at the scandalized stares he drew from the relatively few people he passed on the back streets. He couldn't understand this new capital, which seemed not to be a real city at all. It reminded him of the jubilee courts of ancient kings he'd once seen near

Men-nefer, where all the "buildings" that surrounded them were in fact nothing but handsome facades.

He pounded on Aha's gate and was met by the porter, who somehow recognized him under his disfiguring injury and cried in shock, "Lord Hani! Come in, come in! What's happened, my lord?"

"A run-in with wild animals," Hani said wryly. "Is my son home?"

"Lord Hesy-en-aten is at the Hall of Royal Correspondence, my lord. But I know he would want you to come in and let Lady Khentet-ka bandage your wounds."

Hani dragged himself wearily over the threshold. He smelled something delicious cooking, and his stomach growled eagerly in response. He realized it must be lunchtime, although his days on the boat, subjected to the endless and repetitive interrogations, had begun to spin around him a time all their own—the cocoon of the spider around its prey. The servant led him into the elaborate salon and sat him down in a fine chair that had to be Aha's. Hani eased his weight onto the cushion with a groan.

"One moment, my lord. I'll get the mistress of the house." The servant scuttled off into the rear of the residence.

Hani grunted with pain as he shifted in the chair.

At that instant, the front door banged open, and the loud, cheery voice of Neferet called from the vestibule, "Iry? Nobody's at the gate? Hello!"

She burst into the salon with her medical basket over her arm, braids bouncing, mouth pursed for some call, but stopped in midstride when she saw her father. Her eyes grew wide in horror. "Papa! Oh no! What happened to you?" She ran to his side and knelt beside him then hugged him until he winced and pried away her fingers. "Oh, Papa!" Her eyes filled with tears. "What...?"

"This is what a smart mouth gets you, my duckling. Learn from this lesson." Hani tried to smile, but the side of his face was too swollen, and he had the feeling his effort came out a ghastly grimace.

Neferet was regrouping rapidly; eyebrows knit in concentration, she started to dig in her basket. "We need to clean that wound, Papa. Here." She brandished a stick about the length of a hand. "Chew this."

"What, are you going to do surgery?" he cried, alarmed, drawing away from the stick.

"No, Papa. It's willow. The bark helps ease pain and keeps the red down. And this"—she produced a little faience pot with a wax stopper—"is water-lily tea. I'll get you a cup."

She sprang to her feet just as the servant returned from the inner house. "My lord, your pardon, but Lady Khentet-ka is confined to bed. She's expecting any day, you know. Permit me to get one of the serving girls to help you."

But Neferet forestalled him with a disgusted wave. "I can take care of him, Iry. Just get me some water and some cloths, please."

With a look of discomfort, the man slipped off to the kitchen. Neferet, gazing at her father with brows crumpled in pity, took his hands. "Oh, Papa, if you could see yourself. What happened?"

"The *medjay* thought I might know something about the whereabouts of your uncle."

"The *medjay*!" Her eyes grew round. "They should have asked me. I know where he—"

But Hani pressed an urgent hand over her mouth, his heart hammering. He hissed, "By all the gods, my love! Don't let anyone hear you say that. You *don't* know; do you understand? The person you think it is just found him a place to stay."

She looked mutinous but shrugged.

"I'm serious, Neferet. You see what they did to me. They mustn't have any reason to think you know anything at all, do you hear?"

"All right, Papa."

"And besides, we don't want to get that person into trouble." He fixed her with his good eye.

"I understand."

The servant returned with a pitcher and basin and a stack of ripped-up old shirts that served for rags. Neferet wrung out one of the cloths and began to dab gently at Hani's cheek. He twitched in spite of himself.

"I'm sorry, Papa, but if I don't press, I can't get the blood off. What did he hit you with?"

"His fist," Hani muttered.

After a moment's earnest cleansing, Neferet asked, almost as if ashamed of her curiosity, "Did they have a baboon, Papa?"

"They did, my love. He was the nicest one among them. We became friends."

She sat back on her heels. "What does their fur feel like?"

"I don't know, duckling, I didn't pet him. That wouldn't have seemed respectful. He was quite a dignified fellow."

315

She screwed up her eyes and flared her nostrils and hunched her shoulders in what Hani took to be an imitation of a baboon. "Did he look like that?"

"More or less, yes." He laughed and regretted it as his ribs spasmed.

The door opened once more, and male voices could be heard from the vestibule. Hani recognized Aha and Pa-kiki, who must have returned from the Hall of Correspondence together.

"Aha! Pa-kiki!" cried Neferet, surging up and running out to greet them. "Guess who's here and what happened to him?"

Her voice dropped as she related in breathless detail the juicy news of the morning. Hani's two sons burst into the room, their faces aghast.

"Father!" cried Aha. "You must have nothing to do with that man!"

"Who? Mahu? It wasn't by choice, I assure you."

"No. Uncle Amen-em-hut. He'll drag us all down with him."

Hani squeezed his firstborn's proffered hand. "As it happens, they're looking for him for something he didn't even do. But Mahu's uninterested in that little fact. That would mean he'd have to find the real culprit."

"Papa." Pa-kiki dropped to his knees at his father's side. "They didn't hurt you badly, I hope?"

"No, son. The worst, I think, is from when I nearly fell backward down the gangplank. I must be pretty badly bruised."

He could tell by the children's faces that they, too, were

thinking of Baket-iset's terrible accident and how easily their father could have been broken forever by such a fall.

"Stay where you are," said Aha, laying a hand on his shoulder. "I'll tell them to bring you a table here, and we'll all eat. Where is Khentet-ka?"

"In bed again," said Neferet with a roll of the eyes. To her father, she mouthed, "She's just lazy."

Aha called the kitchen servants, and before long, they'd brought out the folding tables, and everyone sat on stools around their father and tucked into the lunch. Hani felt he could have done with something a little simpler and heartier, but it was certainly delicious. Aha didn't appear to be suffering from insufficient food.

"Where are the children?" Hani managed painfully through a mouthful of ornate marinated vegetables. Chewing required more movement of the cheekbone than he'd realized.

"With Khentet-ka's mother," Aha explained. "It's gotten too hard for her to watch them all the time. And even with a nurse—all the yelling and noise. She needs a lot of rest."

Neferet rolled her eyes again.

"So, what did the *medjay* want with you, Papa?" asked Pa-kiki after they'd finished all but the dried dates.

"They wanted to know what I knew about Uncle's whereabouts. It seems someone has been posting death threats against the king, using his name."

His sons drew back in outrage.

"But I pointed out to them that it wasn't Uncle, because he had no writing implements. He was shut up in our boat shed for weeks."

"*Our* boat shed?" cried Aha, appalled. "Stay away from him, Father."

"I only happened upon him by accident, son. But the point I want to make is that they're accusing Amen-em-hut of something he didn't do. And they didn't like it much when I pointed that out."

"Well, I don't like *them*," cried Neferet with spirit. "Their baboon is better than all of them." She made her baboon face again, but it drew no laughs.

"Stay away," Aha hammered, his plump face crimson and a bit wild. "That Lord Mahu is a dangerous fellow. No one who is anyone likes him, but he's useful, so he has the king's ear."

"Yes," said Hani dryly. "If the king wants false charges leveled against someone, I'm sure he's useful."

"Father, surely you don't think—"

"I don't know what to think. I offered to look at these mysterious broadsides and see if the handwriting was Amen-em-hut's, but Mahu wasn't interested."

Pa-kiki was listening to everything with his mouth open. "This doesn't seem right to me," he said finally.

❦

Lord Ptah-mes's yacht did indeed reach Akhet-aten before the police boat. After storming into the police barracks in search of his father-in-law, Maya and the others found themselves cooling their heels. They retreated to the Hall of Correspondence and, the following day, appeared once more at the *medjay*'s headquarters. And they came... not just like any old petitioners but in Lord Ptah-mes's chariot with servants running at their side. People fell back as they passed in the street—Ptah-mes erect and concentrated, the reins in his red-gloved hands, Mery-ra braced wide legged beside him, and Maya peering over the bar of the box, the lappets of his wig flying back with the speed. He thought he'd die of excitement. *How many people, even scribes, ever have the chance to ride in a chariot?* His mother would faint when he told her about this.

They arrived in a flurry of dust and clattering hooves, and Ptah-mes left the vehicle in the care of his servants. Bystanders gathered shyly to catch a look at the luxurious car of tooled leather and steam-bent wood and the high-strung, priceless horses. The three men strode into the three-story tower of the police office as if they owned it, demanding to speak to Lord Mahu. He had, in fact, returned late that morning.

Mahu appeared in the reception hall, looking rumpled and in a bad mood. "Who is it who wants to see me?" he said ungraciously.

"I am Ptah-mes son of Bak-en-ren-ef, high commissioner of the northern vassal states and former vizier of the Upper Kingdom. I understand you have one of my men in your custody," said Lord Ptah-mes loftily. He was considerably taller than Mahu, perfectly groomed, and decked with all his gold of honor, and he'd put on his frostiest grandee face.

"And who would that be, my Lord High Commissioner and former vizier?" Mahu managed to make the titles sound like an insult.

"Hani son of Mery-ra."

"Wrong. He's not in my custody anymore. But he could be coming back if he doesn't learn better manners."

Ptah-mes said coldly, "I should warn you that by

impounding members of our king's foreign service, you endanger the security of the kingdom, my lord. I hope you'll be mindful of that the next time you're tempted to lay hands on him."

"I'll certainly be mindful of that, my lord," said the chief of police sarcastically.

"What did you arrest him for, anyway?" demanded Mery-ra. "He's committed no crime in Akhet-aten."

"And who are you?"

"His father. Military scribe under the God's Father, Lord Ay."

Maya shot a surprised look at him but then dropped his eyes. In a manner of speaking, it was true. Ay was head of the entire cavalry.

"He's a person of interest in our investigation of the sedition of his brother-in-law." Mahu glared from face to face. "I don't suppose any of you chaps happen to know where Amen-em-hut is hiding?"

"Oh, of course," Lord Ptah-mes said, his voice thick with sarcasm. "He's probably under my sheets with all the other seditious priests."

Now, there's sangfroid, Maya thought admiringly. But it cut a little close to the bone. He could see Ptah-mes was angry or perhaps afraid—his nostrils were tense and pale and his lips compressed. Still, his expression of bored contempt had never changed. Mahu, on the other hand, was livid, his bushy eyebrows drawn down, his mouth rippling in what wanted badly to become a snarl. *This could degenerate fast*. Maya felt uneasy.

Evidently, Mery-ra had picked up on the brewing collision too. "Come, my lord," he said under his breath, plucking Ptah-mes by the sleeve. "We're clearly going to get no satisfaction here." He turned away.

Maya made as if to follow him, swallowing hard. *This Mahu fellow exudes violence. He'd love nothing better than to have us pounded into pulp.*

Ptah-mes lingered an instant, eyeing the dumpy police chief up and down. "I'll certainly make known to our lord king in my next private audience how insolent his servants have become."

Mahu's color drained a little, but he responded coolly, "You do that, Lord Ptah-mes."

They left in a dignified procession. Once out in the street, Maya blew a relieved breath. Lord Ptah-mes stood chewing his lip, his eyes narrowed, as he pulled his gloves back on.

Mopping his forehead beneath his wig, Mery-ra said, "Hani might be at Aha's. Why don't we check? You don't have to come with us unless you want to, my lord. You've already done more than mere friendship could demand."

"I'll come."

Maya suspected he wanted to know if Hani had been made to talk. They mounted the chariot again, and Maya hung onto the rail for dear life as they galloped through the scattered properties of the southern city, the grooms or guards or whatever they were running tirelessly at their sides. *The clatter of hooves, the rattle of harness, the thunder of wheels! Oh, what a story this will make!*

Hani was stretched out on the bed he'd formerly occupied at Aha's house, trying in vain to find a position that didn't

321

hurt. He supposed he'd have to turn the bed back over to Neferet that evening in any case. He could sleep with Pa-kiki perhaps.

He cursed himself for a fool. He'd disobeyed the cardinal rule of the diplomat and lost his temper. The veiled threats against Nub-nefer and the children had been too much. And now he'd made an enemy in a high place. Just what he needed—another enemy in a high place.

One might have thought that, with the minimal sleep Hani had enjoyed during his days on the boat, he would have fallen asleep easily. But his mind was spinning, and the ache of his cheek and his back—which seemed to have been badly scraped, as he found out under the water of a shower—made him restless. The children had all returned to their respective jobs after lunch, and in the absence of the mistress and her children, the house was unnaturally silent, not livened by the whisper of trees or the twitter of birds. This was a city of the dead, for sure.

His thoughts had finally begun to drift and float somewhere between waking and drowsing when a pounding on the door brought him once more to attention. He heard the bare footsteps of the doorman pad through the quiet house and the sound of the door being unbolted.

"Is Hani here?" his father cried.

"I'm here," he yelled back, unsure if he could be heard. With a teeth-gritting effort, he pulled himself up to a sitting position on the edge of the bed. Even as he struggled to his feet, he heard the steps of several men clattering through the salon, and the door flew open.

"Hani! Thank the Hidden One you're alive!" Mery-ra growled, throwing himself on his son.

Hani yelped. "Easy, Father. I'm black and blue from one end to the other. Maya!" he said over Mery-ra's shoulder. "Lord Ptah-mes! What...?"

"Your father told me the police had taken you," Ptah-mes said, grim. He clapped Hani a little shyly on the arms. "We came up as fast as we could."

"In fact," Maya added, his face red with excitement, "we beat their boat here. You should have seen our grand entrance into the police office!"

"What did they do to you, son? That scum Mahu just said you're a person of interest in Amen-em-hut's case."

Hani and Ptah-mes sat on the bed while Maya and Hani's father crossed their legs and settled on the floor at their feet. Hani proceeded to tell them all about the interrogations—day after day of the same questions—and how it had suddenly come to him that Amen-em-hut couldn't be guilty of posting calls to arms because he'd spoken to no one and had no writing implements.

Ptah-mes nodded in slow motion, his face drawn.

Mery-ra said caustically, "They just want a scapegoat. The king's probably after Mahu to produce a nose and a pair of ears."

"Don't let them be yours, Hani," said Ptah-mes in a grave voice. "I wonder if you wouldn't be safer somewhere in Kharu."

"I'm beginning to think so, my lord. But safety isn't everything." Hani was troubled to see how pale Ptah-mes's face grew all of a sudden and how fixed his features became. *I hope he doesn't think I'm accusing him of playing it safe.* "It was brave of you three to walk into the lion's den like that. I could have been lying, bloody, in a closet somewhere."

"Shall I leave you all here?" Ptah-mes asked, rising. "Or would you prefer to return to my house?"

"I came here because I thought it might be the more expected place," Hani said, bending painfully and heaving to his feet. "I didn't want to lead the police to you if I were followed—make them believe we were anything more than colleagues. What do you think, my lord?"

"You're probably right." Ptah-mes turned back to the others from the doorway. "Take some time off to recover, Hani. You can use my boat if you want it to go back to Waset. And I'll send for you if anything comes up." He forced a preoccupied smile and left. They heard his precise footsteps clicking through the salon.

The three men listened to him open and shut the door. The house fell silent again. "He's worried," said Hani.

"What's a man like that got to worry about?" Maya snorted. "You should have seen us, my lord. We drove up to the police barracks in a chariot! A chariot! With horses and everything!"

"They don't go very fast without horses, son," said Mery-ra drolly.

"And outrunners! And he had on driving gloves! I've never even seen gloves before."

"I think everyone should see gloves at least once before they're twenty-seven," said Hani, struggling against a laugh that he knew would hurt. But then he thought of Ptah-mes, and his laughter died. *He's worried that his wife is the one behind the death threats.*

CHAPTER 11

S OME TWO MONTHS LATER, ON a brisk morning in the midwinter second month of the season of Peret, Hani and his younger son and his father sat ensconced in the salon around a brazier. Maya had gone down to the farm to await Sat-hut-haru's lying-in. Hani himself was eager to be off to the country—not that he could be of any service to his daughter in this most feminine of endeavors, but he wanted to support her by his presence. Coincidentally, Aha's latest child was probably due to see the light of day at the same time. However, Hani and Mery-ra had awaited the arrival of Neferet and Pa-kiki before taking off for the south. At the moment, Neferet was still sleeping, and the three generations of men, providing for themselves in the absence of the mistress of the house, were enjoying toasting chunks of bread over the coals.

"Papa, would you be terribly disappointed if I tried for a post as a military scribe?" Pa-kiki said, his cheerful face earnest. He'd brought Neferet back for the trilogy of holidays in Waset that commemorated the parade of the goddesses to and from Mut's temple. Needless to say, there would be no celebrations, at least outwardly. But not even the Hall of Royal Correspondence had dared deprive its scribes of their days off.

"Why would I be disappointed, son? Your grandfather and I both served as military scribes."

"Oh, I don't know. Aha always says…" Pa-kiki lowered his eyes and trailed off, perhaps realizing that Aha was at odds with the other scribes in the family on this matter.

"What does he say?" Mery-ra demanded. "Out with it? That we're inferior?"

"Well, he says there are more opportunities for advancement working directly under the vizier, but frankly, Papa, it's as boring as can be."

Hani clapped his son on the shoulder. "Not the dream job you expected, eh, son? Well, there's nothing wrong with transferring to the army if there's a post open. It's often interesting, that's for sure. You'll travel. You may find yourself in dangerous situations."

Pa-kiki's little brown eyes were alight. "That sounds more like it! All I do now is copy court cases for the archives. I suppose it's important to somebody, but I'd rather be out there on the front lines!"

Hani smiled. "It's not *always* that interesting, though. You'll do your share of copying documents there too."

"And who said you can't advance? I think Aha's real problem is that an army scribe might have to get his hands dirty now and then. You might have to mobilize and live in a camp and get a suntan." Mery-ra grinned wickedly. "You might have to miss a few meals, and what you get are not always very good. Your brother likes his comforts."

Hani had to fight back a snort. Mery-ra had the boy figured out. But then he remembered Ptah-mes saying the vizier saw Pa-kiki's enrollment in the ranks of the chancery as a sign of the family's loyalty. How would he view his efforts to transfer? Nothing was simple anymore.

"How do I go about looking?" Pa-kiki asked.

"Let me sniff around. There's a big garrison in Akhet-aten, but the main headquarters of the army are still here in Waset and in Men-nefer." Mery-ra reached out and shook the boy's shoulder. "Let old Grandfather work his magic, eh, my lad?"

Before Pa-kiki could even express his gratitude, Neferet had appeared among them, rubbing her eyes. "Good morning, everybody. When are we going down to the farm?"

"As soon as you've eaten, my duckling. And washed your face."

The girl settled herself on the floor beside her father's stool. "Can I have some bread, please?"

He'd just passed her the basket with chunks torn from a dryish pot-shaped loaf when A'a called from the door, "My lord, the diplomatic pouch has arrived."

"Ah," Hani said, getting to his feet. "Let me look at these before we take off." He made his way to the vestibule, where the doorkeeper presented him with a leather sack of clay tablets and a single folded papyrus. He brought them back into the salon and reseated himself, drawing a tablet from the bag. "Let's see what's new with Aziru's children."

"You read his mail?" Neferet cried.

"Yes, my dear." He laid a warning finger to his lips. "King's orders." His eyes skittered over the impressed characters, and he said to Pa-kiki as he read, "You'll need to learn foreign languages if you want to travel." He laid down the tablet and selected the papyrus bundle. Then he noticed the seal. "*Yahya.* Something from the vizier. Well, I'd better not read this one." He thought that this might finally be the summons Aziru was waiting for. The gods knew Hani was eager to have his house back as well.

"I'll take these up to him and be right down. I suppose they're out of bed by now. It's halfway through the morning."

Hani trudged up the stairs, humming a shapeless little tune. He hadn't given much thought to the situation, as it was inevitable, but it had been uncomfortable to have strangers under his roof day and night for so many months. At the top of the steps, he called out, "Lord Aziru? I have your mail."

The landing was silent. Not a snore broke the quiet from any of the rooms. He went up to the roof and glanced around, but nobody was sleeping there—not at this time of year. He returned and knocked at the door where Aziru stayed. No one roused. Gingerly, he pushed it open. The room was empty, the bed made. *If he's not here, the others won't be either. Strange.*

The Amurrites weren't prisoners, he reminded himself. They were free to spend time in the city or even travel. But so far, with the exception of their hunting party, they had made it back every night, late though it sometimes was. Hani supposed he had a kind of responsibility to see that nothing happened to them, since they were royal guests even though they lodged with him.

His tune silenced, he stumped back downstairs and called the housekeeper. "When was the last time you saw Lord Aziru and his men?"

The woman looked anxious, wringing the towel. "I made the beds yesterday morning, my lord. They hadn't been used this morning, so I didn't do anything up there. Is something wrong?"

"Did they say anything about traveling?" *Maybe they found themselves some girls at the beer house*, he thought. *They've apparently only been gone a night.*

The woman shook her head. "Not to me, my lord. Maybe to A'a."

"Trouble, son?" asked Mery-ra from across the room.

"I doubt it. Aziru's not here, and usually, he lets someone know when they'll be gone. But it's no cause for worry." He grinned. "I only hope they're not hunting more ostriches, although those plumes were worth something." What he really hoped was that they hadn't fallen afoul of some of the violent malcontents who prowled the city by night. Aziru himself was the only one among them who seemed to speak much Egyptian.

"I'm ready now, Papa. Can we go?" Neferet was bouncing around with her accustomed impatience.

"Why don't you all go? I'll come down when I've found Aziru."

"Do you need a hand, Hani?" his father asked.

Pa-kiki chimed in, "I'll stay too. We can cover more territory."

Hani shot Mery-ra a look of mock surprise. "Father, you don't want to be there when Sat-hut-haru presents you with a grandson?"

"It won't be *my* face she's searching for while she's screaming in pain," Mery-ra said matter-of-factly.

Pa-kiki looked appalled. "Screaming in pain?"

329

Hani reminded him, "Childbirth is grim, son. Show your mother a little appreciation. 'She had a heavy load in you, but she did not abandon you.'"

Pa-kiki licked his lips, his eyes wide.

"Of course," his grandfather said, "you'll see some screaming in pain in the army too."

But Hani said firmly, "I want one of you to go with Neferet. Choose between you who that will be." He made for the door.

"Pa-kiki will go with his sister," Mery-ra decided unilaterally. "I'll come with you."

They split up then, Hani and Mery-ra making for the gate while the children gathered their baggage and prepared to find a ferry.

"Where are we heading?" Mery-ra asked once the two men were standing in the street.

"I thought the beer house might be a place to start." Hani stared around the empty lane. It was chilly still, and he wished he'd thought to bring a cloak.

"It's a little early in the morning, don't you think?" Mery-ra said.

"Not if they spent the night there. The place has rooms, I'm told."

They set off past the empty villas and crumbling mud-brick walls with their peeling whitewash. Every time Hani witnessed the ruin into which his beautiful City of the Scepter was falling, the sight was a spearpoint of pain through the heart. He saw his father shaking his head and suspected he was having a similar reaction.

"You know," Mery-ra said as they walked. "I'm going to sell your cattle and convert them into grain or bronze.

It will be easier to take up to Pipi now that the weather is cooler."

"Good idea," Hani replied, preoccupied.

After a while, Mery-ra asked, "Why aren't we taking the litter?"

"Because I want to look around. Our friends could be anywhere."

The nearest beer house was fairly reputable, a chosen gathering place for visiting merchants or even royal functionaries en route from one town to another. From the outside, Hani couldn't even tell if it were open at this matutinal hour. The gate to the courtyard was closed, but then he saw that only a reed mat hung in front of the door. The two men pushed in, blinded for a moment by the sudden lack of light. Nothing but the high barred windows and the rear door into the open kitchen court illuminated the room, which was heavy with smoke from the kitchen fires and the lingering fug of sweat and spilled beer.

Hani cast his eyes around. He saw only a few people seated at the little low tables, eating—an older man, sitting by himself, and a pair of tall foreigners in short dark woolen tunics and ankle boots, their hairy legs stretched out before them. One of them was clean-shaven, and the other had a collar of beard around his jaw. Their hair was cut at shoulder length. Hani nudged his father to a corner seat, not so close the foreigners would notice but close enough to hear them.

There's something familiar about those clothes. He chose a stool facing the room so that he could see the staircase up to the bedchambers and also the front door. The darkness of the corner would make them inconspicuous.

"Order beer and some bread," he said to Mery-ra under his breath. He strained his ears toward the two men, who were speaking softly one to the other. He was unable to see them well, but they were strapping, rough-faced fellows. *Soldiers, or I miss my mark.* Hani couldn't tell if they were carrying arms. There was no reason to think they had anything to do with Aziru, but they'd piqued his curiosity. One raised his voice in a growl of laughter, and Hani heard his words. *Mitannians. I was right.*

"I don't see your Amurrites," murmured Mery-ra.

"No, but those men of Naharin interest me. Kiya said two Mitannian mercenaries approached her with the blackmail threat."

A potbellied little man brought them their beer and set its stand between them.

"You drink first," Mery-ra said, "or we'll crack heads lunging for the straws."

"No, go ahead, Father. I want to listen to these two fellows." He found himself speaking in a near whisper.

A flicker of movement in the stairwell drew his eye, and Aziru descended, knotting his belt, his brother and secretary behind him. *Well, that was incredible luck*, Hani thought. *The first place we looked.* Instead of hailing them, though, he kept his head averted. From the corner of his eye, he watched them make their way across the room and draw up stools with a screech around the little table where the Mitannians sat.

"There are your friends," Mery-ra pointed out—he, too, adopting a barely audible tone.

"I saw. Keep your face down and act casual. They haven't spotted us."

Aziru had his back to Hani, who couldn't easily make out his words but detected the intonation of Amurrite. The bearded Mitannian replied in the same language. "What shall we tell him, my lord?"

Aziru said something else, and the men nodded.

"He'll want it in writing, I expect," said the Mitannian.

Aziru laughed sarcastically, a sound Hani knew only too well. The Amurrite said audibly, "Not likely. We'll do all that when I finally get back. I'm not sticking around here much longer, I'll tell you. Once I'm gone, let the king do his worst."

"Pretty insulting, isn't it?" the clean-shaven Mitannian snorted. "My lord is making a good choice."

They fell silent. Hani lowered his face over his bread, his thoughts darkening. *What have I just heard?*

After a while, during which time Hani assumed the Amurrites were eating and drinking, he heard a clink of metal thrown down on the table, and Aziru and his followers made their way, without a word, to the staircase and disappeared from sight. The bearded Mitannian scraped the pieces of silver off into a bag and rose from the table. Followed by his fellow, he strode toward the curtained front door and departed, with never a glance at the two Egyptians bent over their breakfast. Hani gave them a bit more time, then he laid a little something on the table for their meal and beckoned his father to the exit.

"What was that all about?" Mery-ra said once they were out in the sunlight of the street.

"Some kind of transaction. Aziru seems on the point of leaving Kemet, audience or no. He said the king could

333

do his worst afterward. He doesn't seem afraid of the consequences."

Mery-ra shot his son a sharp glance. "Is he going over to the Hittites, do you think?"

"It could be interpreted that way. I'd probably better let Lord Ptah-mes know." Hani stared down the street as if he could see the foreigners retreating. "I'm just as interested in those Mitannians. If they're Kiya's mercenaries, they may be serving as intermediaries. Naharin is our ally, supposedly. No one would suspect them of working for the Hittites."

"If they're the same people as Kiya's blackmailers, weren't they working for the queen? Surely she's not in the pay of Kheta!"

Hani shrugged. "Mercenaries work for whoever pays them. They have no other loyalties." But admittedly, things seemed suddenly more complicated. "I need to talk to Keliya, if he's still in the Two Lands. He probably knows all of his countrymen around here."

They strode along the half-deserted streets, where beggars lounged in the shadows. *He stays with Mane when he's here. The last man I want to see. Maybe Mane'll be in Wasshukanni.*

Mane's substantial Theban house wasn't far from Hani's own. Since he was almost always missioned to the Mitannian capital, he hadn't bothered to build in Akhet-aten either.

Hani and his father approached the gate identified on the lintel as Mane's and knocked. The porter let them in and disappeared toward the house to notify his master. A moment later, Mane bloomed in the doorway, round and beaming, his arms extended. "My friend! What brings you here—and voluntarily, eh?" he burbled happily, giving

Hani a knowing wink. "Ah, your father, right? Come in, gentlemen, come in." He beckoned them up the path and into his vestibule. It was a richly appointed place. Mane was well recompensed not only by their own king but also by Tushratta, at whose court he'd served for years. Mane seemed sometimes more Mitannian in his loyalties than Egyptian, but in recent years, Hani could understand that only too well.

"I'm actually here to talk to Keliya, if he hasn't left yet," Hani said. "I wasn't sure how much of your business about seeing him off was true and how much was for the *medjay* trailing me."

Mane laughed. "He's here, he's here. Although, in fact, he will be leaving soon." He called to a servant, "Go fetch Lord Keliya." Mane bade Hani and Mery-ra take seats in his lofty salon. A middle-aged woman as round as her husband was sitting there. "Do you mind, my dear? Business." She rose, smiling, and made her way elsewhere.

"I've never met your wife," said Hani.

"You never come to see me," Mane scolded him merrily. His eyes sharpened, and he lowered his voice. "Any movement on our little project?"

"I need to bring you up-to-date. We may well have the solution in hand."

Mane's eyes widened. "Well done, my friend. I had confidence in you."

"You can trust my son to get things done," said Mery-ra proudly.

Hani heard footsteps on the stairs, and Keliya appeared, his long face garlanded with a smile. "Hani! I hope this means good news!"

The two men embraced, and Hani introduced Keliya to Mery-ra. The Mitannian emissary was nearly ten years Hani's junior but looked older—a long, thin, stooped fellow with droopy eyebrows and a retreating hairline, who had the air of having scarcely raised his nose from the scribal table in his life.

"I think the news is good. My father is aware. Do you mind if he hears us?"

"Not at all," Keliya said.

Hani proceeded to describe his idea to promote the queen and the way she and Ay had received the plan upon the recommendation of her physician. The two men hung on his words, nodding, *hmm*ing, and raising an occasional eyebrow.

"Did she seem to like it? Was she willing to relent in her campaign against Kiya?" Mane asked eagerly.

"I think she was interested. Whether she'll relent, I couldn't say. But I painted the direst of pictures if anything should happen to Tushratta's daughter."

"Let's hope she doesn't realize how straitened things are for him at the moment," Keliya said with a sigh. "But it sounds optimistic, doesn't it?"

"I think so," Hani said. "Actually, Keliya, I had something else I wanted to ask you about. Do you know the two Mitannians who brought our girl's blackmail message?"

"I think I know who they are, yes. They were, as they told her, veterans of her father's army turned sell swords. At some point in the past, they were bodyguards for that Abdi-ashirta, leader of the *hapiru*."

"So it was the same two men? I may have seen them this morning." Hani found this identity troubling, although that could explain why Aziru had dealings with them. "Do you know if they're still working for the queen?"

"Hani, I *never* knew they were working for the queen," said Keliya with a twisted smile, "or I could have saved you a lot of investigation."

What if they weren't *working for the queen?* Hani thought suddenly. *What if she sent the first message with Kha-em-sekhem, but someone else sent the second one through the mercenaries? What if someone else tried to have me killed? Then again, why complicate the affair unnecessarily?* It was unlikely two people had wanted to ruin the hapless Mitannian princess... unless someone wanted to see the alliance with her father broken wide open. A chill ran up Hani's back.

"Say, old friend, what happened to your face?" Mane asked.

"The *medjay* shared a little hospitality with me." Hani grinned ruefully. His cheek had only recently reached the point that grinning wasn't a source of excruciating pain.

Keliya looked anxious. "They aren't after you about our girl, are they?"

"Oh, no," said Mery-ra. "That's only one of the many nefarious deeds my son is up to."

"They wanted to know the whereabouts of my brother-in-law," Hani explained.

"Ah, yes." Mane nodded. "I remember. Never found him, have they?"

Hani shook his head. "And that's why I was so reluctant to get involved with you two. I never knew when I was being followed." Somewhere inside him, an idea was creating pressure, wanting to emerge. He changed subjects abruptly.

"Keliya, is there any way to trace the movements of those mercenaries—see where they've been over the last year or two?"

"Not unless they're registered diplomats or merchants, and that seems unlikely."

Gloom had gathered over Hani like his own personal storm cloud. He'd thought he had everything figured out, but maybe Kiya wasn't out of danger after all. Maybe *he* wasn't out of danger.

Hani and his father took their affectionate leave, and Hani promised to come again before Keliya departed for his homeland. Once out in the street, Hani said, "I think I need to report to Lord Ptah-mes what we overheard in the beer house. You don't have to come unless you want to."

"If he's in Waset, I'll come."

"We'll start here. I'm not sure whether he's back for the holidays or not."

They turned toward the riverfront and continued south. The day was warming up pleasantly. A skylark spiraled overhead, pouring out its contagiously joyful song.

"You don't often see those fellows over the city," observed Hani, his face upturned to receive the notes. "There must be a lot of overgrown patches now to attract them."

The doorkeeper informed the two men that Lord Ptah-mes was indeed home, and before long, the high commissioner came out to join them on the portico. "Do you mind talking outside? We can sit by the pool in the sun. I don't think it will be too cold."

Hani and his father followed their host through the garden to a large pool surrounded by palms. At nearly midday, the winter sun had claimed much of the area. Ptah-mes led them to a pair of stone benches, where he took a seat on one, Hani and Mery-ra settling upon the other.

"My lord, I went to the beer house in our neighborhood this morning"—he saw a slight smile draw out the corner of Ptah-mes's mouth and added quickly—"looking for Aziru, who didn't come home last night. He was indeed there. We ordered a beer and stayed inconspicuous while Aziru sat down at table with a pair of Mitannians, whom I believe to be mercenaries. Maybe the same ones who were Abdi-ashirta's bodyguards several years ago."

"The ones Yanakh-amu paid to turn on him?"

"I don't think these men did. But their Egyptian fellows, who had been part of Yanakh-amu's troops, were, in fact, the ones who assassinated Abdi-ashirta."

Ptah-mes nodded thoughtfully. "You believe these men have remained in the pay of Abdi-ashirta's son, do you?"

"I don't know. They seemed to be bringing him a message from... from someone else." Hani proceeded to repeat to his superior what he'd heard the men saying in Amurrite.

Ptah-mes's face grew increasingly serious as he listened.

"The irony is, a summons from the king probably arrived this morning, just as Aziru is about to give up. As soon as he gets back, I'll present it to him," Hani finished. "And then he can legitimately be on his way."

"And what will his next action be, I wonder?" Ptah-mes's mouth turned down bitterly. "Is he preparing to jump the fence? I wouldn't be surprised if your mercenaries brought him word from the king of the Hittites."

"That was my own feeling, Lord Ptah-mes," Hani said, "although I heard no mention of them in that conversation."

"Of course, it was almost impossible to hear anything," Mery-ra added.

"And if that's so," Hani said, "this adds a new wrinkle to the matter of the Beloved Royal Wife."

"I thought you had determined the queen was behind that," said Ptah-mes, looking up sharply.

"She was certainly behind the note Kha-em-sekhem was paid to leave. But was the second message the same person's work or another's? It seems the same two mercenaries may have presented themselves to Kiya with a demand for action on behalf of Naharin. Whether Kiya honored it or not, she would be ruined, and with her fall would come the inevitable rupture of the Mitannian treaty. Nobody would profit but the queen... or Kheta Land. Were our sell swords already in the pay of the Hittites?"

Mery-ra let out a groan.

"This Shuppiluliuma of theirs is smart, if he's behind it." Ptah-mes chewed his lip in thought.

Hani nodded in reluctant admiration. "And well informed. He must have someone in the palace keeping him abreast of the Beloved Wife's peccadilloes."

"Hittites are forbidden in the Two Kingdoms at the moment, but if people saw a Mitannian, he'd be the last person they'd suspect of agitating for the enemy of his homeland," Ptah-mes murmured pensively.

The men sat in silence, digesting the ramifications of this idea.

"Find out who is paying these Mitannians and what Aziru is planning," said Lord Ptah-mes finally.

Hani grimaced. "That's not going to be easy, my lord."

340

Ptah-mes gave him a strange twisted smile. "Nothing ever is."

⁂

Aziru and his men returned to Hani's house shortly after lunch while Hani and his father were still sitting at table in the salon.

"Ah, Lord Aziru," Hani called. "The diplomatic pouch came in this morning." He picked up the bag from the floor at his side and held it out to the Amurrite, forcing himself not to mention the letter from the vizier.

Aziru snagged the sack with a polite tip of the head. He pawed around the contents then drew out the letter and passed it to his secretary. In a mumbling undertone, the fellow read it to his master in the Egyptian in which it was written. From the corner of his eye, Hani saw the Amurrite's face light up, then Aziru threw back his head and hollered with a laugh of relief—or maybe irony.

"Finally! Well, Hani, you won't be sorry to know the king will receive me at last. I can get out of your hair. How long has it been? Nine months?"

"You could have had a baby to show for all that waiting," Mery-ra said amiably.

Aziru chuckled, the happiest Hani had seen him for nearly that long. In Amurrite, he explained to his brother what the letter contained, and they both crowed in appreciation. Together, still smiling from ear to ear, the three men trooped up the stairs.

Mery-ra said under his breath, "Now he can go home and switch allegiance to Kheta."

Hani shushed him with a glance up the staircase. *I*

wonder how much truth I'd get from the king of A'amu if I asked him point-blank whether he intended to remain faithful to Kemet. Hani pondered whether he needed to remain accessible to the Amurrite contingent until they got back from the capital and made their final departure.

"I got a letter from Pipi," his father said after a while. "He's coming down with the horse, then he'll accompany me back to Men-nefer with the grain barges. Your guest bedrooms won't go empty for long."

"Were you ever going to tell me this?" Hani shot him an accusing look. "What if Aziru hadn't left?"

"I'm telling you now. I just got the letter. And the girls are all at the farm anyway. He said Mut-nodjmet really wanted to see Sat-hut-haru's baby."

"When are they coming?"

"He didn't mention, but I assumed not long after the letter left his hands."

As if on cue, there were voices in the vestibule.

Mut mother of us all, Hani thought. *Say that isn't Pipi!*

But it was Maya. The secretary's loud, excited voice shouted, "It's a boy! It's a boy! Lord Hani! I have a son!"

Hani and Mery-ra rushed into the vestibule to find Maya dancing up and down, with A'a chortling and waving his hands as if it were his own son who had been announced. Hani threw himself on Maya and picked him right up in a joyous hug, which Mery-ra joined from the outside.

Realizing belatedly that his action might have been offensive, Hani set Maya back down, his face burning but wearing an inextinguishable grin. "And the mother's doing well, I hope?"

"Perfectly well, my lord, and enjoying her perfect,

beautiful son! Lady Nub-nefer and Neferet have built her bower, so I pretty much had to leave anyway. I won't get to see them again for fifteen days."

"We missed her," Hani said reluctantly to Mery-ra. "We'll have to wait till she's out of seclusion now."

"I vote for a celebration with the happy father," Mery-ra said.

"And grandfather and great-grandfather," Maya added magnanimously. He was beaming from ear to ear, still posturing back and forth as if he were dancing inside.

Mery-ra charged to the kitchen, where Hani heard him ordering the servant girls, "A jar of that wine from Kharu!"

"Does your mother know yet?" Hani asked.

"No, but I'm going there next. It's her first grandchild, of course."

"It's a great day, my friend." Hani had to admit that he'd been so overwhelmed by everything that was happening that he'd barely stopped to worry about Sat-hut-haru's lying-in. She was young and healthy, but still, safe childbirth was never a given. *Thank you, Bes. Thank you, Great One. Let them continue in good health.*

Mery-ra came toddling back in managing three cups of wine, two of which he extended, splashing, to the others. "To the mother and her son. And the father," he offered, and the three men drank. "Are you still going to name him Amen-hotep?"

"I am," Maya said with big smile of pride and something close to defiance sparking in his eyes. "Let them try to stop me."

"I suppose Nub-nefer is having all the proper sacrifices of thanksgiving made," Hani said, but then he realized the temple of Mut was no longer open. He turned to his father, confused. "What does one do now?"

"I've seen offerings at the gate of the Ipet-isut. I think people are continuing to honor the gods even without a liturgy happening." Mery-ra shrugged. "Maybe the Hidden One and his family will realize we haven't rejected them, even if... *some* people have."

"Who could we ask?" Maya said. "One of the Prophets?"

"Not the Third one," Mery-ra cautioned. "I don't want to see Amen-em-hut until everything has cleared up."

"I think we need to stay away from all of them," Hani said uneasily, thinking of the *medjay* lurking on his traces. We'll leave gifts at the gate like everyone else."

"Well," Maya said, once he had finished his wine with a slurp. "I'm off to tell Mother the news. I'll be back." He handed the cup to Mery-ra and hitched up his kilt.

They bade the new father a jovial goodbye, and he swaggered out through the garden.

"Ammit take it," said Hani, mostly to himself. "I want to go down to the farm and be with everyone. But I have to wait here until Aziru has departed."

"And until Pipi has arrived, which could be any day," Mery-ra added.

"Let me at least write a note to Nub-nefer and Sat-hut-haru. Maya can take it back with him and read it to them—from safely outside the bower, of course."

⁂

Later that afternoon, Maya burst once more into Lord Hani's salon, his mood thunderous.

"What's wrong?" Hani cried, seemingly unnerved.

His bitterness an icy knot in his stomach, Maya cried, "My mother is moving to Akhet-aten. She's selling the workshop—the house where I grew up."

"I suppose it's only good business," Hani said reasonably. "Akhet-aten's where her work is now."

Maya glared at the floor. *This is unpardonable.*

"Why don't you buy it and you and Sat-hut-haru and the little one move there? It must be bigger than where you are now. You could convert the workshop and put a garden in the courtyard—"

"It's the idea of it," Maya broke in, aggrieved. "That's where all my memories are. She's... she's throwing it away, as if it meant nothing to her."

"People don't always have the luxury of living where they want, Maya. Look at the big exodus of bureaucrats when the capital moved—all these empty houses around us. Those people can't have been happy to pick up roots like that—you know how Thebans are. But they couldn't lose their jobs."

Maya pounced. "But you didn't move, Lord Hani. It took a choice, an act of the will. It wasn't all about gold."

Hani, evidently seeing he couldn't win, shrugged helplessly. "Maybe the king won't continue to patronize her if she's too hard to get to."

"Then let her rent it out but not get rid of it. The little one won't ever know his father's house. He won't share any memories with me." Maya's face was hot as a brazier, and he felt it wouldn't take much to squeeze tears out of his eyes. Somehow, the excruciating timing of this betrayal had walloped him hard. His mother was cutting his past out from under him just as he prepared to hand it along to the

345

N. L. HOLMES

future. He'd hardly slept all night after she'd hit him with the news, and he was barely in control of himself.

"Why don't you buy it?" Hani asked again.

"She's never going to find a buyer." Maya continued to rage, stalking around, bristling with furious energy. "The whole city is emptied out, full of properties nobody wants. Why does she have to leave now, of all times? The little one will never get to see his grandmother. Doesn't she even care?"

Hani reached out and took Maya by the shoulders, stopping him in his tracks. "Why don't *you* buy it?" he said for the third time. "Say what you will about her intentions; this would save the house and its memories. If you need help, we can do something for you."

Maya melted. He knew that Lord Hani had already stripped his country property of cattle and grain to pay his brother's debts. He bit his lip, contrite. "I couldn't ask that, my lord. Maybe I can put together enough, pay her a little at a time."

"I think that would be a wonderful, responsible thing to do." Hani was smiling his warmest gap-toothed grin. "You can make that a comfortable house. With the workshop, it will be really substantial. The wall around the property is in great shape. And there are two courts, if I remember correctly. You can have a beautiful garden and a service court. For your chariot!"

Maya froze, not quite knowing if he was being mocked. But Hani's laugh was working its way up from his belly, and Maya burst into laughter himself. The two of them howled happily.

"All right," said Maya at last, his anger dispersed, all business now. "I'll talk to Mother."

He started to go but turned back at the door, a niggling anxiety rising. "What if Sat-hut-haru doesn't like the idea?"

"Didn't you say she loved the house?"

That was true. "I'm off," Maya resolved.

He'd gotten no farther than the door when A'a came rushing in, excusing himself as he brushed past. Maya turned after him, miffed and prepared to snap at him, but he heard the porter cry to Hani in the salon, "My lord, your brother is here with two horses. What shall I do with them?"

Maya's eyes popped open wide. *Two horses?* Had the irresponsible Lord Pipi bought two horses instead of the one his brother was sacrificing to pay off?

Hani went rushing out with A'a in his wake, and Maya peeled off after them. There at the gate stood Pipi and his daughter, holding the two horses awkwardly by their halters. Maya didn't know which to look at first—Mut-nodjmet or the animals. The girl, whom he remembered from only a few months before as heavy and unattractive, had lost weight, and now her extraordinary bosom was set on a worthy pedestal. Her small waist gave purpose to the swell of her, her neck looked longer, her face wasn't so shapeless, and her features not so overwhelmed by fat cheeks. He could hardly absorb the transformation and had to close his mouth by an act of the will.

Then there were the horses. *Beasts of grandeur!* He kept his distance—they were enormous, with their big barrels and hard feet. *But the elegance of those heads! The eyes like ripe olives! Their russet coats with silky black legs!* Suddenly, he could understand Pipi's folly.

Pipi held out his arms to Hani as if to forestall any comment, and the two brothers embraced. Hani took the girl in a fatherly hug—Maya tried not to imagine too hard what that must be like—and cried, "Pipi! Mut-nodjmet! By the Lady of Beauty, girl—she's transfigured you! What... what happened?"

"Grief, Uncle," she said shyly. But her smile had found a sparkle of self-confidence, almost coquettishness, that had never set it alight before. She felt beautiful... and she had become beautiful.

Perhaps if I felt tall... Maya thought wryly.

"Pipi, what are these?" Lord Hani asked a little less enthusiastically. He extended a hand and petted the nose of one of the horses.

"They're horses, brother."

"In the plural." Hani's voice was carefully neutral.

"I was afraid to tell you. It seemed so stupid to have bought one—what would you and Father think if you knew I had two of them? But by the seven-headed demons, Hani, one horse can't pull a chariot." Pipi held out his hands in a helpless gesture of reason.

Hani pursed his lips and peeked under the two animals' bellies. "They're mares, Pipi. Mares don't pull chariots."

Pipi looked dumbstruck. He exchanged a stare with Mut-nodjmet. "What do they do, then?"

"They have foals," said Hani.

Pipi seemed to deflate. Still, he said gamely, "But that's good, isn't it?"

"I don't know, Pipi. Horse breeding is a royal monopoly."

"You mean it's illegal to own a mare?" Pipi's eyes widened in horror.

"No, no. Well, I don't know. Lots of things are illegal these days that I never would have believed."

One of the horses lifted her tail and deposited a big gob of manure in the path. Maya suppressed a snicker that threatened to overwhelm him.

Hani, maintaining his aplomb with remarkable success, asked, "So, do we in fact owe twice what you named?"

"No, no. That was for both of them. It wasn't a bad price for two, was it?"

"I'm not sure Father's friend will be interested in two mares," Hani said with a sigh.

Pipi brightened. "What about that rich friend of yours—the one with the yacht?"

"No, Pipi. We can't ask him. He's done too much for us already." Hani turned to the doorkeeper, who stood marveling on the path well up toward the house, and bellowed, "A'a, call Lord Mery-ra."

A'a disappeared into the doorway. Maya's efforts to control his laughter had become painful. A ripping snort finally escaped him. He closed his eyes and shook his head, but hilarity was a rising tide inside him that had reached Flood stage. He managed to get out, "I'd better go, my lord," and lurched for the gate. Once outside, he started to laugh so hard he nearly fell down in the street.

※

Pipi and Mut-nodjmet went up to the farm with Maya the next day while Mery-ra set off in Hani's litter to ask his colleague whether he wanted two mares. Aziru and his men had taken the ferry for Akhet-aten. Thus, Hani alone remained in Waset, trying feverishly to think of a way to identify the master of the two Mitannian mercenaries. He wondered if they were actually staying at the beer house or if they had simply come to meet Aziru. It occurred to him that the best way to find out was to ask.

Winter had given them a fine crisp morning and a flaming eastern sky, and Hani wondered what the bloody glow presaged. Through the quiet streets he strode, with a cloak knotted around his shoulders, taking pleasure in the solitude and the satisfying effort of walking. A few merchants had started to set up their stalls in the marketplace, but it was still a holiday, and a holiday without celebration. Most people would be sleeping late, he supposed. He saw beggars at the edge of the open space who had never been there before. *Probably most of them were hard-working employees of the temples or their properties just a few years ago.* His ebullient mood began to dim.

Hani found the beer house open. Led by a group of dark-skinned men from the south, a caravan of pack donkeys was emerging from the wicket gate, eager to be off before the day grew older. Hani saluted with a friendly hand as he threaded through them and made his way into the common room. Warmth immediately surrounded him, although no braziers were lit. He shrugged out of his cloak and seated himself at the same corner location that he and his father had occupied before. No one else seemed to be around, and in fact, he had to knock on the table to attract the attention of the potbellied servant who emerged sleepily from the kitchen.

Hani said quietly, "A jar of beer, my friend. And"—he

laid a copper bangle on the tabletop and pushed it toward the man—"some information."

His eyes round and all at once wide-awake, the servant reached out a hand and snatched up the bracelet. "How can I help you, my lord?"

"I'm looking for two Mitannian men. Soldierly types, tall. One of them bearded, the other not. Hair down to their shoulders. They're wearing short tunics and boots. Does that say anything to you?"

The man looked around him furtively. "I'm not supposed to talk about our guests, my lord, but... yes. That says something I understand."

"Are they still here?"

More and more uneasy, the servant nodded. He was on the upper edge of middle age, slack looking rather than fat, his shaved gray-stubbled head bare. No doubt, he was weighing how much it was worth to lose his post at such a point in his life.

"I'm in the king's foreign service," Hani said reassuringly. "Sit down. You needn't be afraid. The government wants to keep track of foreigners in the country, that's all."

Somewhat appeased, the servant edged himself onto a stool. "They're here, my lord. They could come down any minute."

"Excellent." Hani smiled, although he had no idea what he would do if the men entered and saw him there. Assuredly, they would recognize him if they had been the ones who'd shot at him in the Mountains of the West.

"Have they met with anyone here, do you know?"

Casting his eyes at the staircase, the servant nodded nervously. "Three other foreigners with beards. They've

351

met several times. The other people stayed the night here recently."

Hani nodded. "I'm aware of that. Anyone else?"

"I don't know, my lord. I'm not always on duty in the common room."

"How long have the two men been here?"

"They come and go. This last time... maybe six months. Since well before the Flood. But then they left for a while, even though they continued to hold their rooms. Now they're back."

Hani wondered why the men were holed up in Waset rather than the capital if their business had been with the queen. Increasingly, he was convinced it had not been. Aziru was in Waset. But surely, he had nothing to do with the plot to ruin Kiya. "Anything else of interest?" he asked.

The man seemed distinctly twitchy at this point. He shook his head. "Nothing, my lord."

Hani rose and said quietly, with his friendliest smile, "If you think of anything, I'll be in from time to time. Pass me word, all right?"

With a bobbing of the head, the servant assured him he would.

"Forget the beer. We'll talk later." Hani cast an uneasy glance at the stairs. Thinking he heard footsteps on the treads, he made his way quickly to the exit.

In the street once more, he narrowed his eyes, threw his cloak over one shoulder, and glanced all around him. He hadn't learned much he didn't already know, except that the Mitannians had been in Kemet for a long time, coming and going. They might well have made a trip to Kheta and back.

But what are they really involved in—some defection of Aziru? The plot against Kiya? Both? And were they the ones who shot at me? If so, why—and why only once? Perhaps it was a warning and not an attempt on my life. I'd just spoken to Kha-em-sekhem and Kiya. Somehow, that provoked the attack. They must have been afraid I was getting close to something.

His mind wrapped in these thoughts, Hani drifted through the back streets, between crumbling blocks of empty houses and small workshops with gates hanging and courtyards silent. There were beggars here, too—more than he'd ever seen—sullen looking and importunate. He thought of In-hapy, forced to sell her ancestral home and move to the soulless City of the Horizon. Little by little, his outrage mounted in a tide of cold bile. It occurred to him that Amen-em-hut might have the right idea. Surely, a ruler who could do this to his own people had forfeited the benevolence of the gods.

The world suddenly tilted as a weight hit Hani's back. One of the beggars had leaped on him and locked his arms across his throat. Hani staggered, choked by the man's mass. Another beggar rose up out of the shadows of an alley, his grimy rags camouflaged against the grimy wall. The second man ran at Hani from the front, a stout stave raised in his hands.

Hani gasped in terror. *Where did they come from? I didn't even see them, I was so engrossed in my reflections.*

A thought flashed through his mind in a panic: *If he hits me in the head with that, I'm dead.* He tried desperately to cry out, but the man behind him was cutting off his air. Nothing emerged but an inhuman noise of fear. Hani summoned a burst of strength. Folding in half, he dragged

353

the man over his back like a cloak. The oncoming attacker dared not strike for fear of hitting his companion. Once the pressure from his throat was relieved, Hani threw the man over his head. He fell on top of the fellow, who let go in an effort to protect himself from the ground. Now the other beggar was upon him, snarling with effort. The staff whistled through the air as he slashed back and forth. Hani dodged by rolling to the side. He scrambled to his feet and threw his cloak at the man on the ground, entangling him.

Hani backed out of range with the agility of the desperate. He was panting, his heart hammering. He and the man with the staff circled one another watchfully, but Hani was aware that the companion might attack him from behind. Two against one were bad odds. Realizing this might be his last moment, he yelled, "Help! Watchman!"

Beside him, he was conscious of a streak of olive brown, and out of nowhere, a furry body the size of a large dog with a thin tail hurled itself silently upon the man with the stave, latching onto his leg with all four agile paws. The fellow began to scream as the animal sank its fangs into his calf. The man on the ground scrambled to his feet and took off running with the baboon at his heels. Hani could hear his shrieks—whether of fear or pain, he couldn't say. The wounded man collapsed to the ground with a moan, hugging his shin, and Hani, his chest heaving, turned to look at his savior.

It was the young policeman from the boat, the one who'd kept the baboon on a leash. He came jogging up, the leash over his shoulder, a bronze rod in his hand, and knocked the wounded attacker sprawling. He bound his wrists and ankles then he gave him a few more blows for good measure. Hani grinned at him, panting, as he picked up his wig. "I never thought I'd be glad to see you people again!"

The policeman chuckled. "Thank Cub. He knew you were in trouble and made me hurry after you. He'll immobilize the other fellow." He started off after his animal to arrest the second attacker.

Hani called after him, "You were following me?"

The young man nodded, smiling. "Aren't you glad?"

CHAPTER 12

A T LEAST HIS ATTACKERS HAD not been the two Mitannians—if they'd been trained killers, Hani would have been dead. But the men were cleaner and better fed than the beggars they were posing as. *Some unemployed workmen, eager for any chance to earn a loaf of bread,* Hani thought, not altogether unsympathetically. Cub had put them in a bad way with his massive fangs more than half as long as a man's finger. The fellows would think twice about a life of crime.

While the policeman chased down the second man, Hani squatted at the side of the first one, who rocked and moaned in anguish. He wasn't young. "Did someone pay you to attack me in particular, or were you just looking to rob anyone who passed?"

"You're the one who just left the beer house? It was us we was supposed to put out of action."

"To kill me?"

"Just to rough you up. To scare you." The man's face was screwed up in pain.

A likely story. That staff was a serious weapon. "Who paid you?" he asked in a gentler voice.

The man's eyes flicked to the side, where Hani saw the policeman and Cub approaching with the second man, hands tied and feet trammeled. He was limping badly, and blood ran down his calf. "Some man. A foreigner."

Hani knew he didn't have much time. "Where was he from, do you know?"

"I don't know. He spoke good Egyptian."

Ammit devour him. Hani had only a few more minutes before the policeman arrived and took his interlocutor from him. "Did he have a beard? A mustache or not? Clean-shaven? Quick—what did he look like? Young or old?"

"Light skin. Beard with mustache. Youngish. Good-looking. Not real tall."

Cub walked up to Hani with dignified steps and sat in front of him, fixing him with his close-set, melancholy eyes, his hands hanging over his knees. Hani, suspecting he'd gotten all he was going to get from his attacker, greeted the animal gravely. "Thank you, son of Djehuty. You're a worthy addition to the forces of order."

The young policeman laughed. "He likes you, all right. I've got to take these characters in to the station now. You want to come and accuse them formally?"

"No," said Hani, surprising even himself. "They're not hardened criminals, and Cub has already punished them. No need to cut off their noses or ears too. Would your fellow officer object if I touched him? My daughter wants to know what his fur feels like."

"Just move slow and talk to him, like you did. Here. I'll put his collar back on."

Once the animal had been secured, Hani reached out gently and stroked the frizzy, unexpectedly coarse fur of the baboon's mane. Cub, in turn, extended a hand and laid it on Hani's shoulder. They looked into each other's eyes in a moment of understanding that almost brought Hani to tears; he felt so honored.

He got to his feet slowly. "How much longer are you going to be following me around?" he asked with a friendly smile.

The policeman shrugged. "Until I'm ordered to stop, my lord. But unless you show signs of being up to something interesting, probably not much longer."

Hani drew off one of his faience rings and passed it discreetly to the officer. "Buy some treat for Cub. You two saved my life."

The man accepted it with gratitude, and Hani set off for home. He told himself, marveling, *I think Aziru just tried to have me killed.*

❧

Since, for a brief while at least, Hani could be sure he wasn't being followed, he headed for Ptah-mes's house to report what new things he'd found out—or suspected—about Aziru.

Lord Ptah-mes was sitting in his salon, reading a beautifully illustrated scroll. As usual, he was dressed as if he were prepared for a royal reception. He looked up, seeming pleased to see Hani. "How's it going, my friend?" he asked amiably.

"Well enough, my lord. I've learned a few more things that might interest the vizier." After reminding his superior about the meeting he'd overheard between the king of Amurru and the Mitannian mercenaries, he recounted what the servant had told him on his second visit to the beer house—the comings and goings of the two sell swords—and the subsequent attack in the street.

Ptah-mes's arched black eyebrow dropped pensively. "Ungrateful bastard. What's that all about, I wonder?"

"It may not have been Aziru, of course. But I wonder if he didn't recognize me in the beer house after all. The Mitannians could see me over his shoulder. Maybe they said something about a man watching them too closely. Aziru doesn't have much longer to pull off his transfer of allegiance and get out of here. It would have looked as if I'd simply been attacked by some of the violent disaffected of the city."

"Do you think it was he the first time, then?"

Hani pondered that idea. "No. He would have had no reason then. That has me confused. I assumed it was the queen, but now I don't know whose hire these Mitannians are in."

"Let me say to you what I've said so often before, Hani. Be careful." Ptah-mes looked serious, his lips pursed in thought.

Hani pondered this, equally troubled by the harm someone seemed to wish him. Then he brightened. "Ah, I must tell you, my daughter has given birth to a son. I need to make the offerings, but I'm not sure how anymore. Someone said we could just leave them at the gate of the Ipet-isut."

"People seem to be doing that. We can ask my wife

before you go. But congratulations, Hani. Your secretary is the father?"

"Yes, my lord. And then my brother has returned with two horses he's trying to sell. Even with Aziru leaving, it's never boring."

Hani chuckled, and Ptah-mes smiled, an expression that warmed his severe face and made it attractive. "Perhaps I could look at your horses—"

"Oh, Lord Ptah-mes, don't feel any obligation. You've done so much."

"No obligation, but one never knows. They might be something I'm interested in."

"As you wish. They're at my house for the moment."

"Let's call Apeny and see what she says about offerings." Ptah-mes rose and moved elegantly to the inner door, where he called out, "Apeny, my dear. Are you there?" Hani was unable to interpret his tone, which was neither rancorous nor affectionate. The "dear" seemed to have only neutral meaning.

The mistress of the house emerged, as perfect as a figure from a tomb painting. "Hani, how delightful. Has Ptah-mes offered you anything to drink?"

"It was a business meeting, my lady. And I'm on my way out, but thank you," Hani said with a bow.

Ptah-mes said, "His daughter just bore a son, and Hani wants to know how one goes about making the offerings these days."

"Why, congratulations!" she cried, taking Hani by the hand in that perfect blend of warmth and reserve that seemed to be the mark of the household. "May Mut the mother of us all smile upon her and her child." She laid a reflective finger to her cheek. "I can let you into the courtyard of the temple. That would be safer. One never knows who's going to take something sitting outside the wall."

Ptah-mes's face grew sharp, his eyebrows taut. "I'm not sure that's a good idea, my dear. The police are following him."

"Although at the moment, they've let me go. I have a few hours at least before they put the tail back on me," Hani said mildly, not wanting to seem to side against his friend. Then he remembered. "Wait, I have no offerings with me." He wouldn't have time to go home before the police detail was back at work.

But Apeny said smoothly, "We can take care of that. I'll get some grain or a haunch of meat from the pantry. Ptah-mes, let him pick some of your flowers, won't you?"

Hani could sense the tension rising between Ptah-mes and his wife like the shimmering of the air over the desert. He shot Ptah-mes a look that tried to say, *I don't have to do this if you don't want me to*, but the high commissioner's face had taken on a mien of neutrality that was no more expressive than a cucumber. He led Hani to the garden and directed one of the gardeners to cut an armload of anything that was blooming or fruiting in the winter season. They filled a basket, and Lady Apeny joined them in the garden with a jar of wheat.

"You're too kind," Hani said, looking from one to the other. "I'll pay you back for this."

But they simultaneously urged him not to think of it.

"I've called the litter bearers," Lady Apeny said. "That will be more discreet."

"Are you so sure the temples are not under observation?" Ptah-mes asked his wife with a pointed look that belied his courteous tone.

"I know my way around, my dear."

Hani couldn't wait to get out of the freezing atmosphere of their dialogue. The litters were brought up, Apeny mounted one and Hani the other, and they departed, curtains drawn. Hani's last glimpse of Ptah-mes revealed him standing as stiff as a statue in the garden path, his features frozen.

⚜

This was grossly imprudent, Hani thought uneasily as the litter swayed along. He felt rather as if he'd been trapped into an act of folly. Hani might easily have discharged his offering otherwise; he wondered if Lady Apeny was trying to prove something to her husband, perhaps. He peeked through the linen curtains of the litter and saw that they were passing the facade of the Ipet-isut, that majestic, superhumanly high wall that undulated like the waters of creation around a sacred space as vast as a city. He felt the hairs on his arms stand up. Even abandoned and locked, the Greatest of Shrines was alive with the power of the divine.

The litters passed the southern pylon and continued to the desert side of the enclosure, facing the Gem-pa-aten. Hani's litter stopped, and the bearers set it down. He dismounted to find they'd drawn up beside a small service gate, probably used for emergencies. It had been barred and sealed, but the seals were broken, and the bar was propped against the wall.

Hani's throat was tight, and droplets of sweat beaded his forehead despite the cool of the day.

"My lady, I'm not purified. I can't enter the temple," he whispered to his companion.

But she replied with perfect graciousness, "The whole precinct is deconsecrated, Hani, and the sacred images have been removed. I certainly wouldn't take you somewhere you couldn't respectfully go. Nub-nefer would never forgive me, would she?"

She knocked, and someone opened the door without showing himself. To Hani's relief, they stepped into a courtyard. Before him stretched an enormous rectangular lake—the sacred lake that his wife had spoken of but which Hani had never expected to see. All around were small buildings—or buildings that appeared small against the immensity of their surroundings—clustered as in a miniature city. Magazines, perhaps, or workshops or offices. But behind them, dwarfing them, rose the divine mansion of Amen-Ra, towering walls and pylons of yellow stone rosy in the late-afternoon sun of winter, with the golden tips of multiple obelisks skewering the sky.

"You may lay down your offerings, Hani. May the Hidden One and the Great Mother grant your grandchild long years of life, prosperity, and health," Apeny said quietly. Hani knelt and laid the basket and the jar on the sacred ground. On this very spot, the first dry earth had risen from the primal flood. He remained there, his nose to that earth, his hands over his eyes, overwhelmed by the holiness of it all and the magnificence and the vastness. Waves of power lapped him until he cringed under it. This great god would not be disrespected forever. Hani got to his feet, breathing hard.

Apeny said with gentle courtesy, "Are you all right? You look pale."

"This was a great privilege, my lady," he murmured.

She smiled with deep warmth, and they turned back toward the door. Three men stood there—two burly and older, one small and slim and about Hani's age.

Hani widened his eyes in shock. "Amen-em-hut? *This* is where you are?"

His brother-in-law extended his arms, and the two of them embraced. The priest was beaming, looking considerably healthier and better fed than when Hani had last seen him. He turned to the other men. "Here's Hani, my sister's husband, whom I spoke of. He can be trusted."

The taller of the two said in a deep voice, "I am Mai, First Prophet of the Hidden One."

"And I am Si-mut, Second Prophet," said the shorter man.

So, here are the silent crocodiles. They haven't given up at all. "Honored, my lords," said Hani with a bow. He shouldn't be here, shouldn't know that these men were gathered in the shuttered temple. But far from feeling fear, he rejoiced that their resistance to oppression was strong.

Mai said in his profound voice, "Your brother-in-law has told us of your courage, your aid to him. The Hidden One counts on such men to return him to the light, Hani."

"I think the majority of the people of the Black Land are with you, Lord Mai. The king's new religion offers nothing to anyone but himself." Hani spoke more boldly than he'd ever dared.

The high priest smiled grimly. "I was appointed by the Osir Nefer-ma'at-ra. Much as he revered the King of the Gods, he'd already begun to look with mistrust at the power of the divine household. Our present ruler fears us mightily, and like anyone who is afraid, he has tried to kill us off. But the lord of the universe will not be contained. This king is not the living Haru but a man. His days will end. The gods will triumph."

"May it be so, my lord. May my new grandson, at least, see the return of our old ways."

Amen-em-hut took him by the arm and said quietly, eyeing Hani's face with concern. "Is it true the police got hold of you, my brother?"

"They did. And they've been following me. I only had a respite today because of... circumstances. I was able to tell them honestly that I didn't know where you were. Now I suppose I'll have to lie." He said it humorously, although it was a serious consideration.

"Ah, but I don't live here," said his brother-in-law with a matching crafty smile. "You can still speak the truth if they ask."

The high priest said, "Hani, you shouldn't leave the temple precinct until after twilight. In the meantime, let us talk." He indicated one of the small buildings within the enclosure and led the way in his heavy tread, with Hani and the other priests and Lady Apeny trailing him. They entered what appeared to be a chancery, the walls lined with shelves of papyrus rolls, and took their seats cross-legged on the floor in a circle.

These men of great power and wealth were all dressed plainly, with no jewels or insignia of office. They could have walked the streets without anyone recognizing them at all. Mai was somewhere between Hani's age and Mery-ra's, a tall, stocky man with a jowly face, stubborn jaw, and thick nose. There was something generically middle-aged about his appearance—Hani felt he had no idea at all what the priest had looked like in his youth—but his narrow eyes were fierce and intelligent. This was not a man who was going to hold his tongue forever. Si-mut was softer, plump and scholarly looking, his bulbous eyes ringed with shadow. But his gaze, too, was penetrating, despite the frequent blinking. Hani had only ever seen them in procession, from afar. Beside them, Amen-em-hut, with his handsome, animated face, looked young and light. The high priests were men of substance in every sense, rooted in ages of tradition. They were scions of the greatest families of Kemet and had served at the highest levels in the government. They'd wielded power second only to the king's.

Why did I ever think little Shu alone was keeping the fire alight? Hani realized a great weight had lifted itself from his heart.

Lord Mai began to speak, and the others fixed upon him attentively. "Hani, my friend. Your brother-in-law has sung your praises as a man of honesty and piety. He understands your need to keep a low profile, to maintain your credibility in the government. Many of ours have taken the same approach, and it's valuable—perhaps more valuable, in the long run, than the role of those who are designated to speak out, to keep fanning the flames." He nodded at Amen-em-hut then turned back to Hani. "I speak to you in frankness, trusting that you're a man of discretion. I'm going to tell you some things that may offend you as a member of the king's foreign service, but I beg you to consider them in the larger framework of things. The cosmic framework."

Lord Mai seemed to await an acknowledgment from Hani, who tipped his head. His heart was pounding heavily as if in expectation of something dangerous—or something wonderful.

The First Prophet continued. "We hope to destabilize the administration, Hani. Both abroad and at home. You've no doubt noticed the dissatisfaction in Waset these days. If the entire kingdom were that outraged, the king wouldn't last a fortnight. He has already dealt a death blow to the economy by shutting down the entire temple system, but that's a slow-acting poison. We want to provoke something more immediate—something that will cost him the support of the army."

"The Hittites," said Hani under his breath. Suddenly, things made sense.

Lord Mai's wide lips spread in a predatory smile. "I see you follow me. We have pushed the treaty with Naharin to a rupturing point—although, as you know, the king himself has let it languish until it's a mere dead letter. We have agitated among the northern vassals to seek their alliances elsewhere."

"Forgive me, my lord"—as a member of the foreign service, Hani felt he had to object—"but this seems very like treason against the Two Lands. Conspiring with a foreign government? Soliciting rebellion among the vassals?"

Si-mut spoke up, his voice hoarse and high-pitched. "We're not conspiring, Hani. Ironically, our enemies of Kheta are more pious than the king of the Two Lands. They are devout worshipers of the sun and see in our Ra one more avatar of their own Ishtanu. They are enthusiastically in favor of the restoration of the rights of the Hidden One. But we have promised them nothing. At most, they want to become our ally, our trading partner—something that a new administration would favor. We imagine a world where the great powers are friends, not enemies. Is this disloyalty, do you think?" He blinked his myopic eyes like a great thoughtful owl.

"Still," Hani said dubiously, "it's easy enough to call for an end to the king. But who will replace him? The Great Queen, if she survives him? That's no improvement. A half-witted brother? One of his daughters? She would be ruled by some man."

"Yes, she would," said Mai with a thin smile. Amen-em-hut, at his side, shot Hani a triumphant look. "And she would need a husband. Any prince who worships the sun and longs for the restoration of Amen-Ra would do, wouldn't he?"

Hani stared at his lap, trying to absorb all this. Part of him was horrified. *Does this mean what I think it means? They're undermining everything I work for daily. How can this not be treason?* Yet as Mai had said, it might be for the greater good of the kingdom. Part of Hani approved.

"Have you any questions?" Si-mut asked in his reedy owl voice.

Hani looked up, overwhelmed by a sudden urge to grin. "Do you have an agent in the household of the King's Beloved Wife, by any chance?"

"We do," Mai said. "The royal palaces are full of our people. As you might imagine, not many of the king's intimates—even his own family—are really convinced by his new religion. They fear, as any right-minded person would, the consequences of turning our backs on the powers of heaven."

"Will you persist in trying to ruin the princess Kiya, my lord?"

"Her homeland is collapsing without any help from us, and the king is doing nothing. Many people in the military are scandalized. Our work there is over."

Hani thought for a moment. "Then, was it you who tried to kill me—or warn me away—in the City of the Dead?"

"Not at all, Hani. I swear by the *ka* of my mother."

Hani filed that answer away for further reflection. "Who has really been writing those calls to arms with Amen-em-hut's name on them?"

Lady Apeny smiled proudly. "I have. My secretaries have made copies that have been distributed as far north as Per-wedjyt in the marshes of the Great Green and south into Wawat."

"But why use his name, my lady? The police are ready to punish him for something he didn't even do."

Lady Apeny looked regretful, but then her cool self-control returned. "No one would listen to a woman, Hani. And… out of respect for members of my family who might find it hard to accommodate such notoriety, I—we—decided a false name was wiser."

"I wish it really was me." Amen-em-hut looked quite exalted, his cheeks flaming. "But as you know, I had no way to write them or get them out. That will change now."

369

"Your wife thinks you're dead," Hani said sadly, and Amen-em-hut's face fell.

Mai said in his grave tones that would have made a divine pronouncement of the most banal remark, "We're all paying a price, Hani, even those of us who seem to be acquiescing in evil. But if we're victorious, it will have been worth it."

Hani heaved a sigh, conflicted in spite of himself. "What is it you want of me, my lords... and lady? Why have you confided your actions to me in this way? What if I report you?"

"You won't, any more than my husband would," said Lady Apeny, "because you have a conscience. You're caught between your oath to the king and what you know to be the real path of moral right." Her cool expression softened, and she looked at him with pity. "It's a hard place to be. I've seen it up close. And it's harder by far if you think you are alone."

"What we want is this," said Si-mut. "A man we can trust in the Hall of Royal Correspondence—"

"Trust to do what?" Hani interrupted, uneasy. "Subvert our foreign policy?"

"What exactly is our foreign policy, Hani?" asked Mai pointedly.

Hani found he had no answer.

"You speak many languages and have an excellent rapport with foreign rulers. When the time comes, their support or blind eye may be the difference between success and failure. Until then, just do your job. If you can figure out what it is."

Hani's head felt so heavy he could hardly hold it up—it

was packed dense with ideas that rattled and clamored, demanding to be examined. He needed desperately to reflect, to straighten out his raging thoughts. He looked at the faces of those around him—serious middle-aged people, not youthful fanatics but men and women with experience and power and wealth who had committed their lives to a cause that exacted a real sacrifice. All Aha's talk about corruption and venality in the priesthood—he didn't see it here.

Mai rose, and the others followed. Hani brushed off the seat of his kilt and let out a deep breath.

Lady Apeny said, "I'll send you back to your home in my litter, Hani. I need to stay for a while." She took his hands warmly. "I do hope you'll consider our offer."

"If all you require of me is to do my job and long for the restoration of the Hidden One in my heart, then consider me your servant, my lady, my lords." Hani made a full court bow, with his hand to his mouth. Passing by the sacred lake that sparkled like a living thing under the dying sunlight, he exited by the same door through which he'd entered. Behind the glimmering golden tips of the obelisks, evening was sinking deep into a twilight the color of dry blood.

What a day this has been, he thought.

❧

By the time the litter and its bearers had deposited Hani at his house, it was nearly fully dark. He drifted into the kitchen and asked the cook to make him a simple little something, regretting mightily the absence of the family. He was aching to talk to Nub-nefer or his father about the

371

strange, thought-provoking events of the day. Nub-nefer wouldn't leave Sat-hut-haru until her days of purification were over. He hoped his secret encounter with the priesthood wouldn't embolden her to become active against the administration after he had worked so hard to convince her to stay silent—although she might be proud of him, thinking he'd finally committed himself to standing against the Aten and his solipsistic cult. But in fact, Hani didn't know what had actually changed in his heart. Perhaps he'd foreseen with greater clarity the ultimate—the inevitable—triumph of the Hidden One.

And the attack in the streets. *Why would Aziru have paid someone to kill me after all the months of hospitality I showed him? Is the vassal king that determined to keep his dickering with the Hittites secret?* It wasn't that much of a secret that the northern principalities were on the verge of bolting. Shuppiluliuma was at their doorstep, and their suzerain, hundreds of *iteru*s away, couldn't be troubled to raise a finger. Jumping ship was probably evidence of Aziru's good sense. The priests' work on that front, encouraging Aziru and his men to defect, had been only too easy.

Hani settled down to a lonely meal. He spied Qenyt on the porch and hoped that she, at least, would join him, but she seemed bent on some hunt. He was draining the last of his beer when A'a coughed at the entrance to the vestibule.

"My lord, the high commissioner is at the door. Shall I let him in at this hour?"

"But of course!" cried Hani, rising hastily and straightening his clothes. He stuck his wig back on, wondering what could have brought Ptah-mes to his door so late.

The commissioner stood in the doorway, immaculate as ever, his impassive face giving no clue as to the gravity of his mission. Hani's heart skipped a beat in anxiety. "My lord, be welcome. Can I offer you something to drink?"

"Later perhaps." Ptah-mes smiled, but it was a strained effort. "You wouldn't happen to know where my wife is, would you?"

"Ah," Hani said, relieved. "Probably. She sent me home in one of the litters and said she'd be delayed at the temple. I, uh, I saw my brother-in-law there."

Ptah-mes's face darkened, but he asked lightly, "Should I be worried?"

"No, no. The other prophets were there too."

"Don't let her drag you into anything, Hani."

"I'm an adult, my lord," Hani said with a smile. His superior seemed brittle and on edge. Hani sensed he needed comforting, but Ptah-mes wasn't a man one could throw an arm around and give a squeeze. Hani lowered his voice. "Your wife admires you very much, my lord. She sees you as a man of conscience."

Ptah-mes stared at him, an eyebrow raised skeptically. "She said that?"

"She did."

Ptah-mes looked unsettled. He was silent, as if pondering Hani's words, then seemed to shake off his reflective mood and said in a brighter tone, "Since I was alone, I thought I'd come look at those horses of your brother. My men have torches. That should be enough light to get a basic view."

"Of course. They're in back." Hani added, "I'm alone, too, my lord. The family is all in the country, and Aziru's still in the capital."

"That's where I should be," Ptah-mes murmured as the two men made their way through the kitchen into the dark service court.

"Iuty!" Hani called out. "Bring us some torches, will you?"

Ptah-mes said, "My men are in your street. Let me get them."

"No need, I think."

Iuty appeared after a moment with a flaming brand in either hand and accompanied the two scribes to the cowshed, where Hani had penned up the horses. Hani opened the door and gathered the halters from a hook at the side. He managed to slip one onto each long muzzle without embarrassing himself too badly and led the docile creatures out into the light. They stood there, blinking and swishing their tails. Occasionally, one of them stamped a foot.

Ptah-mes raised an appreciative eyebrow. "Nice, actually. But they're mares." He moved over to the horses and examined each of them in turn—bending to feel their legs, looking into their mouths, sweeping his hand down the smooth expanse of their necks. Hani was amused to see his urbane superior handling animals with such familiarity. Ptah-mes looked finally at the brands on their rumps then stared up at Hani. "They're stolen. You'll never be able to sell them."

Hani's stomach did a flop into his throat. "Stolen?" he cried, stunned. "How do you know?"

"The brands have been changed. Look here—a bar has been added to cancel out the first image. See? The new scar crosses the old scar right there." Ptah-mes pointed with a carefully groomed forefinger. "They've been stolen from the royal stud farm."

"Oh no!" Hani couldn't conceal his horror. "This is all I need!" He was so distraught that he laughed, a sound that had more pain than humor in it.

"How did your brother come by these?"

"He bought them from some itinerant dealer in Men-nefer. Of course, Pipi knows even less than I do about horses. He'd be an easy mark for any swindler." Hani put his face in his hands. "So much for getting my gold back."

"Get them off your property, Hani. Throw them in the river. Kill and eat them. But burn those hides." Ptah-mes was dead serious, Hani saw.

"Can I give them back to the king? Tell some cavalry officer I found them wandering?"

"If you dare. He or his agent might wonder where that happened. I'd get rid of them."

That's because you're rich, Hani thought, a spark of resentment alight in his breast. *I had to strip my farm to pay for those beasts, and I need to recoup my expense.* But he knew Ptah-mes was right. "Well, there's one crisis that's back in operation after I thought I'd resolved it."

"I'm sorry I can't help you." Ptah-mes looked regretfully at the horses.

"Oh, you have helped me, my lord. I would innocently have taken them to market and ended up in some well with my nose cut off for horse thieving. Mahu would have enjoyed every minute of it!" Hani turned to Iuty. "Put the girls up for me, will you?" To Ptah-mes, he said, "Can I offer you some beer? Have you eaten?"

"Yes to the first. No to the second. But don't bother with anything. I'm not hungry."

That's why he's so svelte. I'm always ready to eat.

They returned through the kitchen, where Hani instructed the servant to bring out two pots of beer, preferably something nicely flavored with herbs. They took their seats in the only fancy chairs in the salon. *I may have to sell these.* He tried to harden himself against that idea.

"Time to go back to the capital," Ptah-mes said with a sigh, smoothing his perfect pleats mechanically. He managed a smile, no doubt so Hani wouldn't feel sorry for him. "When will your family be back?"

"Nub-nefer—not until Sat-hut-haru is out of her seclusion, and probably my niece as well. I'll take Neferet and Pa-kiki back to Akhet-aten whenever they return. I'm not sure when my father and brother and Maya plan to come home. They won't have much to do in the country, with the new mother's bower set up in the middle of things."

Ptah-mes nodded.

Hani remembered that his superior had mentioned children of his own. "Do you have sons or daughters, my lord?"

"Five daughters, all of whom are chantresses of Amen-Ra, and two sons. The eldest is a priest." Ptah-mes gave a snort that edged close to bitterness. "They have as little to do with me as they can."

Ai, thought Hani, with a pinch of the heart. *He deserves more happiness than that.* It was true that Ptah-mes wasn't a cuddly fellow—he had perhaps been a cold father. But he was a good man, generous and fair; Hani couldn't imagine that he'd ever mistreated his children so as to earn their hatred. *Are they, too, estranged because of his participation in the present administration?* Watching his superior and friend sitting, straight backed but weary looking, across from him, a dispirited absence of expression on his fine-boned face, Hani thought, *He isn't an easy person to know. He seems to be full of contradictions.*

The servant girl brought their beer, set up stands beside both of them, then left.

"To our master, the Lord of the Two Lands," Ptah-mes said in a tone dangerously close to sarcasm. The men put their lips to their straws and drank.

Hani was uncertain whether to tell Ptah-mes the details of his meeting with the priests; he couldn't read the strange mood the man seemed to be prey to and didn't want to aggravate his tense relationship with his wife. They sat in silence, drinking from time to time, Hani casting a friendly smile at the high commissioner whenever he saw his eyes emerge from their distant focus.

After some while had passed, Ptah-mes rose. "It must be getting late. I'll give you back your evening, Hani. I'm sorry about the horses."

"Me, too, my lord, but that's the way it is. I'll get rid of them. Thank you for your diagnosis."

He clapped Ptah-mes's arm with a comradely hand and saw the other man's dark eyes warm.

Ptah-mes laid his hand on Hani's. "Thank you for the beer. I'll see you in the capital soon, I expect." He turned and made his way to the door, where A'a opened it for him with a respectful bow.

Hani heard his footsteps crunching off down the path.

"May Khonsu give you safe travels, my lord," he called from the door.

◈

The next morning, Hani was watching the ducks dive for bread balls in the pond when there came a commotion of talking and laughter from the gate. He swung the panels open without waiting for A'a and found his father, Pipi, Pa-kiki, Mut-nodjmet, and Neferet rocking with hilarity. Neferet pounced on him immediately, her arms in a crushing hug around him. "Papa! You have to see little Tepy! He's so adooorable!"

"Tepy? He's Tepy?" Hani inquired laughingly of his father over her head.

"That's right—'the first.' Of many, one hopes. And it makes a good nickname for Amen-hotep," Mery-ra said in approval.

Pa-kiki grinned. "At least people won't always be asking him why he's called that."

Flashing a knowing look at Pa-kiki, Mut-nodjmet stifled a giggle.

"I owe my life to a monkey, son" Hani said. "No unkind words about them."

Everyone stared at him in surprise. "What's happened now?" Mery-ra asked, catching his eye.

"I'll tell you later."

"Was it...?" Neferet made her baboon face.

"Yes. His name is Djehuty's Cub, and I petted him for you. His fur is surprisingly coarse, although it looks soft." Hani combed his daughter's bangs with his fingers.

"We're going back to Akhet-aten today, right?" She looked up at him.

"Afraid I'll have to wait for Lord Aziru to return, little duck. But Pa-kiki can take you down."

"Let's get our bags put up," said Mery-ra, leading the procession into the house.

"Wait a minute, Father." Hani put out a hand to stop him. "And you, too, Pipi. I need to tell you something."

While the others clumped off into the back of the house, the three men remained in the vestibule.

"Lord Ptah-mes came by last night to look at the horses," Hani said under his breath.

Pipi's eyes lit up eagerly. "Is he interested?"

But Hani shook his head in warning. "He said they're stolen from the royal stud farms and that we'll never be able to sell them. He said we'd better destroy and eat them and conceal the evidence of their brands."

Pipi's jaw dropped, the very picture of horrified.

Mery-ra rolled his eyes. "Why does this not surprise me? There's no such thing as half a disaster. Thank the gods I didn't show them to Pa-aten-em-heb."

"What are we going to do?" cried Pipi in a high-pitched voice. "That bastard gold changer will destroy and eat *me*."

"Calm down, son," said Mery-ra, patting the air. "I've already charged the wagons with your grain and bronze *deben*s. We're taking them up to Men-nefer as soon as Mut-nodjmet is ready to leave. *You* have nothing to worry about. Hani, on the other hand..." He cast a reluctant glance at his firstborn. "They're probably worth a year's wages each, would you say?"

"At least we won't starve this year, between them and

the ostrich." The situation was so ridiculous that Hani had to laugh. "Maybe we can sell the meat in the market. Barter the skins for bread."

"Make fly whisks out of the tails," Mery-ra suggested. "Wigs out of the manes."

Despite their chagrin—or perhaps because of it—the men laughed crazily.

"What's so funny?" Pa-kiki asked as he stuck his head into the vestibule from the salon.

Wiping his eyes, Hani recounted the story of the doomed horses.

"What a shame. Horses are so beautiful." The youth dropped his gaze then looked back up at Hani, his little brown eyes sparkling. "Speaking of beautiful, have you seen Mut-nodjmet?"

Pipi beamed proudly. "She's changed, hasn't she?"

"I should say so. *Iy*, she's really gorgeous! I mean," he protested quickly, "she always was. But now..." Pa-kiki cleared his throat, his face growing red. "We talked quite a lot at the farm. She's a very intelligent girl. I like her sense of humor. And loving—you should have seen how she handled Tepy."

"Of course. She's one of us," said Mery-ra with a broad smile. He clapped his younger son on the shoulder.

Pa-kiki kept fishing for his father's eye, a daft grin on his lips. "I mean, a man could do worse." He clearly wanted to be reassured.

"A man could do much worse," Hani agreed amiably.

"I don't suppose she could stay around a little longer, Uncle? Do you have to get back to Men-nefer immediately?"

"I do," Pipi said, "but if your mother is agreeable, Mut-nodjmet could stay longer."

"I'd like to get to know her better." Beaming, the youth drifted on back into the salon and away.

They watched him go, Hani full of tenderness for the boy, whose heart was attached to his eyes.

"Can cousins marry?" asked Pipi.

Mery-ra said, "Of course. Why, brothers and sisters can marry."

"I think you're confusing us with the royal family, Father," Hani said.

"You're telling me your friend Ptah-mes and his wife aren't brother and sister?"

Scandalized, Hani said, "Father, how lurid!"

"I'll bet anything she's his father's love child or the other way around."

The conversation was getting uncomfortable. Hani felt disloyal making a joke of Ptah-mes's staggering marriage. The truth was, he admired both Ptah-mes and his wife. He said blandly, "How can we know? Maybe all those high nobility look alike."

Suddenly, he was painfully conscious of how much he wanted to see *his* wife. And the older girls. He wanted his Amurrite guests gone and his family back where they belonged. "How many more days until Sat-hut-haru and Tepy leave their bower?"

☥

In the afternoon, Pa-kiki and Neferet returned to Akhet-aten. Mut-nodjmet went with them, because she had yet to see it, and Aha's new baby must have been born by that point. The young people headed off gaily to the riverside in search of a ferry. Hani thought with a smirk that Aha was going to find himself with three hungry adolescents on his hands instead of two. Hani would need to make another offering at the Ipet-isut, he supposed, but outside the gate seemed to be sufficient. His police tail was probably back in effect.

To complete the cascade of events, Aziru and his entourage arrived at the house, talking loudly and laughing with the high good humor of men who were headed home after too long a time. Aziru stopped to greet Hani, who was writing a letter to Nub-nefer in the salon. "Well, Lord Hani," he said with his most charming and sincere-seeming smile. "At last you're rid of me. We'll pack tonight and leave tomorrow. The king, as eager suddenly to be rid of me as you no doubt are, has actually lent us a state boat as far as the delta of the River. I thank you for your hospitality. That hunt was something to tell my grandchildren about."

Hani smiled, his relief unfeigned. "I wish you a safe journey, my lord. Salute your beautiful homeland on my behalf." He stared directly into the dark-lashed, foxy eyes of the Amurrite, who sustained his look with the shared understanding of their long mix of friendship and antagonism. Hani said more quietly, "Why did you have me attacked in the street, Lord Aziru? Didn't you like the food you were served?"

Aziru froze for a moment but gathered his smile quickly, even if his face reddened. He'd caught the reference to sharing bread and salt, which should have bound them in unbreakable friendship. "Oh, that was you? How awkward.

Let's say it was a hasty reaction to being spied on, eh? Nothing fatal was intended."

"The Mitannian agents of Kheta must have told you we were sitting behind your back, I suppose," Hani said with bland amiability.

"Is that who they were?" Aziru asked innocently.

Hani just smiled. "I forgot to tell you the police were following me. Those poor men were pretty badly bitten by the *medjay*'s baboon."

"Life plays strange tricks, doesn't it?" Aziru grinned. He was a handsome fellow—more than a little wicked looking—with his almond-shaped eyes and neat beard. Hani found his sarcasm a bit abrasive, but he wished him well as king of the newly established A'amu. "I somehow never got around to buying those horses I intended to take home, but—"

"You're looking for horses?" A crazy hope tinkled in Hani's head.

"To enrich our breeding stock. I actually have an export billet for them, but I never got to the king's stud farm. Not, the gods know, because I didn't have time. I'll have to send an agent back here at some point. Soon. Before—" Aziru eyed Hani's suddenly eager face and asked quizzically, "Why?"

"It happens that I have two mares from the royal stud farms in my cowshed, Lord Aziru. I don't suppose you'd like to look at them?"

Aziru laughed richly. "You never cease to amaze me, Hani. This is surely the last word in hospitality!"

Hani led him through the kitchen into the court. "Wait till you see them first. You're under no obligation, of course, but it would save your agent a trip back. Before..." Hani knew that Aziru would understand his meaning: *before you cease to be a vassal of the Two Lands.*

Hani swept the indignant geese ahead of him and out of the way and opened the door of the cowshed. The mares looked up with their mild brown eyes. He slipped their harnesses on and led them out into the light. Aziru's face brightened appreciatively, and he began the same inspection Lord Ptah-mes had performed the other evening—lifting their feet, parting their lips, running his hands over them.

"Someone hasn't curried these girls for a while, but they seem to be in good health. Very nice stock. I'd be interested... considering that I owe you some kind of reparations anyway." Aziru grinned. "May I trot them around?"

"Of course."

One at a time, Aziru led them around the court, increasing his speed and watching their legs as they trotted then cantered in a circle. He listened to their chests and put his ear to their nostrils. He obviously knew what he was about. "Not bad at all, Hani. Before I ask you the price, tell me why you have two horses with marked-out royal brands in your barn?" His expression was both amused and curious.

"It's a long story, my lord," Hani said with a rueful quirk of the mouth. "Let's just say that my brother doesn't know much about horse trading. Are those brands going to cause trouble for you?" *Not that he cares, once he's outside the borders of Kemet.*

"No, no. I have a billet for horses from the royal stud farm, after all. And at this time of year, I think a nice trapper will keep the girls warm, don't you? That way, no one will ask unnecessary questions." Aziru threw back his head and laughed, as if he could scarcely believe the good fortune of this coincidence. "Now, break the price to me gently."

Aziru didn't even flinch at the amount. Perhaps Pipi had gotten a good price after all, since the animals had been unsalable.

"This may delay our departure a day or two. I need to buy some equipment and hire some grooms." The Amurrite's eyes sparkled naughtily. "I hear Mitannians make the best grooms."

"That's what I hear, too, my lord," Hani said. *And his Mitannian accomplices will get to leave the country under diplomatic immunity.* "I'll be heading for the capital tomorrow, so if we don't see one another before your departure, please give my best to your brother. His attentions were a nice diversion for my daughter."

"Mutually, my lord. Perhaps we'll meet again." His white teeth bared in a smile, Aziru made his way back into the house while Hani put up the horses.

"Better to bear your foals in A'amu than be eaten in Waset," he told the animals and chuckled. *There's the first entry in my new "Aphorisms for Horses."* He was eager to share the good news with Pipi and his father.

❖

Lord Hani and Maya were sitting on the deck of the ferry, en route to the capital. Lord Hani was supposed to be working on some documents for the Hall of Correspondence, but he kept losing his train of thought. Maya had rarely seen his father-in-law so distracted. The gods knew *he* was distracted as well, with visions of his little son and his beloved wife floating in front of the words he was supposed to be writing. He couldn't wait until the days of seclusion were over and he could hold them both in his arms. Little Tepy—the first of many sons!

"I might as well stop this, Maya," Lord Hani finally said with a sigh. He rubbed his face with his hands. "I need to organize my thoughts."

"Six more days till we can see Tepy and the women, my lord," Maya said, grinning.

"I should drop in on Aha and congratulate him, too, if Khentet-ka has, in fact, given birth. We may have crossed their messenger on the water."

"These are great days," Maya said, unable to wipe the grin from his face.

Hani laughed that deep belly-bouncing chuckle of his. "Yes, they're turning out that way. Little by little, everything is resolving. Pipi could hardly contain himself when he found out about Aziru and the horses. He kept saying it was too good to be true."

"Great days. Great days," Maya continued to murmur, stroking his gold amulet of Bes.

"Let's count our blessings, Maya. Here are the problems we've had this year and their outcome. You might take notes."

Maya fished around for a potsherd and wrote, *Lord Hani's Problems*, at the top. "This isn't a very big sherd, my lord. I hope you haven't had too many problems."

"No," Hani agreed. "Few but serious. One…" His voice dropped. "Who was blackmailing Lady Kiya, and how do we stop them?"

"Ah," crowed Maya. "We know what happened there. It was the queen."

But Hani held up a hand in warning. "Yes and no, my friend. As it happens, there were two blackmails going on. The first was the queen's. We'll see if that's resolved or not. If she doesn't take up the suggestion we made to her, then I'm out of ideas. It can still go either way."

"There were more?" Maya looked at him dubiously, his pen floating over the potsherd.

Hani nodded. "The one brought by our Mitannian friends was a wholly different attempt. It seems to have been engineered by the Hittites, enabled somehow by the... let's call them the Crocodiles. They consider their work finished, so we need fear no more on that score."

Maya looked up, confused. "The Hittites were blackmailing her? The crocodiles?"

"Ah," said Hani. "You've missed some things while you were at the farm. I'll fill you in when we're done. Subproblem: who tried to kill or frighten Hani during his investigation of the blackmail? Still unresolved. The Crocodiles deny responsibility. Along with that comes the death of Kha-em-sekhem. Unresolved, although I've been assuming it was the queen."

Maya caught up to him with a flourish. "Second?"

"The disappearance of Amen-em-hut, which is now resolved."

"You know where he is, my lord?"

"No, but I know *that* he is. Alive, well, and as subversive as ever. And by no means alone."

Maya said with a bit of heat, "Too bad Lady Anuia can't hear that. She's given up. She thinks he's dead."

"I know," said Hani, his eyebrows drooping sadly. "We may have to do something about that. Put it under Unresolved. Third problem."

Maya scribbled, *Three*.

"Pipi's debt. Resolved. I never thought I'd be grateful to Aziru, but somehow, our mutual self-interests converged here. I may even be able to get myself a small yacht after all. Wouldn't it be nice not to have to rely on public ferries?"

In the back of his mind, Maya thought reluctantly that Hani buying a yacht would probably mean no more trips on Ptah-mes's beautiful vessel. Maya wrote, *Resolved*, and turned the potsherd over. "Is there a four?"

"Yes. Mut-nodjmet's broken heart." Lord Hani chuckled. "That may be taking care of itself. The Lady of Love has touched the heart of Pa-kiki. We'll see how things develop."

Maya smiled with the tolerance of a man who knew about such things. "Resolved," he said as he wrote. He raised his pen. "Anything else?"

"Five: Aziru's questionable loyalty. I'm not sure this constitutes a problem, because everyone pretty well knows he's planning to go over to Kheta, and no one, from the king on down to myself, really cares. May Ammit take me if I see why Nefer-khepru-ra was in such a furor to make him come to Kemet if it was just to insult him into the enemy camp. But that's another problem, one I can't solve." Hani's face went sour for a moment, then he brightened. "Ah, subproblem: who attempted to kill or discourage Hani after he began to investigate Aziru? By his own admission, that was Aziru. Probably with the collusion of those Mitannian henchmen of Kheta. But they won't bother us anymore—they're going back to A'amu with him. Let's hope they're more loyal to Aziru than Abdi-ashirta's guards were to him."

Maya looked up, goggling at Lord Hani in disbelief. "Mitannians working for the Hittites? That's like lambs in the employ of wolves."

"They're mercenaries, Maya. Men without loyalties. And who would be less likely to be suspected of being on the side of the wolves than a lamb?"

Maya shook his head and snorted. "Crocodiles, wolves, lambs, horses! Where are your favorites, the birds?"

"The Great Queen and the Beloved Wife are ducks, remember? Brawling for the favor of their drake." The two men laughed hilariously. Freedom—at last—from most of the anxieties that had been haunting him for months seemed to have made Hani effervescent. "Now, read out the unresolved issues, if you will, please, my friend."

Maya scanned the potsherd and read aloud, "Attempt on Hani and death of Kha-em-sekhem. Maybe the queen's blackmail. Lady Anuia."

Hani crawled to his feet, grinning. "Lord Ptah-mes recently said I'd be safer in Kharu, and it looks like he was right. And then there's the police trailing me. But that's probably going to end soon, I've been told."

"Now that you have a friend on the force," Maya said with a wink.

"You mean Cub? I'm grateful to that boy."

"Oh, one more unresolved issue, my lord." Maya's smile tarnished, and he could taste the bitterness in the back of his throat. "Maya's childhood home being sold out from under him."

"I thought you were going to buy it."

Maya hung his head, twisting his mouth. "That's going to be a little hard now, with a baby to take care of." He looked up quickly. "I know you'd help us, Lord Hani, but I feel I've asked enough of you. I may just have to make my peace with this… this betrayal." In spite of himself, Maya still felt a burn of anger and humiliation inside at the thought.

Hani nodded slowly. "Whatever you think, Maya." He hitched up his kilt. "We've worked long enough. I have a gourd full of wine, if you'd like to share some."

They reached the capital to find it in something of a state of ferment. Hani couldn't think of any upcoming major festival likely to be celebrated in the Horizon of the Aten, but there were workmen sweeping the streets and garlanding the lion-bodied images of the king along the processional road. Banners hung over the bridge into the palace precinct and flew from the two royal buildings face-to-face on either side of it.

"Is someone receiving the gold of honor, I wonder?" Hani asked himself.

At his side, Maya said sarcastically, "It's been a whole year. About time for another jubilee."

"Not hot enough. Wait till midsummer." Hani shocked himself with the openness of his cynicism these days. Maybe it was because he knew how many were suffering the present administration in seeming silence while working to undermine it. Looking around at the arid, swept processional way, he said, "Where do we go first? I think

I'd like to see if Mane's around. Once we get to Aha's, we may be there for a while."

Accordingly, they passed under the bridge and turned right, bypassing the small state residence and entering the cluster of drab cubes that housed the Hall of Royal Correspondence. In the court, clutches of Hani's colleagues talked together animatedly. He approached a knot of several men with Maya in his wake. "Anyone seen Mane son of Pa-iry?"

One of the scribes said, "He's with the Mitannian delegation. They're getting ready for the queen's elevation. All the foreigners are making some sort of presentation, same as at a real coronation."

Hani exchanged a quick look of knowing satisfaction with his secretary. To the other scribe, he said genially, "You'll have to forgive me, I've been down at my farm. What's going on?"

Another man said with an edge of tartness, "They're crowning her as a second king or something like. We're going to have two of them at once now."

"A coregency," explained the first man.

"He-king and she-king?" Hani said with a smile.

"That's it," said the second man. "This must have come up pretty quickly. They didn't even tell us in advance we had the day off."

Hani laughed conspiratorially and turned away. He caught Maya's eye. "Resolved," he whispered. "Let's find Mane."

The scribes directed him to the courtyard of the reception palace not far away.

"They're doing the coronation today?" Maya cried as they passed through the splendidly decorated pylons.

"Surely not. But soon. This may be a rehearsal. If it's not at the Ipet-isut, I don't know what the ceremony even consists of."

Within, the vast court was planted with rows of palm trees that led the eye toward the entrance like a hall of columns. *The king certainly has a strong artistic sense.* Hani saw assemblages of exotically dressed men and women gathered here and there and heard snatches of music as he and Maya passed. Everyone seemed to be practicing their presentations at once. He cast around for men of a Mitannian-looking stamp, and sure enough, there were Mane and Keliya talking at the edge of the group. A line of women in bright woolen dresses were playing tambourines and dancing. Hani waved at his friends, who looked up in delight.

"Hani," cried Mane. "Join us. You can be a Mitannian for the day." Keliya stood, smiling, behind him.

"I thought I'd pass myself off as one of the dancing girls," Hani said. "Speaking of girls, how is…?"

"About ready to pop. I don't know if she'll be able to take part in the celebration or not." Mane looked conspiratorial. "Whatever possessed Nefer-khepru-ra to crown his wife a king, eh?" He nudged Hani in the ribs.

"We've had women kings before," Hani said modestly. "Both of you, I need to know something from our girl. Any chance of seeing her?"

"Now?" Keliya scratched his beard. "Maybe now's the best time, in fact, while everyone is busy."

"I can take him," Mane said. "You're head of the Mitannian mission. You need to stay."

Mane peeled off, an energetic little round figure, and Hani and Maya followed in his brisk wake. Lady Kiya was established on the deep colonnaded porch with other women, presumably the king's concubines and lesser wives, and a bevy of servants who fanned the warmth of a brazier toward her offered her fruit, laid out a choice of shawls for her perusal, and in general pampered the Beloved Royal Wife. Kiya was enjoying the role of a very pregnant woman. She seemed no longer to be worried about whose child she carried. Even from a distance, Hani saw the happiness in her face—the sparkling eyes, the flushed cheeks. This was the antechamber of her triumph, with the queen neutralized as a rival. Now all Kiya needed to do was produce a male child.

Hani and Maya waited respectfully in the court while Mane approached the royal wife's chamberlain. The official carried the message to Lady Kiya. Her gaze grew wide, and she scanned the edge of the crowd. She saw him and beckoned.

"Wait for me here, son," Hani said to Maya, and he climbed the steps to the portico. In the presence of the Beloved Wife, he made a deep obeisance, hand to mouth, and looked up into Kiya's merry eyes.

"You did it, my friend," she said softly. "She'll never give me another thought. Except when I bear the king's heir. How can I thank you, Hani?"

"Just with an honest answer or two, my dear lady, so I can understand what has happened." He stared at her, seeing her as the very young girl she still was. "Who killed the sculptor?"

Her face fell. She glanced fearfully at the servants, who'd stepped away to allow her more privacy, then back at Hani. She managed a transparent air of innocence. "How would I know?"

"I think you do, my lady. Honest answers, please. Clearly, nothing is going to happen to you as a result." He spoke gently as if to a frightened animal.

"He was dangerous," she said, hanging her head. "He could have revealed things. And I thought he was blackmailing me. Maybe he even said something to those other people, the veterans."

Hani was saddened by this ruthlessness but not surprised. Kiya had spent her entire life at someone's court, where murder was as common as a drink of water. Her family, in particular, was a seething snake pit of fratricide. At least, she had the grace to look ashamed.

He said, "And so I suppose you wanted to warn me away, too, when I started investigating? But you were the one who asked me to find out who was after you, my lady."

"Yes, but I panicked, Hani. Suddenly, I was afraid it all was going to come out. You'd find out I had lied to you about the time and everything." Her voice dropped to a husk of itself, and Hani had to fasten his eyes to her lips. "Nobody must ever suspect."

He nodded his understanding. He couldn't demand more honesty of her than he himself displayed often enough in diplomatic discussions.

"I only wanted to scare you," she pleaded, her sweet plum-shaped face more beautiful than ever with her incipient motherhood. It was hard to hold anything against such a face.

"I take it you didn't send the Mitannians after me." He thought she didn't need to know that they'd been the agents of anyone other than the queen.

"No, no. I was afraid of them. It was just some people who... who do things like that." She smiled uncertainly.

Hani nodded. "You've answered my questions, Lady Kiya. I wish you a safe and happy childbirth."

"You must let me give you something, Hani." She turned, dug about in the chests behind her, and produced a marvelous gold cuff bracelet, which she forced on him. "I'm grateful."

Hani accepted it with a deep bow. *Heavy. Priceless. There sits my yacht.* He backed away down the stairs into the courtyard, and Mane and Maya stepped up to his side.

"What did she give you, my boy?" asked the emissary to Naharin.

Hani held out the bracelet as they all walked away through the tree-shaded court. Mane whistled. "Your wife will love that."

"Yes, she will," said Hani, suddenly conflicted. His yacht had disappeared into the mists again.

He saw Maya's goggling eyes. *There's his mother's house.* He rolled the bracelet up carefully in the end of his cloak and pinned it under his arm.

They left Mane once more with the Mitannians, and Hani and Maya made their way through the southern residential sections of town to Aha's gate. They were admitted to the garden, where in spite of the lingering chill, the young people had congregated.

"Papa!" cried Neferet, rising and hurling herself on him. "Pa-kiki and Mut-nodjmet want to get married! Isn't it wonderful?"

"It is indeed." He looked over her head at the happy pair, who sat beaming at him, red-faced with beatitude, their arms around one another's waists. "No one can say they haven't known each other long enough." He winked at his son then turned to Neferet. "You're not at Djefat-nebty's side today, my duckling?"

"She gave me the day off. She said we'd be busy as soon as the queen and Lady Kiya have their babies. Which is aaany day now."

Hani exchanged a puzzled look with Maya. "Doctors do that? I thought it was for sisters and aunties to deliver babies."

"But, Papa, these are the king's women. You can't be too careful." Neferet sounded so grown-up that he had to remind himself she was barely fourteen. "It will be another sort of experience for me."

"I'll say," he said, thinking of his father's remarks about screaming in pain. "Where is Aha?"

"He's at the temple of the Aten, Papa," said Pa-kiki. "He said he had work there, but I think he wanted to get out of the house."

"Ah, yes, speaking of childbirth—has Khentet-ka had hers yet? We hadn't received a message by the time we left Waset."

"Not yet," Neferet assured him. "Her mother said I could help her, so I'll have some experience when the queen and the Beloved Wife go into labor."

"It's a great year for babies," Maya murmured at Hani's side, his mouth spread in a wide smile of satisfaction.

"Well, Maya, you and I can head back to Lord Ptah-mes's house for the evening and return to Waset tomorrow. Unless you want to stay for the coronation." He shot his secretary a teasing quirk of the mouth, which Maya returned knowingly.

"The staff of the Hall of Correspondence is off until after the ceremonies," Pa-kiki said, "but I'm not sure we'd have time to get home and back. I'm thinking of quitting anyway."

"I wouldn't until your grandfather finds you a post in the military, son. It might look like a protest, and this family needs to minimize its appearance of rebellion." Hani clapped him on the shoulder unoccupied by Mut-nodjmet. The boy would find something to do with his time in Akhet-aten; that was clear. "See everyone soon. Let me know when Aha's little one comes along."

They all bade the two men a cheerful goodbye, Neferet giving him her usual rib-cracking hug, and Hani and Maya regained the street.

"When do the royal scribes ever work?" Maya said with a snort.

"We could ask ourselves that, too, eh, my friend? We may have to request another assignment to Kharu just to get some rest." They marched along with their mismatched strides. Hani said, "By the way, Kiya admitted that it was she who killed Kha-em-sekhem and had me attacked as a warning."

Maya lifted his eyebrows and puckered his lips.

397

"Whew. Like that insect that kills her mate. And she looks so innocent."

Hani said thoughtfully, "I suspect it *is* a sort of innocence that believes murder solves anything. As if the Judge of the Soul doesn't see."

They continued in silence, their steps ringing softly on the hard-packed ground of the street. The bracelet, wrapped in multiple turns of the hem of Hani's cloak, slapped against his hip at every stride. Hani wondered if he ought to offer the jewelry to Pa-kiki and Mut-nodjmet to help them get started.

"Do you think your mother might be willing to appraise this piece of gold Lady Kiya gave me?"

"I'm sure she would, my lord. She may even have made it."

"Let's be sure to see her when we get back."

Maya gave a *psh* of annoyance, his good humor evaporating instantly. "She may be here. She said she's already starting to set up the new workshop."

"Well, let's ask someone where it is."

"She said she's just south of the royal warehouses along the river."

We were just near there, thought Hani, surprised. *Didn't you even want to say hello to her?* He pivoted, and the two scribes directed their footsteps northward once more. Ahead, Hani saw the vaulted roofs of the royal magazines and long, low warehouses, like a scatter of logs, toward the waterfront. Maya craned his neck, and Hani did the same. A small construction site in a pocket of unoccupied ground caught his eye. No one was at work, but scaffolding was still set up in front of a half-erected mud-brick wall.

"Is that it, do you think?"

"No idea," Maya said tersely.

They stepped inside the still unwalled precinct and found an arrangement similar to the Theban workshop: a small house and a double courtyard divided by a barnlike studio.

"In-hapy!" Hani called. "Are you here?"

At his side, Maya maintained a stubborn silence.

After a moment, the little goldsmith appeared in the door of the freshly whitewashed house. Beneath the habitual scarf, her face brightened in delight. "Lord Hani! Maya, my son! How do you like our new workshop?"

She waddled out to greet them on her bowed legs, arms extended toward her son. He drew away, brow thunderous. She turned apologetically to Hani. "Welcome, my lord. None of the workmen is here yet. I'm just watching over the progress on the wall. We can't move our supplies up here until that's secure."

"We wanted to see how your new place was going, In-hapy," Hani said cheerfully, ignoring his secretary. "And I just received a beautiful piece of gold jewelry I'd like to have appraised." He unrolled the hem of his cloak and held out the cuff.

In-hapy took it in her stubby fingers and turned it around, lips pursed. She laughed. "Why, that's one of ours. I can tell you exactly what it's worth. It's solid gold, heavy. Are you wanting to sell it, my lord?"

"Er, not yet. I need to think about it."

She turned sorrowfully toward her son. "Maya's not very happy about this move. But what can I do, Lord Hani? The king's chamberlain has hinted that if we aren't easier

399

to get to, he's going to take his custom elsewhere. And anyway," she looked up at Hani, her worn face sly, "I have something else to do with the old place."

"No doubt!" Maya snapped. "All my childhood memories mean nothing to you, clearly." He would hardly look in his mother's direction.

"I was going to give the house to you, my love—to you and Sat-hut-haru and little Tepy," In-hapy said, beaming at Maya. "And I'll even have it reworked to however you want it laid out. The people doing the building here are good men, and I'd like to keep them employed awhile longer."

Maya gaped at his mother, his eyes round as doum fruit. "Seriously? You were going to *give* it to us?"

"You'll get it someday. Why not now, when you're young and could use some help?"

He threw himself on his mother, squeezing her in his short arms, weeping with happiness. Hani watched, touched and a little sorrowful. *The children never seem to realize how much we love and sacrifice for them until they have children of their own.*

At last, Maya's tearful—and no doubt guilt-tinged—words of thanks had been accomplished.

"Will you stay here by yourself tonight, In-hapy?" Hani inquired kindly. "I'm sure our host would accommodate you."

But she waved him off, rolling her eyes. "Oh no, my lord. I've heard about that man and his fancy palace. No, no. Too rich for my blood. I'll be safe here tonight. There's a door, at least."

"Maybe I should stay with her," Maya suggested, enveloping her shoulders with a protective arm.

"Good idea, my boy. I'll see you in Waset, then." Hani rolled up his bracelet, and with a light step, he set off once more for Ptah-mes's house.

⸙

Five days later, Hani reached Waset to find that Sat-hut-haru and her little son had been released from their seclusion. They and Nub-nefer and Baket-iset were already at the house when Hani walked in. He embraced his wife joyfully, savoring her warmth and the sweet smell of bergamot and lilies she always seemed to exude. "My love! It seems like it's been forever since I've seen you!"

She looked up at him with a piquant smile. "Now you know how I felt when you used to be away for months at a time, Hani." She snuggled against him. "Here we are, reunited again. How were the others in the capital?"

"Well. Neferet is going to attend the royal lyings-in with Lady Djefat-nebty. Aha's wife hasn't given birth yet. Pa-kiki—ah! Pa-kiki and Mut-nodjmet want to get married."

Nub-nefer laughed. "I saw this coming. They were inseparable at the farm. I guess this means we'll be seeing more of your brother." She shot Hani an amused glance. "Better practice your dancing, my dear."

"I don't suppose Father's back yet?"

She shook her head. "Come say hello to the girls. They've missed you. And greet a certain small someone you haven't met yet."

She took him by the hand and led him toward the salon, but Hani stopped her and unrolled his cloak. "Wait, my dove. There's something I want to give you. It was payment for services rendered to the King's Beloved Wife." He held

401

the magnificent bracelet out toward Nub-nefer, who gasped at the sight of it. "Pure gold, like you. Maya's mother made it."

His wife took the cuff in her hands, turning it over and over, admiring the craftsmanship of the fine appliquéd decorations in wire and granules, marveling at the weight. "This is worth a fortune, Hani. Maybe we should give it to Pa-kiki and Mut-nodjmet instead, to start their household."

Hani laughed. "That went through my mind. But I wanted my lady to have it. If she passes it along, then both my wishes are fulfilled."

Nub-nefer strained up on her tiptoes to kiss him. Her voice trembled with emotion. "Thank you. *You're* my gift from the gods, Hani."

They started again toward the salon. Hani slipped out of his sandals and said under his breath, "Speaking of the gods, I never told you—I saw Amen-em-hut again."

Nub-nefer looked up, her eyes alight and eager. "Is he well? He looked so pitiful when I saw him last."

"Oh, yes. Back in form." Hani's voice dropped still lower, and he said into her ear, "He and the other priests are quietly mounting a rebellion. And Lady Apeny. But please, dearest, don't breathe a word to anyone. I only tell you this because I know how happy it will make you."

She threw her arms around her husband and locked him there in silent ecstasy. Finally, she admitted, "Hani, I told Anuia he's alive. It wasn't fair to keep her in the dark. She had started to languish, and the children need her."

"How good is she at dissembling her happiness?" he asked uneasily.

THE CROCODILE MAKES NO SOUND

"She's been golden. One would say she's just bravely carrying on as a widow."

"Good. One more thing resolved."

She looked at him curiously, but they'd entered the salon, where both girls cried out simultaneously, "Papa!"

Hani knelt first at the couch of Baket-iset and bent to kiss her. "My swan! How I've missed you and your insights. I've had to judge people on my own, and I haven't always done well. How are you?"

She beamed, a beautiful young woman of intrepid spirit, impeccably made up and coiffed, thanks to the loving attentions of her mother. "Wonderful, Papa. I'm an aunt again!"

"I hope you won't miss that Abdi-urash too badly. He was probably married anyway."

Her smile wavered painfully but she forced it bright once more. "Not at all, Papa. It was just a diversion."

My poor broken dove, Hani thought, his throat constricted. *So little happiness comes your way, and you relinquish it so bravely.* Rising, Hani turned to his second daughter, who sat in his chair with a wee rosy bundle in her arms.

She was glowing with pride as she stretched her face up for a kiss. "Here is Tepy, Papa. Say hello to Grandfather, my little man."

She handed up the naked baby, holding his head carefully. He waved his tiny hands and made a cooing noise but didn't cry. Hani took him in his arms, marveling at the small creature in whom his own blood ran. Tepy already had a scalp covered in dark fuzz—curly, like Hani's. Hani could feel tears starting to burn in his nose.

403

"Cover him, Papa. It's chilly." Sat-hut-haru rose, wrapped his loopy-woven blankets around the child, tucked them in with tender fingers.

Nub-nefer, at Hani's side, put her arm around her husband. "In-hapy said she doesn't think he's going to be a dwarf."

"What difference does it make?" Sat-hut-haru demanded, a little defensive.

"None at all, my love. Maya should be home any day now, by the way. He stayed the night with his mother, who was in the capital overseeing the construction of the new workshop." Hani watched the baby's stirrings with delight. He looked up at his daughter. "She's giving him the old place here in Waset for you and your family."

Sat-hut-haru's eyes grew wide with excitement. "Oh, she's so generous! Maya was sick at the thought of losing that house. And it's the sweetest little place, Papa. We can fix it up so nicely. I bet if we bring in River mud, we can even have a beautiful garden."

"I'm sure you can, dearest," said Nub-nefer, melting with affection. She inserted her finger into Tepy's diminutive fist. "What does our little man think of that, eh?" She took the baby from Hani's arms and rocked him back and forth, and a look of contentment spread on Tepy's face.

He's perfectly satisfied with his life. "I completely agree," Hani said fervently.

"Agree with what?" Nub-nefer asked, her face still transfigured with the happiness of watching her grandson.

"My life is pretty well perfect."

❖

THE CROCODILE MAKES NO SOUND

The next morning, Hani received a letter, written in a careful schoolgirl hand, from Neferet in the capital. At first, he faced it with misgiving. This was the first time she'd ever written to him. Had something happened to her or Aha or Pa-kiki? He fumbled off the seal—Lord Pentju's, so she had clearly written it at Djefat-nebty's house—and unfolded the papyrus with unsteady fingers.

Dear Papa, he read and began to relax. *I thought you'd want to know: Khentet-ka had another boy! You won't believe this, but they're calling him Pa-aten-mes! I swear I didn't act as disgusted as I felt.*

Hani laughed in spite of himself. The idea of Neferet concealing her feelings was pretty hard to imagine. He read on. Numerous words were written in emphatic red ink:

> *Lady Kiya just had an adorable little girl, but she didn't seem terribly happy. They all said the baby looked just like the king. The Great Queen—or is she a king now?—had a little boy! Everybody was very happy! As Maya would say, it's a great year for babies. Grandfather was right about the screaming in pain, though. Don't tell Mama, but I never, ever, ever want to go through this! May Ta-weret twist off my ears one by one and stuff them down my throat if I do. Be glad you're a man.*

> *Love, Neferet*

**Did you enjoy this book? Here is a taste of the
next Lord Hani mystery, *Scepter of Flint*:**

H OW LONG WILL THIS GO *on? How long will we suffer at* *the hands of an impious tyrant who thinks of no one but* *himself?* Hani thought in disgust.

Hemmed in by an enormous crowd, Hani stood between the lion-bodied images of the king that flanked the main street of Akhet-aten. He was waiting—as it seemed he had so often in the last seven years—for the king and his family to make their appearance. This occasion was the opening ceremony of the Great Jubilee of the Aten. More splendid than even the two previous jubilees Nefer-khepru-ra had held since he'd come to the throne alone, this one had been two years in the making. All the ambassadors of foreign lands, all the mayors of Kemet's vassal states to the north, and all the princes of Ta-nehesy to the south were there to render homage—because Nefer-khepru-ra *was* the Aten. Officially, he was the son and the only priest of the Shining Sun Disk, but Hani had realized long ago that, in fact, the king in his person was intended to be the revelation of the Aten.

One god, one priest, one revelation: him.

Hani ground his teeth at the very thought of Nefer-khepru-ra's theology. Had the king no idea of the havoc his decrees had wrought? The Ipet-isut, the Greatest of Shrines, consecrated to Amen-ra, had been closed, the cult statues desecrated, the priests expelled. The Hidden One's estates had been confiscated, and tens of thousands of priests and workers had found themselves without jobs. Had the king held his celebration in the old capital, Waset, this crowd would have been dangerously hostile.

But the inhabitants of Akhet-aten were handpicked. They were the bureaucrats and tradespeople for whom the king's continued favor had been more important than conscience, and they would applaud him as he demanded.

Yet here I am too, Hani thought with a twinge of cynicism. *And here is my father, and here are my sons and daughter and son-in-law.* Nub-nefer, his wife, had been obdurate enough in her faith to refuse to attend. Sat-hut-haru, Hani's middle girl, had yielded to her mother's stern orders and declined to participate as well.

Hani mopped his forehead. The temperature wasn't extreme in this second month of the winter season. Still, packed in with a dense crowd of perspiring bodies, he was none too comfortable as sweat dampened his armpits and then chilled. The men around him were, like him, scribes and emissaries in the king's foreign office. His friend Mane was at his side, bouncing on his tiptoes, trying to see over the taller heads around him.

"I should be like a crocodile," Mane shouted over the rumble of the crowd. "They keep growing as long as they live. I'd be taller than Keliya by now." Keliya was their mutual friend, the ambassador from Naharin.

Hani laughed. He was of average height and still could see nothing more than the white-clad backs of his colleagues, the linen shirts growing transparent with perspiration. Everyone's big court wigs blocked even more of his view. He wondered if Maya, his son-in-law and secretary, could see anything at all.

Hani eyed the bright, clear sky overhead, blue as turquoise, soft and smooth as the breast of a heron. *Great Ra*, he prayed silently, *put an end to this madness*. A hawk sailed overhead far, far into the cloudless azure distance, and Hani followed it admiringly with squinted eyes. Perhaps it was a magnificent bird… or perhaps it was the god Haru, watching the Two Lands with an all-seeing and protective gaze. *Lord Haru, show us the way of truth.* Hani sighed.

He heard a scuffling noise ahead of him, and suddenly, two men lurched back into the crowd, one of them looking blanched and unwell, leaning on his anxious companion's arm. They forced their way through the throng, and Hani and Mane found themselves pressed forward into the front rank of the spectators.

"We can breathe at last," he said to Mane with a grin.

The great processional way stretched off before him in either direction, the crowd of bureaucrats a bright white-and-black fringe bordering the tall whitewashed walls of temple and palace and sparking with festive gold jewelry. Banners rippled lazily in the scant wind. The sun-scorched street had been swept and the dust held back by a sprinkling of water, but still, it reflected the glare until it was almost impossible to see without a visoring hand. Somewhere to

Hani's right, toward the palace, were the viziers and upper-level functionaries like his own superior, Lord Ptah-mes, high commissioner of northern foreign relations. To his left stood the lower-rank royal scribes and military scribes, including his sons and father.

All at once, trumpets began to bray, chiming in one after the other in a joyous ascending chord. The crowd rustled and murmured excitedly. Around the north wall of the palace, the royal procession came into view, first several army units marching in step to the beat of drums and then the royal family. The king and queen were borne high in their golden carrying chairs on the shoulders of stalwarts decked in plumes and leopard skins. Nefer-khepru-ra gazed straight ahead of him, a slight smile on his lips, and so did the beautiful Nefert-iti Nefer-neferu-aten. They were a splendid couple, he had to admit—and things had reached such a pass in Hani's soul that even that admission was painful. But they were young and good-looking, although the king had begun to grow fat like his father. Decked with jewels, their crossed arms bearing the crook and flail of kingship, they sparkled like the pair of gods they were. Behind them, the royal daughters were borne aloft, pretty girls with shaved heads and the lock of childhood, several of them starting to enter adolescence. The crown prince— the Haru in the nest—who was only two, was carried in his nurse's arms, and other members of the dynasty—the queen mother and more of her children—followed. Clouds of flower petals and bits of fine gold leaf fountained into the air as they passed, tossed by enthusiastic naked children with baskets. The crowd roared its approval, and many spectators lunged forward to collect the falling gold, but soldiers stationed every few cubits held them back with lowered spears.

"Our king does love a spectacle," Mane shouted at Hani, grinning broadly.

Two magnificently dressed servants waved dyed-ostrich-plume flabella at either side of king and queen, and behind the royal carrying chairs marched the king's special friends, the Fan Bearers, each with a single plume on a golden handle. *If real public servants were rewarded as they should be, Ptah-mes would be among them*, thought Hani bitterly. But in fact, his superior had been stripped of his high offices and even of his status of royal friend because he had dared to stand up to the young king when Nefer-khepru-ra had been his father's coregent.

And now the viziers were passing. Lord Aper-el, Hani's higher superior, with his chiseled pale northern face, and his southern counterpart, Lord Nakht-pa-aten, whom Hani knew but slightly. The higher echelon of bureaucrats was peeling off from the crowd to join the procession, and Ptah-mes was in there somewhere—Hani thought he saw his head rising taller than the others at the far edge of the group. Before long, Hani and Mane took their places in line.

The cadence of the drums pounded in his viscera as he began to walk. *I can't wait till this is over*, Hani thought glumly.

⁂

Five days after the opening ceremony of the Great Jubilee, Hani reached Waset, where he defiantly maintained his residence.

"Well, my love? How did it go?" Nub-nefer asked her husband as they embraced.

"Spectacular, as always," he said, bending to smell the perfume rising from her warm natural hair. "I don't know how he has time to do anything but parade around."

ACKNOWLEDGMENT

THE AUTHOR GRATEFULLY ACKNOWLEDGES ALL those who have helped her in the production of this book. To the wonderful women of my writers' group, for their critique and encouragement, my thanks.

To Lynn McNamee and her editorial team at Red Adept—Jessica, Sarah, and Laura—profound gratitude (and Lynn, for so many other forms of help). To the flexible and talented gang at Streetlight Graphics for the cover and map. To my cousin and her husband, my technology guru: thanks, guys. To Enid, who urged me forward by her support, I can't thank you sufficiently. And most of all, to my husband, Ippokratis, who put up with the months of fixation it takes to write a novel, many, many thanks.

ABOUT THE AUTHOR

 N.L. Holmes is the pen name of a professional archaeologist who received her doctorate from Bryn Mawr College. She has excavated in Greece and in Israel, and taught ancient history and humanities at the university level for many years. She has always had a passion for books, and in childhood, she and her cousin (also a writer today) used to write stories for fun.

Today, since their son is grown, she lives with her husband and three cats. They split their time between Florida and northern France, where she gardens, weaves, plays the violin, dances, and occasionally drives a jog-cart. And reads, of course.